VOL. 1

Harmony

VOL. 1

MATHIEU REYNÈS

TRANSLATED BY
MONTANA KANE

INSIGHT COMICS

SAN RAFAEL • LOS ANGELES • LONDON

PART ONE

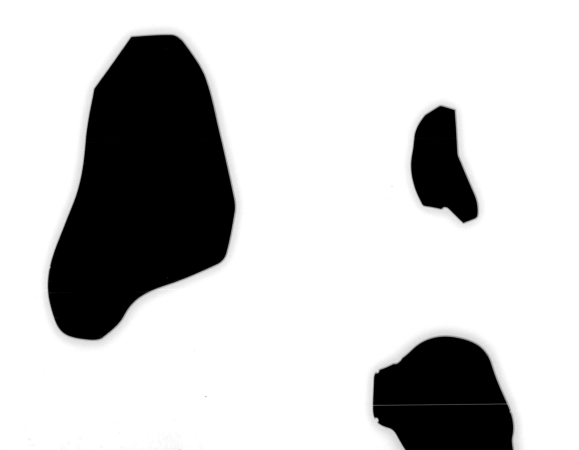

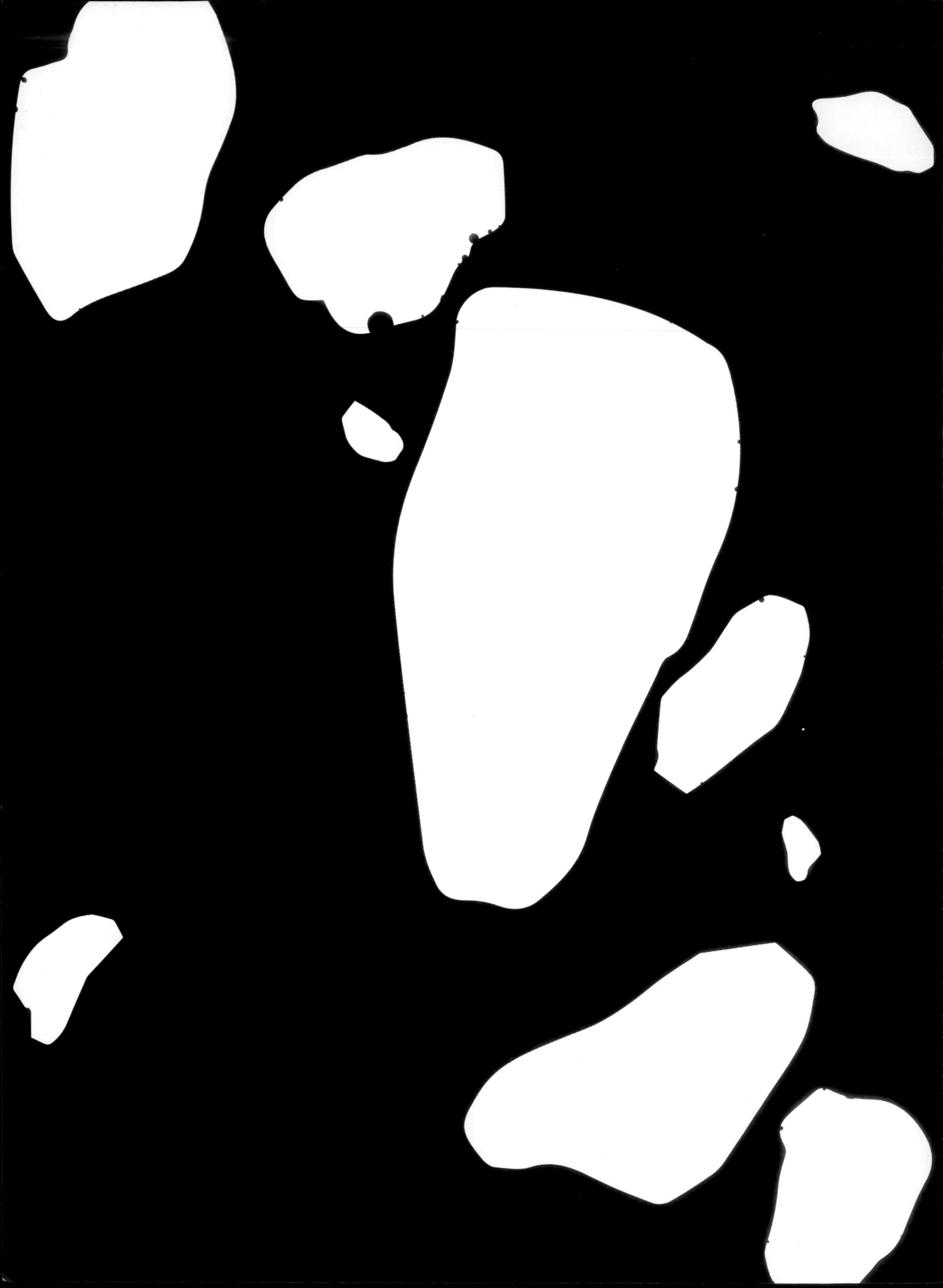

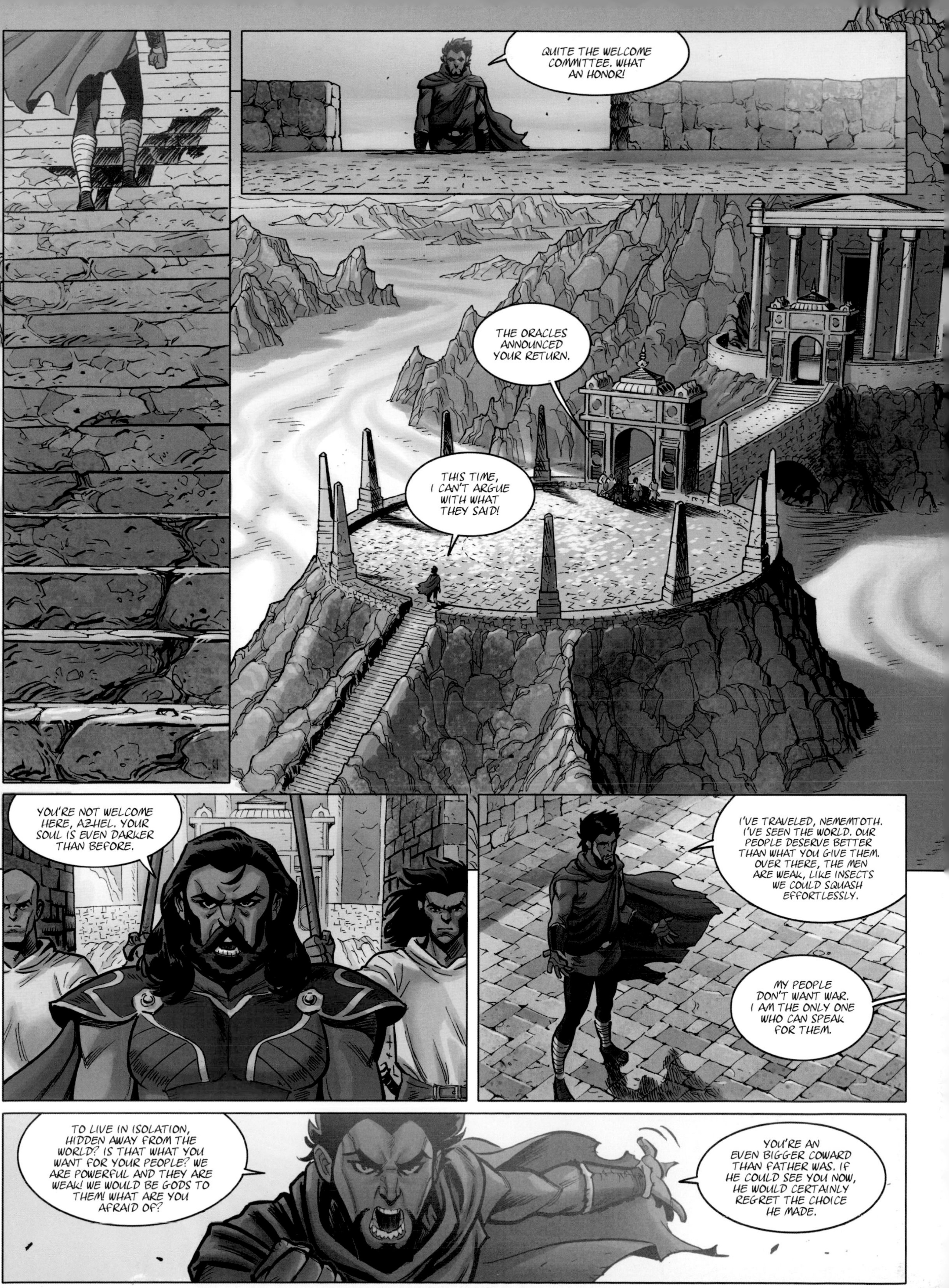
QUITE THE WELCOME COMMITTEE. WHAT AN HONOR!
THE ORACLES ANNOUNCED YOUR RETURN.
THIS TIME, I CAN'T ARGUE WITH WHAT THEY SAID!
YOU'RE NOT WELCOME HERE, AZHEL. YOUR SOUL IS EVEN DARKER THAN BEFORE.
I'VE TRAVELED, NEMEMTOTH. I'VE SEEN THE WORLD. OUR PEOPLE DESERVE BETTER THAN WHAT YOU GIVE THEM. OVER THERE, THE MEN ARE WEAK, LIKE INSECTS WE COULD SQUASH EFFORTLESSLY.
MY PEOPLE DON'T WANT WAR. I AM THE ONLY ONE WHO CAN SPEAK FOR THEM.
TO LIVE IN ISOLATION, HIDDEN AWAY FROM THE WORLD? IS THAT WHAT YOU WANT FOR YOUR PEOPLE? WE ARE POWERFUL AND THEY ARE WEAK! WE WOULD BE GODS TO THEM! WHAT ARE YOU AFRAID OF?
YOU'RE AN EVEN BIGGER COWARD THAN FATHER WAS. IF HE COULD SEE YOU NOW, HE WOULD CERTAINLY REGRET THE CHOICE HE MADE.

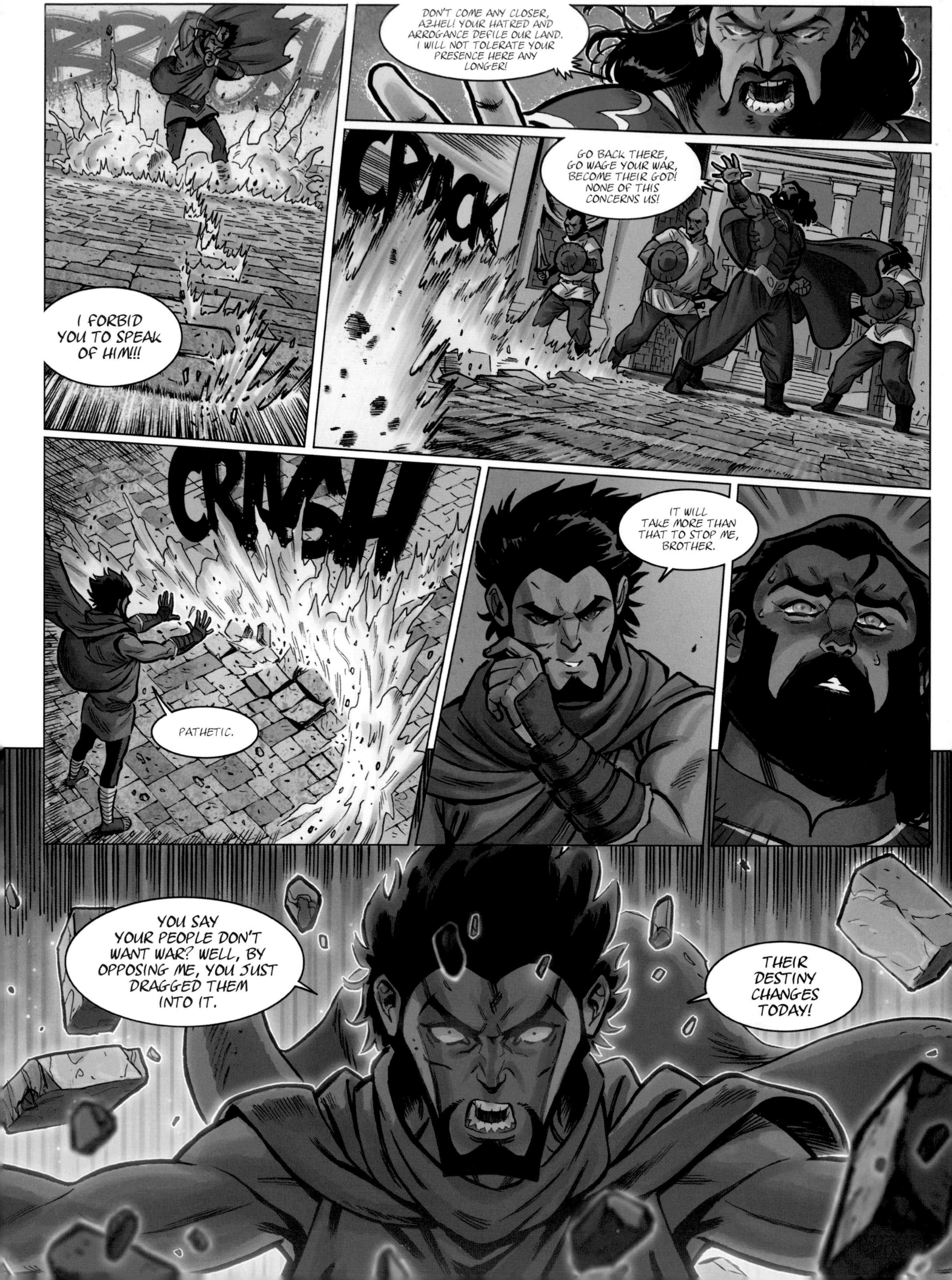
DON'T COME ANY CLOSER, AZHEL! YOUR HATRED AND ARROGANCE DEFILE OUR LAND. I WILL NOT TOLERATE YOUR PRESENCE HERE ANY LONGER!
I FORBID YOU TO SPEAK OF HIM!!!
CRACK
GO BACK THERE, GO WAGE YOUR WAR, BECOME THEIR GOD! NONE OF THIS CONCERNS US!
CRASH
PATHETIC.
IT WILL TAKE MORE THAN THAT TO STOP ME, BROTHER.
YOU SAY YOUR PEOPLE DON'T WANT WAR? WELL, BY OPPOSING ME, YOU JUST DRAGGED THEM INTO IT.
THEIR DESTINY CHANGES TODAY!

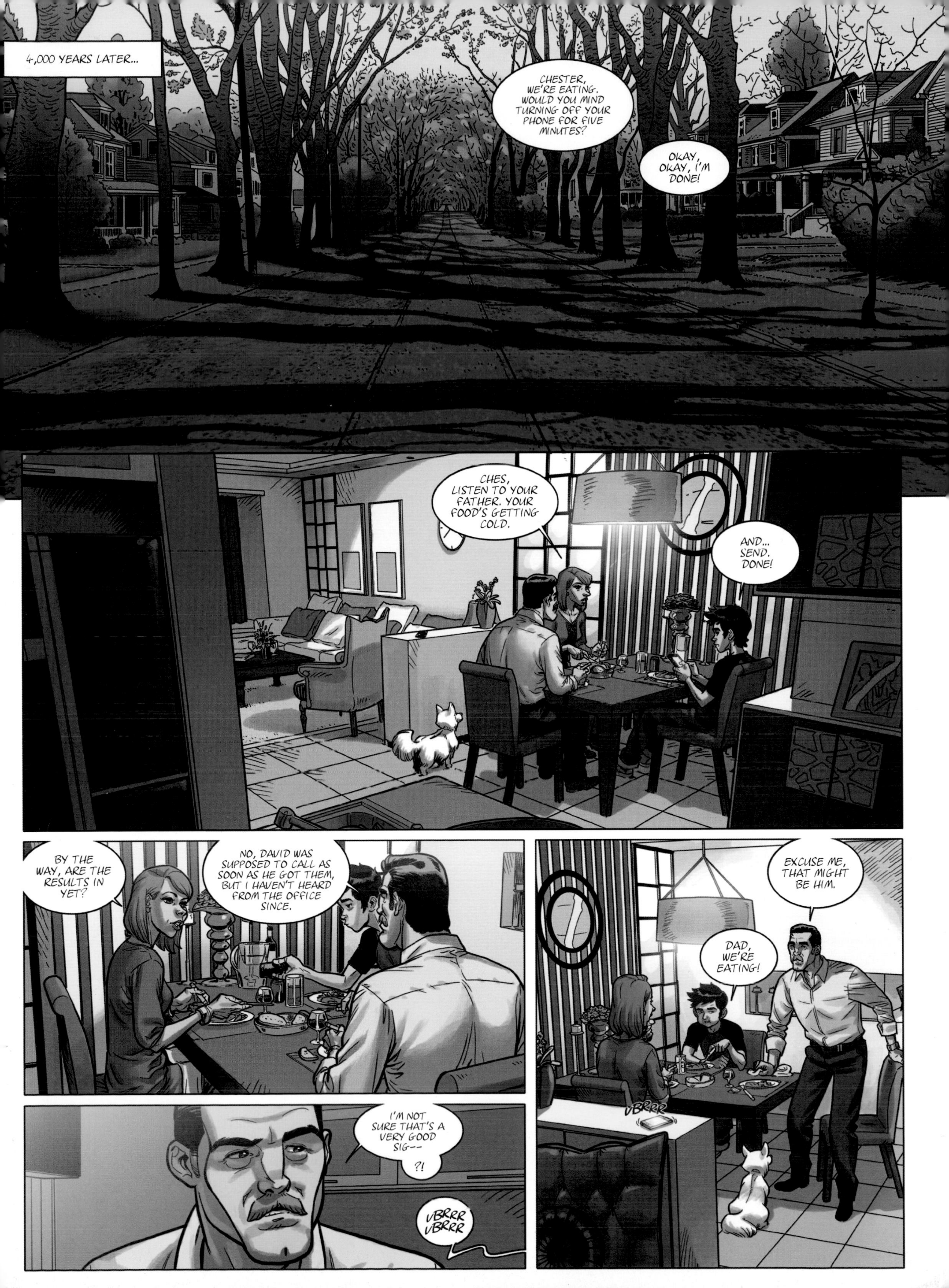

4,000 YEARS LATER...
CHESTER, WE'RE EATING. WOULD YOU MIND TURNING OFF YOUR PHONE FOR FIVE MINUTES?
OKAY, OKAY, I'M DONE!
CHES, LISTEN TO YOUR FATHER. YOUR FOOD'S GETTING COLD.
AND... SEND. DONE!
BY THE WAY, ARE THE RESULTS IN YET?
NO, DAVID WAS SUPPOSED TO CALL AS SOON AS HE GOT THEM, BUT I HAVEN'T HEARD FROM THE OFFICE SINCE.
I'M NOT SURE THAT'S A VERY GOOD SIG--
?!
VBRRR VBRRR
EXCUSE ME, THAT MIGHT BE HIM.
DAD, WE'RE EATING!
VBRRR

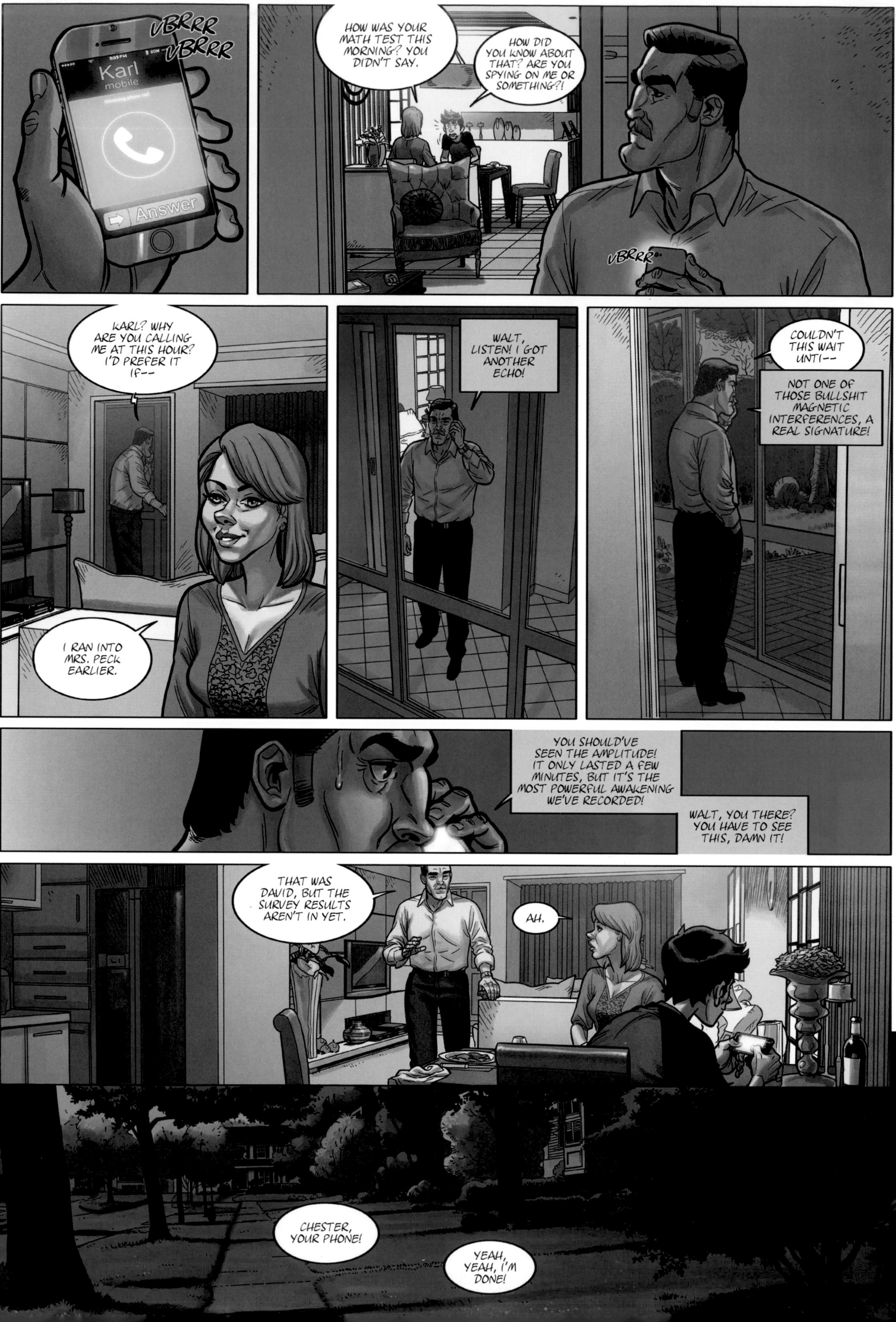
VBRRR
VBRRR
Karl
mobile
Answer
HOW WAS YOUR MATH TEST THIS MORNING? YOU DIDN'T SAY.
HOW DID YOU KNOW ABOUT THAT? ARE YOU SPYING ON ME OR SOMETHING?!
VBRRR
KARL? WHY ARE YOU CALLING ME AT THIS HOUR? I'D PREFER IT IF--
I RAN INTO MRS. PECK EARLIER.
WALT, LISTEN! I GOT ANOTHER ECHO!
COULDN'T THIS WAIT UNTI--
NOT ONE OF THOSE BULLSHIT MAGNETIC INTERFERENCES, A REAL SIGNATURE!
YOU SHOULD'VE SEEN THE AMPLITUDE! IT ONLY LASTED A FEW MINUTES, BUT IT'S THE MOST POWERFUL AWAKENING WE'VE RECORDED!
WALT, YOU THERE? YOU HAVE TO SEE THIS, DAMN IT!
THAT WAS DAVID, BUT THE SURVEY RESULTS AREN'T IN YET.
AH.
CHESTER, YOUR PHONE!
YEAH, YEAH, I'M DONE!

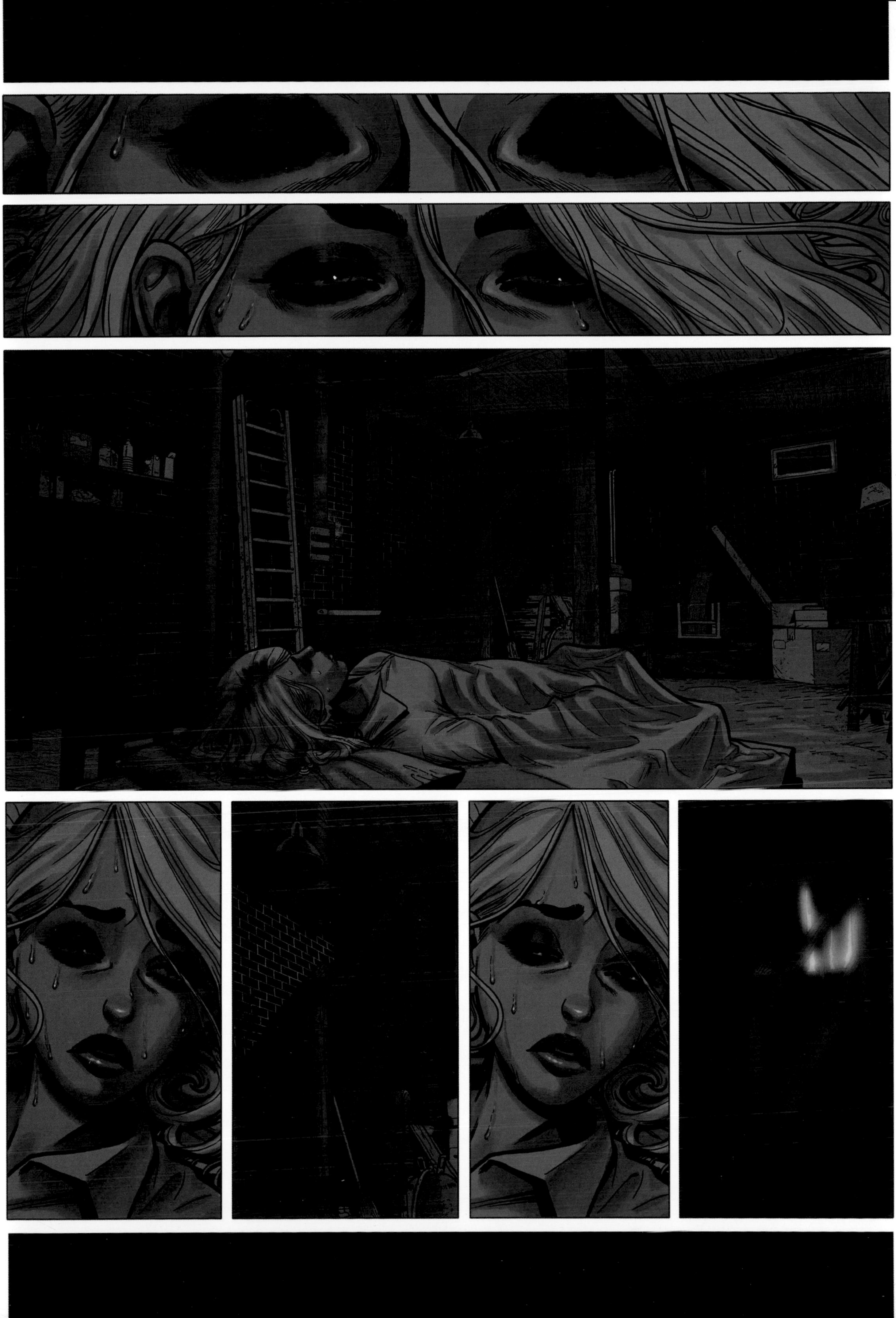

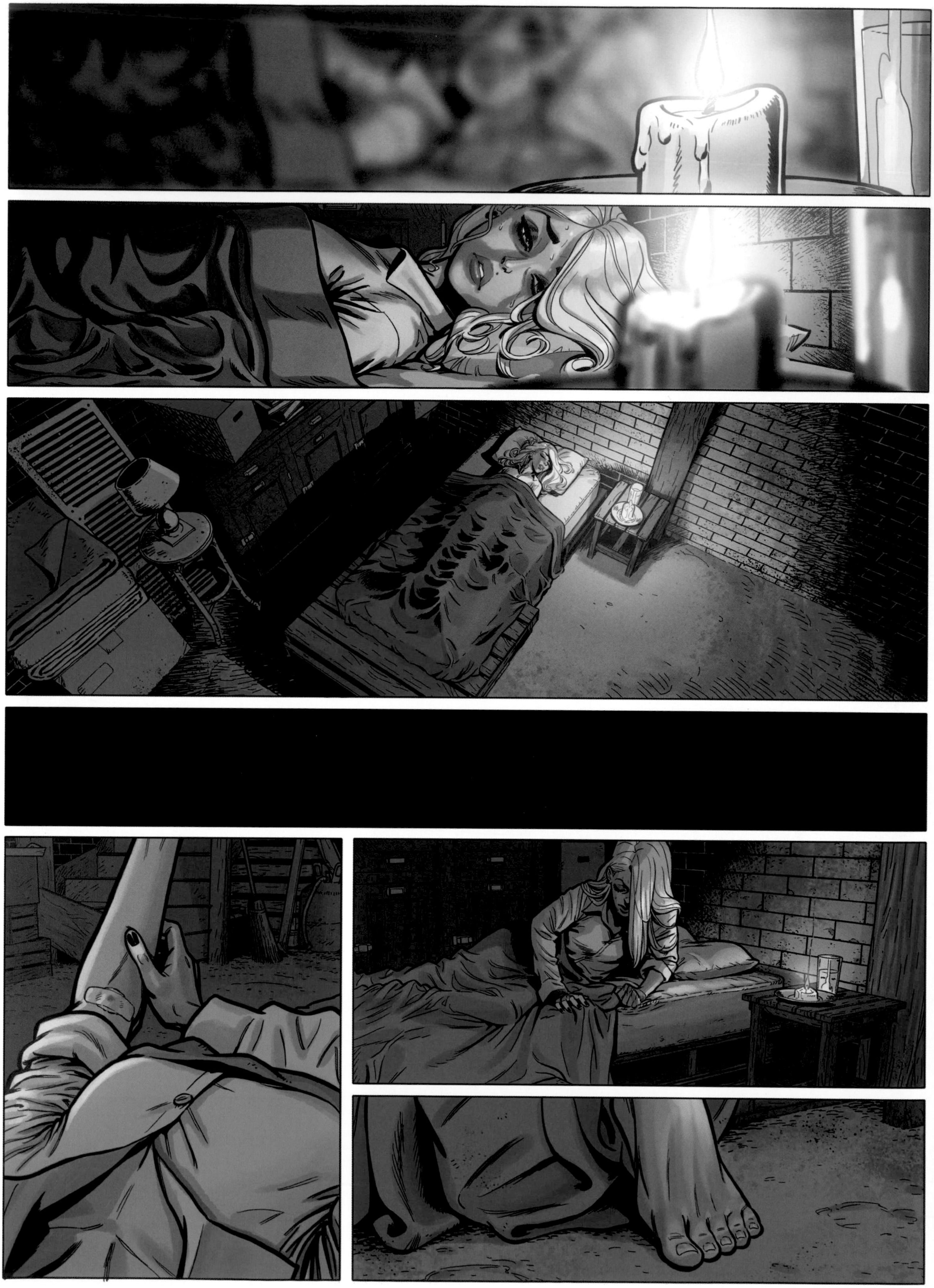

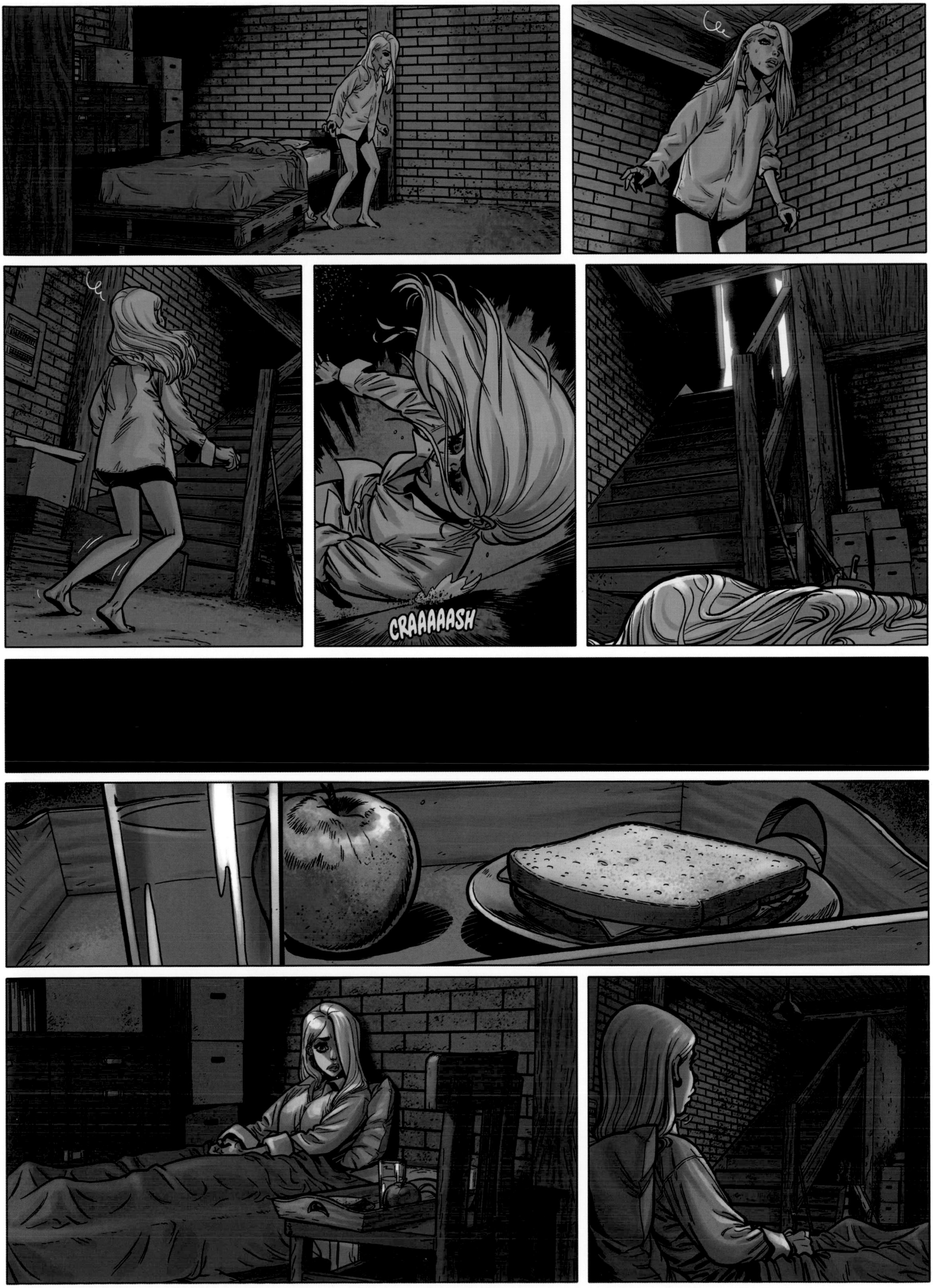
CRAAAAASH

TAKE IT EASY. IT'S BEEN A WHILE SINCE YOU'VE HAD ANYTHING TO EAT.

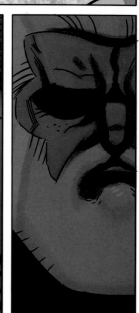

GO AHEAD-- KEEP EATING. YOU NEED TO GET YOUR STRENGTH BACK.

HOW DO YOU FEEL? ARE YOU HURTING ANYWHERE?

OKAY, TAKE YOUR TIME.

I'LL LEAVE THE TRAY.

I'M NITA, BY THE WAY.

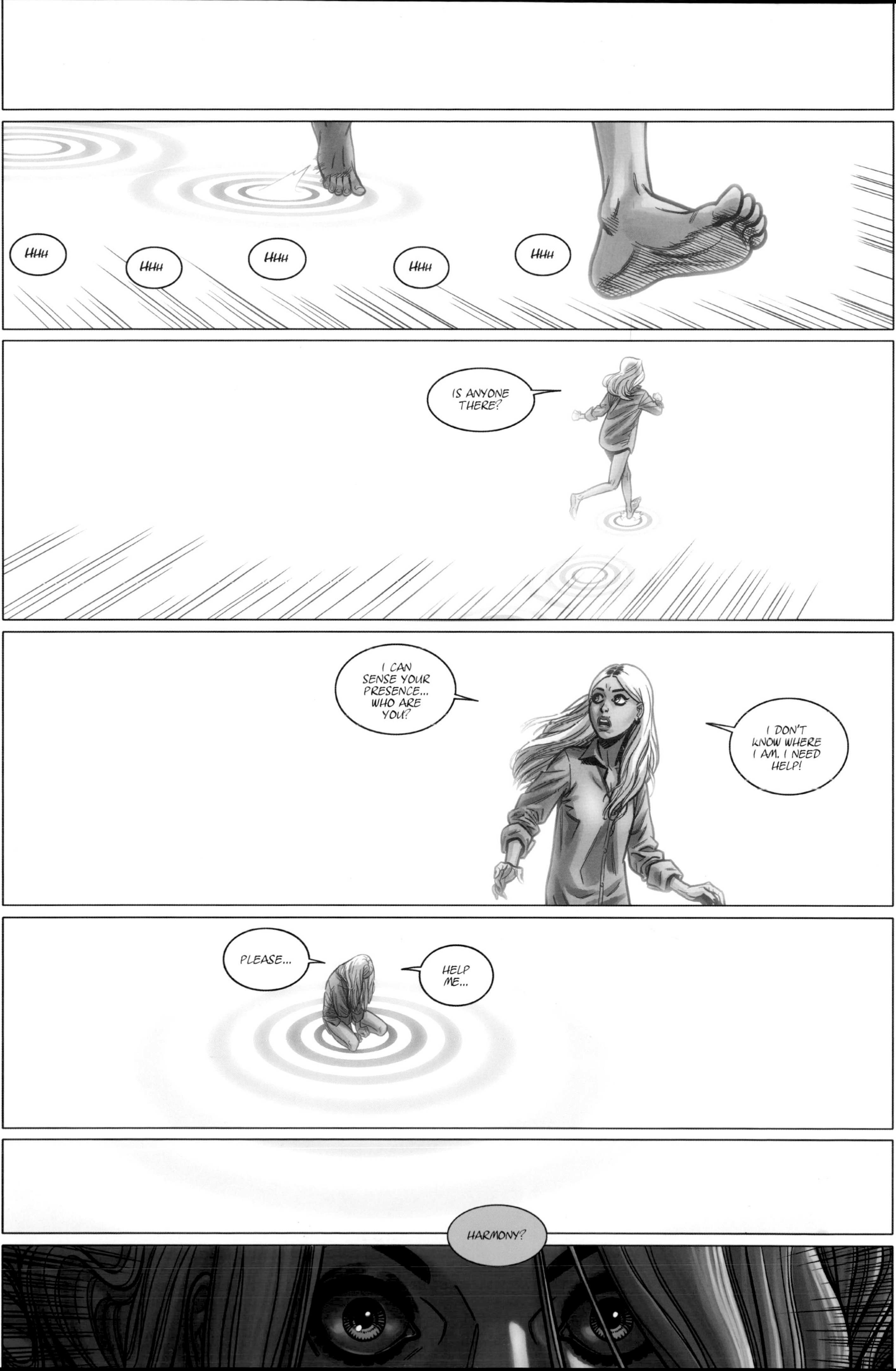
HHH
HHH
HHH
HHH
HHH
IS ANYONE THERE?
I CAN SENSE YOUR PRESENCE... WHO ARE YOU?
I DON'T KNOW WHERE I AM. I NEED HELP!
PLEASE...
HELP ME...
HARMONY?

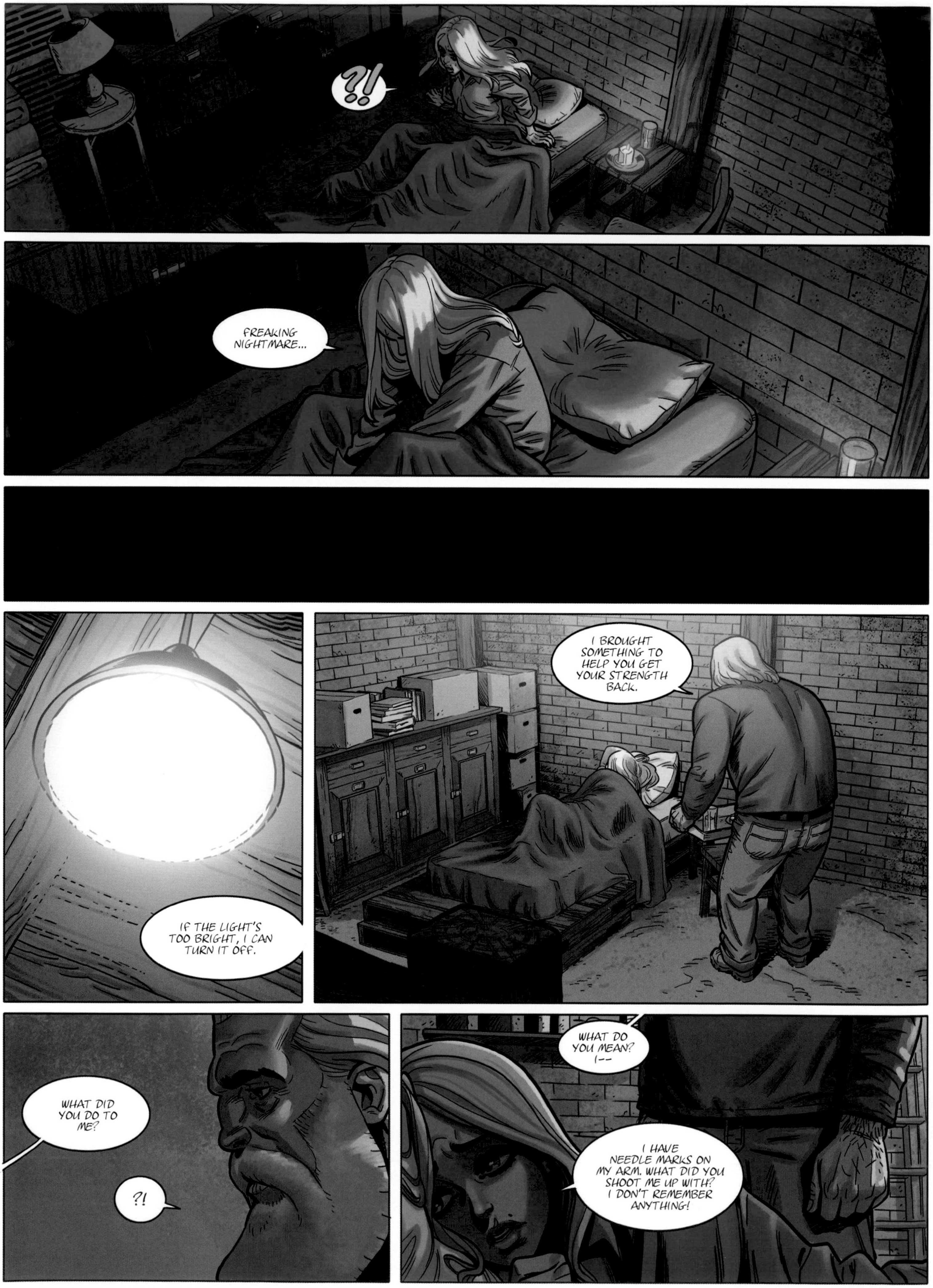
?!
FREAKING NIGHTMARE...
IF THE LIGHT'S TOO BRIGHT, I CAN TURN IT OFF.
I BROUGHT SOMETHING TO HELP YOU GET YOUR STRENGTH BACK.
WHAT DID YOU DO TO ME?
?!
WHAT DO YOU MEAN? I--
I HAVE NEEDLE MARKS ON MY ARM. WHAT DID YOU SHOOT ME UP WITH? I DON'T REMEMBER ANYTHING!

IT'S NOT WHAT YOU THINK... YOU HAD A HIGH FEVER AND--

MY BRAIN FEELS LIKE IT'S LOCKED SHUT.

WHY AM I LOCKED UP IN A BASEMENT?! WHERE ARE WE?

AND WHO ARE YOU?

THAT'S NORMAL--YOU'VE SUFFERED A MAJOR TRAUMA. BUT I'M SURE YOU'LL COME AROUND IN NO TIME. YOU NEED TO REST.

YOU'RE SAFE HERE. AS SOON AS YOU'RE FEELING STRONG AGAIN, I'LL MOVE YOU TO A REAL ROOM.

DON'T WORRY. EVERYTHING IS GOING TO BE--

DON'T TOUCH ME!!!

SORRY, I DIDN'T MEAN TO... I...

I'LL COME BY LATER.

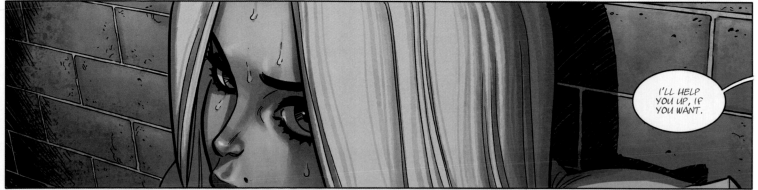

I'LL HELP YOU UP, IF YOU WANT.

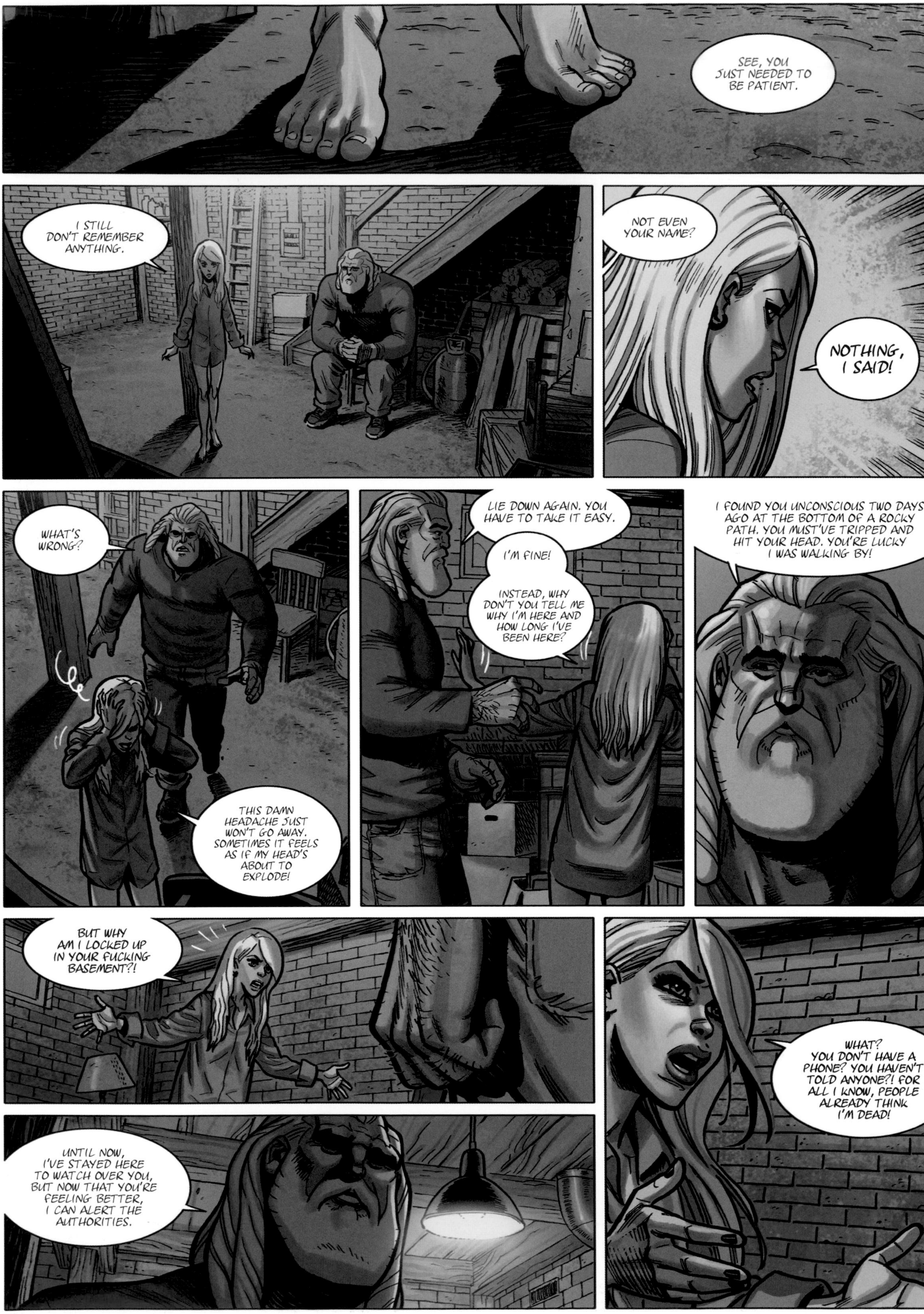
SEE, YOU JUST NEEDED TO BE PATIENT.
I STILL DON'T REMEMBER ANYTHING.
NOT EVEN YOUR NAME?
NOTHING, I SAID!
WHAT'S WRONG?
THIS DAMN HEADACHE JUST WON'T GO AWAY. SOMETIMES IT FEELS AS IF MY HEAD'S ABOUT TO EXPLODE!
LIE DOWN AGAIN. YOU HAVE TO TAKE IT EASY.
I'M FINE!
INSTEAD, WHY DON'T YOU TELL ME WHY I'M HERE AND HOW LONG I'VE BEEN HERE?
I FOUND YOU UNCONSCIOUS TWO DAYS AGO AT THE BOTTOM OF A ROCKY PATH. YOU MUST'VE TRIPPED AND HIT YOUR HEAD. YOU'RE LUCKY I WAS WALKING BY!
BUT WHY AM I LOCKED UP IN YOUR FUCKING BASEMENT?!
UNTIL NOW, I'VE STAYED HERE TO WATCH OVER YOU, BUT NOW THAT YOU'RE FEELING BETTER, I CAN ALERT THE AUTHORITIES.
WHAT? YOU DON'T HAVE A PHONE? YOU HAVEN'T TOLD ANYONE?! FOR ALL I KNOW, PEOPLE ALREADY THINK I'M DEAD!

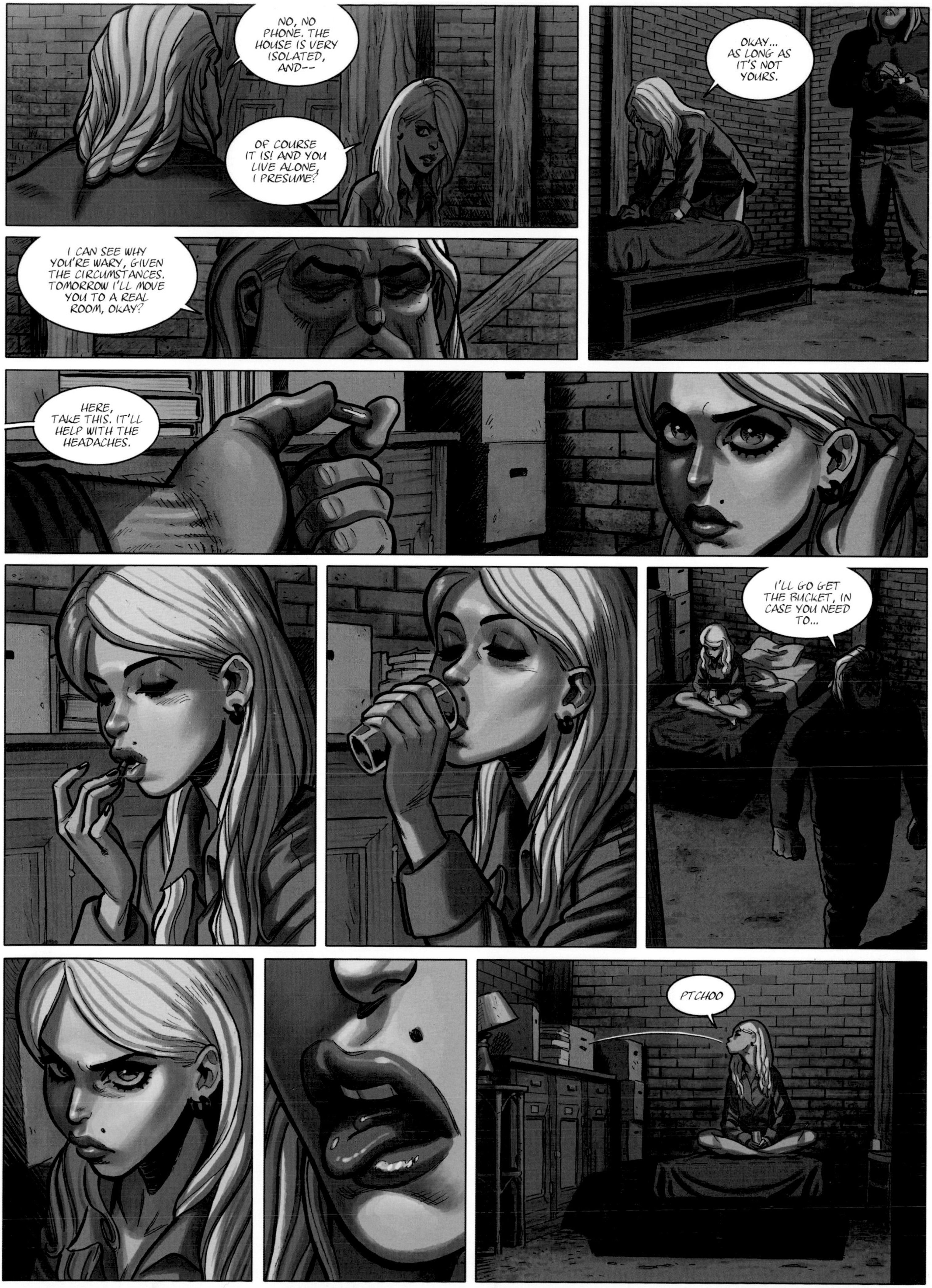
NO, NO PHONE. THE HOUSE IS VERY ISOLATED, AND--
OF COURSE IT IS! AND YOU LIVE ALONE, I PRESUME?
I CAN SEE WHY YOU'RE WARY, GIVEN THE CIRCUMSTANCES. TOMORROW I'LL MOVE YOU TO A REAL ROOM, OKAY?
OKAY... AS LONG AS IT'S NOT YOURS.
HERE, TAKE THIS. IT'LL HELP WITH THE HEADACHES.
I'LL GO GET THE BUCKET, IN CASE YOU NEED TO...
PTCHOO

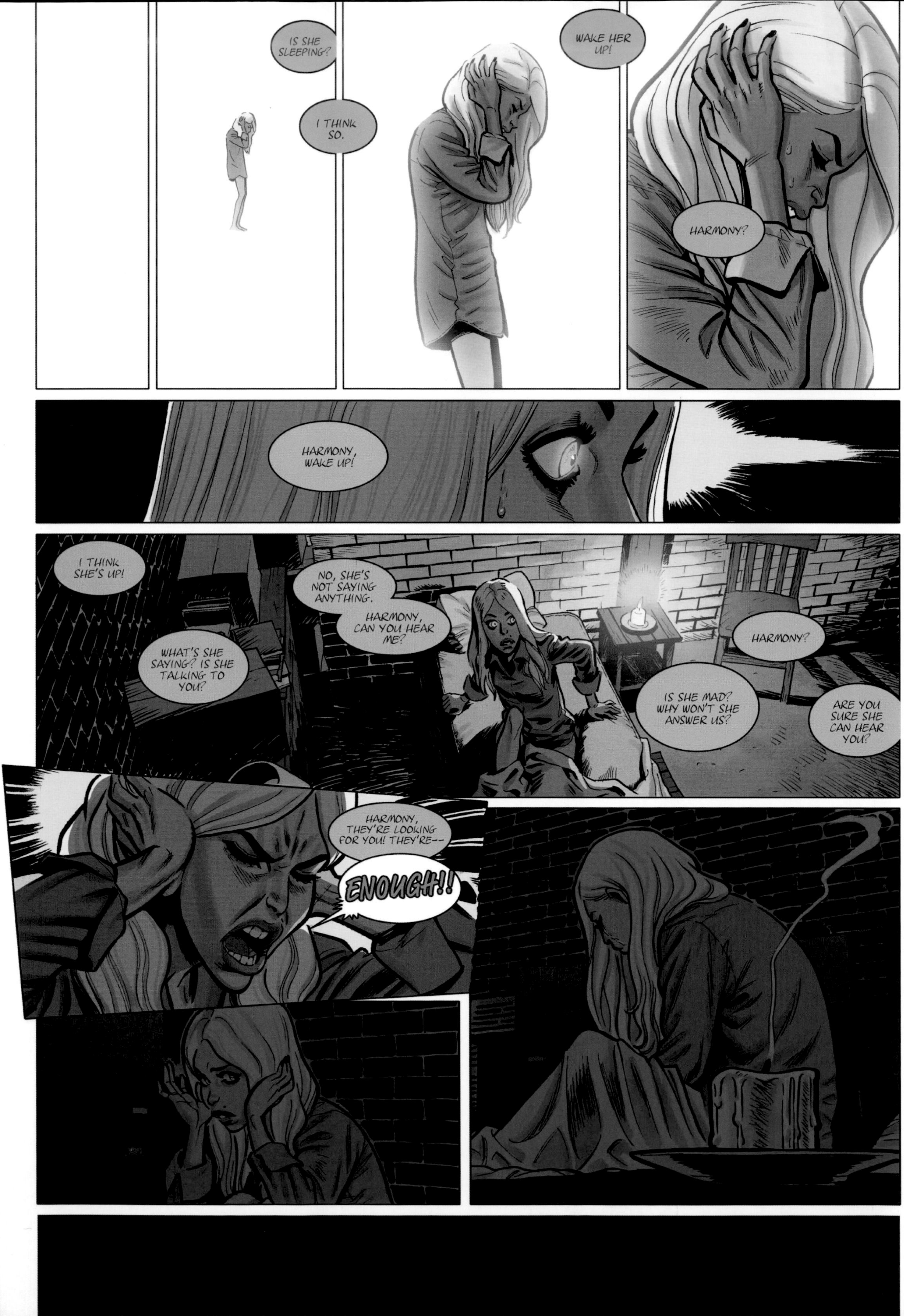
IS SHE SLEEPING?
I THINK SO.
WAKE HER UP!
HARMONY?
HARMONY, WAKE UP!
I THINK SHE'S UP!
NO, SHE'S NOT SAYING ANYTHING.
HARMONY, CAN YOU HEAR ME?
WHAT'S SHE SAYING? IS SHE TALKING TO YOU?
HARMONY?
IS SHE MAD? WHY WON'T SHE ANSWER US?
ARE YOU SURE SHE CAN HEAR YOU?
HARMONY, THEY'RE LOOKING FOR YOU! THEY'RE--
ENOUGH!!

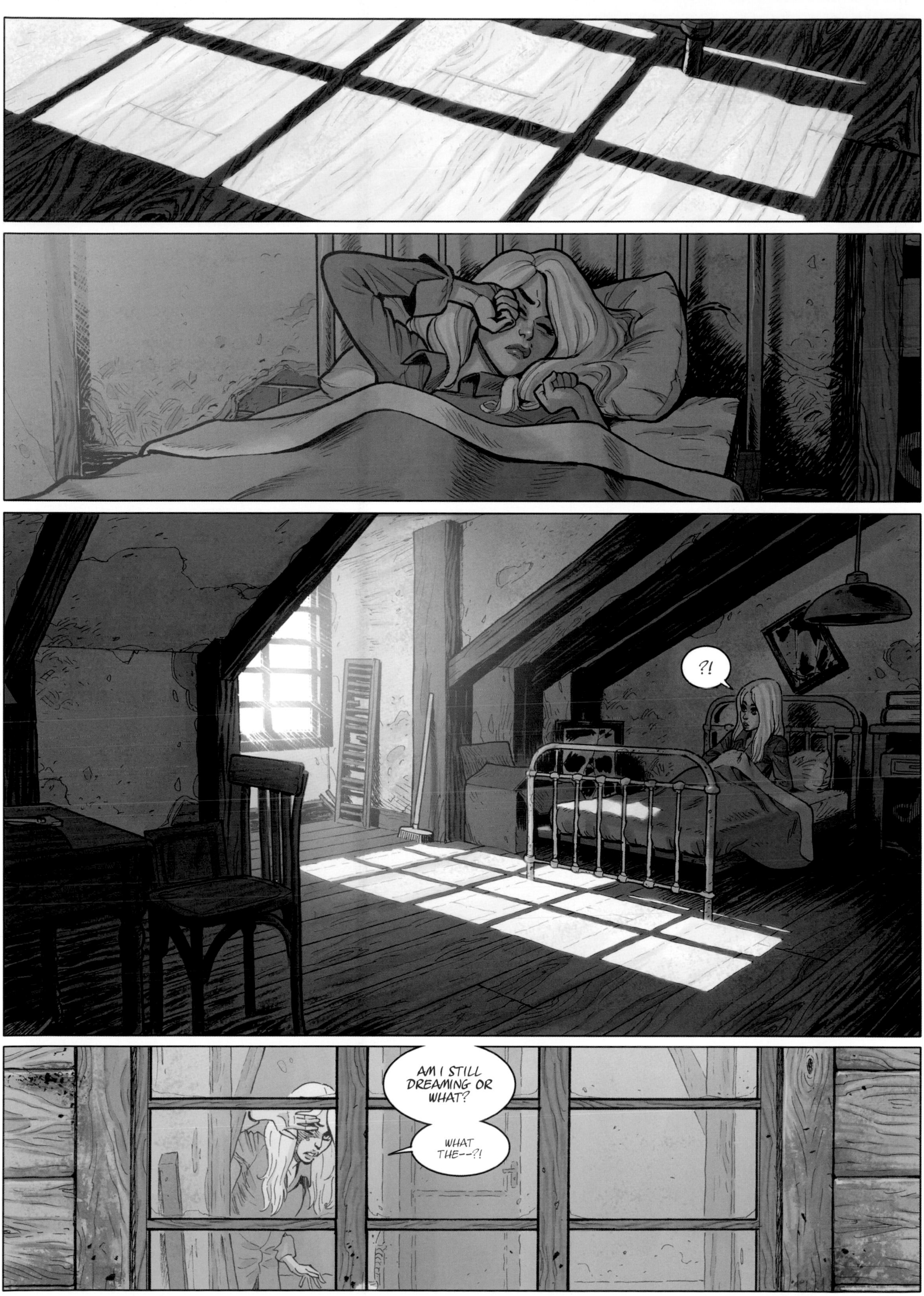
?!
AM I STILL DREAMING OR WHAT?
WHAT THE--?!

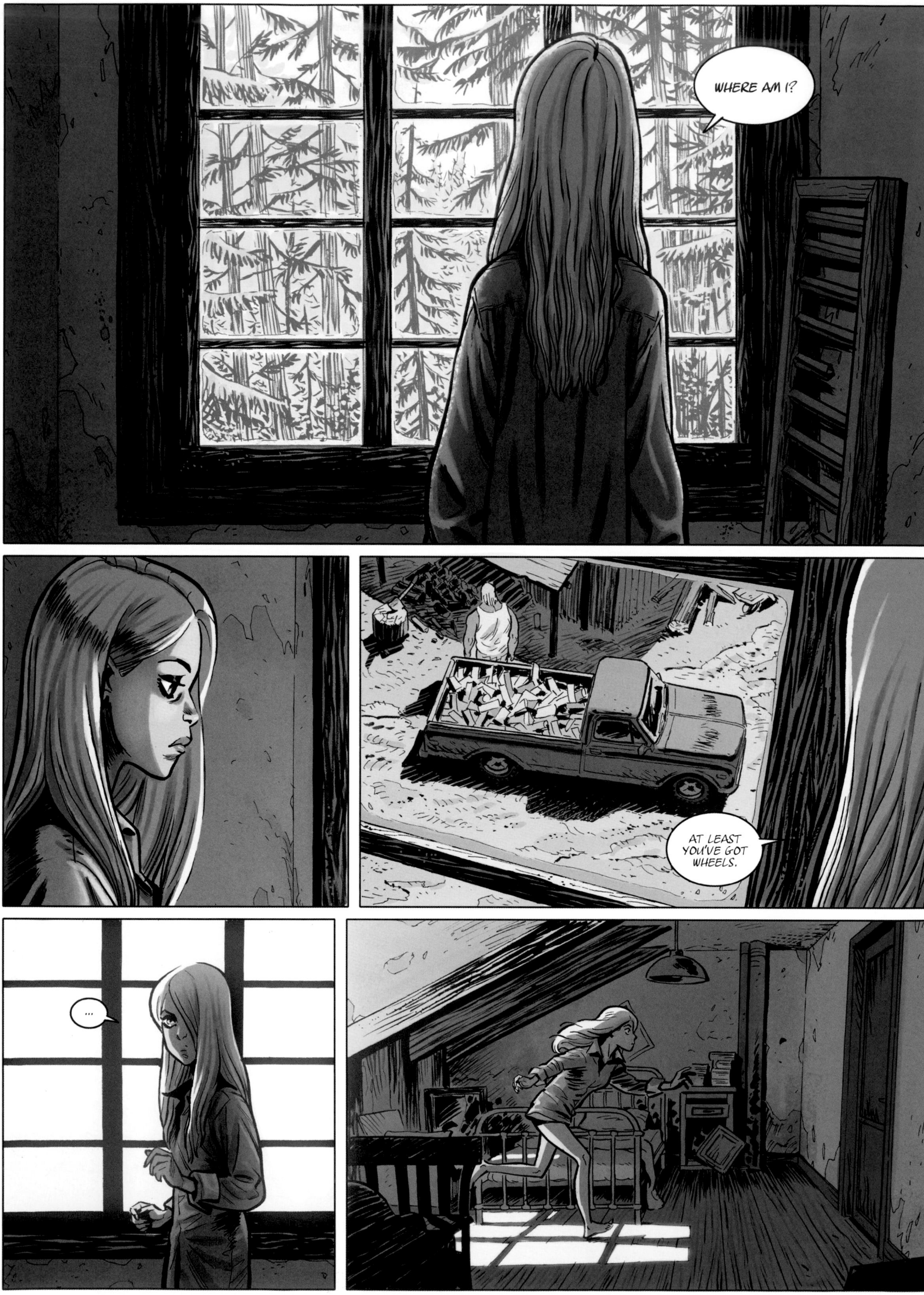
WHERE AM I?
AT LEAST YOU'VE GOT WHEELS.
...

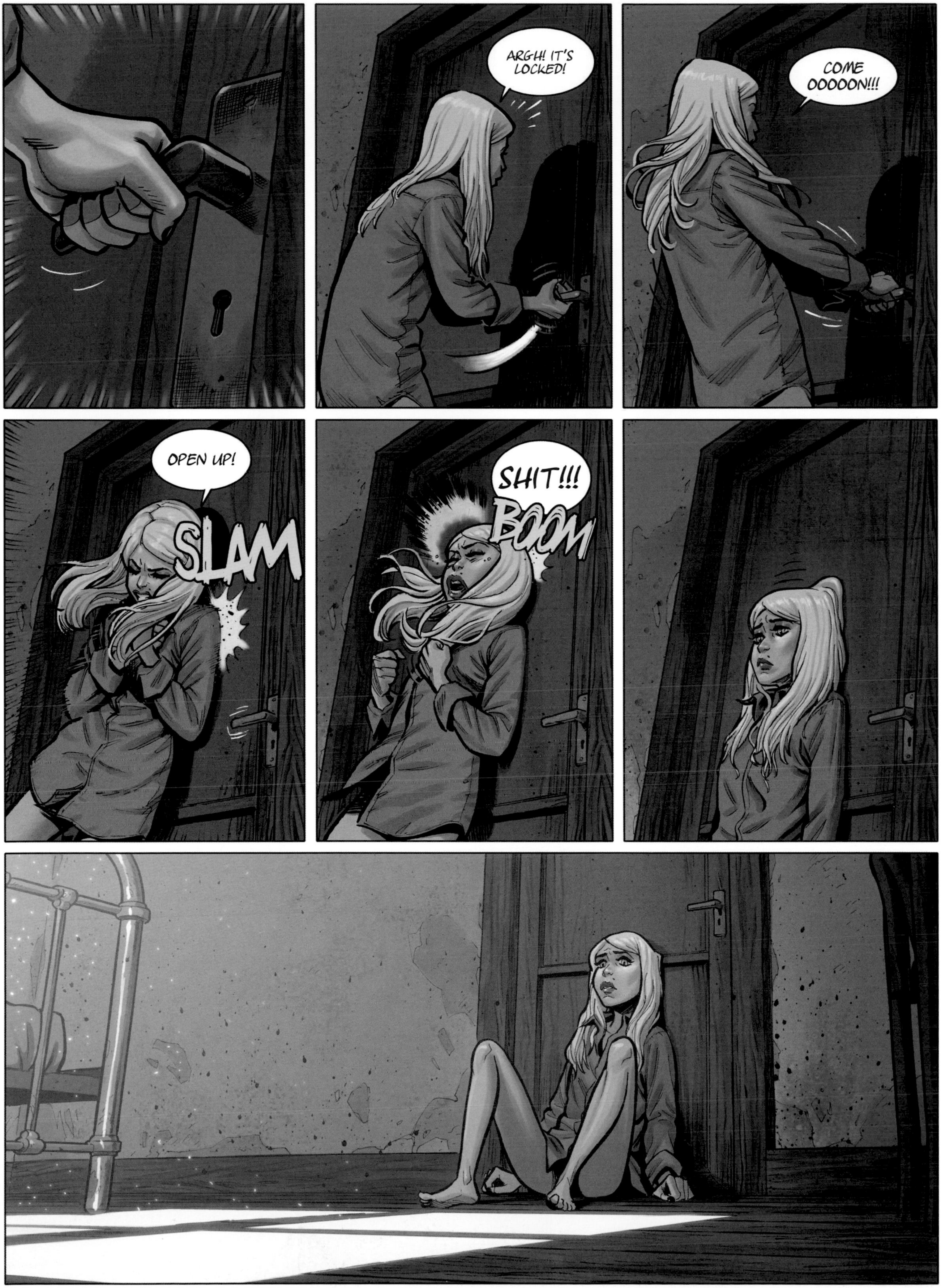
ARGH! IT'S LOCKED!
COME OOOOON!!!
OPEN UP!
SLAM
SHIT!!!
BOOM

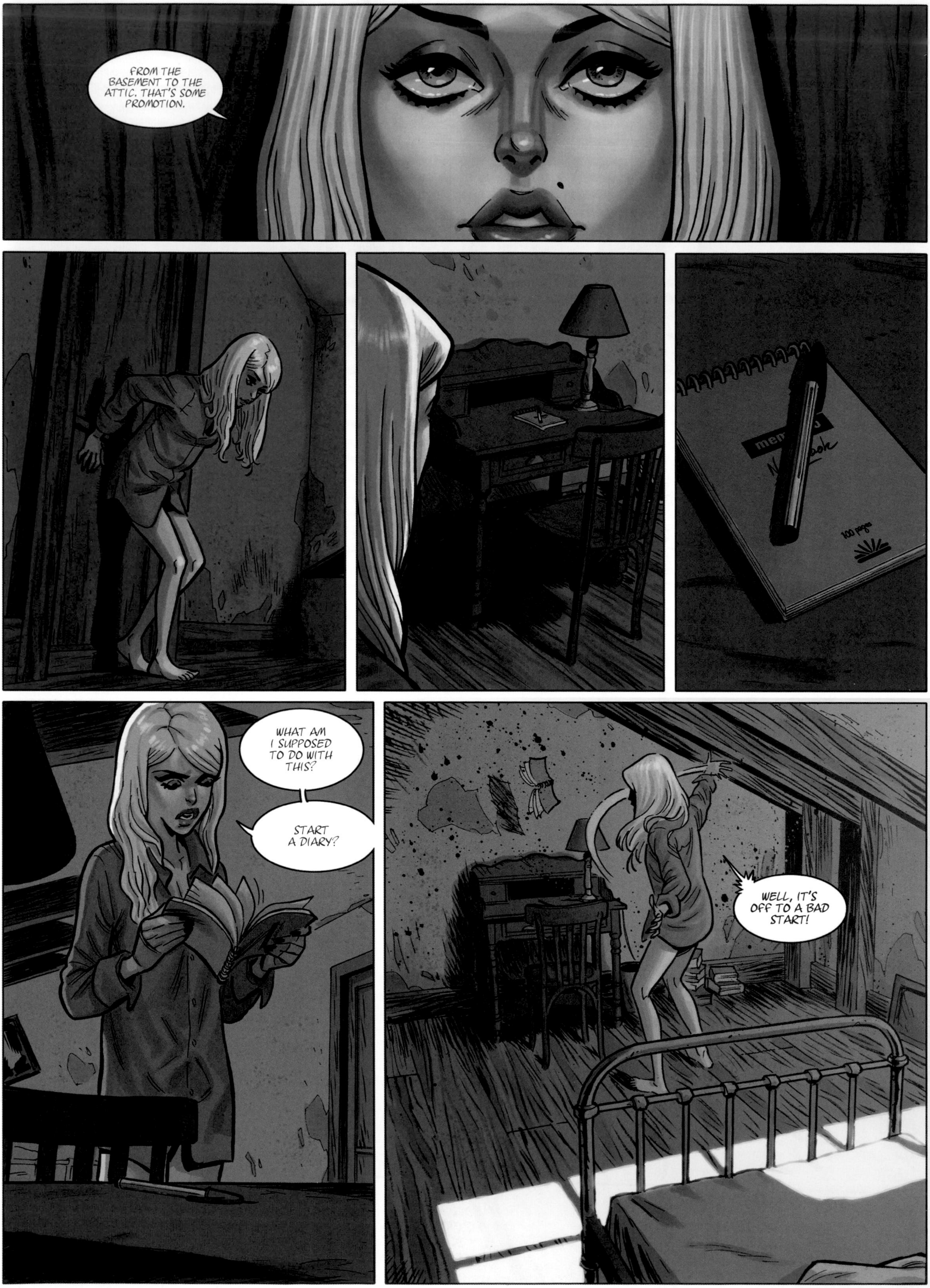
FROM THE BASEMENT TO THE ATTIC. THAT'S SOME PROMOTION.
WHAT AM I SUPPOSED TO DO WITH THIS?
START A DIARY?
WELL, IT'S OFF TO A BAD START!

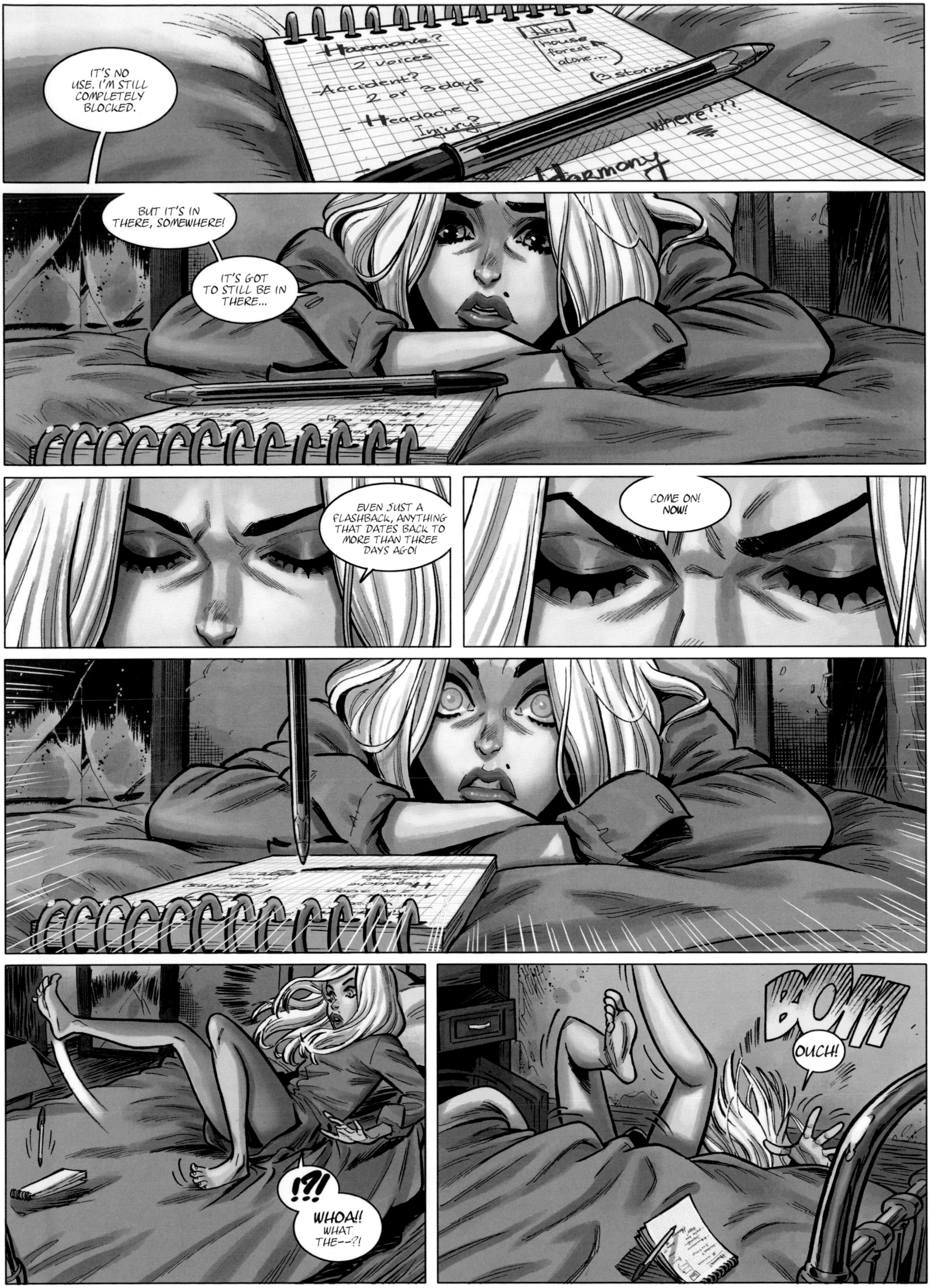

Harmonie?
2 voices
Accident?
2 or 3 days
Headache
Injury?
house
forest
alone...
(3 stories)
where???
Harmony
IT'S NO USE. I'M STILL COMPLETELY BLOCKED.
BUT IT'S IN THERE, SOMEWHERE!
IT'S GOT TO STILL BE IN THERE...
EVEN JUST A FLASHBACK, ANYTHING THAT DATES BACK TO MORE THAN THREE DAYS AGO!
COME ON! NOW!
!?!
WHOA!! WHAT THE--?!
BOM
OUCH!

DID I HALLUCINATE AGAIN OR WHAT?
THAT'S JUST NOT POSSIBLE...
AND YET, IT WAS SUCH A...FAMILIAR FEELING.
Harmonie?
THIS TIME, I REALLY DO THINK I FRIED MY BRAIN!

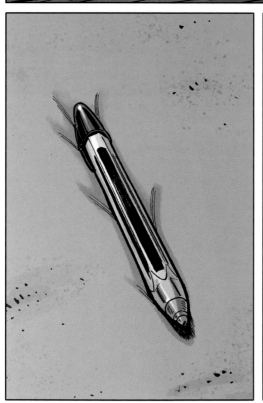

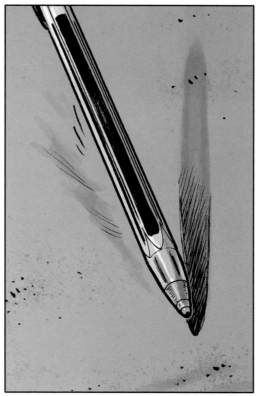

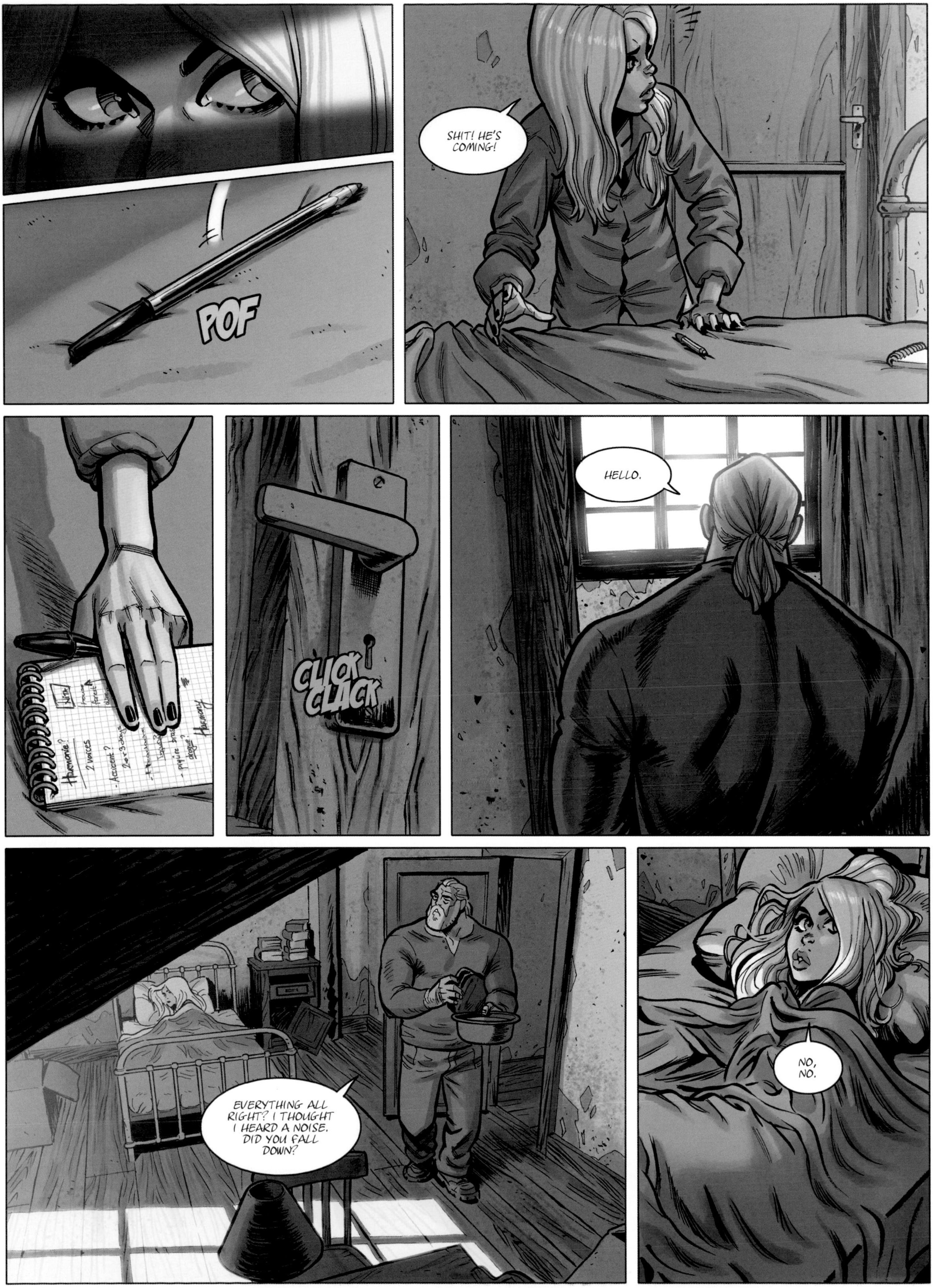
POF
SHIT! HE'S COMING!
CLICK CLACK
HELLO.
EVERYTHING ALL RIGHT? I THOUGHT I HEARD A NOISE. DID YOU FALL DOWN?
NO, NO.

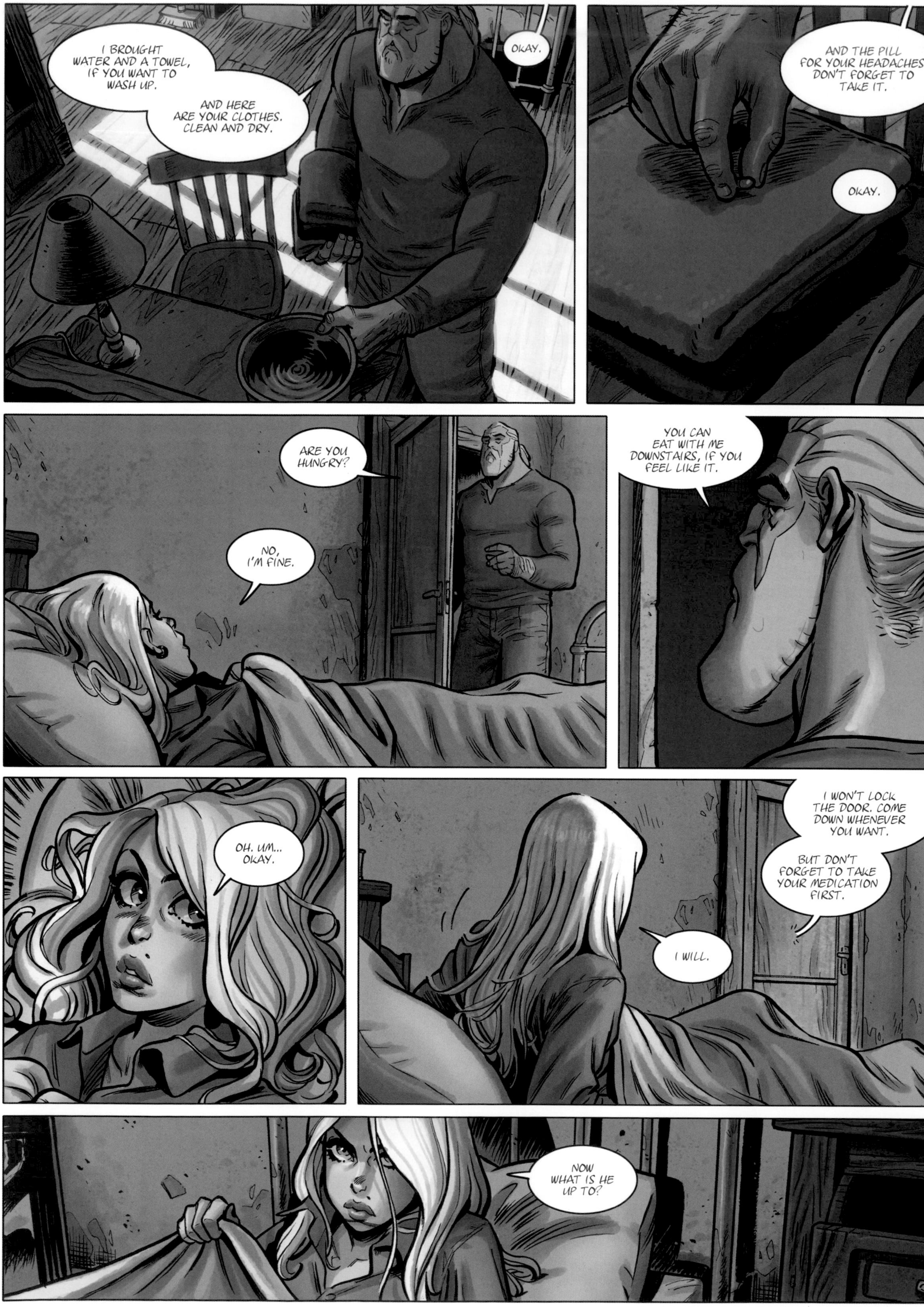
I BROUGHT WATER AND A TOWEL, IF YOU WANT TO WASH UP.
AND HERE ARE YOUR CLOTHES. CLEAN AND DRY.
OKAY.
AND THE PILL FOR YOUR HEADACHES. DON'T FORGET TO TAKE IT.
OKAY.
ARE YOU HUNGRY?
NO, I'M FINE.
YOU CAN EAT WITH ME DOWNSTAIRS, IF YOU FEEL LIKE IT.
OH, UM... OKAY.
I WON'T LOCK THE DOOR. COME DOWN WHENEVER YOU WANT.
BUT DON'T FORGET TO TAKE YOUR MEDICATION FIRST.
I WILL.
NOW WHAT IS HE UP TO?

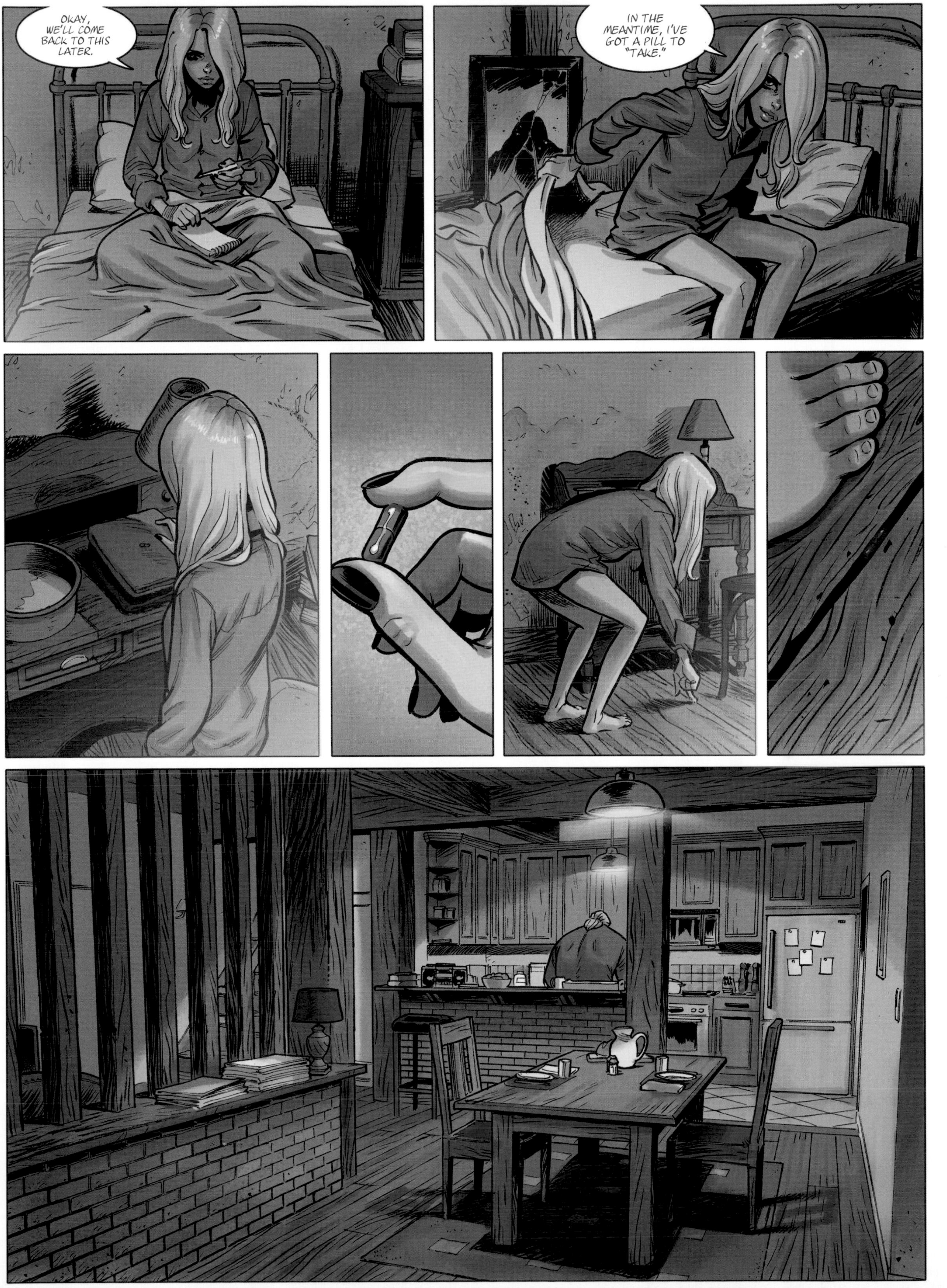
OKAY, WE'LL COME BACK TO THIS LATER.
IN THE MEANTIME, I'VE GOT A PILL TO "TAKE."

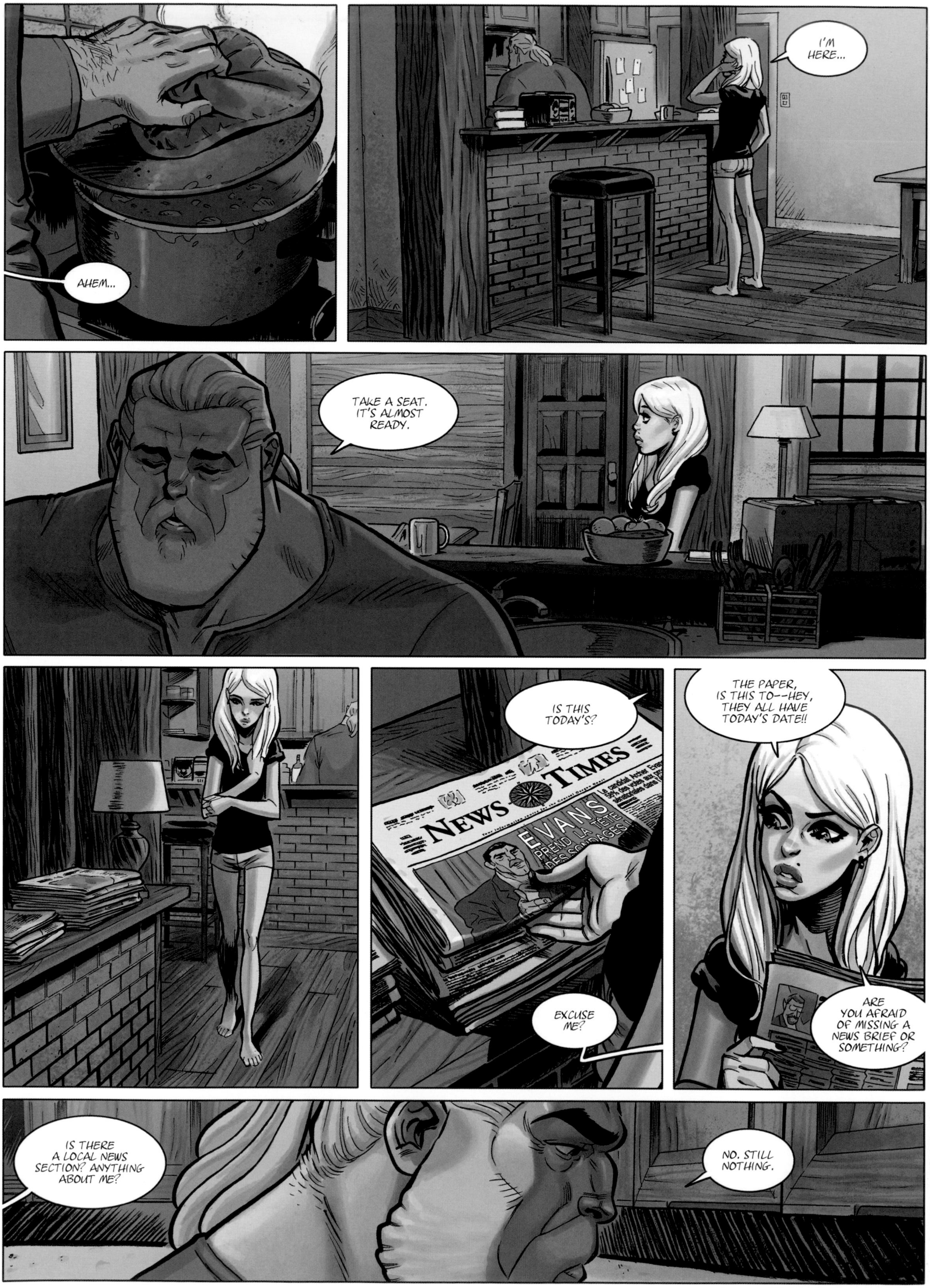
AHEM...
I'M HERE...
TAKE A SEAT. IT'S ALMOST READY.
IS THIS TODAY'S?
NEWS TIMES
EVANS PREND LA TÊTE DES SONDAGES
EXCUSE ME?
THE PAPER, IS THIS TO--HEY, THEY ALL HAVE TODAY'S DATE!!
ARE YOU AFRAID OF MISSING A NEWS BRIEF OR SOMETHING?
IS THERE A LOCAL NEWS SECTION? ANYTHING ABOUT ME?
NO. STILL NOTHING.

HAVE YOU TOLD THE POLICE YOU FOUND ME?

YOU'LL HAVE TO FORGIVE ME. I'M NOT A GREAT COOK.

NOBODY KNOWS I'M HERE, DO THEY?!

I HAVEN'T HAD TIME TO GO ALERT THE SHERIFF YET...

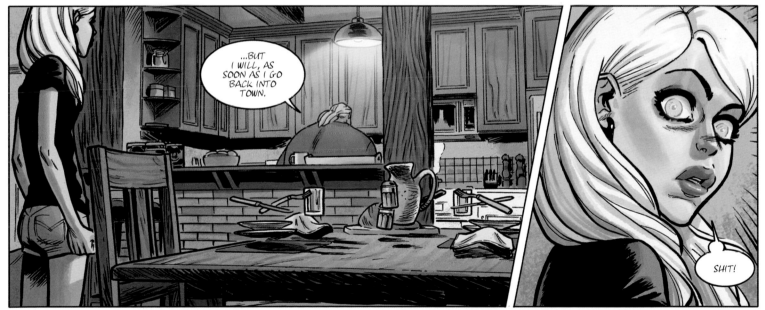

...BUT I WILL, AS SOON AS I GO BACK INTO TOWN.

SHIT!

?!

BLING BLING CLANG TCHING

SORRY, I BUMPED MY KNEE WHEN I SAT DOWN.

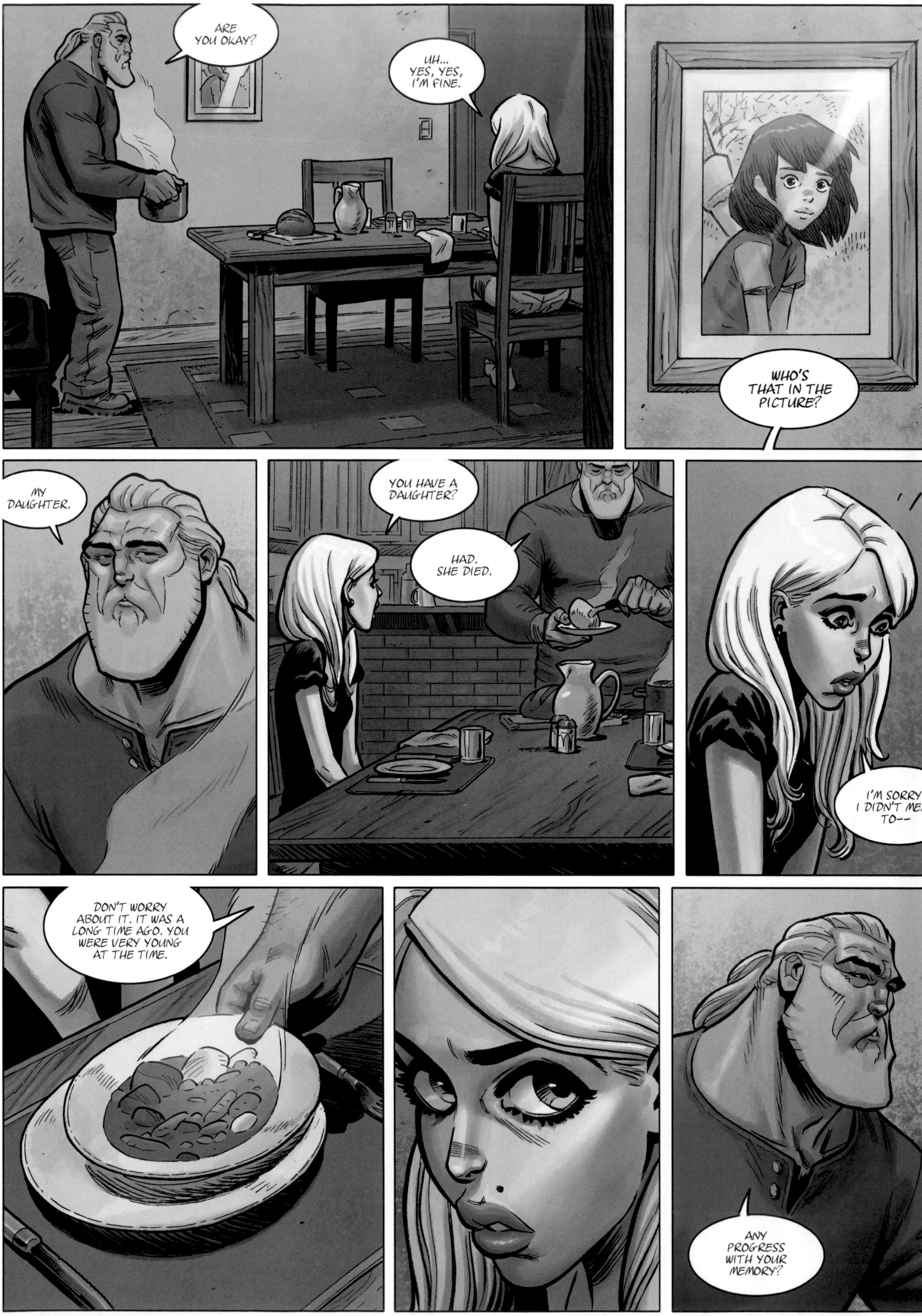
ARE YOU OKAY?
UH... YES, YES, I'M FINE.
WHO'S THAT IN THE PICTURE?
MY DAUGHTER.
YOU HAVE A DAUGHTER?
HAD. SHE DIED.
I'M SORRY, I DIDN'T MEAN TO--
DON'T WORRY ABOUT IT. IT WAS A LONG TIME AGO. YOU WERE VERY YOUNG AT THE TIME.
ANY PROGRESS WITH YOUR MEMORY?

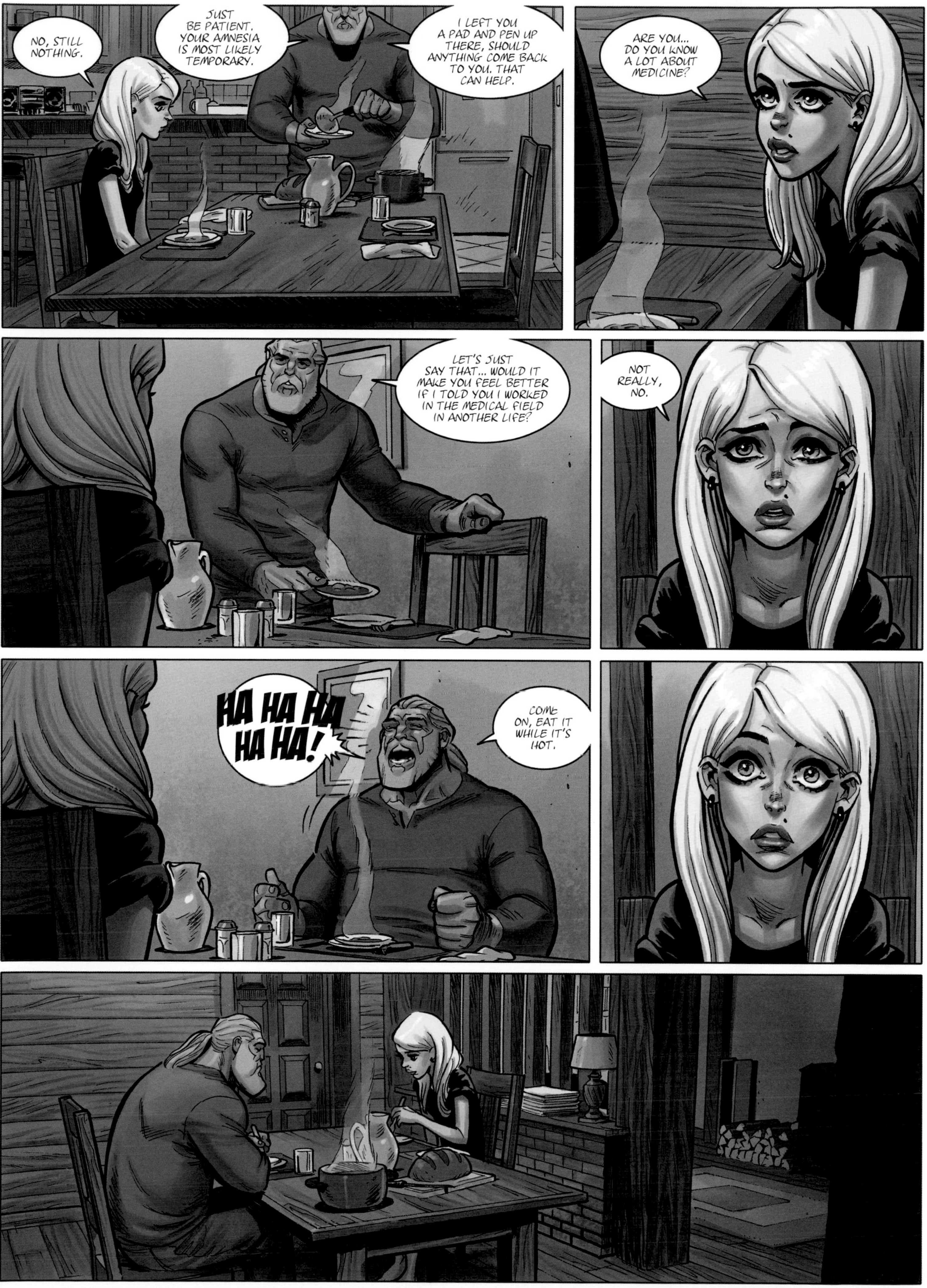
NO, STILL NOTHING.
JUST BE PATIENT. YOUR AMNESIA IS MOST LIKELY TEMPORARY.
I LEFT YOU A PAD AND PEN UP THERE, SHOULD ANYTHING COME BACK TO YOU. THAT CAN HELP.
ARE YOU... DO YOU KNOW A LOT ABOUT MEDICINE?
LET'S JUST SAY THAT... WOULD IT MAKE YOU FEEL BETTER IF I TOLD YOU I WORKED IN THE MEDICAL FIELD IN ANOTHER LIFE?
NOT REALLY, NO.
HA HA HA HA HA!
COME ON, EAT IT WHILE IT'S HOT.

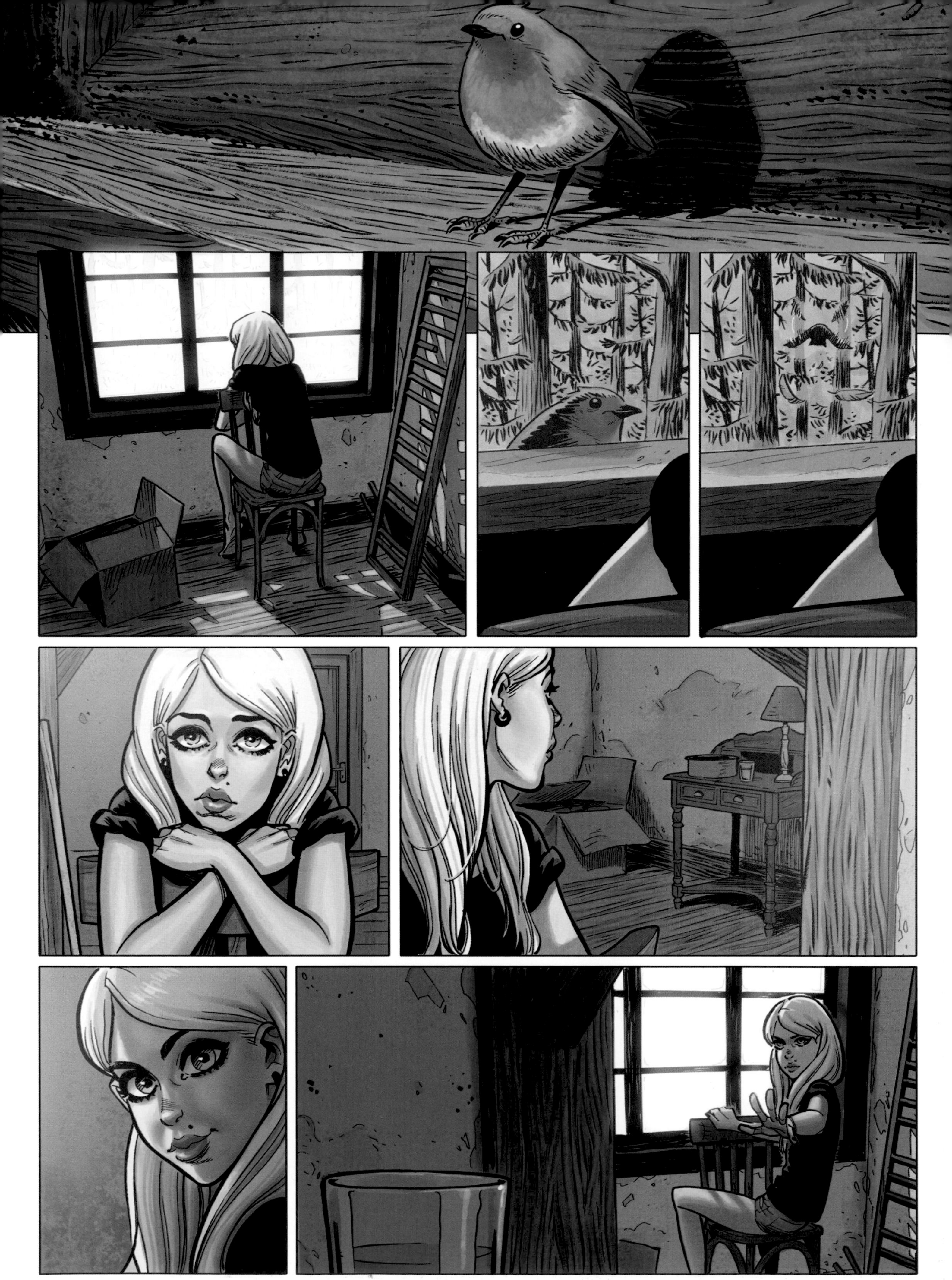

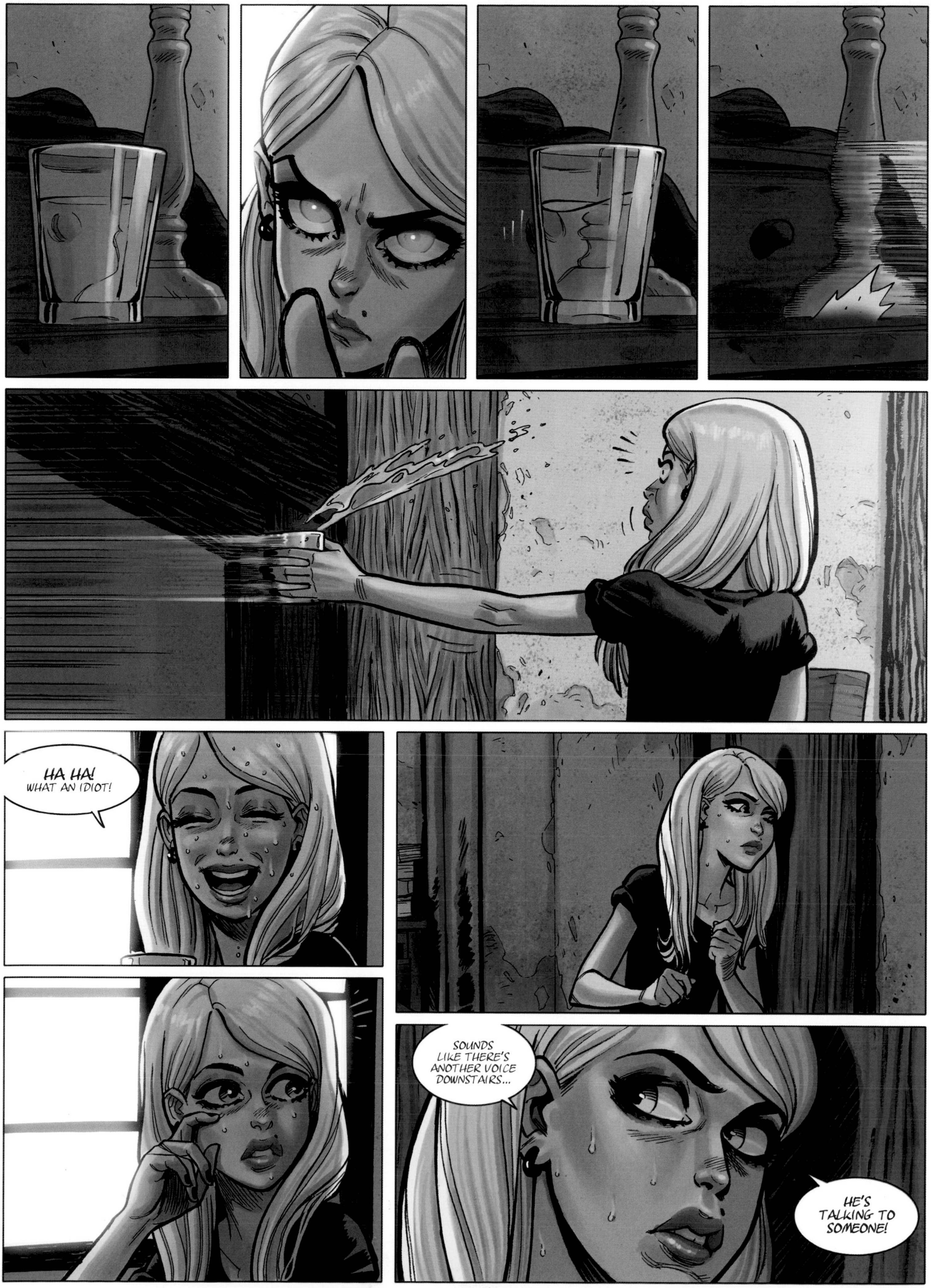
HA HA! WHAT AN IDIOT!
SOUNDS LIKE THERE'S ANOTHER VOICE DOWNSTAIRS...
HE'S TALKING TO SOMEONE!

ARGH! I CAN'T HEAR A WORD THEY'RE SAYING!
THIS FREAKING DOOR IS STILL LOCKED!
WAIT, UNLESS... WITH A LITTLE LUCK...
PERFECT, THE KEY'S IN THE DOOR!
CLACK
YES!
I READ THE PAPERS EVERY DAY, BUT THERE'S STILL NOTHING. IT'S BEEN TOO LONG, SOMETHING'S NOT RIGHT. SOMETHING MUST HAVE HAPPENED... EITHER THAT OR HE CHANGED HIS MIND AND DECIDED TO DISAPPEAR INSTEAD.
I CAN'T LIE TO HER MUCH LONGER. WHAT DO I DO IF HER MEMORY DOESN'T COME BACK?
AND IF IT COMES BACK BEFORE I GET THE CHANCE TO TELL HER, THAT'LL BE EVEN WORSE!

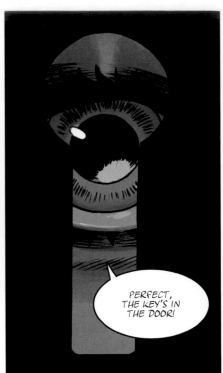

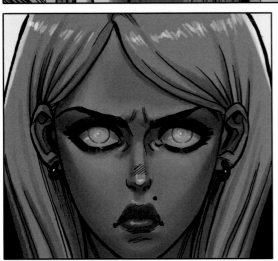

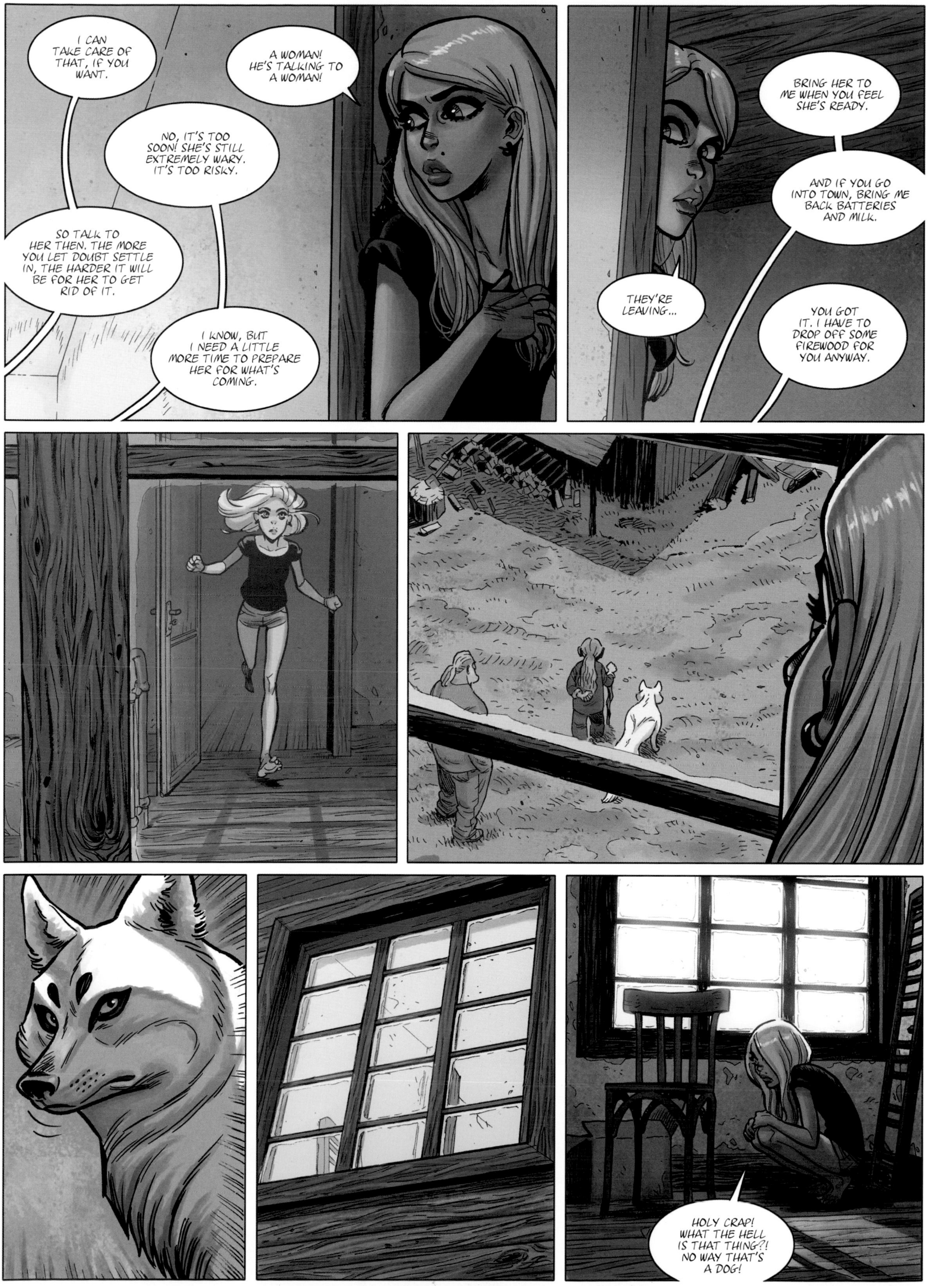
I CAN TAKE CARE OF THAT, IF YOU WANT.
A WOMAN! HE'S TALKING TO A WOMAN!
NO, IT'S TOO SOON! SHE'S STILL EXTREMELY WARY. IT'S TOO RISKY.
SO TALK TO HER THEN. THE MORE YOU LET DOUBT SETTLE IN, THE HARDER IT WILL BE FOR HER TO GET RID OF IT.
I KNOW, BUT I NEED A LITTLE MORE TIME TO PREPARE HER FOR WHAT'S COMING.
BRING HER TO ME WHEN YOU FEEL SHE'S READY.
AND IF YOU GO INTO TOWN, BRING ME BACK BATTERIES AND MILK.
THEY'RE LEAVING...
YOU GOT IT. I HAVE TO DROP OFF SOME FIREWOOD FOR YOU ANYWAY.
HOLY CRAP! WHAT THE HELL IS THAT THING?! NO WAY THAT'S A DOG!

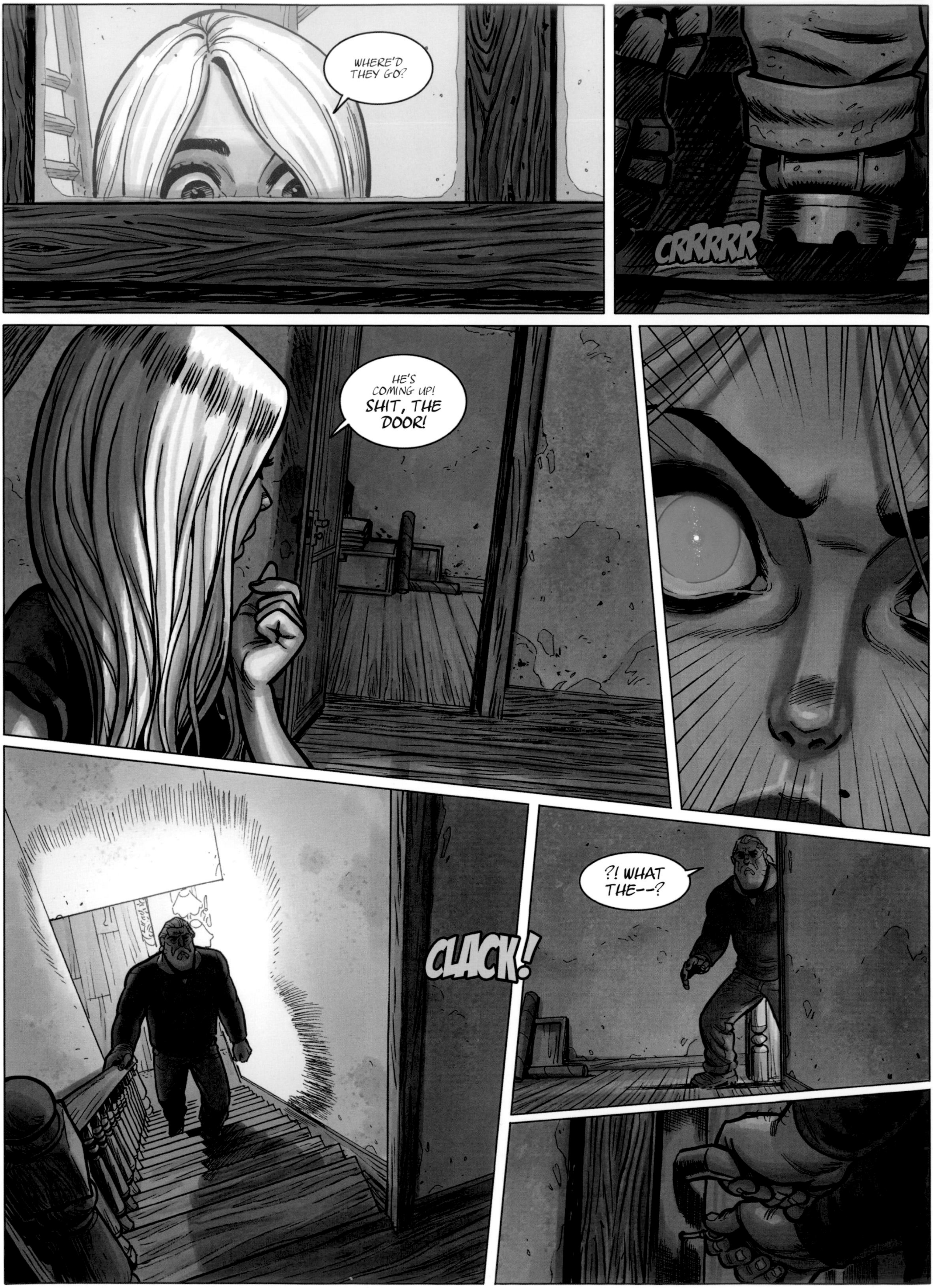
WHERE'D THEY GO?
CRRRRR
HE'S COMING UP! SHIT, THE DOOR!
CLACK!
?! WHAT THE--?

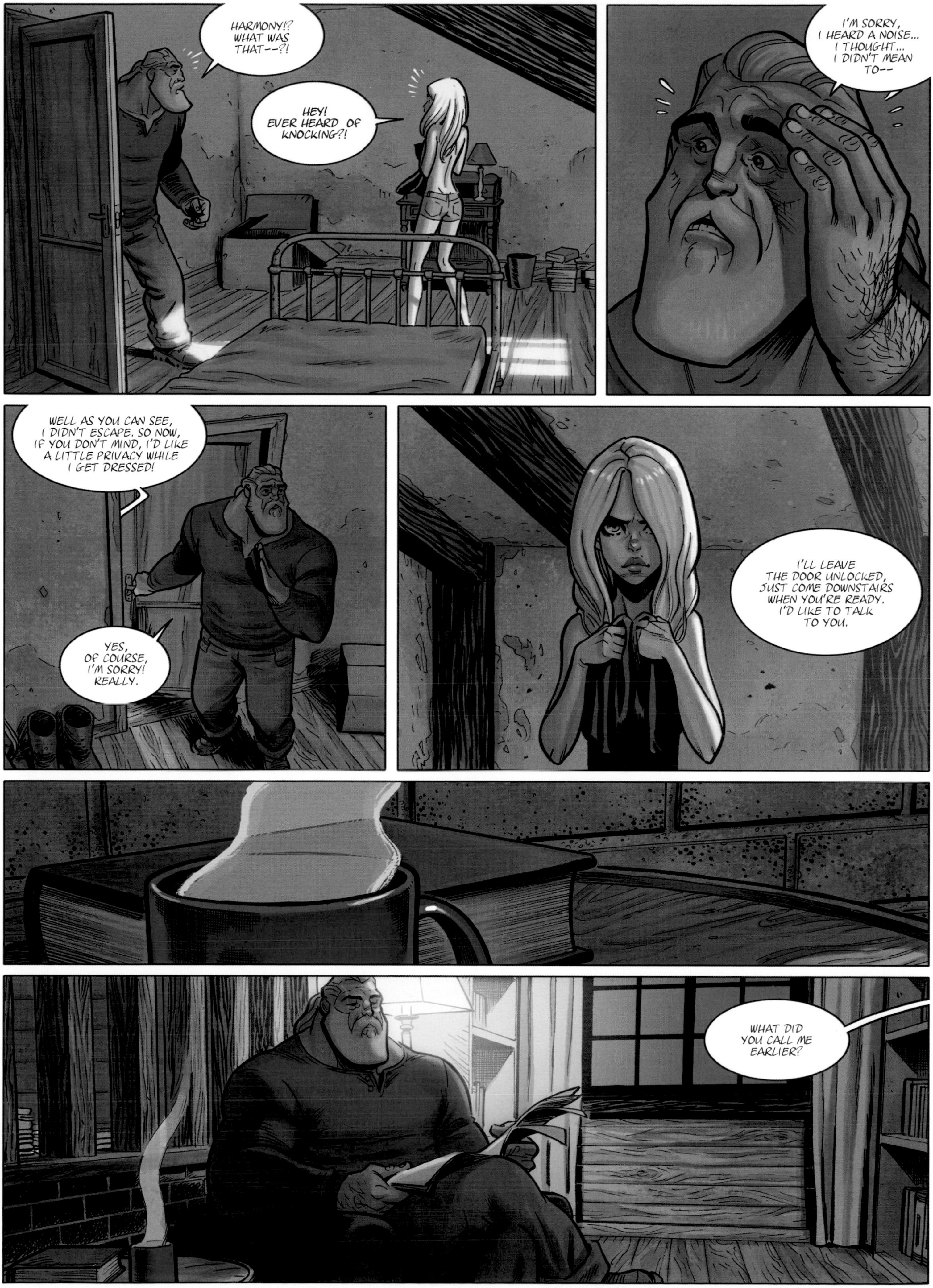
HARMONY!? WHAT WAS THAT--?!
HEY! EVER HEARD OF KNOCKING?!
I'M SORRY, I HEARD A NOISE... I THOUGHT... I DIDN'T MEAN TO--
WELL AS YOU CAN SEE, I DIDN'T ESCAPE. SO NOW, IF YOU DON'T MIND, I'D LIKE A LITTLE PRIVACY WHILE I GET DRESSED!
YES, OF COURSE, I'M SORRY! REALLY.
I'LL LEAVE THE DOOR UNLOCKED, JUST COME DOWNSTAIRS WHEN YOU'RE READY. I'D LIKE TO TALK TO YOU.
WHAT DID YOU CALL ME EARLIER?

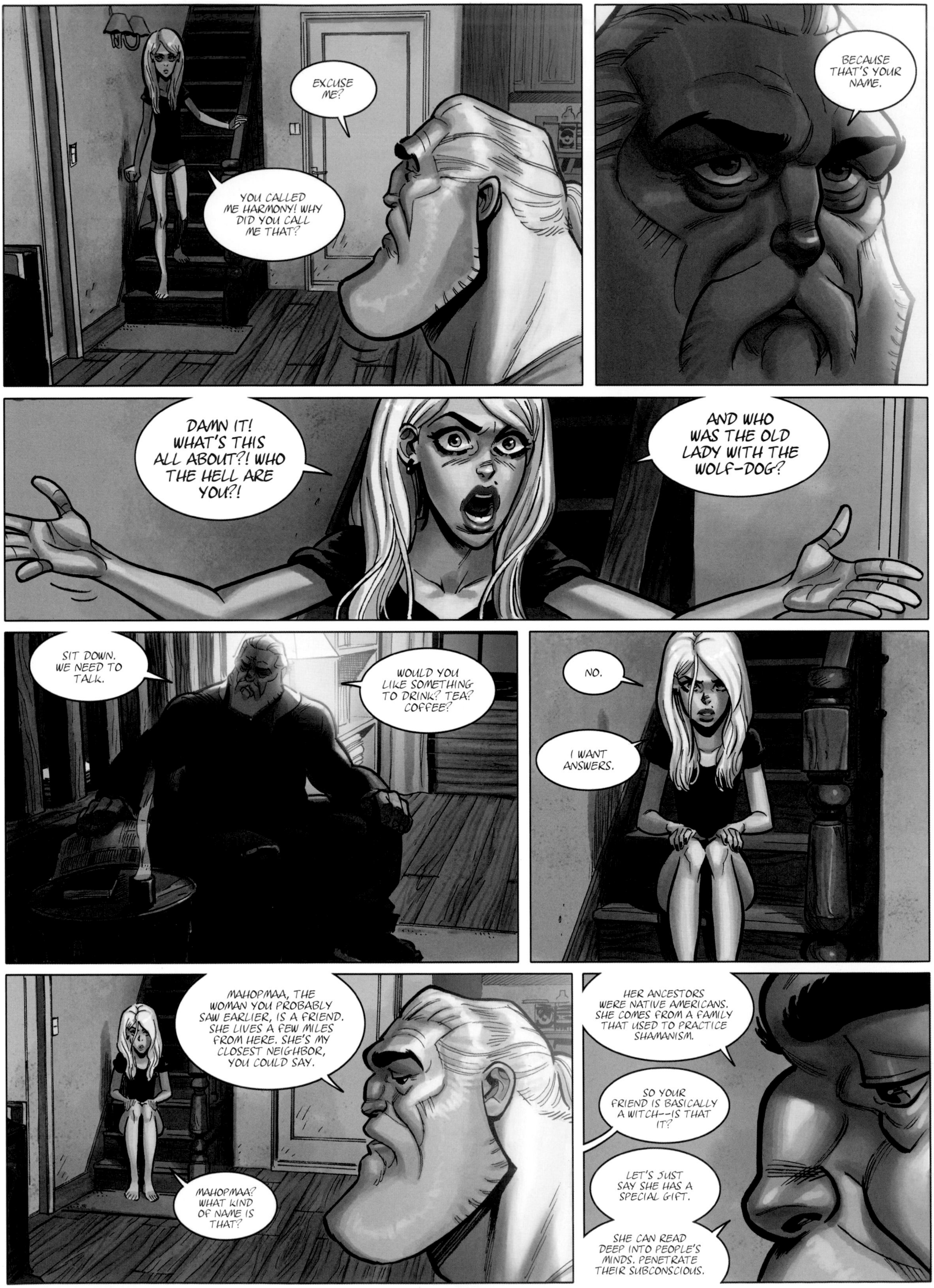
EXCUSE ME?
YOU CALLED ME HARMONY! WHY DID YOU CALL ME THAT?
BECAUSE THAT'S YOUR NAME.
DAMN IT! WHAT'S THIS ALL ABOUT?! WHO THE HELL ARE YOU?!
AND WHO WAS THE OLD LADY WITH THE WOLF-DOG?
SIT DOWN. WE NEED TO TALK.
WOULD YOU LIKE SOMETHING TO DRINK? TEA? COFFEE?
NO.
I WANT ANSWERS.
MAHOPMAA, THE WOMAN YOU PROBABLY SAW EARLIER, IS A FRIEND. SHE LIVES A FEW MILES FROM HERE. SHE'S MY CLOSEST NEIGHBOR, YOU COULD SAY.
MAHOPMAA? WHAT KIND OF NAME IS THAT?
HER ANCESTORS WERE NATIVE AMERICANS. SHE COMES FROM A FAMILY THAT USED TO PRACTICE SHAMANISM.
SO YOUR FRIEND IS BASICALLY A WITCH--IS THAT IT?
LET'S JUST SAY SHE HAS A SPECIAL GIFT.
SHE CAN READ DEEP INTO PEOPLE'S MINDS. PENETRATE THEIR SUBCONSCIOUS.

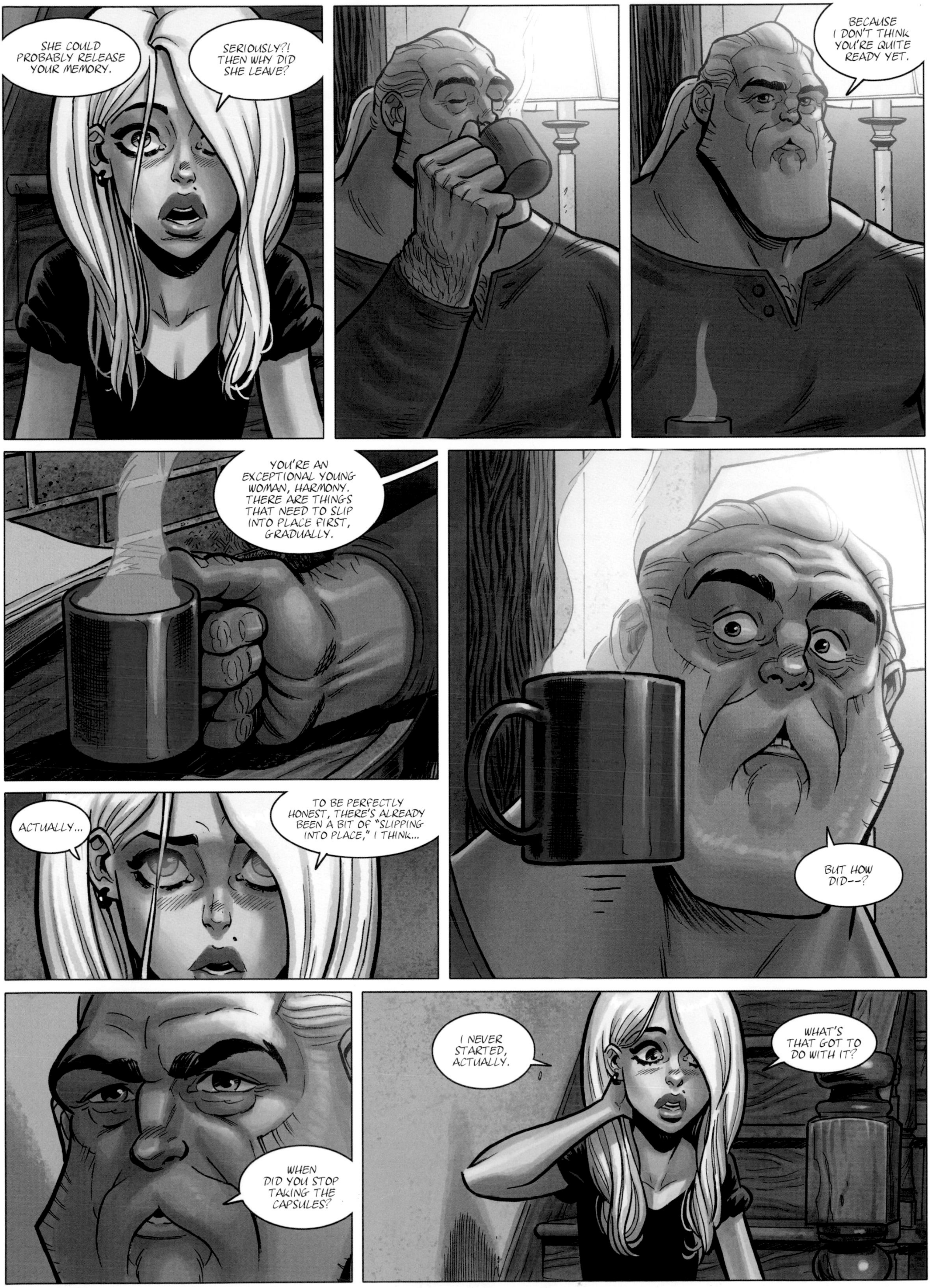
SHE COULD PROBABLY RELEASE YOUR MEMORY.
SERIOUSLY?! THEN WHY DID SHE LEAVE?
BECAUSE I DON'T THINK YOU'RE QUITE READY YET.
YOU'RE AN EXCEPTIONAL YOUNG WOMAN, HARMONY. THERE ARE THINGS THAT NEED TO SLIP INTO PLACE FIRST, GRADUALLY.
ACTUALLY...
TO BE PERFECTLY HONEST, THERE'S ALREADY BEEN A BIT OF "SLIPPING INTO PLACE," I THINK...
BUT HOW DID--?
WHEN DID YOU STOP TAKING THE CAPSULES?
I NEVER STARTED, ACTUALLY.
WHAT'S THAT GOT TO DO WITH IT?

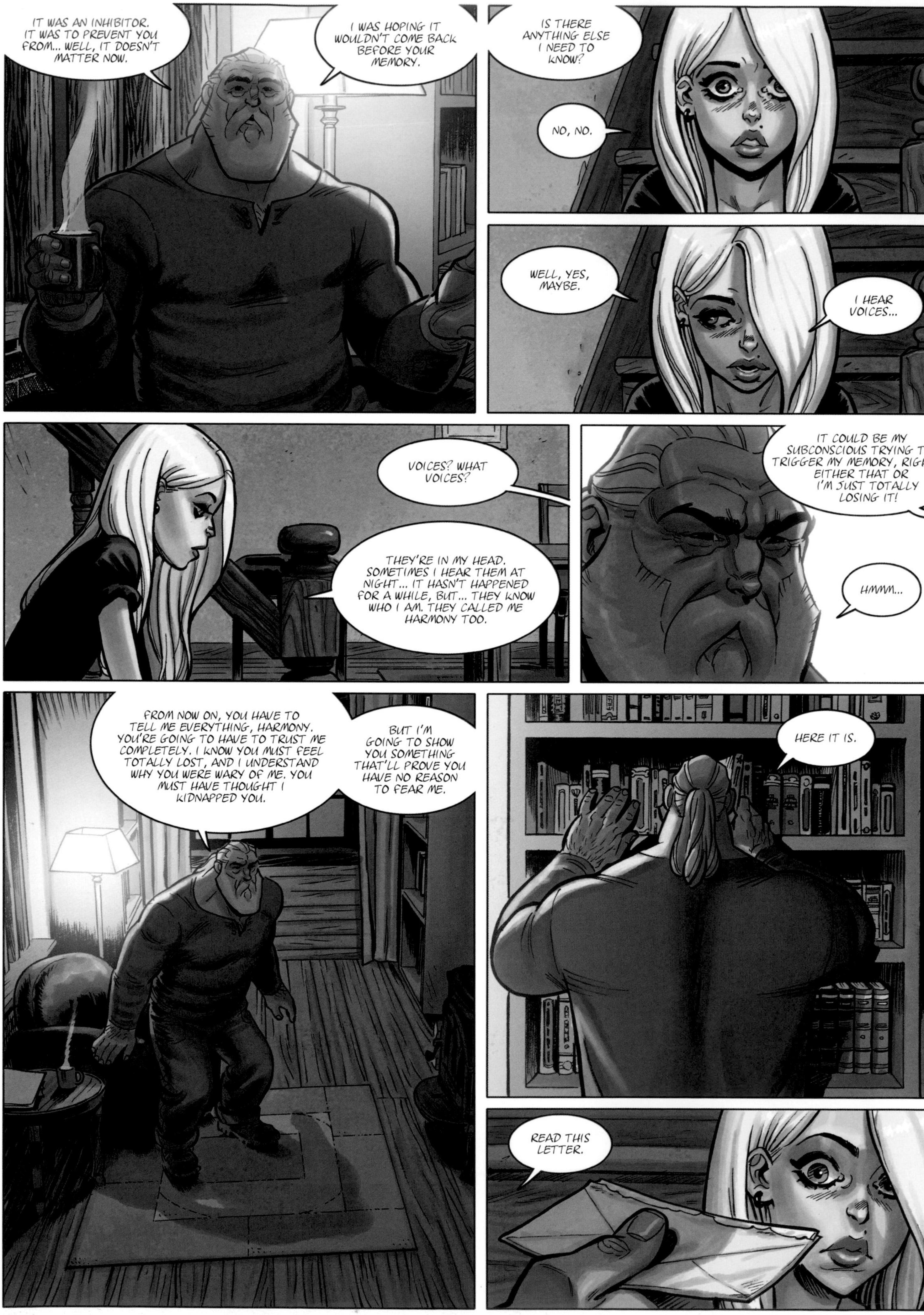
IT WAS AN INHIBITOR. IT WAS TO PREVENT YOU FROM... WELL, IT DOESN'T MATTER NOW.
I WAS HOPING IT WOULDN'T COME BACK BEFORE YOUR MEMORY.
IS THERE ANYTHING ELSE I NEED TO KNOW?
NO, NO.
WELL, YES, MAYBE.
I HEAR VOICES...
VOICES? WHAT VOICES?
THEY'RE IN MY HEAD. SOMETIMES I HEAR THEM AT NIGHT... IT HASN'T HAPPENED FOR A WHILE, BUT... THEY KNOW WHO I AM. THEY CALLED ME HARMONY TOO.
IT COULD BE MY SUBCONSCIOUS TRYING TO TRIGGER MY MEMORY, RIGHT? EITHER THAT OR I'M JUST TOTALLY LOSING IT!
HMMM...
FROM NOW ON, YOU HAVE TO TELL ME EVERYTHING, HARMONY. YOU'RE GOING TO HAVE TO TRUST ME COMPLETELY. I KNOW YOU MUST FEEL TOTALLY LOST, AND I UNDERSTAND WHY YOU WERE WARY OF ME. YOU MUST HAVE THOUGHT I KIDNAPPED YOU.
BUT I'M GOING TO SHOW YOU SOMETHING THAT'LL PROVE YOU HAVE NO REASON TO FEAR ME.
HERE IT IS.
READ THIS LETTER.

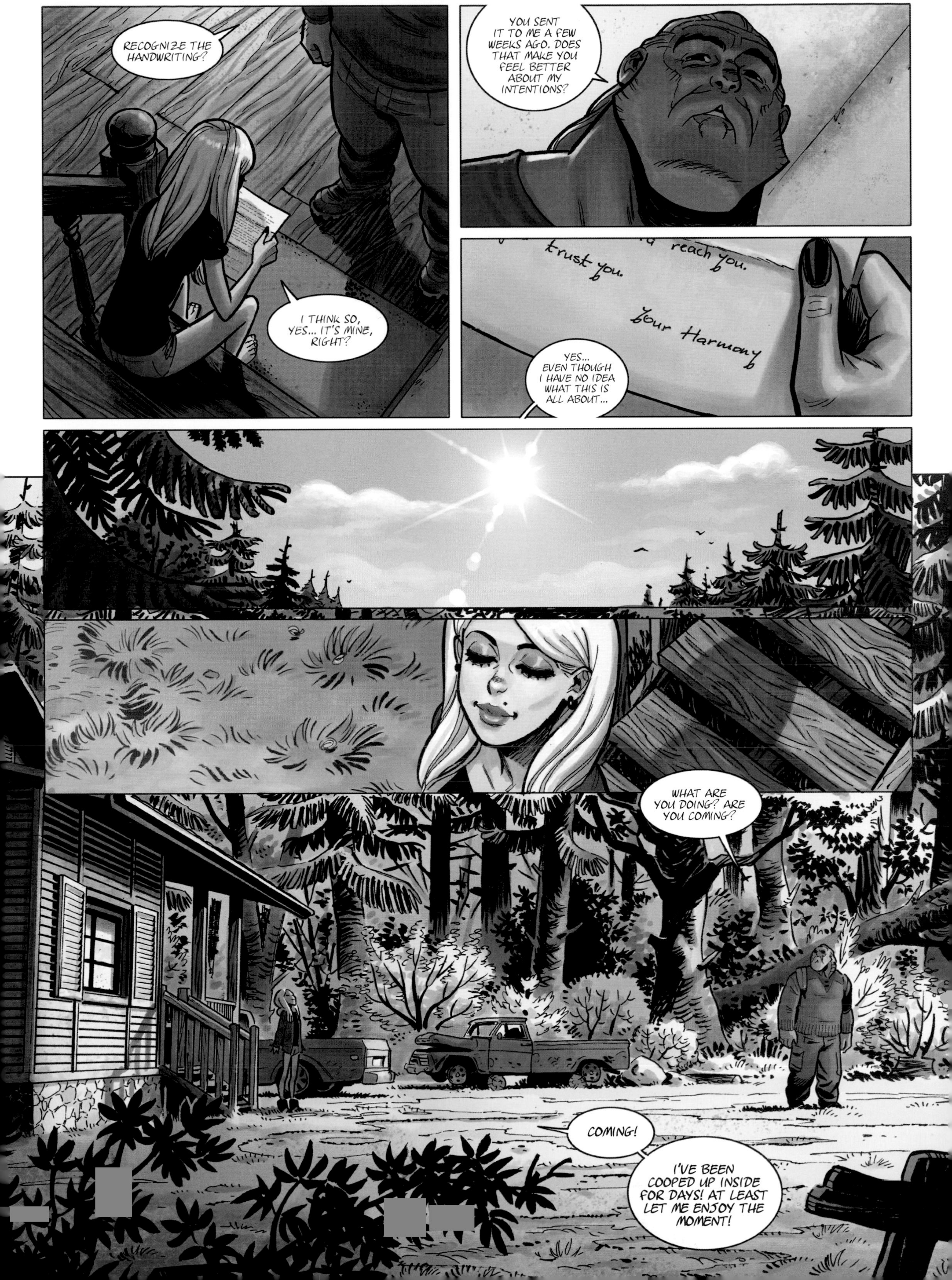
RECOGNIZE THE HANDWRITING?
I THINK SO, YES... IT'S MINE, RIGHT?
YOU SENT IT TO ME A FEW WEEKS AGO. DOES THAT MAKE YOU FEEL BETTER ABOUT MY INTENTIONS?
reach you.
trust you.
Your Harmony
YES... EVEN THOUGH I HAVE NO IDEA WHAT THIS IS ALL ABOUT...
WHAT ARE YOU DOING? ARE YOU COMING?
COMING!
I'VE BEEN COOPED UP INSIDE FOR DAYS! AT LEAST LET ME ENJOY THE MOMENT!

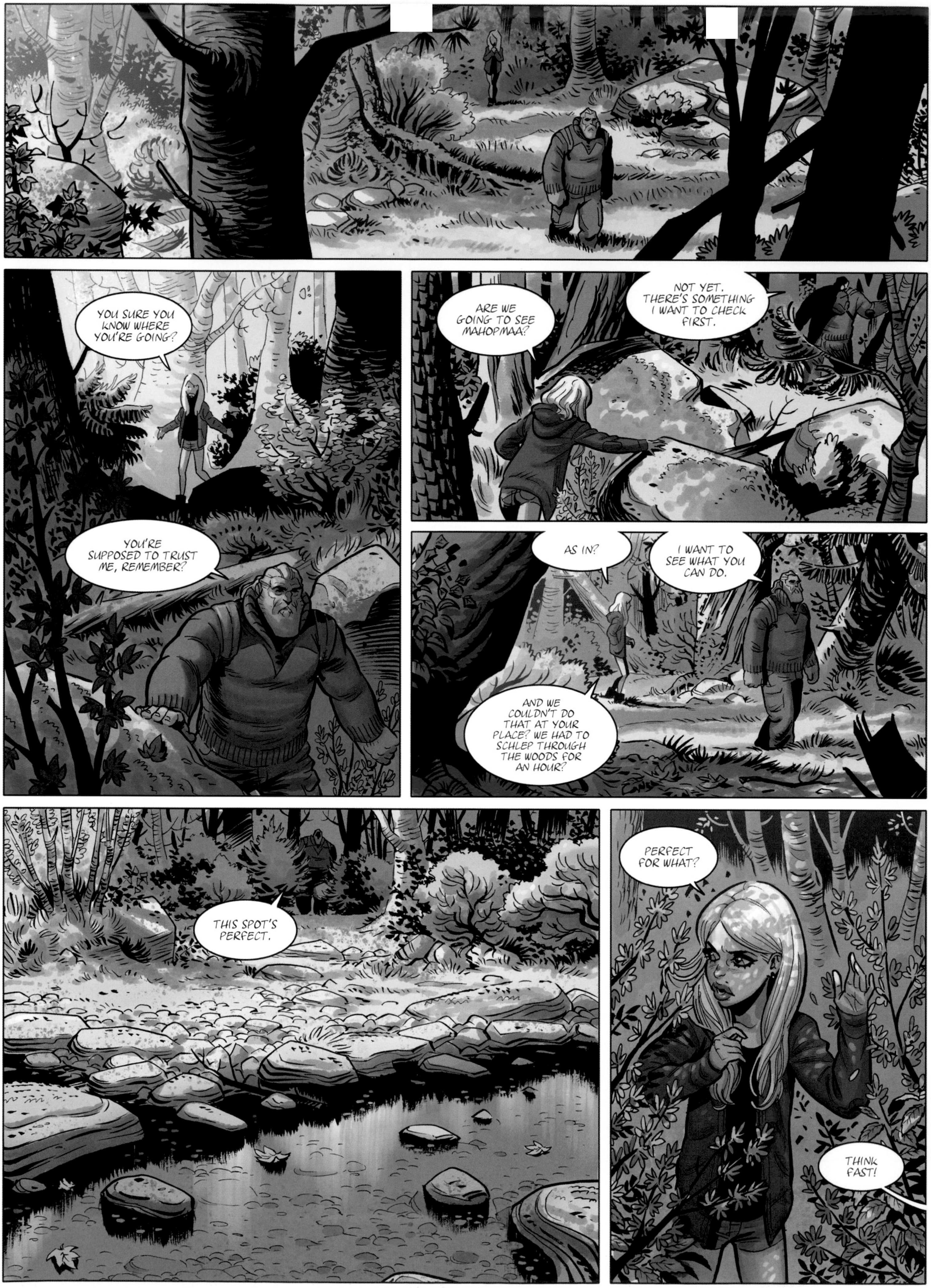
YOU SURE YOU KNOW WHERE YOU'RE GOING?
ARE WE GOING TO SEE MAHOPMAA?
NOT YET. THERE'S SOMETHING I WANT TO CHECK FIRST.
YOU'RE SUPPOSED TO TRUST ME, REMEMBER?
AS IN?
I WANT TO SEE WHAT YOU CAN DO.
AND WE COULDN'T DO THAT AT YOUR PLACE? WE HAD TO SCHLEP THROUGH THE WOODS FOR AN HOUR?
THIS SPOT'S PERFECT.
PERFECT FOR WHAT?
THINK FAST!

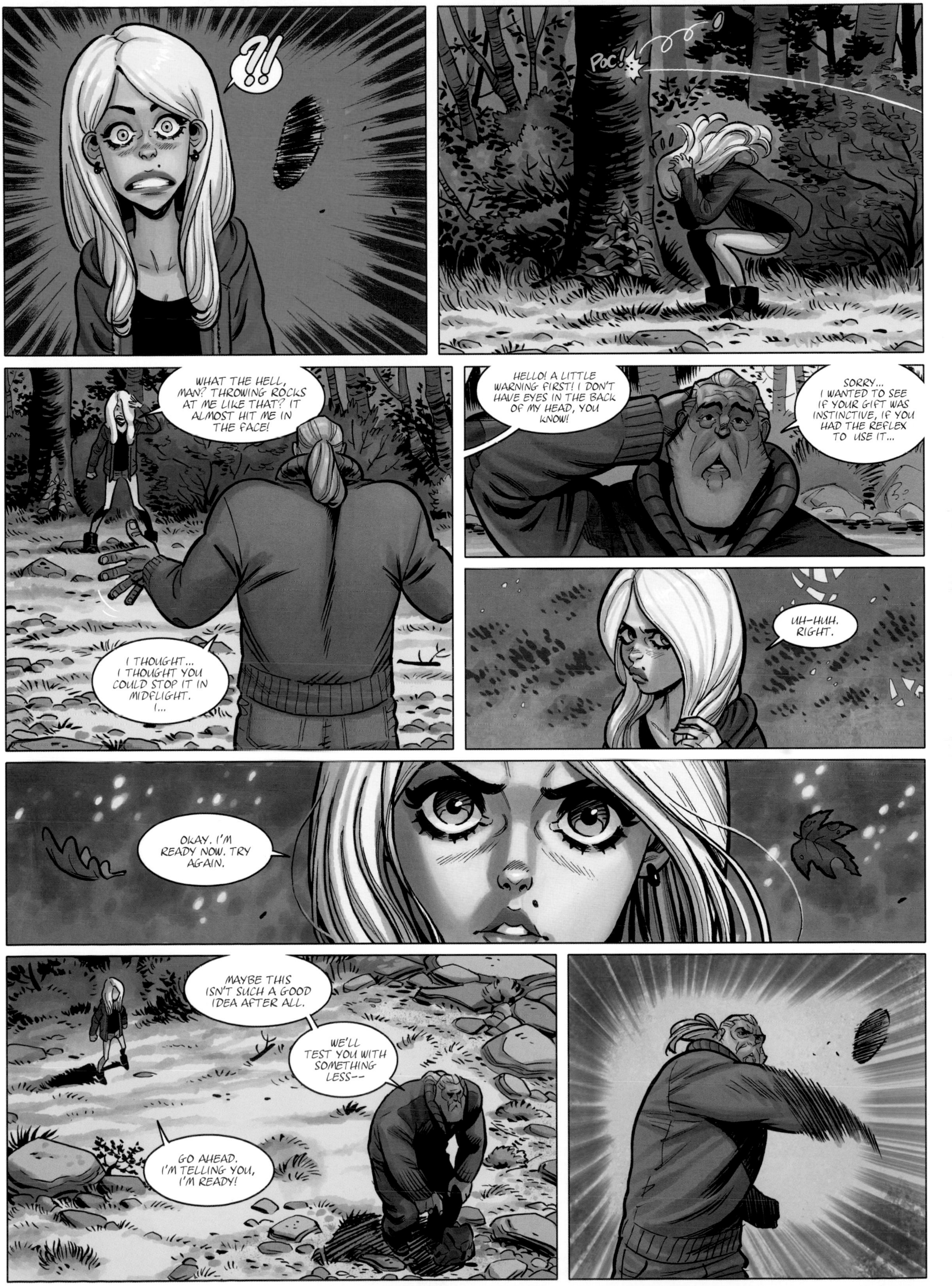
?!!
POC!
WHAT THE HELL, MAN? THROWING ROCKS AT ME LIKE THAT? IT ALMOST HIT ME IN THE FACE!
I THOUGHT... I THOUGHT YOU COULD STOP IT IN MIDFLIGHT. I...
HELLO! A LITTLE WARNING FIRST! I DON'T HAVE EYES IN THE BACK OF MY HEAD, YOU KNOW!
SORRY... I WANTED TO SEE IF YOUR GIFT WAS INSTINCTIVE, IF YOU HAD THE REFLEX TO USE IT...
UH-HUH. RIGHT.
OKAY. I'M READY NOW. TRY AGAIN.
MAYBE THIS ISN'T SUCH A GOOD IDEA AFTER ALL.
WE'LL TEST YOU WITH SOMETHING LESS--
GO AHEAD. I'M TELLING YOU, I'M READY!

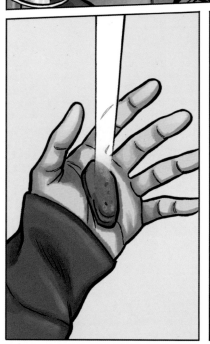

DID YOU SEE THAT?! I STOPPED IT MIDFLIGHT!

YES. NOT BAD, ALL THINGS CONSIDERED.

"NOT BAD"? YOU JUST WAIT--I'LL SHOW YOU WHAT I CAN DO!

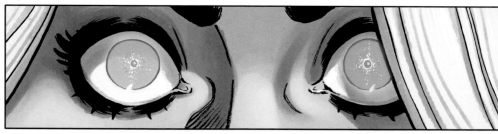

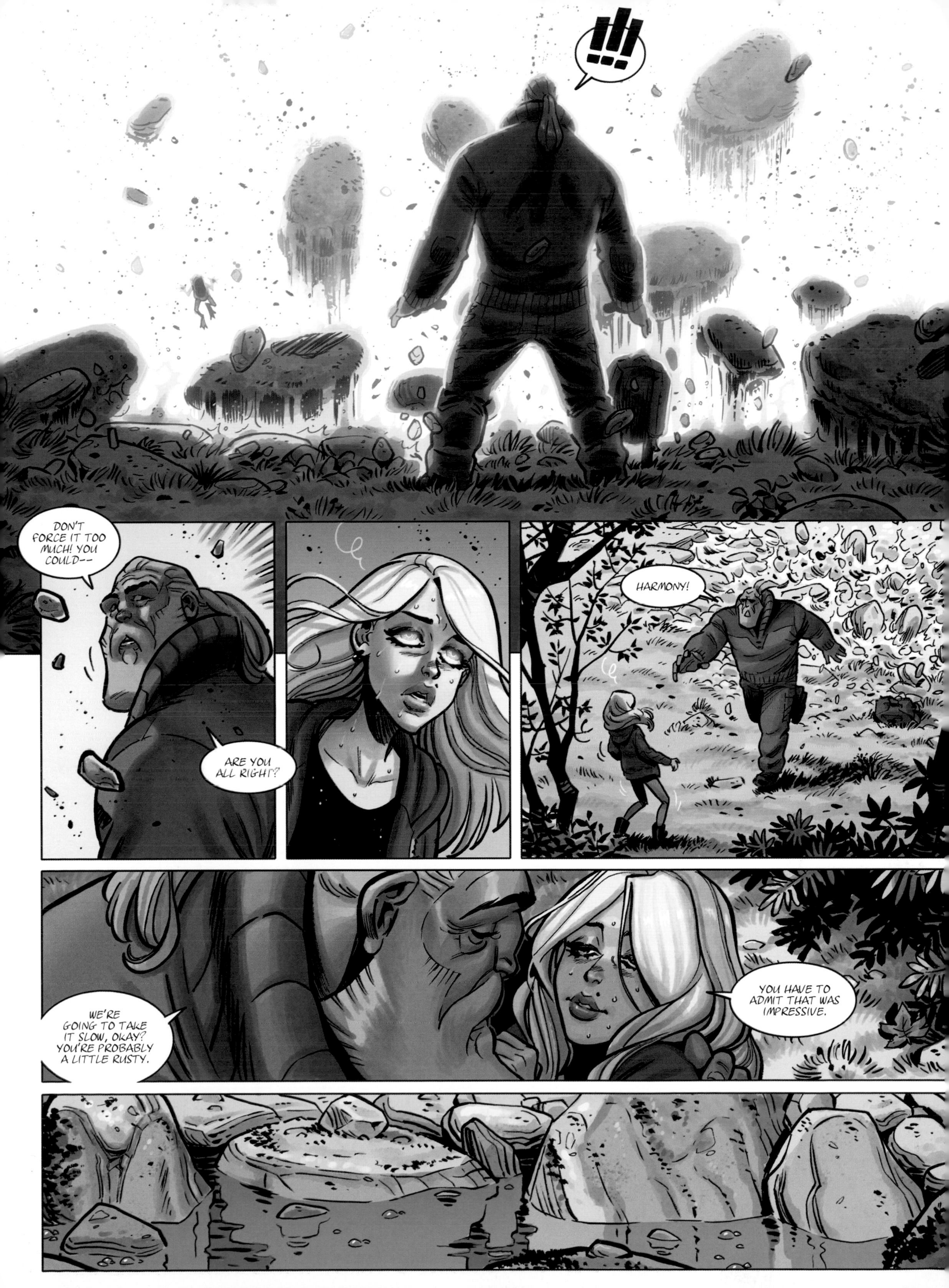
!!!
DON'T FORCE IT TOO MUCH! YOU COULD--
ARE YOU ALL RIGHT?
HARMONY!
WE'RE GOING TO TAKE IT SLOW, OKAY? YOU'RE PROBABLY A LITTLE RUSTY.
YOU HAVE TO ADMIT THAT WAS IMPRESSIVE.

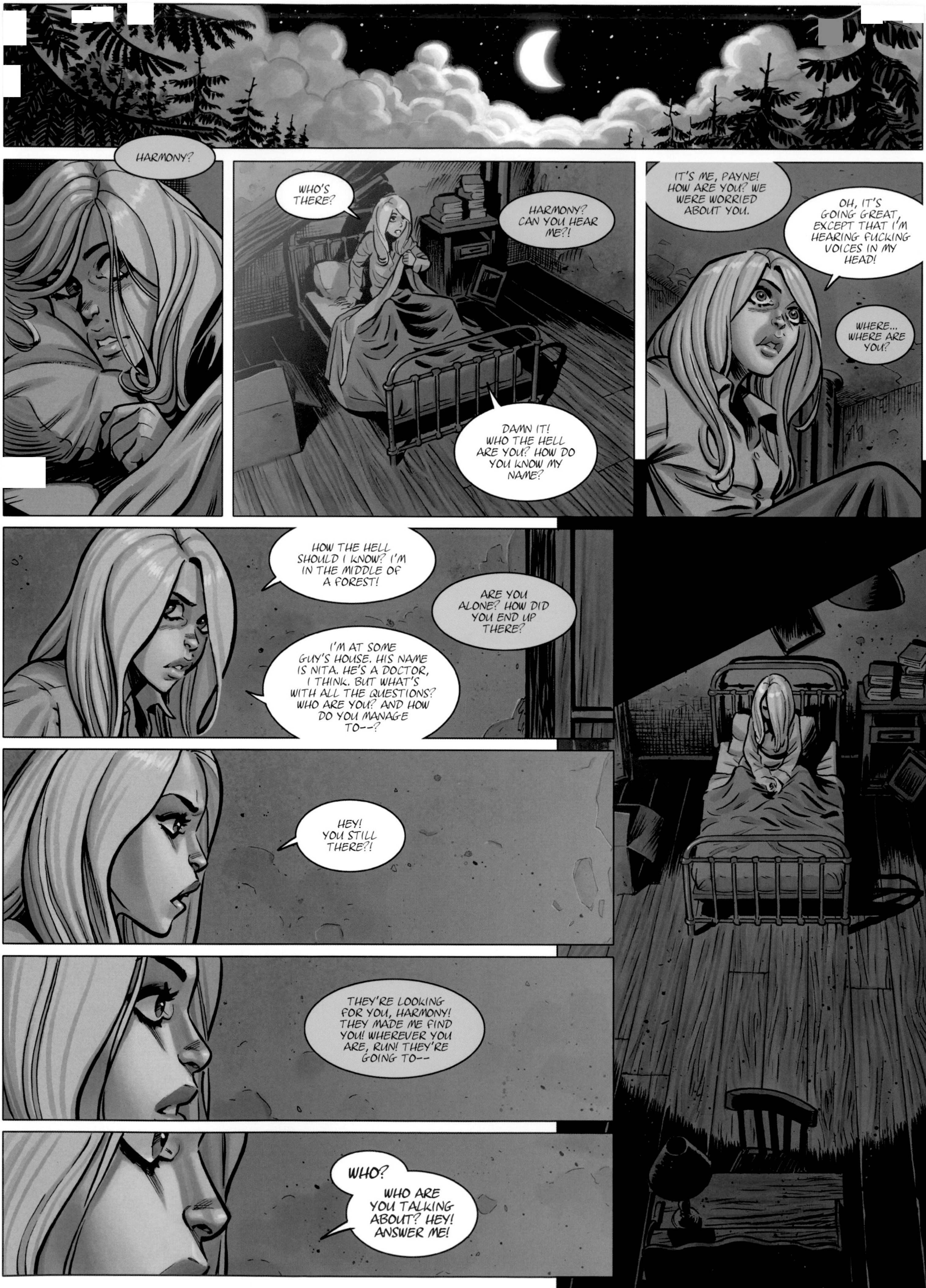
HARMONY?
WHO'S THERE?
HARMONY? CAN YOU HEAR ME?!
DAMN IT! WHO THE HELL ARE YOU? HOW DO YOU KNOW MY NAME?
IT'S ME, PAYNE! HOW ARE YOU? WE WERE WORRIED ABOUT YOU.
OH, IT'S GOING GREAT, EXCEPT THAT I'M HEARING FUCKING VOICES IN MY HEAD!
WHERE... WHERE ARE YOU?
HOW THE HELL SHOULD I KNOW? I'M IN THE MIDDLE OF A FOREST!
ARE YOU ALONE? HOW DID YOU END UP THERE?
I'M AT SOME GUY'S HOUSE. HIS NAME IS NITA. HE'S A DOCTOR, I THINK. BUT WHAT'S WITH ALL THE QUESTIONS? WHO ARE YOU? AND HOW DO YOU MANAGE TO--?
HEY! YOU STILL THERE?!
THEY'RE LOOKING FOR YOU, HARMONY! THEY MADE ME FIND YOU! WHEREVER YOU ARE, RUN! THEY'RE GOING TO--
WHO?
WHO ARE YOU TALKING ABOUT? HEY! ANSWER ME!

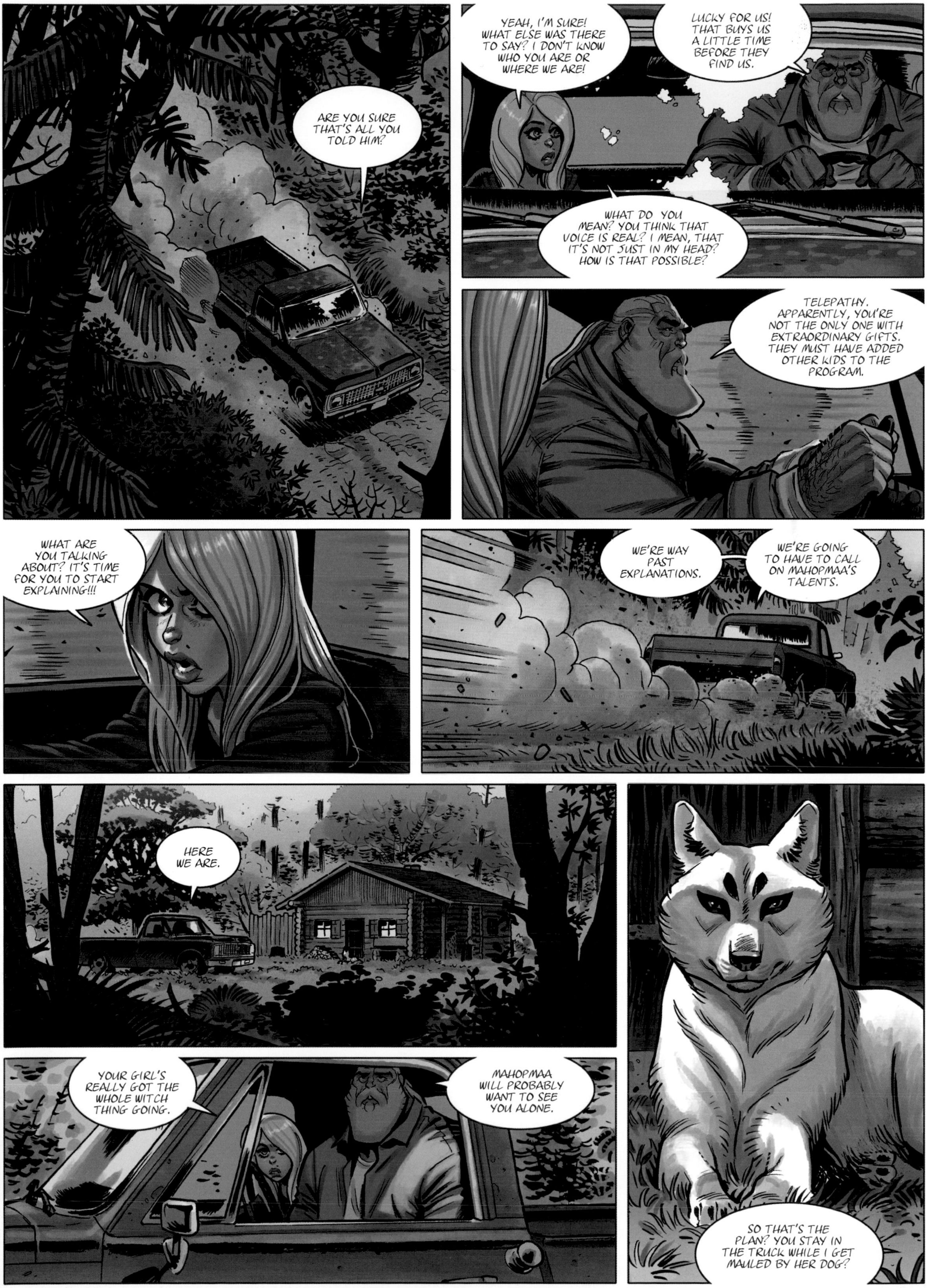
ARE YOU SURE THAT'S ALL YOU TOLD HIM?
YEAH, I'M SURE! WHAT ELSE WAS THERE TO SAY? I DON'T KNOW WHO YOU ARE OR WHERE WE ARE!
LUCKY FOR US! THAT BUYS US A LITTLE TIME BEFORE THEY FIND US.
WHAT DO YOU MEAN? YOU THINK THAT VOICE IS REAL? I MEAN, THAT IT'S NOT JUST IN MY HEAD? HOW IS THAT POSSIBLE?
TELEPATHY. APPARENTLY, YOU'RE NOT THE ONLY ONE WITH EXTRAORDINARY GIFTS. THEY MUST HAVE ADDED OTHER KIDS TO THE PROGRAM.
WHAT ARE YOU TALKING ABOUT? IT'S TIME FOR YOU TO START EXPLAINING!!!
WE'RE WAY PAST EXPLANATIONS.
WE'RE GOING TO HAVE TO CALL ON MAHOPMAA'S TALENTS.
HERE WE ARE.
YOUR GIRL'S REALLY GOT THE WHOLE WITCH THING GOING.
MAHOPMAA WILL PROBABLY WANT TO SEE YOU ALONE.
SO THAT'S THE PLAN? YOU STAY IN THE TRUCK WHILE I GET MAULED BY HER DOG?

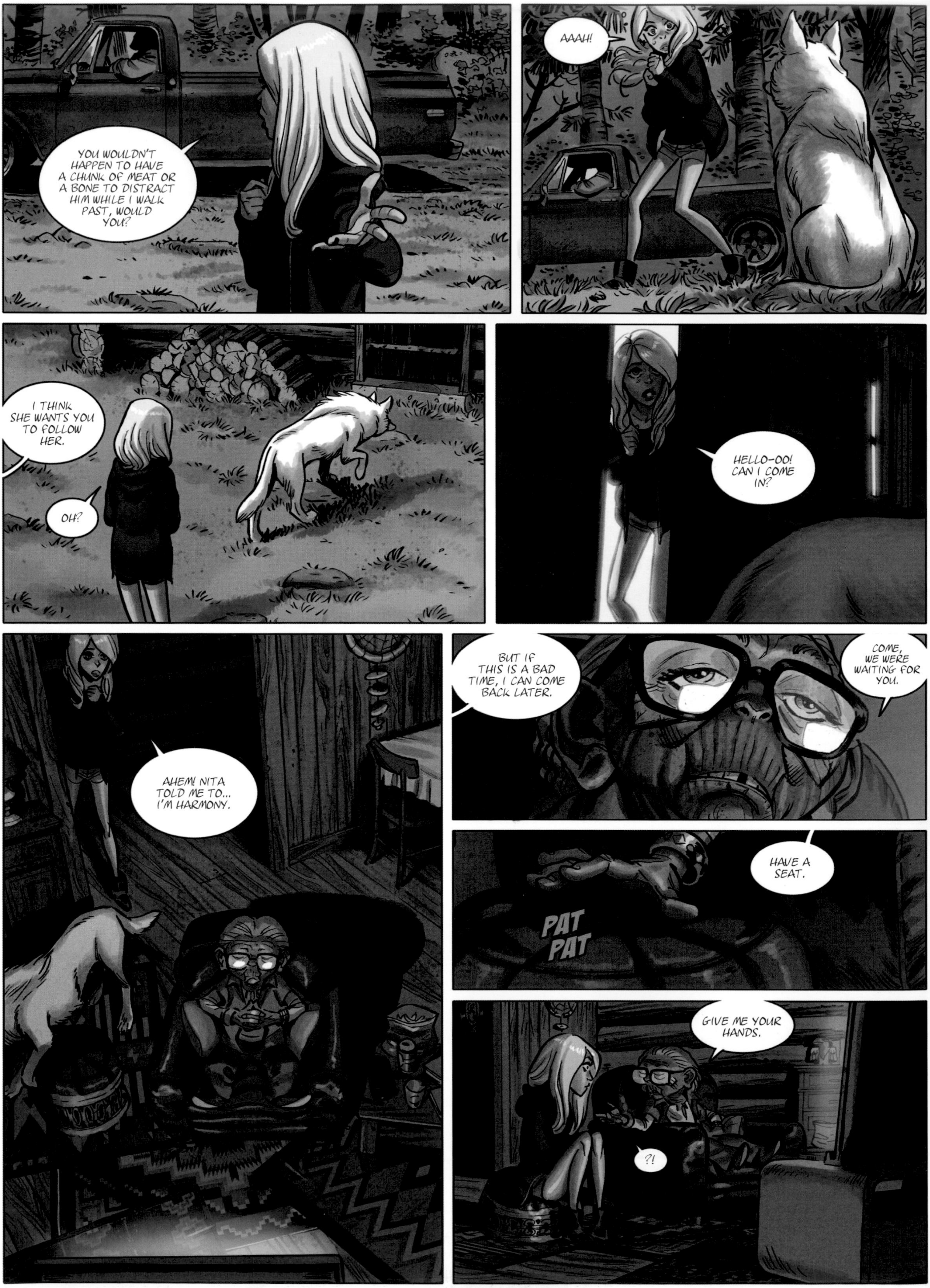
YOU WOULDN'T HAPPEN TO HAVE A CHUNK OF MEAT OR A BONE TO DISTRACT HIM WHILE I WALK PAST, WOULD YOU?
AAAH!
I THINK SHE WANTS YOU TO FOLLOW HER.
OH?
HELLO-OO! CAN I COME IN?
AHEM! NITA TOLD ME TO... I'M HARMONY.
BUT IF THIS IS A BAD TIME, I CAN COME BACK LATER.
COME, WE WERE WAITING FOR YOU.
HAVE A SEAT.
PAT PAT
GIVE ME YOUR HANDS.
?!

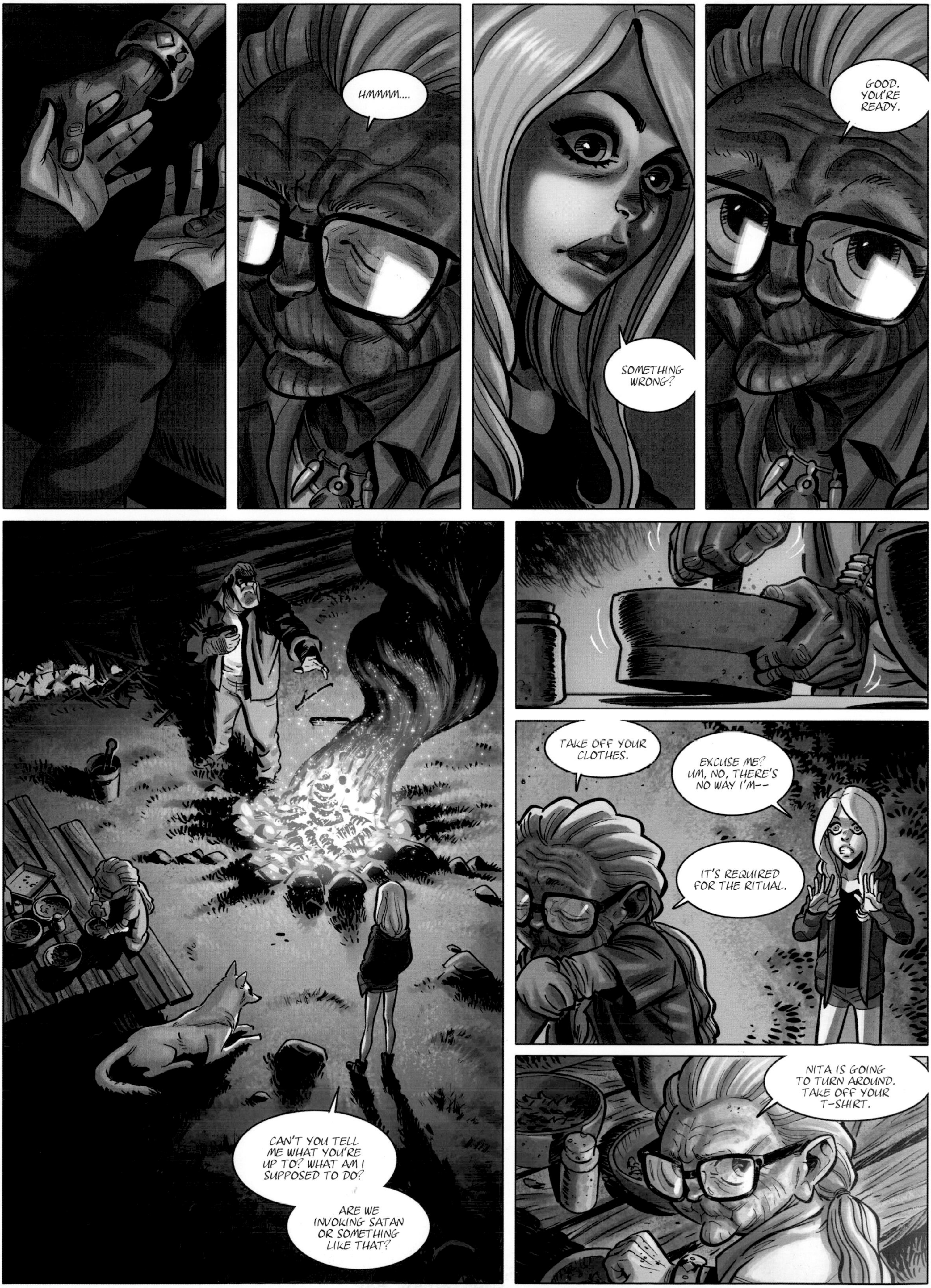
HMMMM....
SOMETHING WRONG?
GOOD. YOU'RE READY.
CAN'T YOU TELL ME WHAT YOU'RE UP TO? WHAT AM I SUPPOSED TO DO?
ARE WE INVOKING SATAN OR SOMETHING LIKE THAT?
TAKE OFF YOUR CLOTHES.
EXCUSE ME? UM, NO, THERE'S NO WAY I'M--
IT'S REQUIRED FOR THE RITUAL.
NITA IS GOING TO TURN AROUND. TAKE OFF YOUR T-SHIRT.

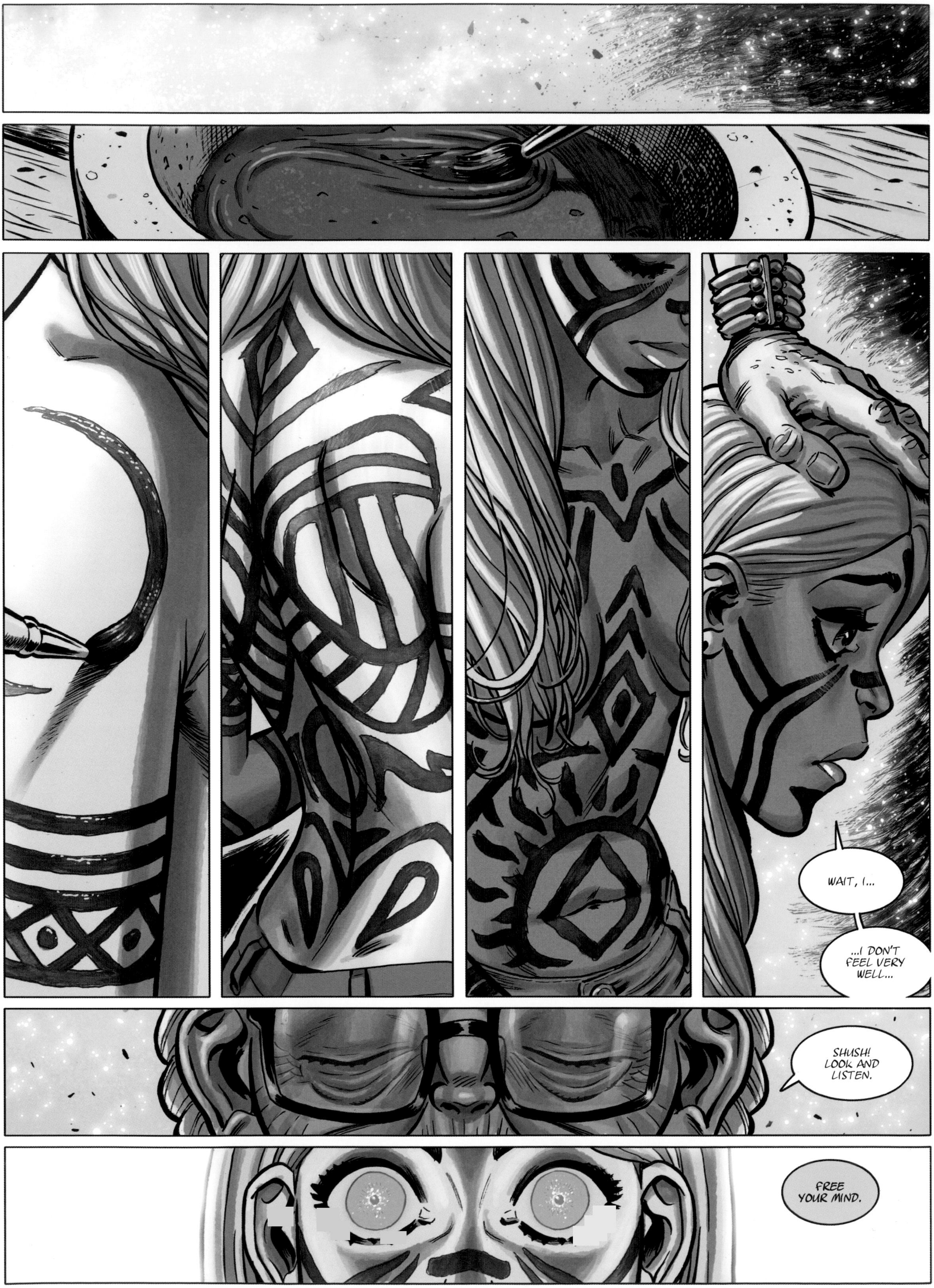
WAIT, I...
...I DON'T FEEL VERY WELL...
SHUSH! LOOK AND LISTEN.
FREE YOUR MIND.

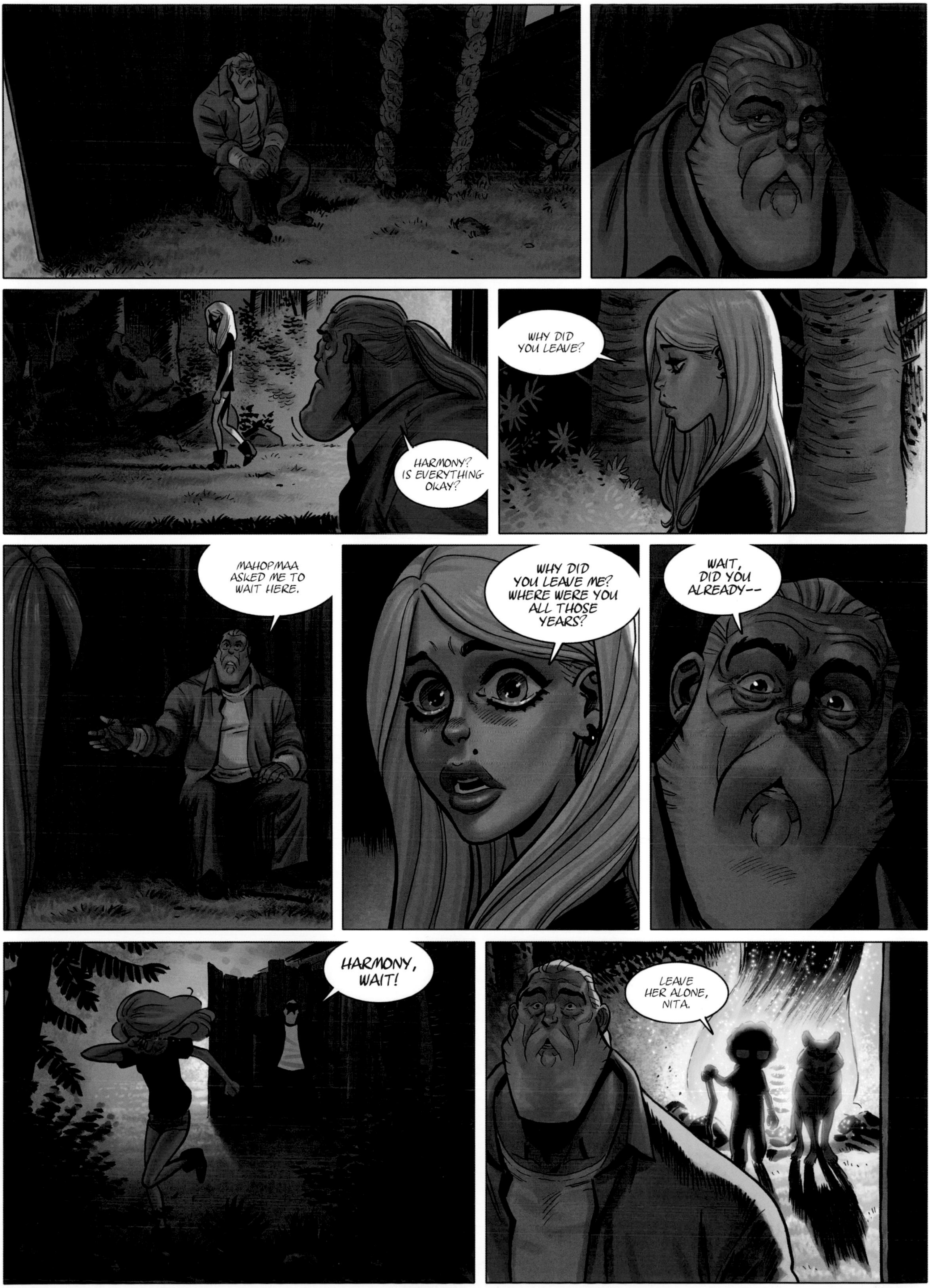
HARMONY?
IS EVERYTHING
OKAY?
WHY DID
YOU LEAVE?
MAHOPMAA
ASKED ME TO
WAIT HERE.
WHY DID
YOU LEAVE ME?
WHERE WERE YOU
ALL THOSE
YEARS?
WAIT,
DID YOU
ALREADY--
HARMONY,
WAIT!
LEAVE
HER ALONE,
NITA.

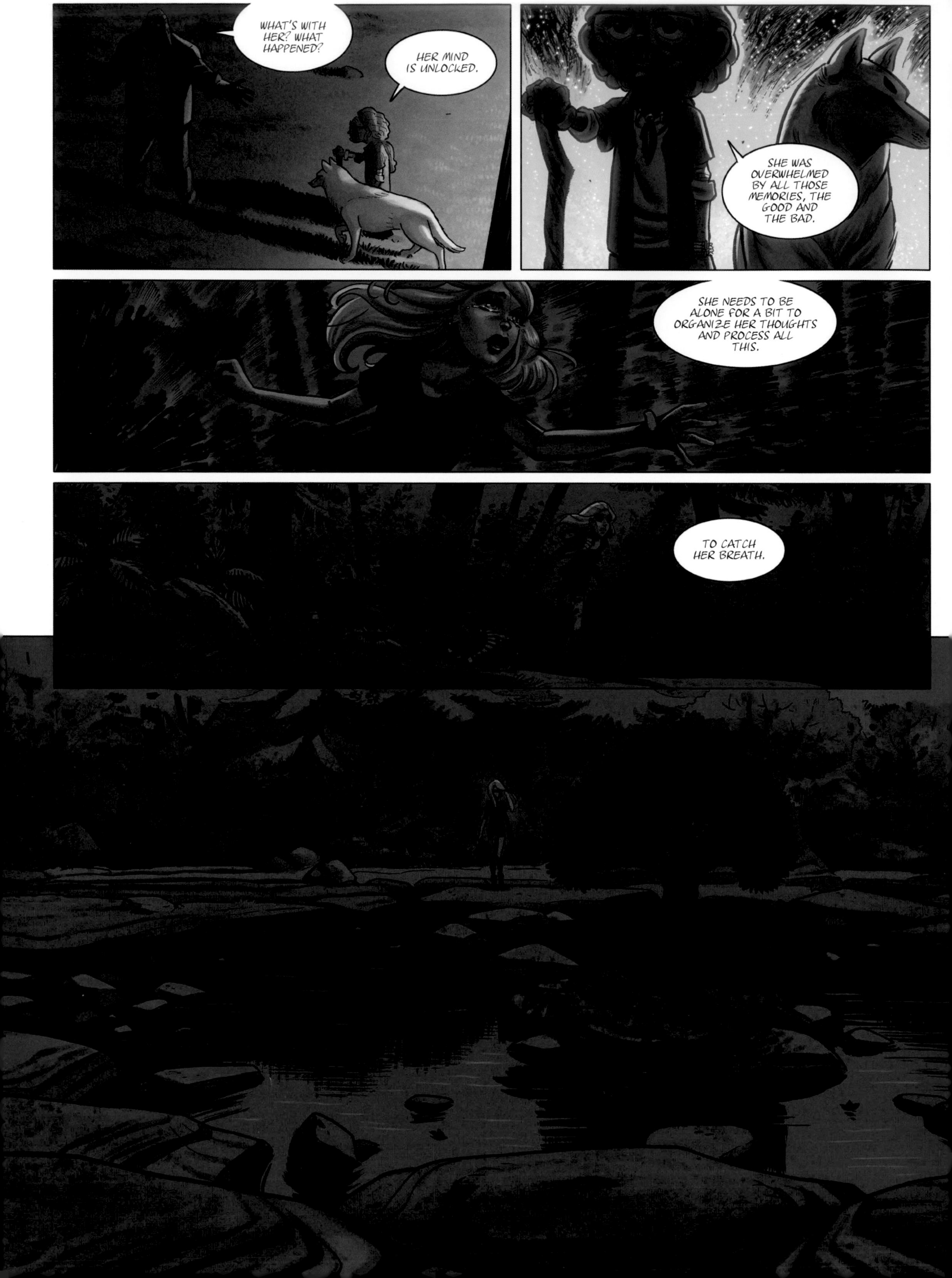
WHAT'S WITH HER? WHAT HAPPENED?
HER MIND IS UNLOCKED.
SHE WAS OVERWHELMED BY ALL THOSE MEMORIES, THE GOOD AND THE BAD.
SHE NEEDS TO BE ALONE FOR A BIT TO ORGANIZE HER THOUGHTS AND PROCESS ALL THIS.
TO CATCH HER BREATH.

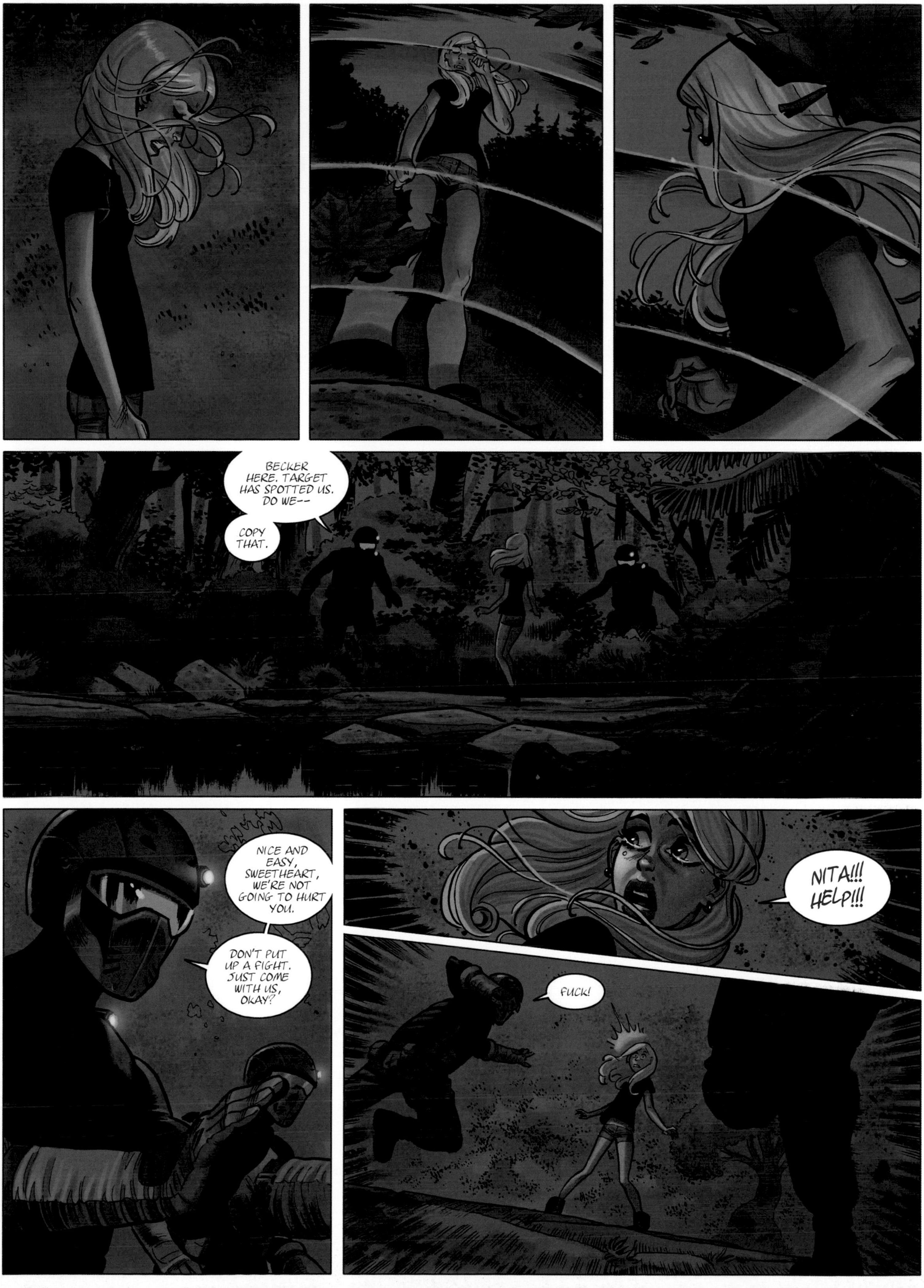
BECKER HERE. TARGET HAS SPOTTED US. DO WE--
COPY THAT.
NICE AND EASY, SWEETHEART, WE'RE NOT GOING TO HURT YOU.
DON'T PUT UP A FIGHT. JUST COME WITH US, OKAY?
NITA!!! HELP!!!
FUCK!

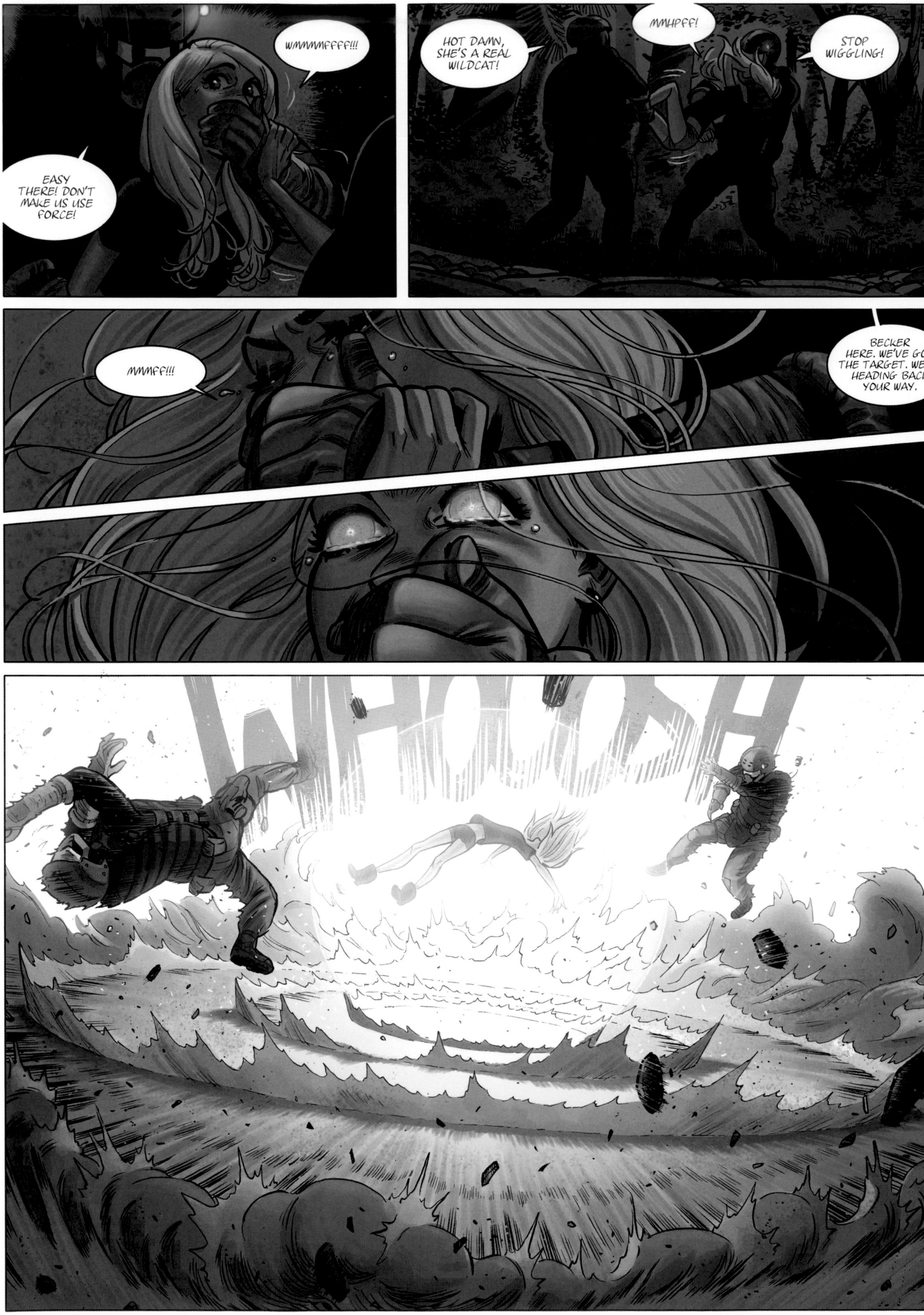
WMMMMFFFF!!!
EASY THERE! DON'T MAKE US USE FORCE!
HOT DAMN, SHE'S A REAL WILDCAT!
MMHPFF!
STOP WIGGLING!
MMMFF!!!
BECKER HERE. WE'VE GOT THE TARGET. WE'RE HEADING BACK YOUR WAY.
WHOOSH

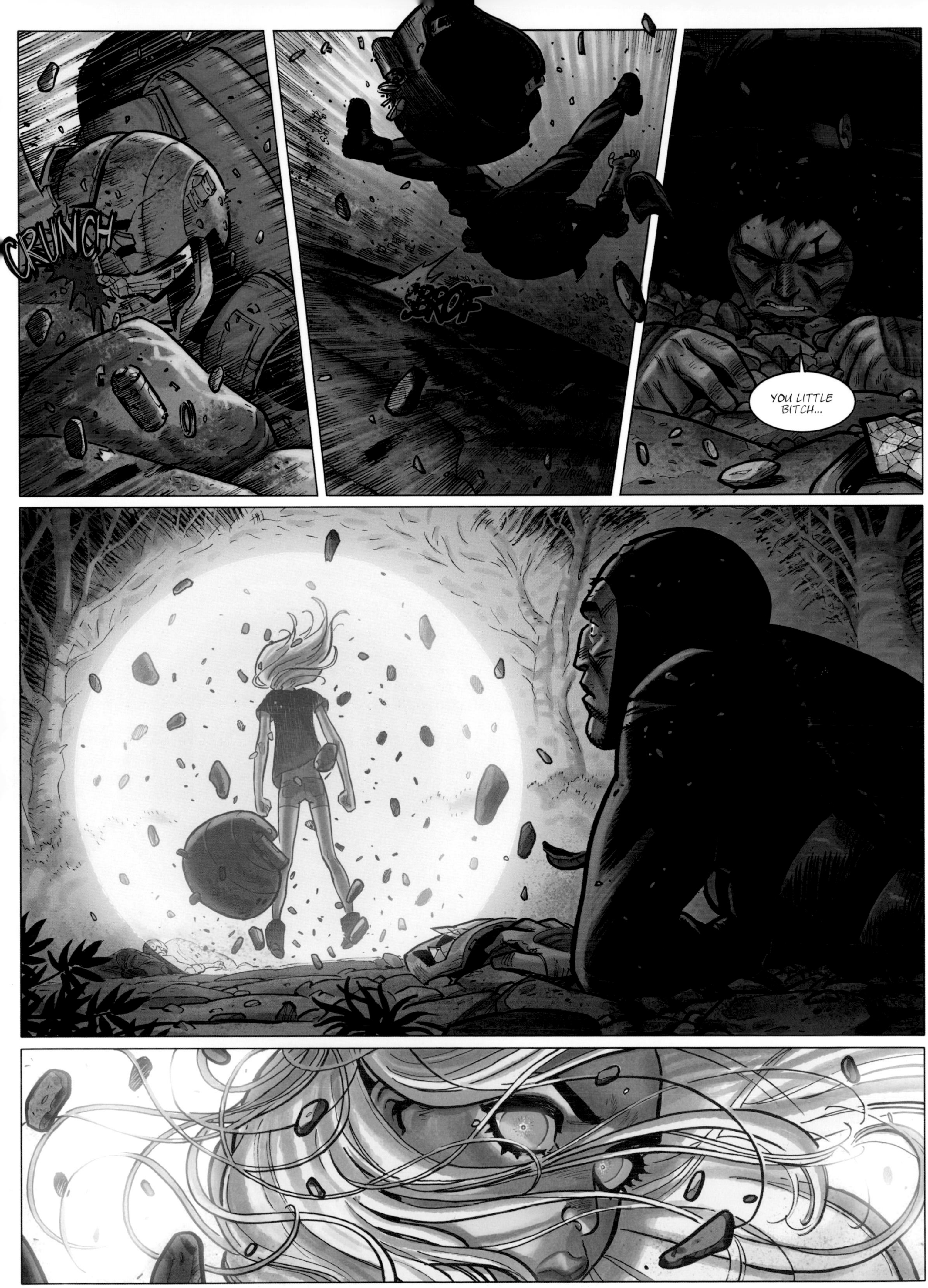
CRUNCH
BROF
YOU LITTLE BITCH...

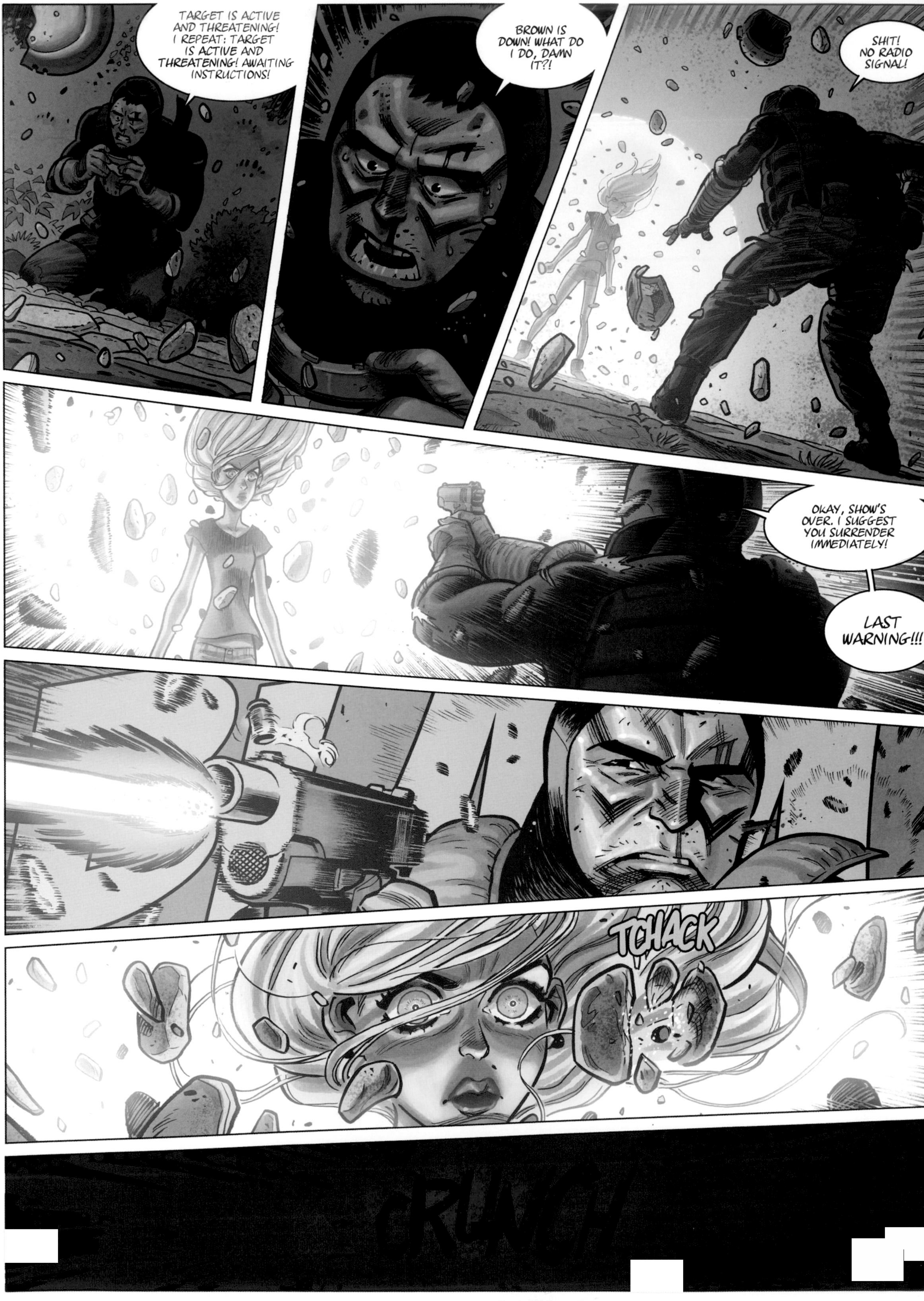

TARGET IS ACTIVE AND THREATENING! I REPEAT: TARGET IS ACTIVE AND THREATENING! AWAITING INSTRUCTIONS!
BROWN IS DOWN! WHAT DO I DO, DAMN IT?!
SHIT! NO RADIO SIGNAL!
OKAY, SHOW'S OVER. I SUGGEST YOU SURRENDER IMMEDIATELY!
LAST WARNING!!!
TCHACK
CRUNCH

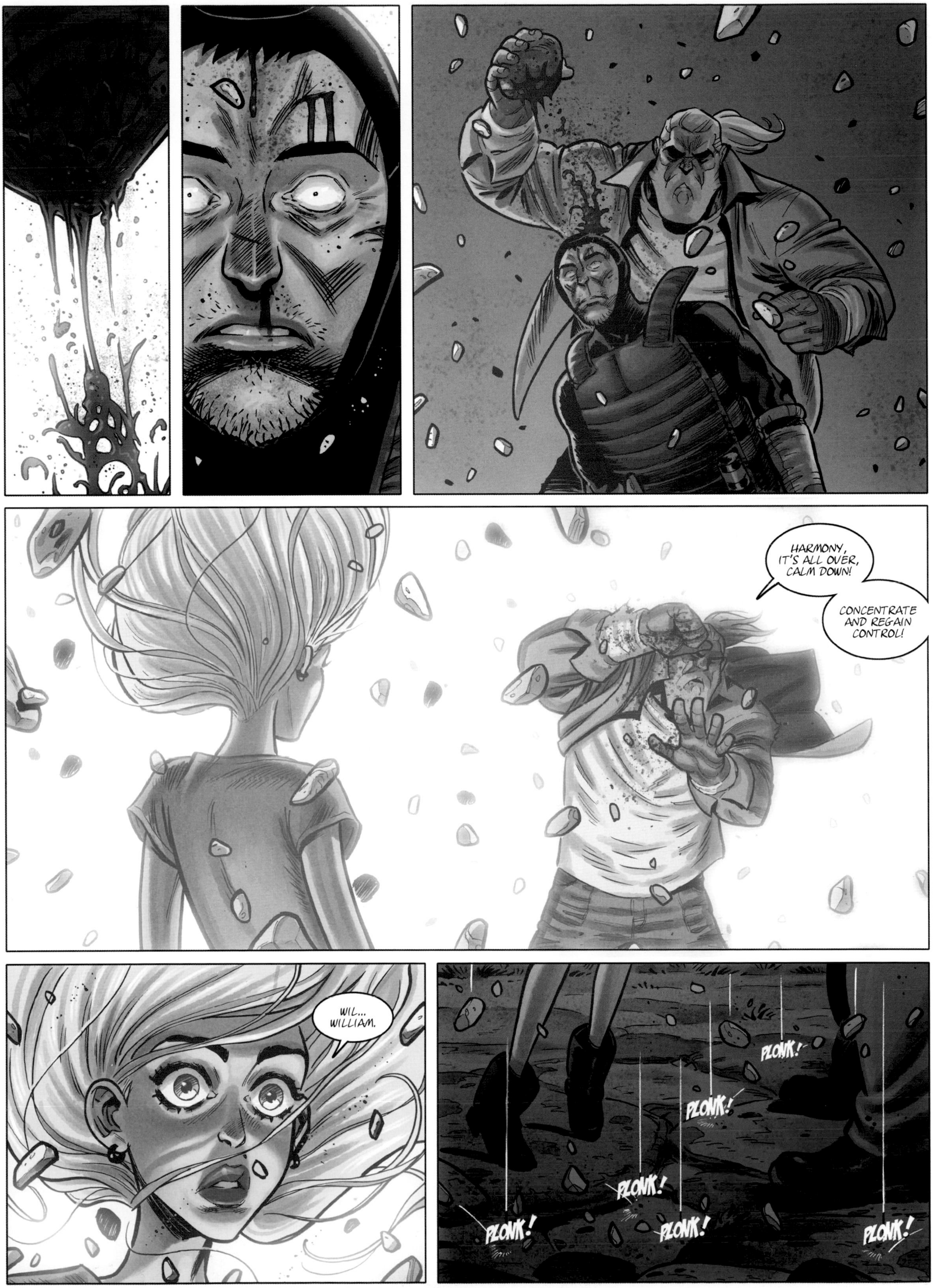
HARMONY, IT'S ALL OVER, CALM DOWN!
CONCENTRATE AND REGAIN CONTROL!
WIL... WILLIAM.
PLONK!
PLONK!
PLONK!
PLONK!
PLONK!
PLONK!

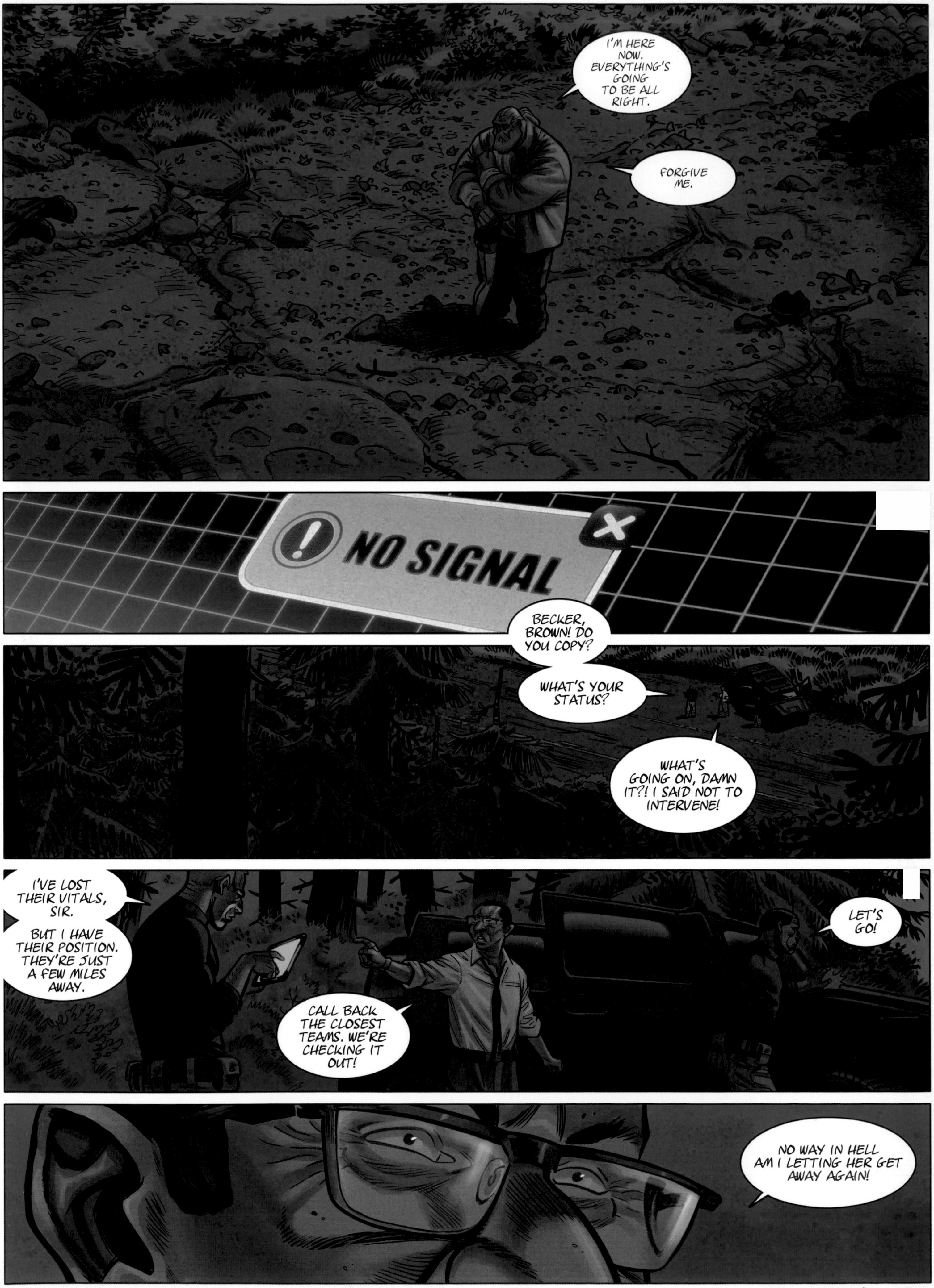
I'M HERE NOW. EVERYTHING'S GOING TO BE ALL RIGHT.
FORGIVE ME.
NO SIGNAL
BECKER, BROWN! DO YOU COPY?
WHAT'S YOUR STATUS?
WHAT'S GOING ON, DAMN IT?! I SAID NOT TO INTERVENE!
I'VE LOST THEIR VITALS, SIR.
BUT I HAVE THEIR POSITION. THEY'RE JUST A FEW MILES AWAY.
CALL BACK THE CLOSEST TEAMS. WE'RE CHECKING IT OUT!
LET'S GO!
NO WAY IN HELL AM I LETTING HER GET AWAY AGAIN!
REYNÈS -05-2015

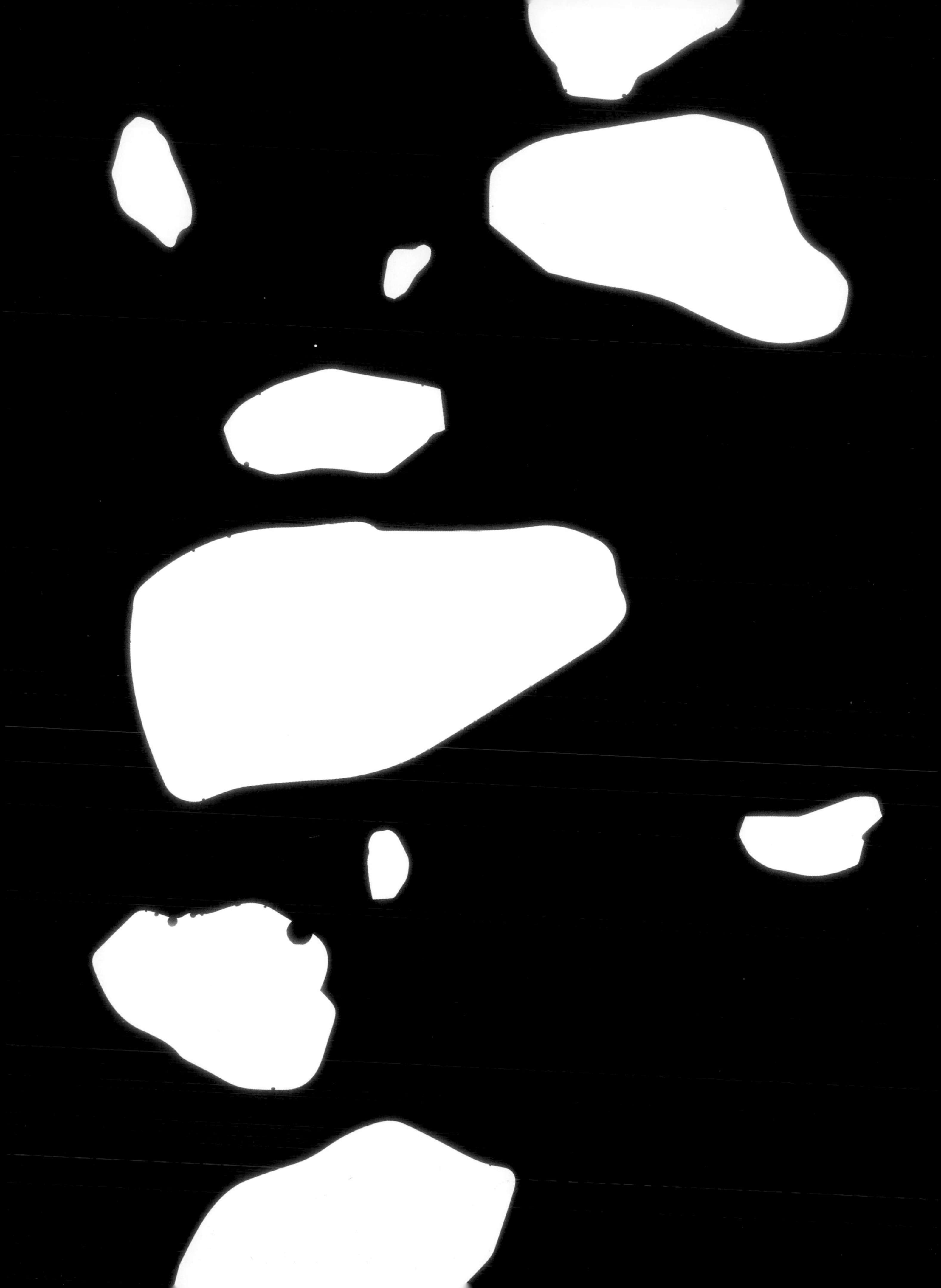

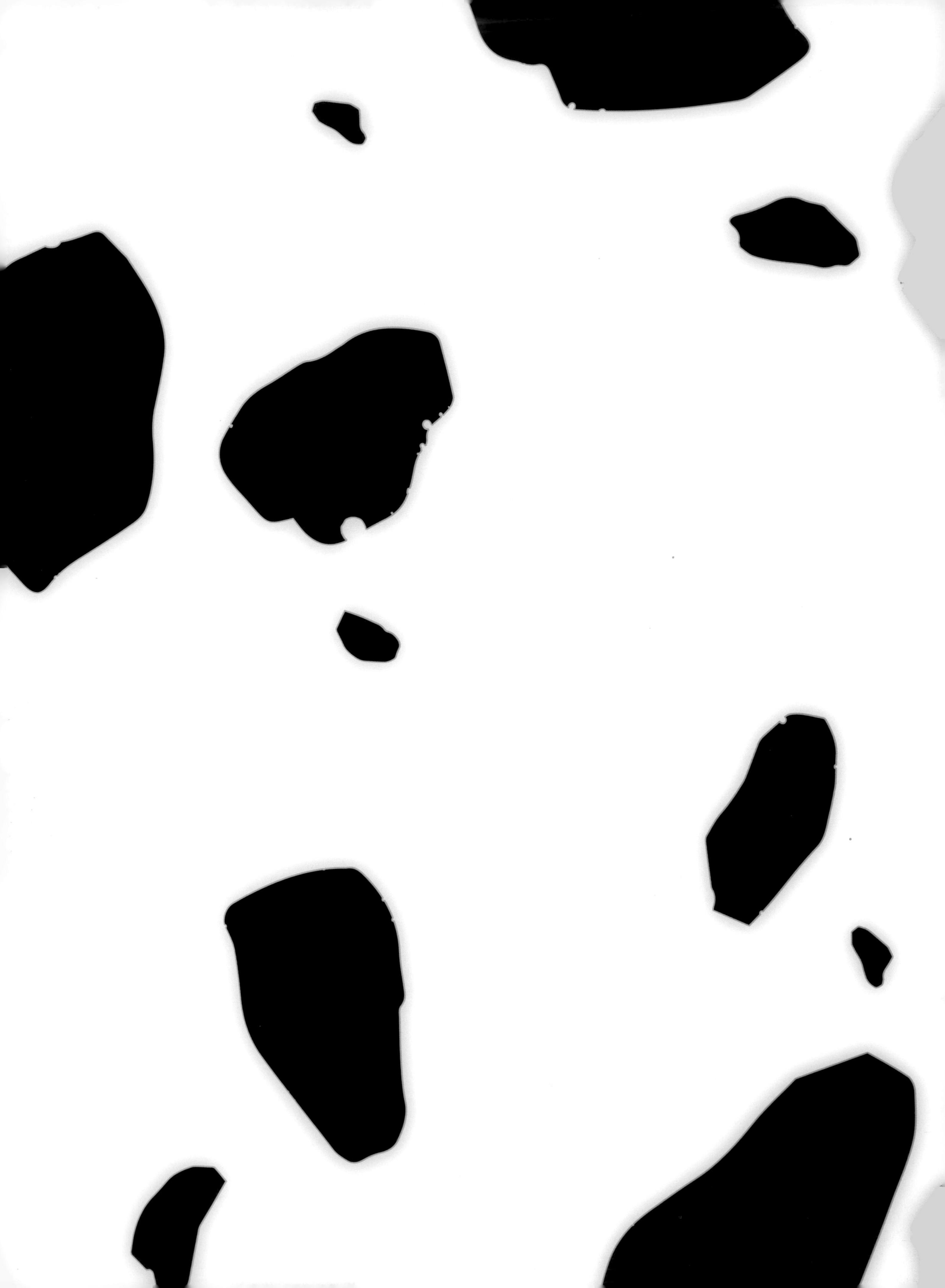

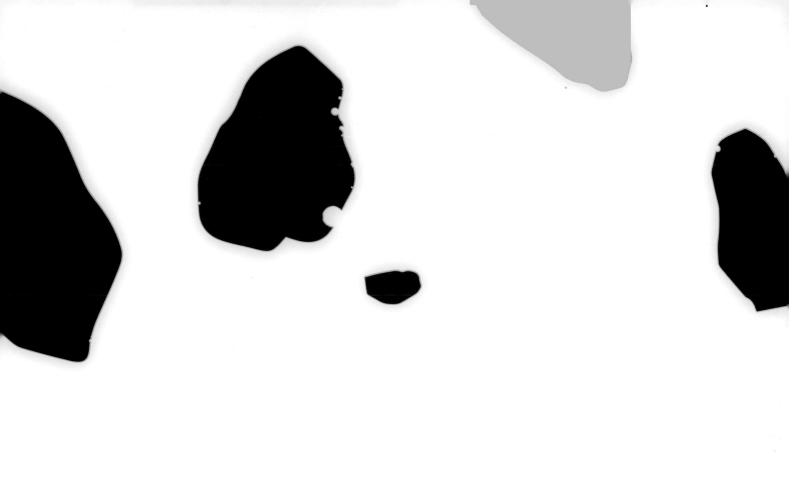

PART TWO

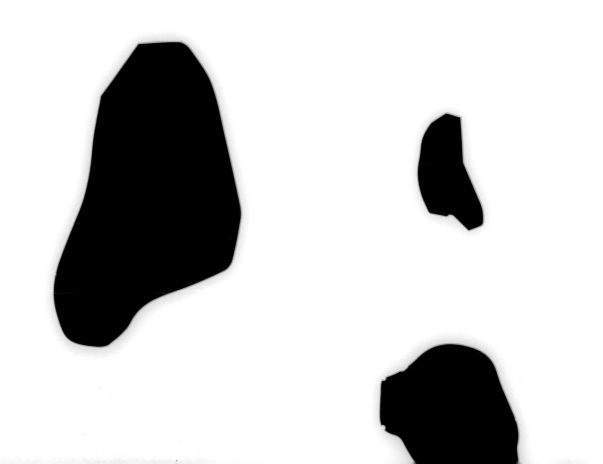

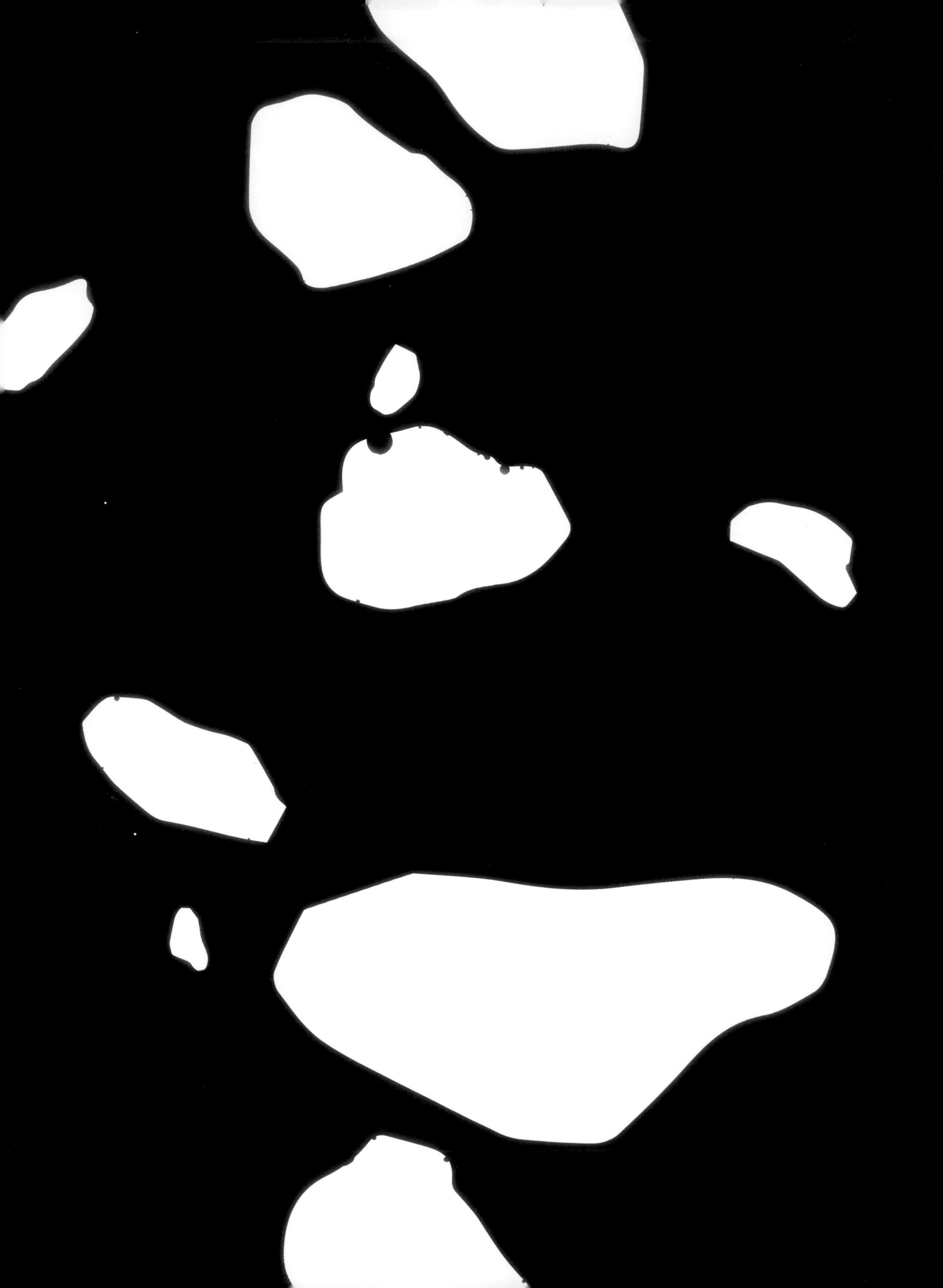

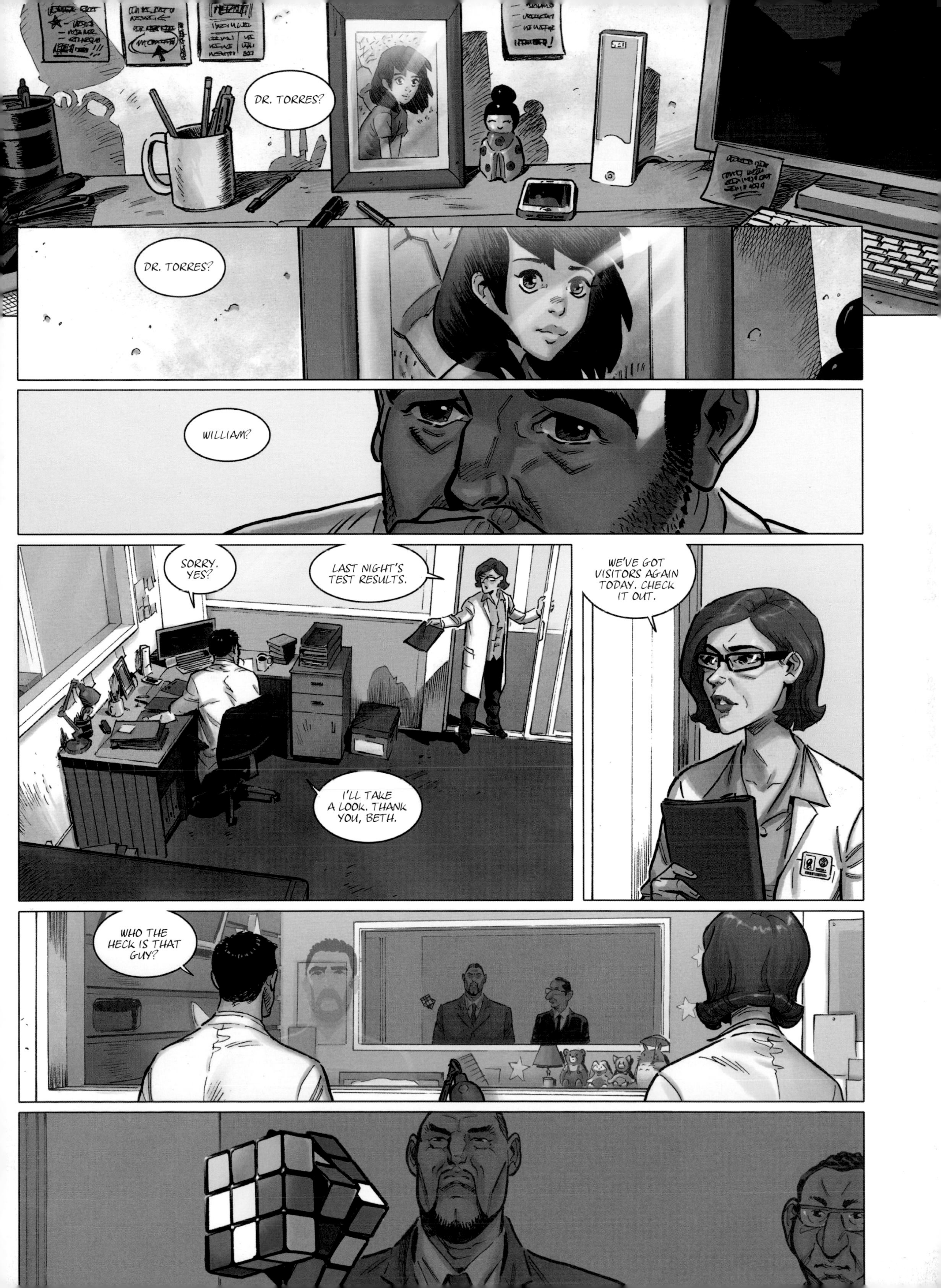

DR. TORRES?
DR. TORRES?
WILLIAM?
SORRY. YES?
LAST NIGHT'S TEST RESULTS.
I'LL TAKE A LOOK. THANK YOU, BETH.
WE'VE GOT VISITORS AGAIN TODAY. CHECK IT OUT.
WHO THE HECK IS THAT GUY?

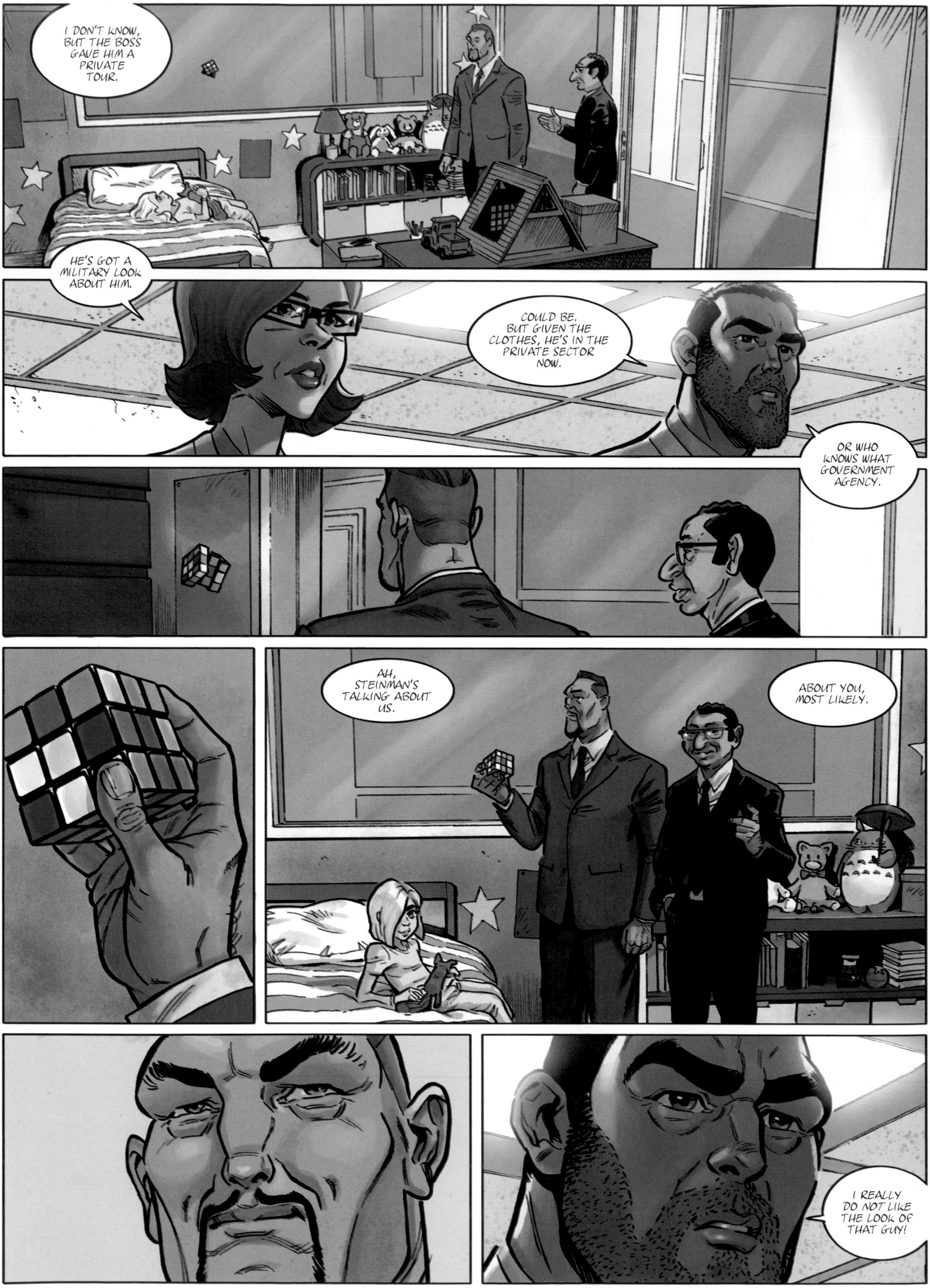
I DON'T KNOW, BUT THE BOSS GAVE HIM A PRIVATE TOUR.
HE'S GOT A MILITARY LOOK ABOUT HIM.
COULD BE. BUT GIVEN THE CLOTHES, HE'S IN THE PRIVATE SECTOR NOW.
OR WHO KNOWS WHAT GOVERNMENT AGENCY.
AH, STEINMAN'S TALKING ABOUT US.
ABOUT YOU, MOST LIKELY.
I REALLY DO NOT LIKE THE LOOK OF THAT GUY!

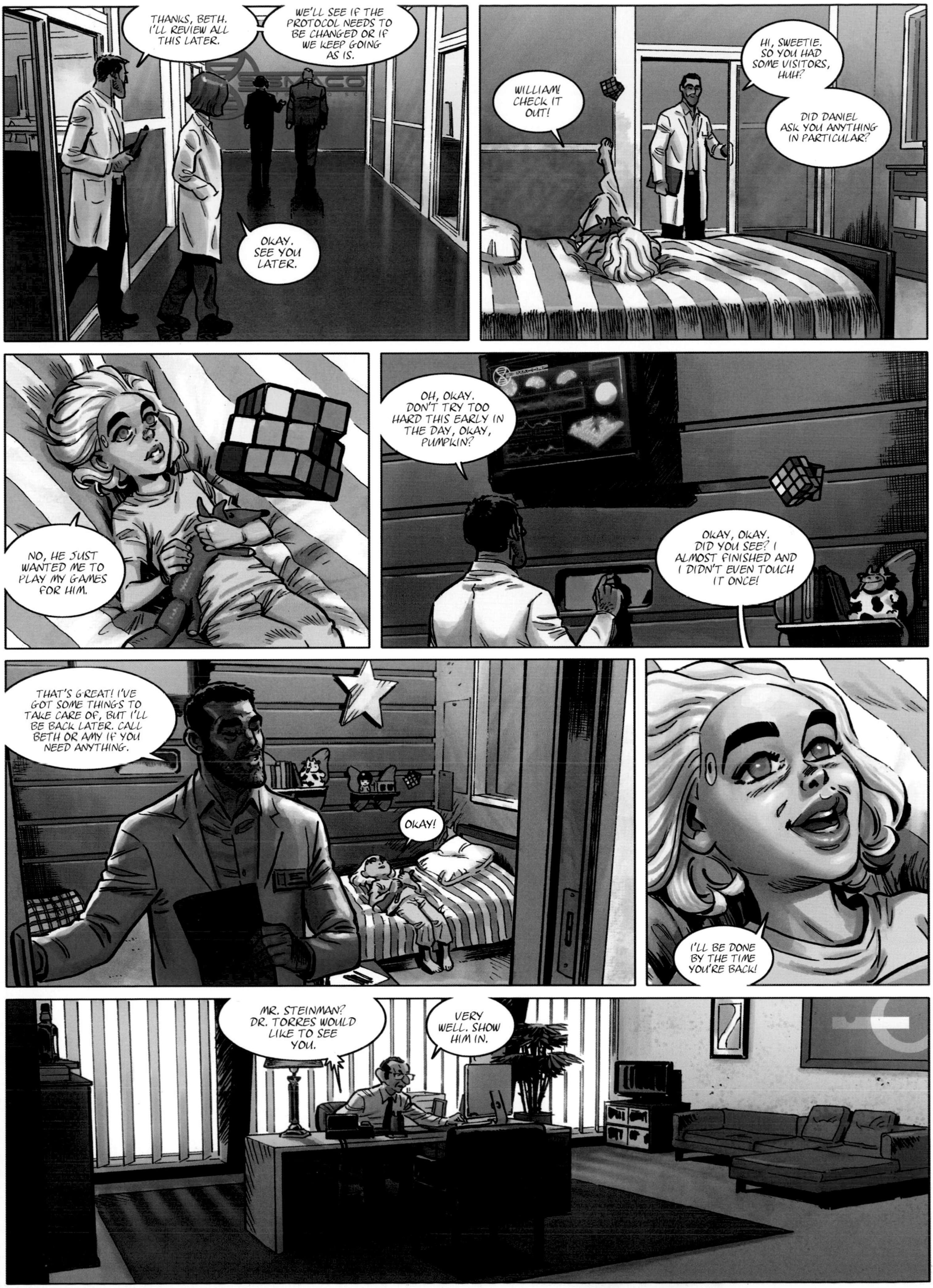
THANKS, BETH. I'LL REVIEW ALL THIS LATER.
WE'LL SEE IF THE PROTOCOL NEEDS TO BE CHANGED OR IF WE KEEP GOING AS IS.
OKAY. SEE YOU LATER.
WILLIAM! CHECK IT OUT!
HI, SWEETIE. SO YOU HAD SOME VISITORS, HUH?
DID DANIEL ASK YOU ANYTHING IN PARTICULAR?
NO, HE JUST WANTED ME TO PLAY MY GAMES FOR HIM.
OH, OKAY. DON'T TRY TOO HARD THIS EARLY IN THE DAY, OKAY, PUMPKIN?
OKAY, OKAY. DID YOU SEE? I ALMOST FINISHED AND I DIDN'T EVEN TOUCH IT ONCE!
THAT'S GREAT! I'VE GOT SOME THINGS TO TAKE CARE OF, BUT I'LL BE BACK LATER. CALL BETH OR AMY IF YOU NEED ANYTHING.
OKAY!
I'LL BE DONE BY THE TIME YOU'RE BACK!
MR. STEINMAN? DR. TORRES WOULD LIKE TO SEE YOU.
VERY WELL. SHOW HIM IN.

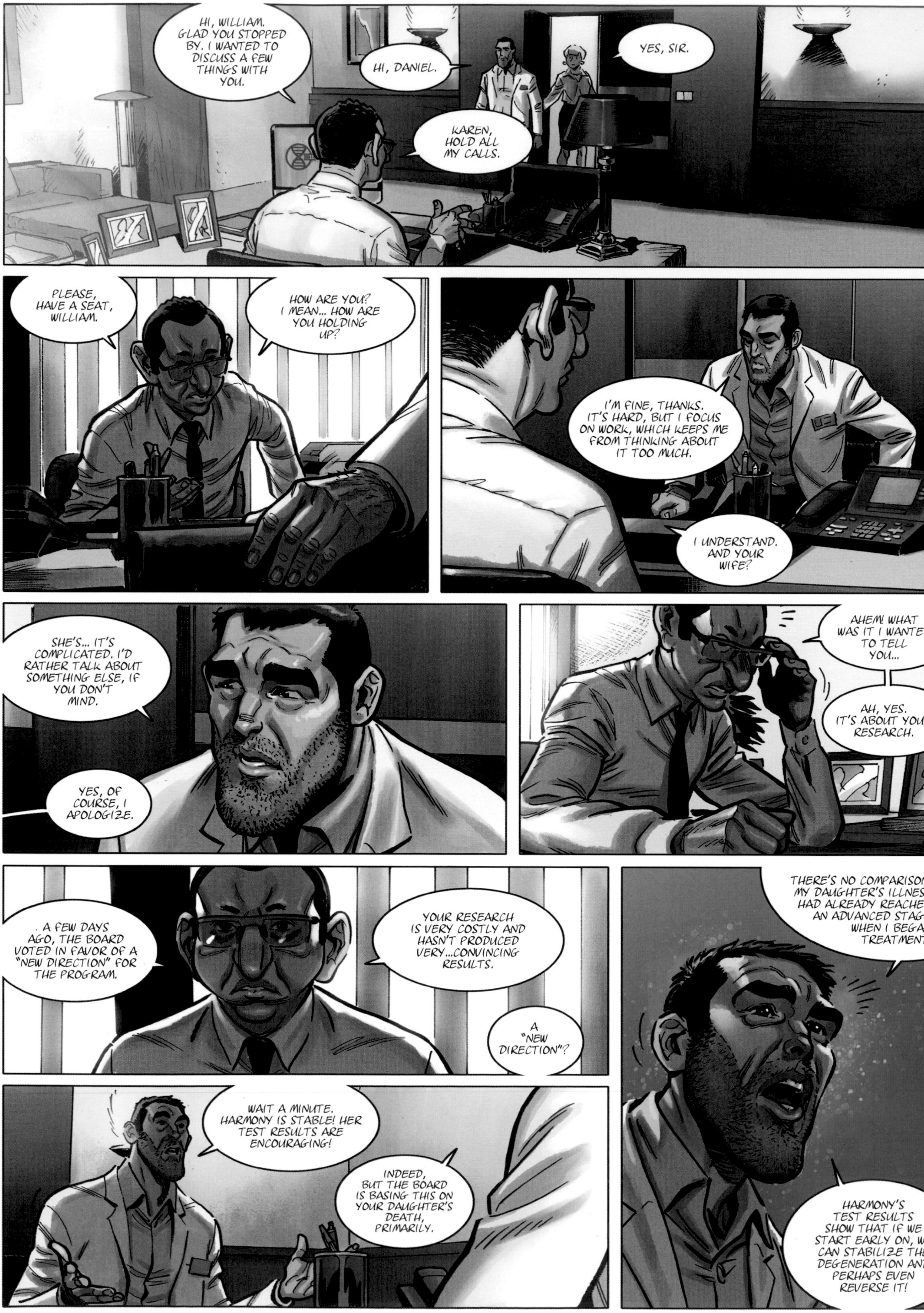

HI, WILLIAM. GLAD YOU STOPPED BY. I WANTED TO DISCUSS A FEW THINGS WITH YOU.
HI, DANIEL.
YES, SIR.
KAREN, HOLD ALL MY CALLS.
PLEASE, HAVE A SEAT, WILLIAM.
HOW ARE YOU? I MEAN... HOW ARE YOU HOLDING UP?
I'M FINE, THANKS. IT'S HARD, BUT I FOCUS ON WORK, WHICH KEEPS ME FROM THINKING ABOUT IT TOO MUCH.
I UNDERSTAND. AND YOUR WIFE?
SHE'S... IT'S COMPLICATED. I'D RATHER TALK ABOUT SOMETHING ELSE, IF YOU DON'T MIND.
YES, OF COURSE, I APOLOGIZE.
AHEM! WHAT WAS IT I WANTED TO TELL YOU...
AH, YES. IT'S ABOUT YOUR RESEARCH.
. A FEW DAYS AGO, THE BOARD VOTED IN FAVOR OF A "NEW DIRECTION" FOR THE PROGRAM.
YOUR RESEARCH IS VERY COSTLY AND HASN'T PRODUCED VERY...CONVINCING RESULTS.
A "NEW DIRECTION"?
WAIT A MINUTE. HARMONY IS STABLE! HER TEST RESULTS ARE ENCOURAGING!
INDEED, BUT THE BOARD IS BASING THIS ON YOUR DAUGHTER'S DEATH, PRIMARILY.
THERE'S NO COMPARISON! MY DAUGHTER'S ILLNESS HAD ALREADY REACHED AN ADVANCED STAGE WHEN I BEGAN TREATMENT!
HARMONY'S TEST RESULTS SHOW THAT IF WE START EARLY ON, WE CAN STABILIZE THE DEGENERATION AND PERHAPS EVEN REVERSE IT!

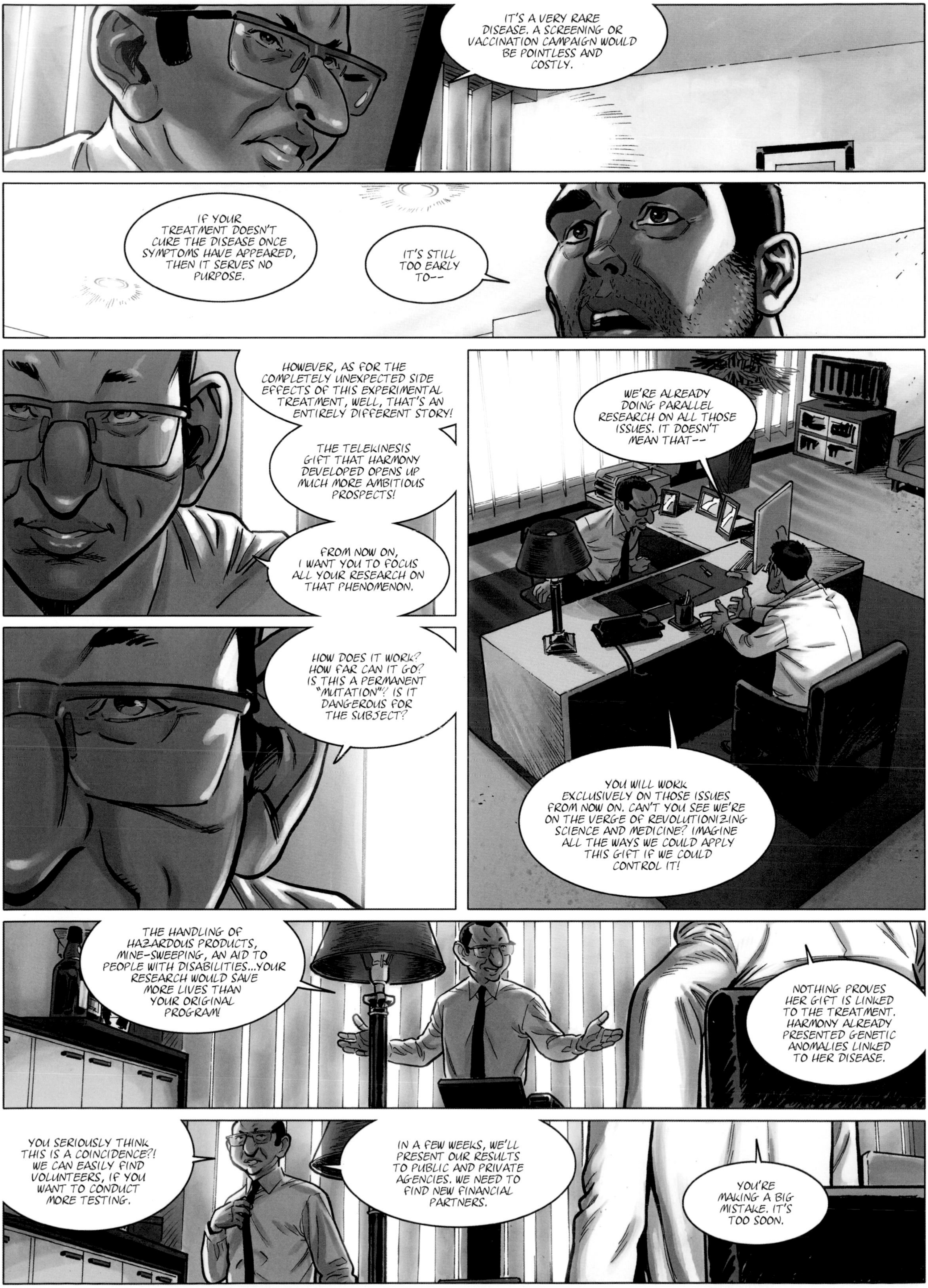
IT'S A VERY RARE DISEASE. A SCREENING OR VACCINATION CAMPAIGN WOULD BE POINTLESS AND COSTLY.
IF YOUR TREATMENT DOESN'T CURE THE DISEASE ONCE SYMPTOMS HAVE APPEARED, THEN IT SERVES NO PURPOSE.
IT'S STILL TOO EARLY TO--
HOWEVER, AS FOR THE COMPLETELY UNEXPECTED SIDE EFFECTS OF THIS EXPERIMENTAL TREATMENT, WELL, THAT'S AN ENTIRELY DIFFERENT STORY!
THE TELEKINESIS GIFT THAT HARMONY DEVELOPED OPENS UP MUCH MORE AMBITIOUS PROSPECTS!
FROM NOW ON, I WANT YOU TO FOCUS ALL YOUR RESEARCH ON THAT PHENOMENON.
HOW DOES IT WORK? HOW FAR CAN IT GO? IS THIS A PERMANENT "MUTATION"? IS IT DANGEROUS FOR THE SUBJECT?
WE'RE ALREADY DOING PARALLEL RESEARCH ON ALL THOSE ISSUES. IT DOESN'T MEAN THAT--
YOU WILL WORK EXCLUSIVELY ON THOSE ISSUES FROM NOW ON. CAN'T YOU SEE WE'RE ON THE VERGE OF REVOLUTIONIZING SCIENCE AND MEDICINE? IMAGINE ALL THE WAYS WE COULD APPLY THIS GIFT IF WE COULD CONTROL IT!
THE HANDLING OF HAZARDOUS PRODUCTS, MINE-SWEEPING, AN AID TO PEOPLE WITH DISABILITIES...YOUR RESEARCH WOULD SAVE MORE LIVES THAN YOUR ORIGINAL PROGRAM!
NOTHING PROVES HER GIFT IS LINKED TO THE TREATMENT. HARMONY ALREADY PRESENTED GENETIC ANOMALIES LINKED TO HER DISEASE.
YOU SERIOUSLY THINK THIS IS A COINCIDENCE?! WE CAN EASILY FIND VOLUNTEERS, IF YOU WANT TO CONDUCT MORE TESTING.
IN A FEW WEEKS, WE'LL PRESENT OUR RESULTS TO PUBLIC AND PRIVATE AGENCIES. WE NEED TO FIND NEW FINANCIAL PARTNERS.
YOU'RE MAKING A BIG MISTAKE. IT'S TOO SOON.

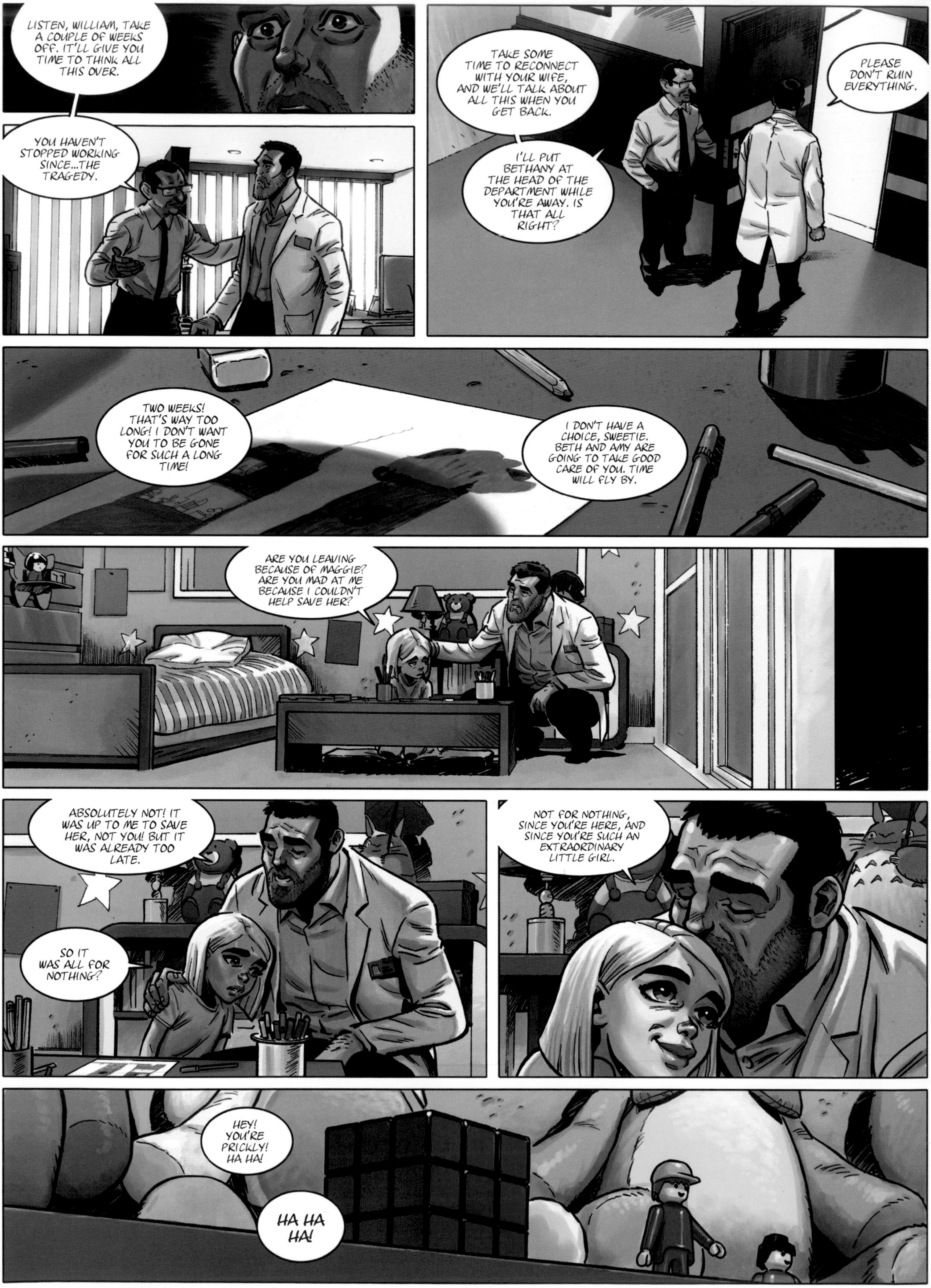
LISTEN, WILLIAM, TAKE A COUPLE OF WEEKS OFF. IT'LL GIVE YOU TIME TO THINK ALL THIS OVER.
YOU HAVEN'T STOPPED WORKING SINCE...THE TRAGEDY.
TAKE SOME TIME TO RECONNECT WITH YOUR WIFE, AND WE'LL TALK ABOUT ALL THIS WHEN YOU GET BACK.
I'LL PUT BETHANY AT THE HEAD OF THE DEPARTMENT WHILE YOU'RE AWAY. IS THAT ALL RIGHT?
PLEASE DON'T RUIN EVERYTHING.
TWO WEEKS! THAT'S WAY TOO LONG! I DON'T WANT YOU TO BE GONE FOR SUCH A LONG TIME!
I DON'T HAVE A CHOICE, SWEETIE. BETH AND AMY ARE GOING TO TAKE GOOD CARE OF YOU. TIME WILL FLY BY.
ARE YOU LEAVING BECAUSE OF MAGGIE? ARE YOU MAD AT ME BECAUSE I COULDN'T HELP SAVE HER?
ABSOLUTELY NOT! IT WAS UP TO ME TO SAVE HER, NOT YOU! BUT IT WAS ALREADY TOO LATE.
SO IT WAS ALL FOR NOTHING?
NOT FOR NOTHING, SINCE YOU'RE HERE, AND SINCE YOU'RE SUCH AN EXTRAORDINARY LITTLE GIRL.
HEY! YOU'RE PRICKLY! HA HA!
HA HA HA!

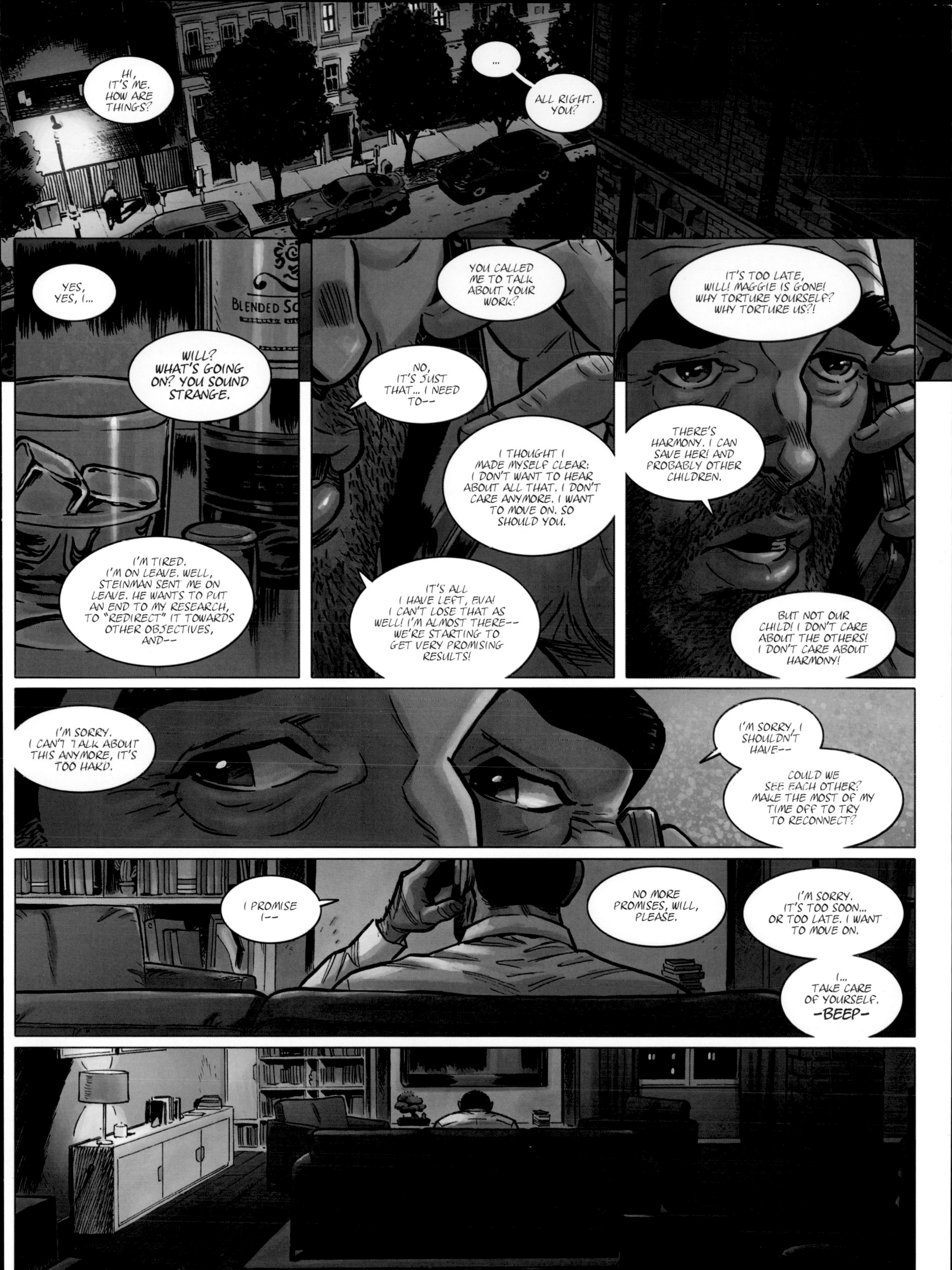

HI, IT'S ME. HOW ARE THINGS?
...
ALL RIGHT. YOU?
YES, YES, I...
BLENDED SC
WILL? WHAT'S GOING ON? YOU SOUND STRANGE.
I'M TIRED. I'M ON LEAVE. WELL, STEINMAN SENT ME ON LEAVE. HE WANTS TO PUT AN END TO MY RESEARCH, TO "REDIRECT" IT TOWARDS OTHER OBJECTIVES, AND--
YOU CALLED ME TO TALK ABOUT YOUR WORK?
NO, IT'S JUST THAT... I NEED TO--
I THOUGHT I MADE MYSELF CLEAR: I DON'T WANT TO HEAR ABOUT ALL THAT. I DON'T CARE ANYMORE. I WANT TO MOVE ON. SO SHOULD YOU.
IT'S ALL I HAVE LEFT, EVA! I CAN'T LOSE THAT AS WELL! I'M ALMOST THERE-- WE'RE STARTING TO GET VERY PROMISING RESULTS!
IT'S TOO LATE, WILL! MAGGIE IS GONE! WHY TORTURE YOURSELF? WHY TORTURE US?!
THERE'S HARMONY. I CAN SAVE HER! AND PROBABLY OTHER CHILDREN.
BUT NOT OUR CHILD! I DON'T CARE ABOUT THE OTHERS! I DON'T CARE ABOUT HARMONY!
I'M SORRY. I CAN'T TALK ABOUT THIS ANYMORE, IT'S TOO HARD.
I'M SORRY, I SHOULDN'T HAVE--
COULD WE SEE EACH OTHER? MAKE THE MOST OF MY TIME OFF TO TRY TO RECONNECT?
I PROMISE I--
NO MORE PROMISES, WILL, PLEASE.
I'M SORRY. IT'S TOO SOON... OR TOO LATE. I WANT TO MOVE ON.
I... TAKE CARE OF YOURSELF.
-BEEP-

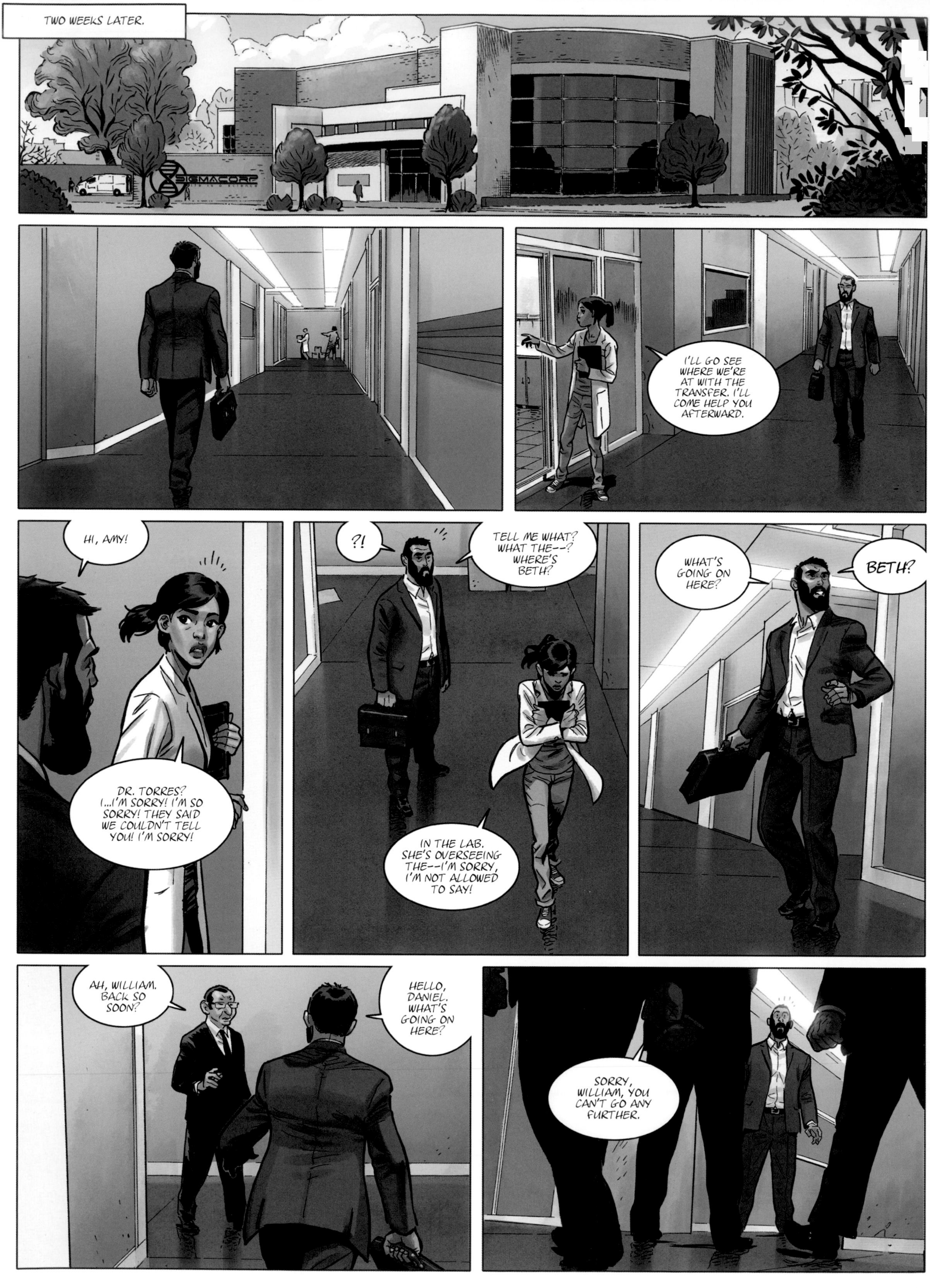
TWO WEEKS LATER.
SIGMACORP
I'LL GO SEE WHERE WE'RE AT WITH THE TRANSFER. I'LL COME HELP YOU AFTERWARD.
HI, AMY!
DR. TORRES? I...I'M SORRY! I'M SO SORRY! THEY SAID WE COULDN'T TELL YOU! I'M SORRY!
?!
TELL ME WHAT? WHAT THE--? WHERE'S BETH?
IN THE LAB. SHE'S OVERSEEING THE--I'M SORRY, I'M NOT ALLOWED TO SAY!
WHAT'S GOING ON HERE?
BETH?
AH, WILLIAM. BACK SO SOON?
HELLO, DANIEL. WHAT'S GOING ON HERE?
SORRY, WILLIAM, YOU CAN'T GO ANY FURTHER.

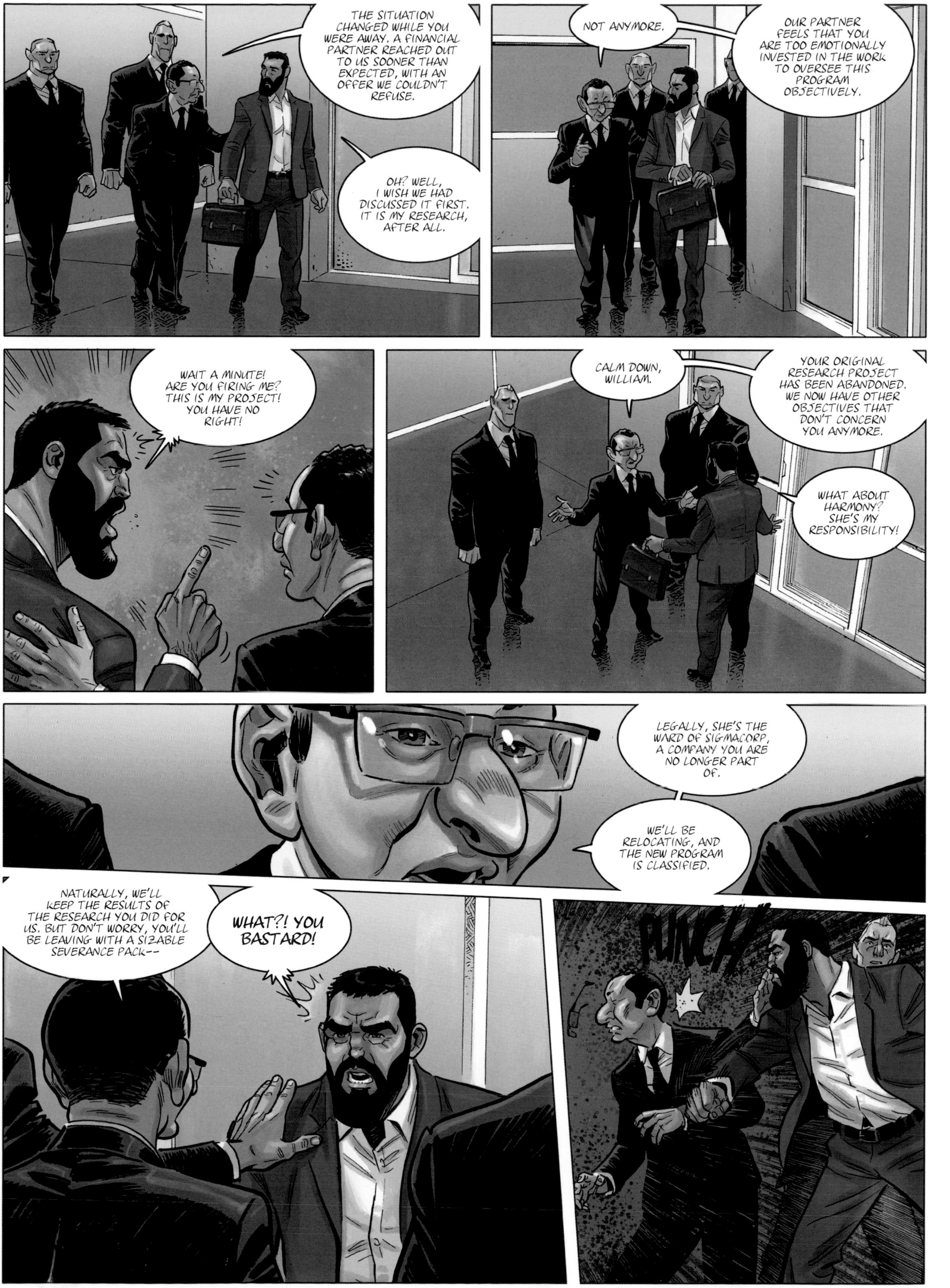
THE SITUATION CHANGED WHILE YOU WERE AWAY. A FINANCIAL PARTNER REACHED OUT TO US SOONER THAN EXPECTED, WITH AN OFFER WE COULDN'T REFUSE.
OH? WELL, I WISH WE HAD DISCUSSED IT FIRST. IT IS MY RESEARCH, AFTER ALL.
NOT ANYMORE.
OUR PARTNER FEELS THAT YOU ARE TOO EMOTIONALLY INVESTED IN THE WORK TO OVERSEE THIS PROGRAM OBJECTIVELY.
WAIT A MINUTE! ARE YOU FIRING ME? THIS IS MY PROJECT! YOU HAVE NO RIGHT!
CALM DOWN, WILLIAM.
YOUR ORIGINAL RESEARCH PROJECT HAS BEEN ABANDONED. WE NOW HAVE OTHER OBJECTIVES THAT DON'T CONCERN YOU ANYMORE.
WHAT ABOUT HARMONY? SHE'S MY RESPONSIBILITY!
LEGALLY, SHE'S THE WARD OF SIGMACORP, A COMPANY YOU ARE NO LONGER PART OF.
WE'LL BE RELOCATING, AND THE NEW PROGRAM IS CLASSIFIED.
NATURALLY, WE'LL KEEP THE RESULTS OF THE RESEARCH YOU DID FOR US. BUT DON'T WORRY, YOU'LL BE LEAVING WITH A SIZABLE SEVERANCE PACK--
WHAT?! YOU BASTARD!
PUNCH!

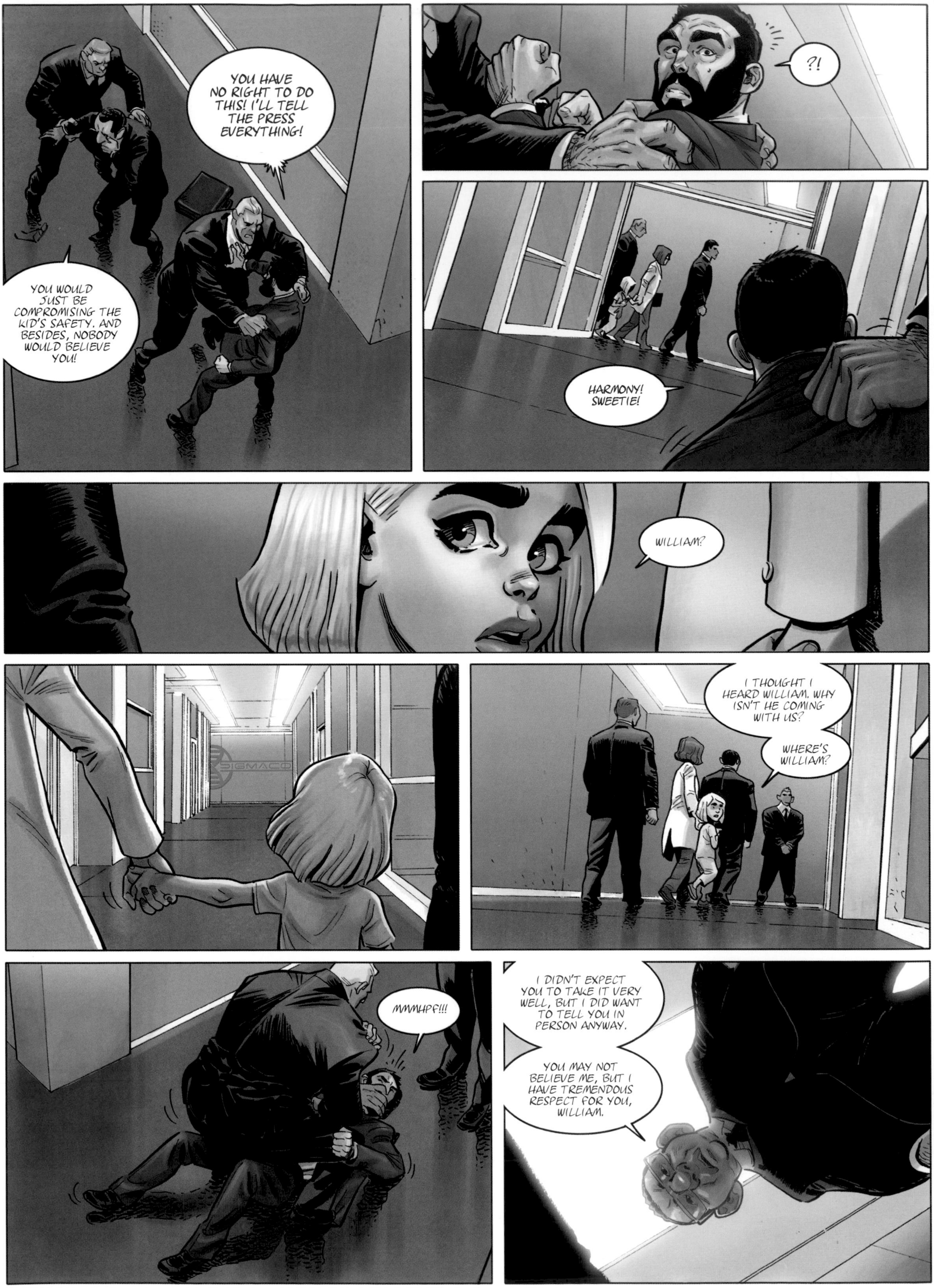

YOU HAVE NO RIGHT TO DO THIS! I'LL TELL THE PRESS EVERYTHING!
YOU WOULD JUST BE COMPROMISING THE KID'S SAFETY. AND BESIDES, NOBODY WOULD BELIEVE YOU!
?!
HARMONY! SWEETIE!
WILLIAM?
SIGMACO
I THOUGHT I HEARD WILLIAM. WHY ISN'T HE COMING WITH US?
WHERE'S WILLIAM?
MMMHPF!!!
I DIDN'T EXPECT YOU TO TAKE IT VERY WELL, BUT I DID WANT TO TELL YOU IN PERSON ANYWAY.
YOU MAY NOT BELIEVE ME, BUT I HAVE TREMENDOUS RESPECT FOR YOU, WILLIAM.

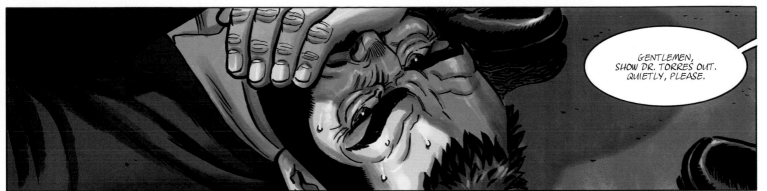

GENTLEMEN, SHOW DR. TORRES OUT. QUIETLY, PLEASE.

YOU'LL PAY FOR THIS!!!

ASSHOLES!

YOU CAN'T JUST TAKE EVERYTHING FROM ME...

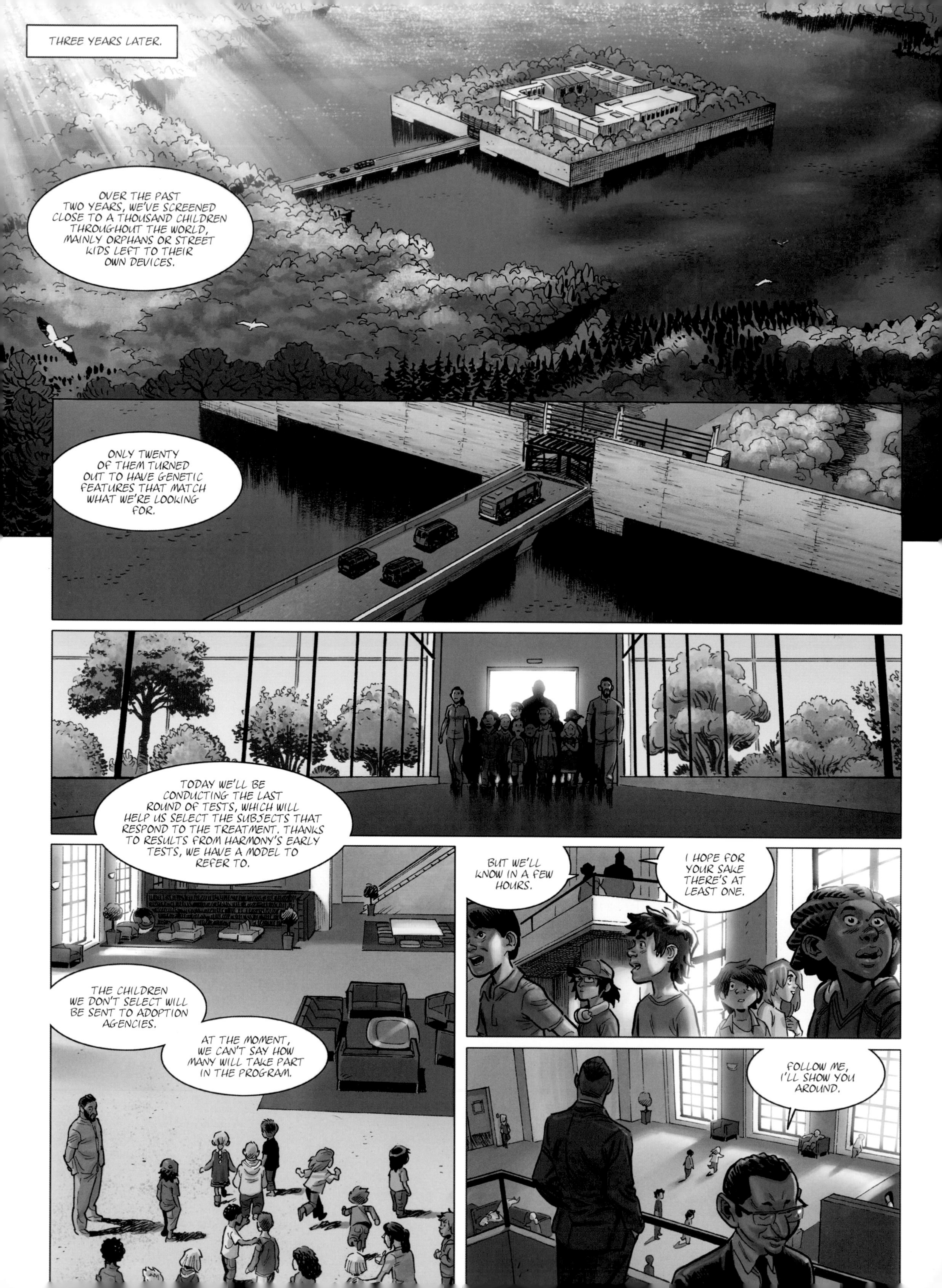
THREE YEARS LATER.
OVER THE PAST TWO YEARS, WE'VE SCREENED CLOSE TO A THOUSAND CHILDREN THROUGHOUT THE WORLD, MAINLY ORPHANS OR STREET KIDS LEFT TO THEIR OWN DEVICES.
ONLY TWENTY OF THEM TURNED OUT TO HAVE GENETIC FEATURES THAT MATCH WHAT WE'RE LOOKING FOR.
TODAY WE'LL BE CONDUCTING THE LAST ROUND OF TESTS, WHICH WILL HELP US SELECT THE SUBJECTS THAT RESPOND TO THE TREATMENT. THANKS TO RESULTS FROM HARMONY'S EARLY TESTS, WE HAVE A MODEL TO REFER TO.
THE CHILDREN WE DON'T SELECT WILL BE SENT TO ADOPTION AGENCIES.
AT THE MOMENT, WE CAN'T SAY HOW MANY WILL TAKE PART IN THE PROGRAM.
BUT WE'LL KNOW IN A FEW HOURS.
I HOPE FOR YOUR SAKE THERE'S AT LEAST ONE.
FOLLOW ME, I'LL SHOW YOU AROUND.

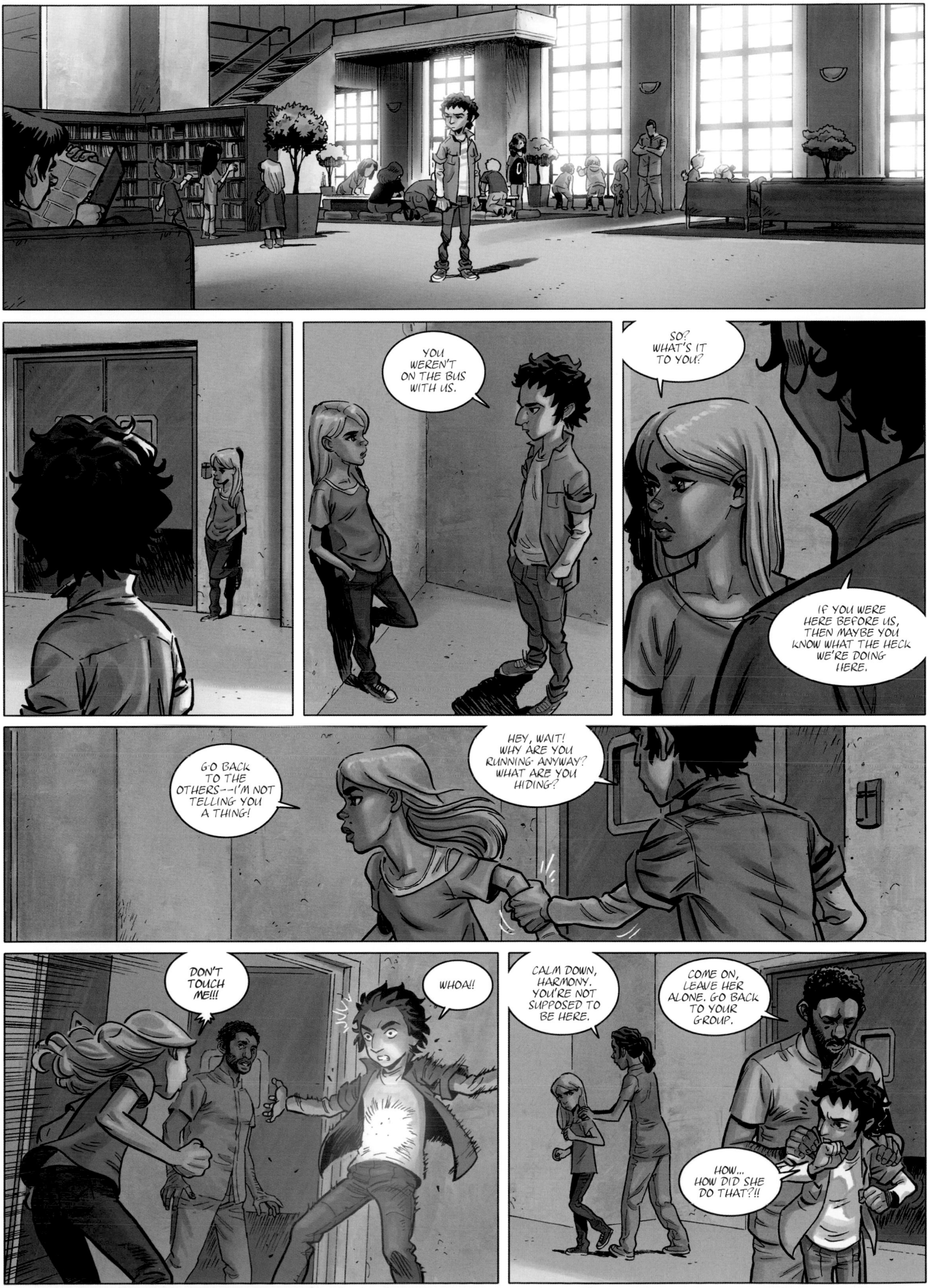
YOU WEREN'T ON THE BUS WITH US.
SO? WHAT'S IT TO YOU?
IF YOU WERE HERE BEFORE US, THEN MAYBE YOU KNOW WHAT THE HECK WE'RE DOING HERE.
HEY, WAIT! WHY ARE YOU RUNNING ANYWAY? WHAT ARE YOU HIDING?
GO BACK TO THE OTHERS--I'M NOT TELLING YOU A THING!
DON'T TOUCH ME!!!
WHOA!!
CALM DOWN, HARMONY. YOU'RE NOT SUPPOSED TO BE HERE.
COME ON, LEAVE HER ALONE. GO BACK TO YOUR GROUP.
HOW... HOW DID SHE DO THAT?!!

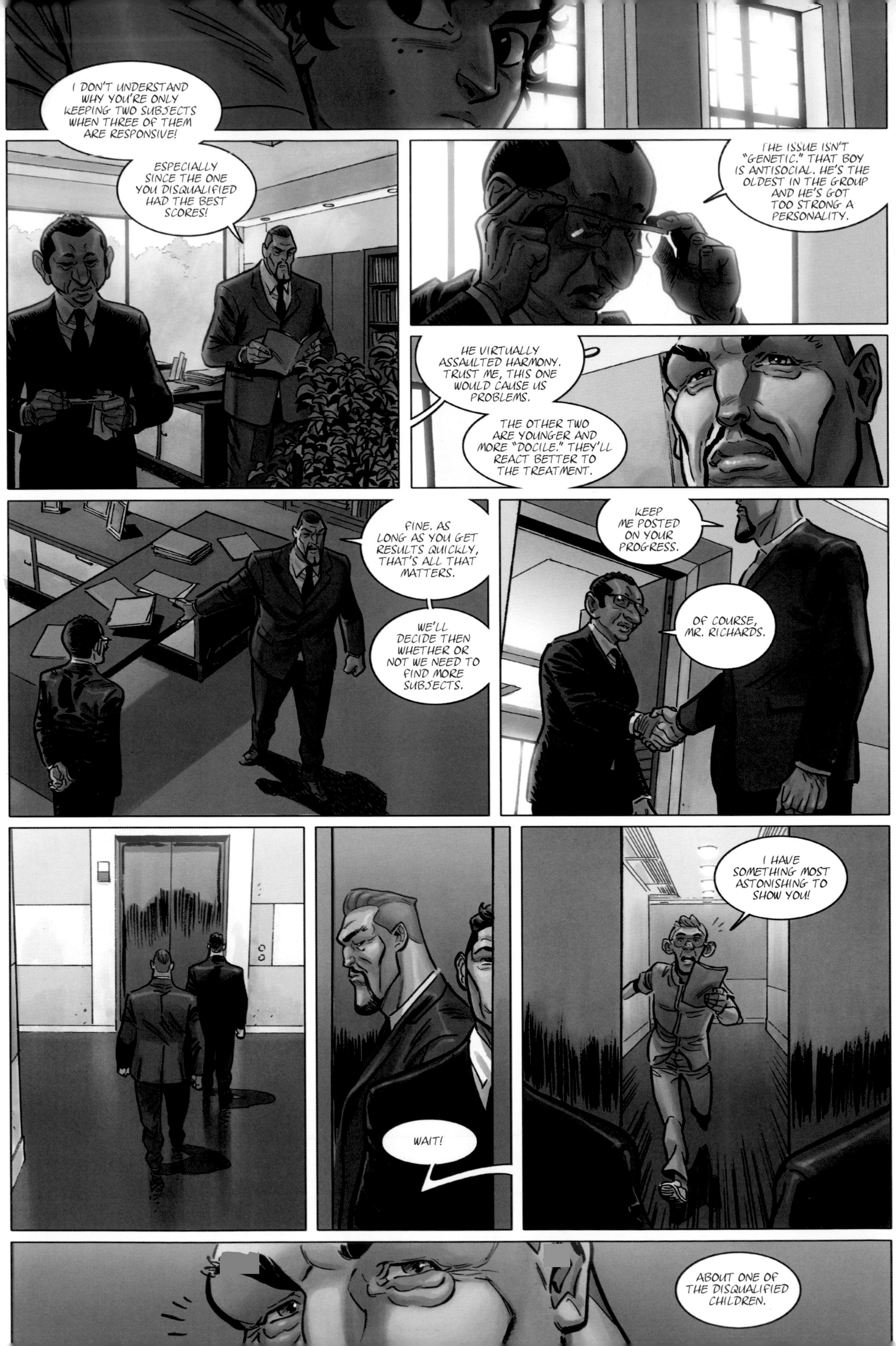
I DON'T UNDERSTAND WHY YOU'RE ONLY KEEPING TWO SUBJECTS WHEN THREE OF THEM ARE RESPONSIVE!
ESPECIALLY SINCE THE ONE YOU DISQUALIFIED HAD THE BEST SCORES!
THE ISSUE ISN'T "GENETIC." THAT BOY IS ANTISOCIAL. HE'S THE OLDEST IN THE GROUP AND HE'S GOT TOO STRONG A PERSONALITY.
HE VIRTUALLY ASSAULTED HARMONY. TRUST ME, THIS ONE WOULD CAUSE US PROBLEMS.
THE OTHER TWO ARE YOUNGER AND MORE "DOCILE." THEY'LL REACT BETTER TO THE TREATMENT.
FINE. AS LONG AS YOU GET RESULTS QUICKLY, THAT'S ALL THAT MATTERS.
WE'LL DECIDE THEN WHETHER OR NOT WE NEED TO FIND MORE SUBJECTS.
KEEP ME POSTED ON YOUR PROGRESS.
OF COURSE, MR. RICHARDS.
WAIT!
I HAVE SOMETHING MOST ASTONISHING TO SHOW YOU!
ABOUT ONE OF THE DISQUALIFIED CHILDREN.

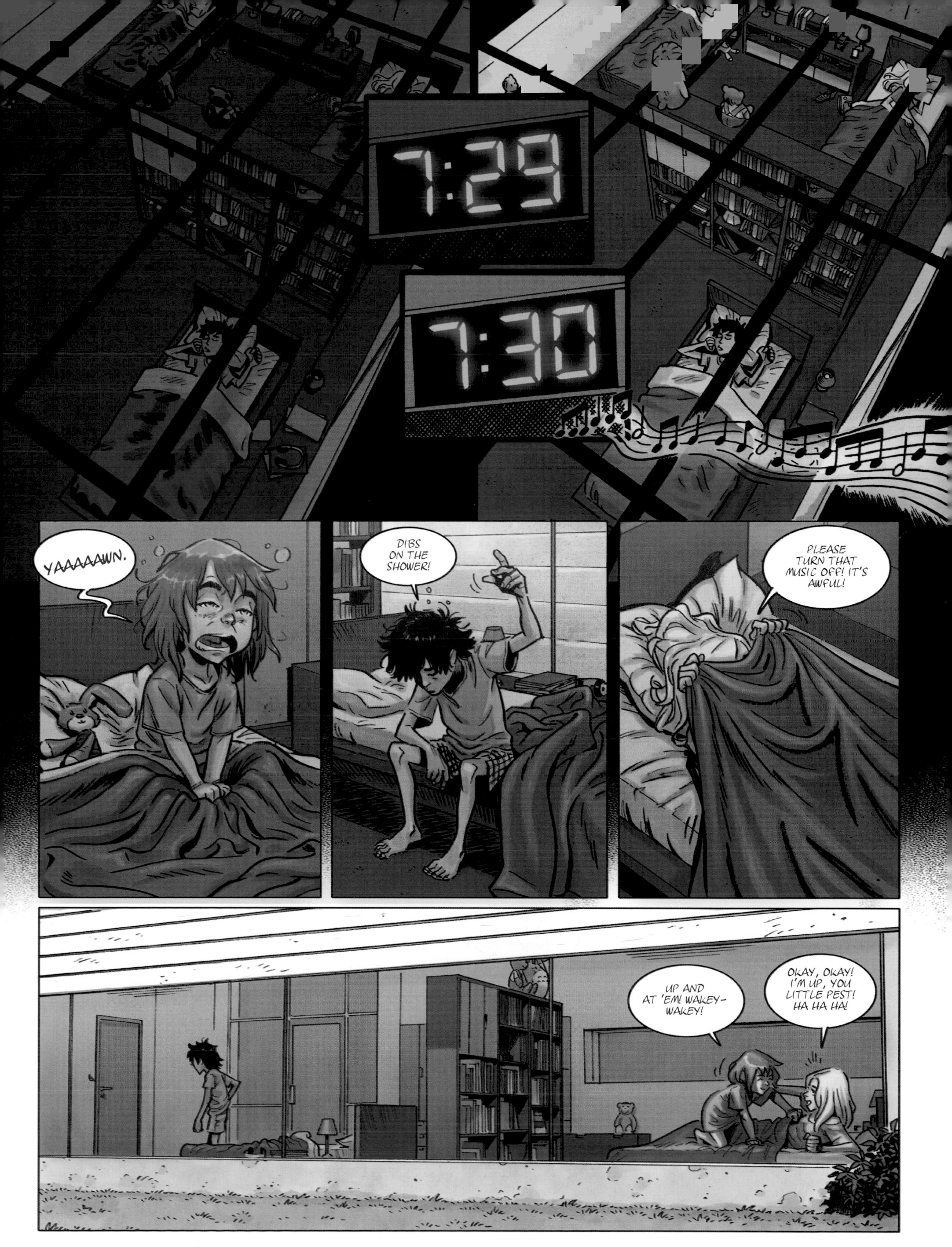
7:29
7:30
YAAAAAAWN.
DIBS ON THE SHOWER!
PLEASE TURN THAT MUSIC OFF! IT'S AWFUL!
UP AND AT 'EM! WAKEY-WAKEY!
OKAY, OKAY! I'M UP, YOU LITTLE PEST! HA HA HA!

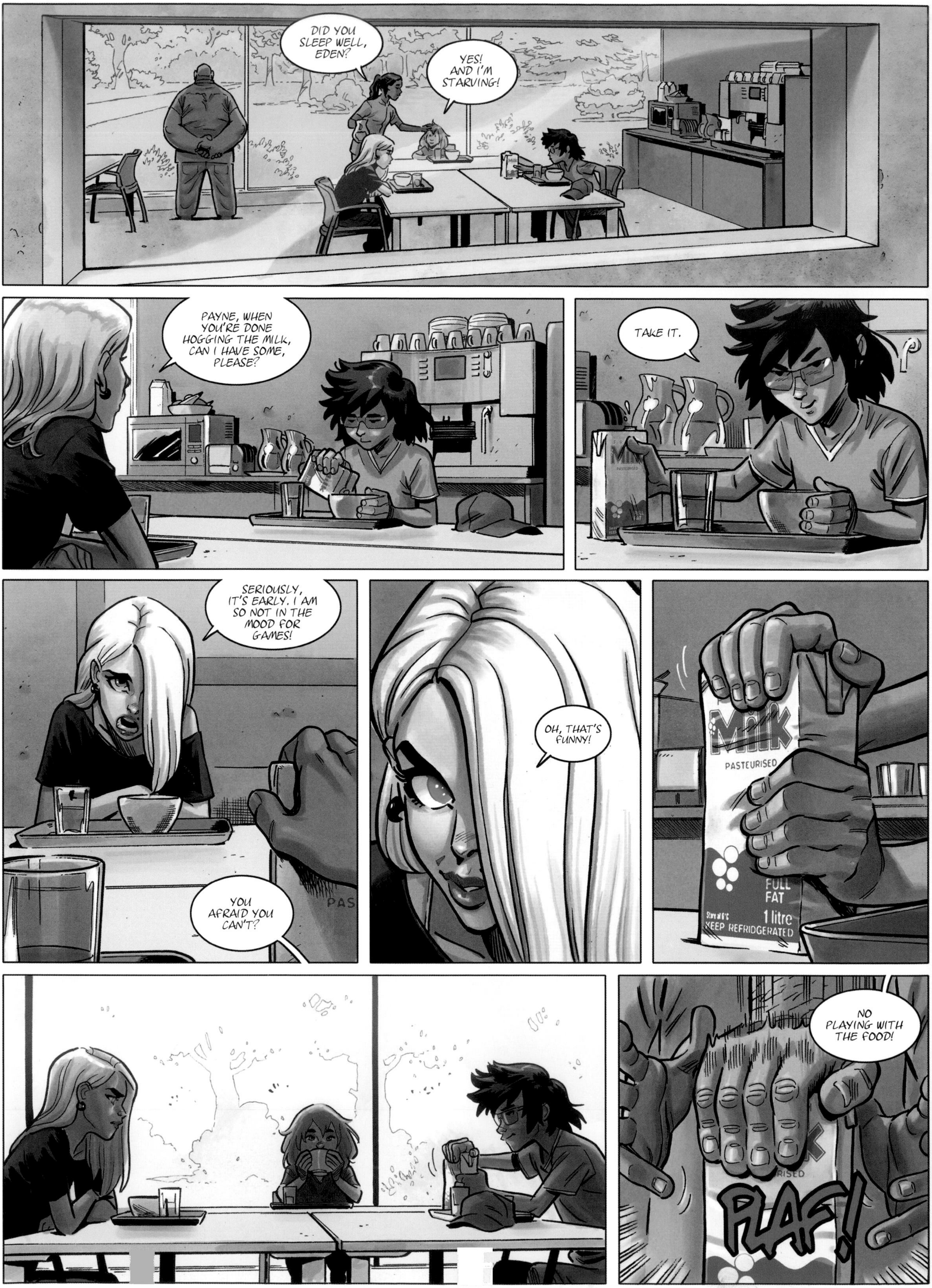
DID YOU SLEEP WELL, EDEN?
YES! AND I'M STARVING!
PAYNE, WHEN YOU'RE DONE HOGGING THE MILK, CAN I HAVE SOME, PLEASE?
TAKE IT.
Milk PASTEURISED FULL FAT
SERIOUSLY, IT'S EARLY. I AM SO NOT IN THE MOOD FOR GAMES!
YOU AFRAID YOU CAN'T?
OH, THAT'S FUNNY!
Milk PASTEURISED FULL FAT 1 litre KEEP REFRIDGERATED
NO PLAYING WITH THE FOOD!
PLAF!

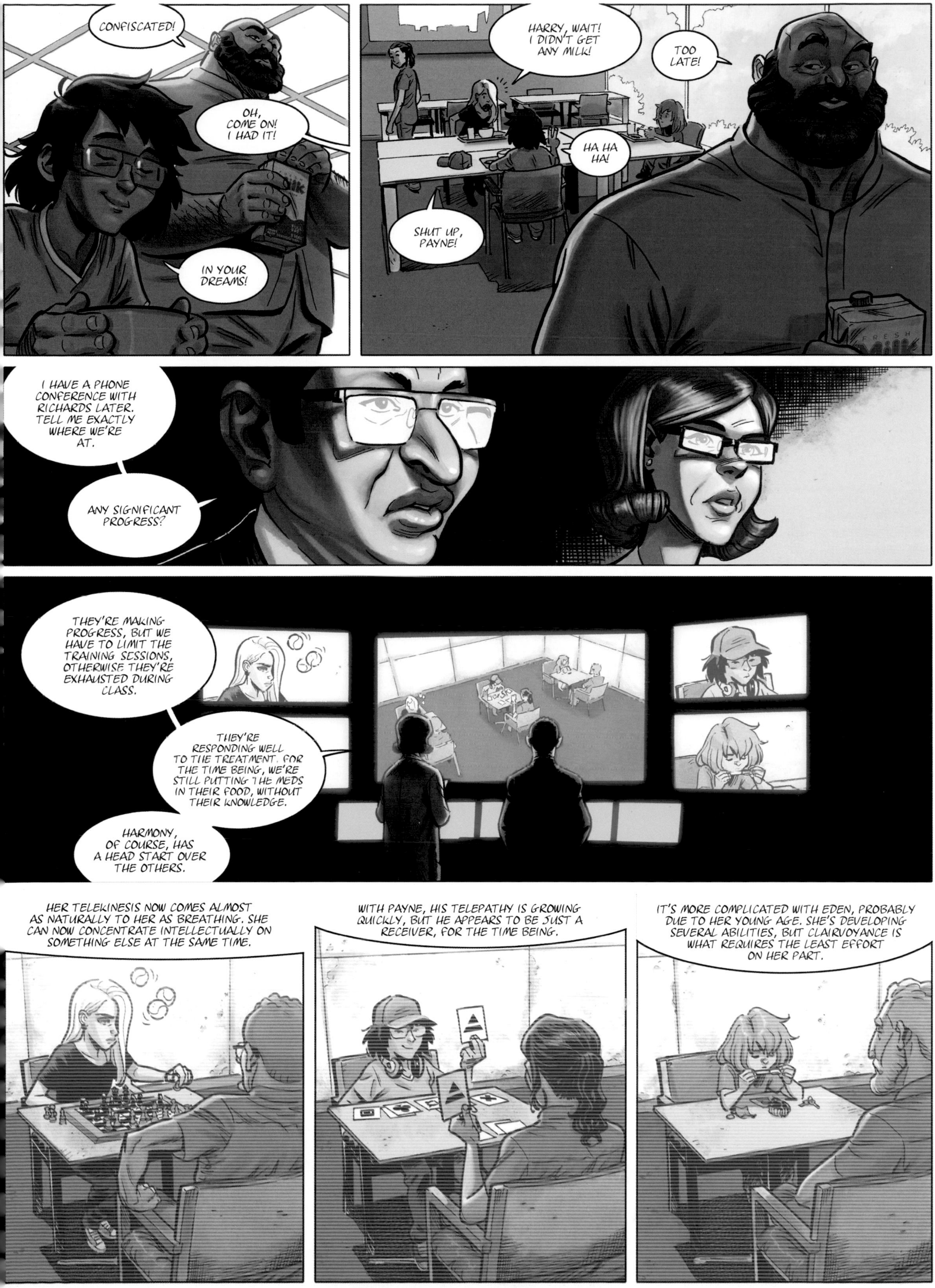
CONFISCATED!
OH, COME ON! I HAD IT!
IN YOUR DREAMS!
HARRY, WAIT! I DIDN'T GET ANY MILK!
TOO LATE!
HA HA HA!
SHUT UP, PAYNE!
FRESH MILK
I HAVE A PHONE CONFERENCE WITH RICHARDS LATER. TELL ME EXACTLY WHERE WE'RE AT.
ANY SIGNIFICANT PROGRESS?
THEY'RE MAKING PROGRESS, BUT WE HAVE TO LIMIT THE TRAINING SESSIONS, OTHERWISE THEY'RE EXHAUSTED DURING CLASS.
THEY'RE RESPONDING WELL TO THE TREATMENT. FOR THE TIME BEING, WE'RE STILL PUTTING THE MEDS IN THEIR FOOD, WITHOUT THEIR KNOWLEDGE.
HARMONY, OF COURSE, HAS A HEAD START OVER THE OTHERS.
HER TELEKINESIS NOW COMES ALMOST AS NATURALLY TO HER AS BREATHING. SHE CAN NOW CONCENTRATE INTELLECTUALLY ON SOMETHING ELSE AT THE SAME TIME.
WITH PAYNE, HIS TELEPATHY IS GROWING QUICKLY, BUT HE APPEARS TO BE JUST A RECEIVER, FOR THE TIME BEING.
IT'S MORE COMPLICATED WITH EDEN, PROBABLY DUE TO HER YOUNG AGE. SHE'S DEVELOPING SEVERAL ABILITIES, BUT CLAIRVOYANCE IS WHAT REQUIRES THE LEAST EFFORT ON HER PART.

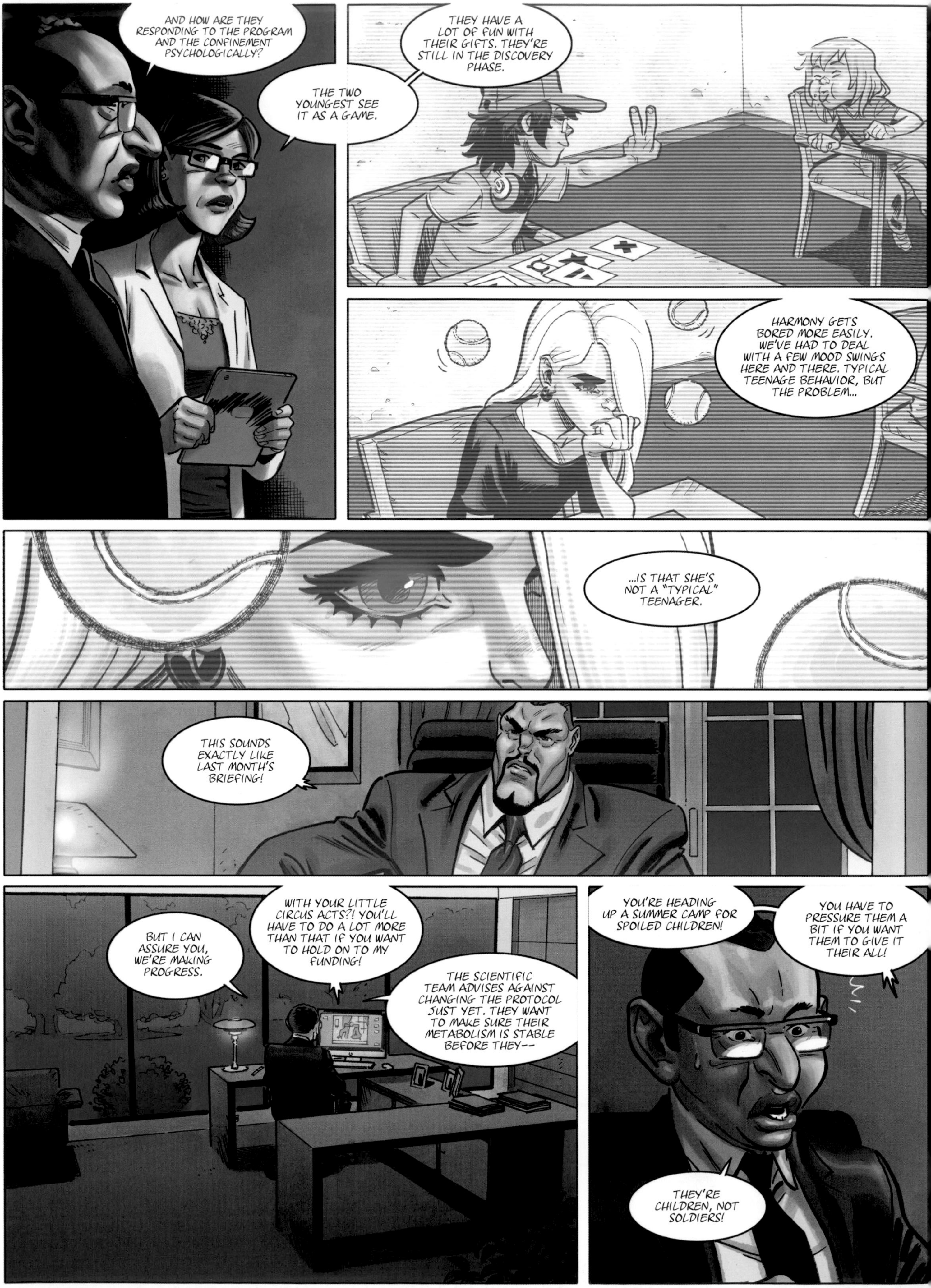
AND HOW ARE THEY RESPONDING TO THE PROGRAM AND THE CONFINEMENT PSYCHOLOGICALLY?
THE TWO YOUNGEST SEE IT AS A GAME.
THEY HAVE A LOT OF FUN WITH THEIR GIFTS. THEY'RE STILL IN THE DISCOVERY PHASE.
HARMONY GETS BORED MORE EASILY. WE'VE HAD TO DEAL WITH A FEW MOOD SWINGS HERE AND THERE. TYPICAL TEENAGE BEHAVIOR, BUT THE PROBLEM...
...IS THAT SHE'S NOT A "TYPICAL" TEENAGER.
THIS SOUNDS EXACTLY LIKE LAST MONTH'S BRIEFING!
BUT I CAN ASSURE YOU, WE'RE MAKING PROGRESS.
WITH YOUR LITTLE CIRCUS ACTS?! YOU'LL HAVE TO DO A LOT MORE THAN THAT IF YOU WANT TO HOLD ON TO MY FUNDING!
THE SCIENTIFIC TEAM ADVISES AGAINST CHANGING THE PROTOCOL JUST YET. THEY WANT TO MAKE SURE THEIR METABOLISM IS STABLE BEFORE THEY--
YOU'RE HEADING UP A SUMMER CAMP FOR SPOILED CHILDREN!
YOU HAVE TO PRESSURE THEM A BIT IF YOU WANT THEM TO GIVE IT THEIR ALL!
THEY'RE CHILDREN, NOT SOLDIERS!

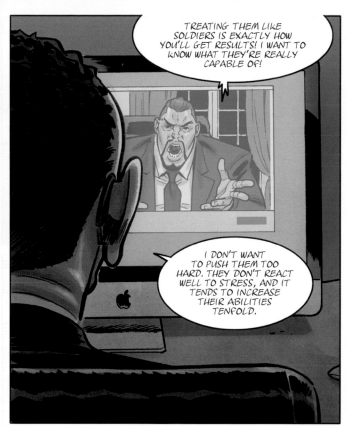

TREATING THEM LIKE SOLDIERS IS EXACTLY HOW YOU'LL GET RESULTS! I WANT TO KNOW WHAT THEY'RE REALLY CAPABLE OF!

I DON'T WANT TO PUSH THEM TOO HARD. THEY DON'T REACT WELL TO STRESS, AND IT TENDS TO INCREASE THEIR ABILITIES TENFOLD.

THAT'S PRECISELY THE GOAL!

HARMONY COULD BE ESPECIALLY HARD TO CONTROL IF--

HA! THAT'S YOUR PROBLEM!

YOU'LL NEVER TAME THEM IF YOU'RE AFRAID THEY'LL BITE!

I THINK IT'S TIME FOR ME TO TAKE OVER.

I'LL CALL YOU IN A FEW DAYS.

RECESS IS OVER, STEINMAN!

BEEP!

ASSHOLE!

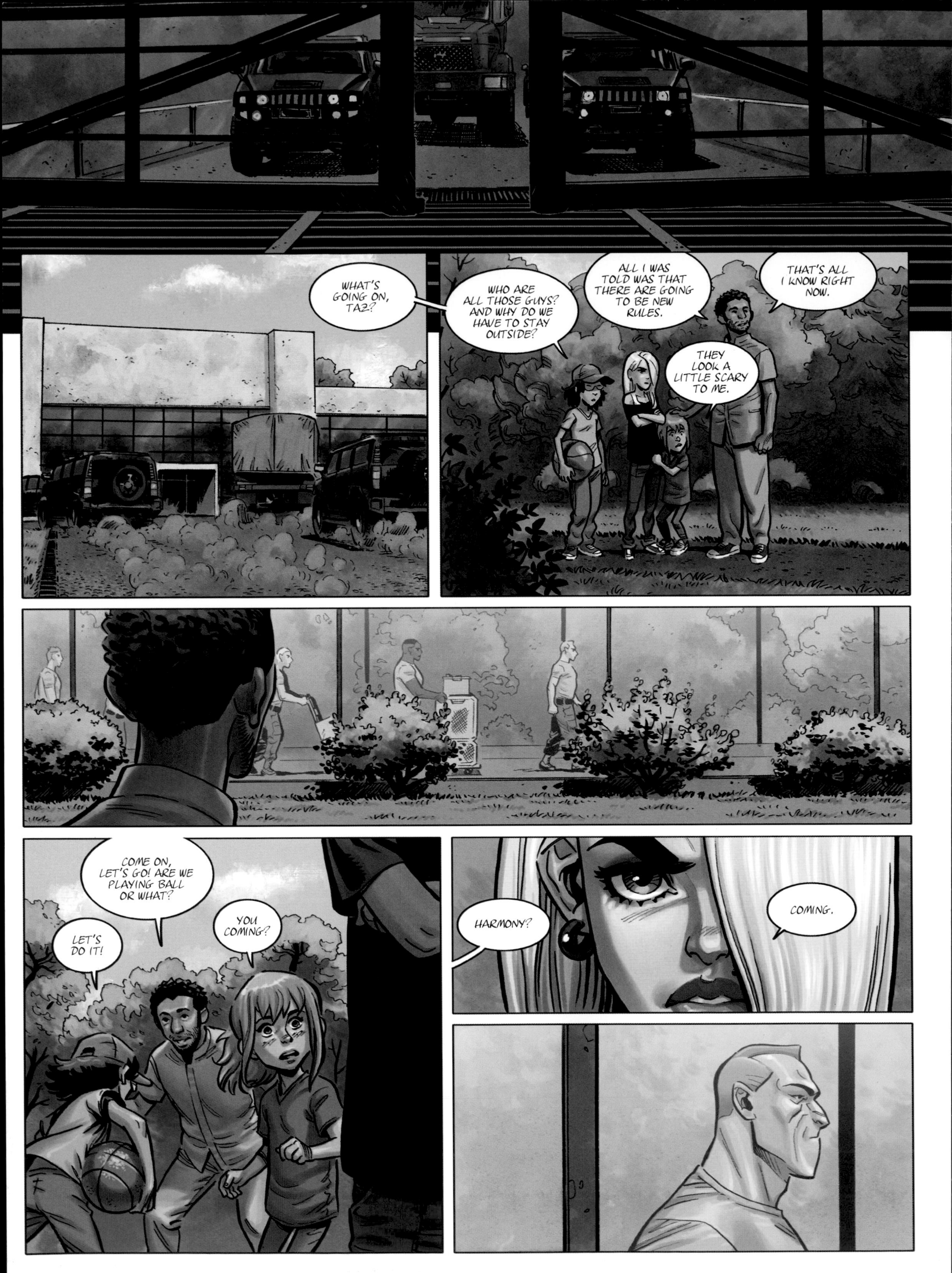
WHAT'S GOING ON, TAZ?
WHO ARE ALL THOSE GUYS? AND WHY DO WE HAVE TO STAY OUTSIDE?
ALL I WAS TOLD WAS THAT THERE ARE GOING TO BE NEW RULES.
THAT'S ALL I KNOW RIGHT NOW.
THEY LOOK A LITTLE SCARY TO ME.
COME ON, LET'S GO! ARE WE PLAYING BALL OR WHAT?
LET'S DO IT!
YOU COMING?
HARMONY?
COMING.

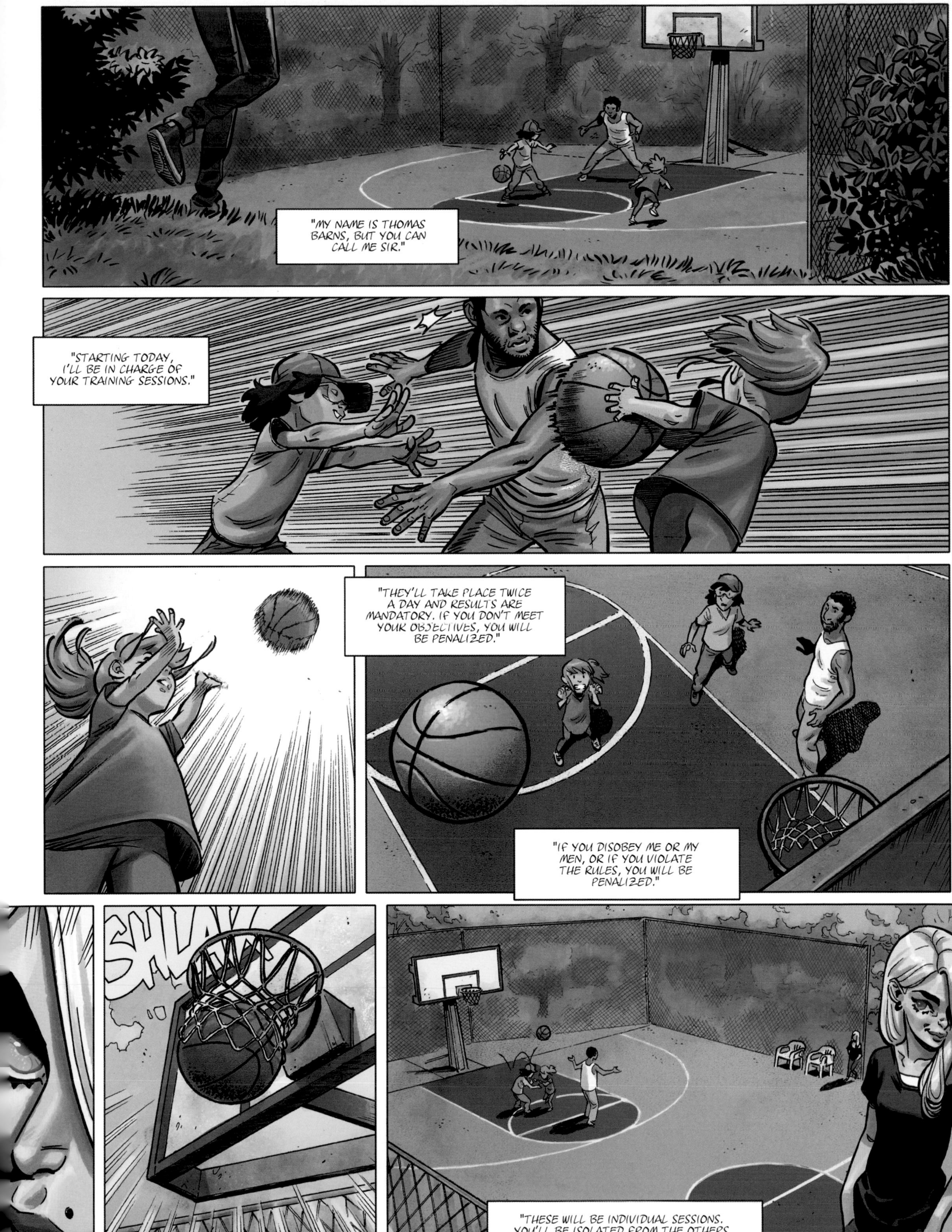
"MY NAME IS THOMAS BARNS, BUT YOU CAN CALL ME SIR."
"STARTING TODAY, I'LL BE IN CHARGE OF YOUR TRAINING SESSIONS."
"THEY'LL TAKE PLACE TWICE A DAY AND RESULTS ARE MANDATORY. IF YOU DON'T MEET YOUR OBJECTIVES, YOU WILL BE PENALIZED."
"IF YOU DISOBEY ME OR MY MEN, OR IF YOU VIOLATE THE RULES, YOU WILL BE PENALIZED."
"THESE WILL BE INDIVIDUAL SESSIONS. YOU'LL BE ISOLATED FROM THE OTHERS IN A ONE-ON-ONE WITH ME. AS YOU CAN IMAGINE, IT WON'T ALL BE FUN AND GAMES."

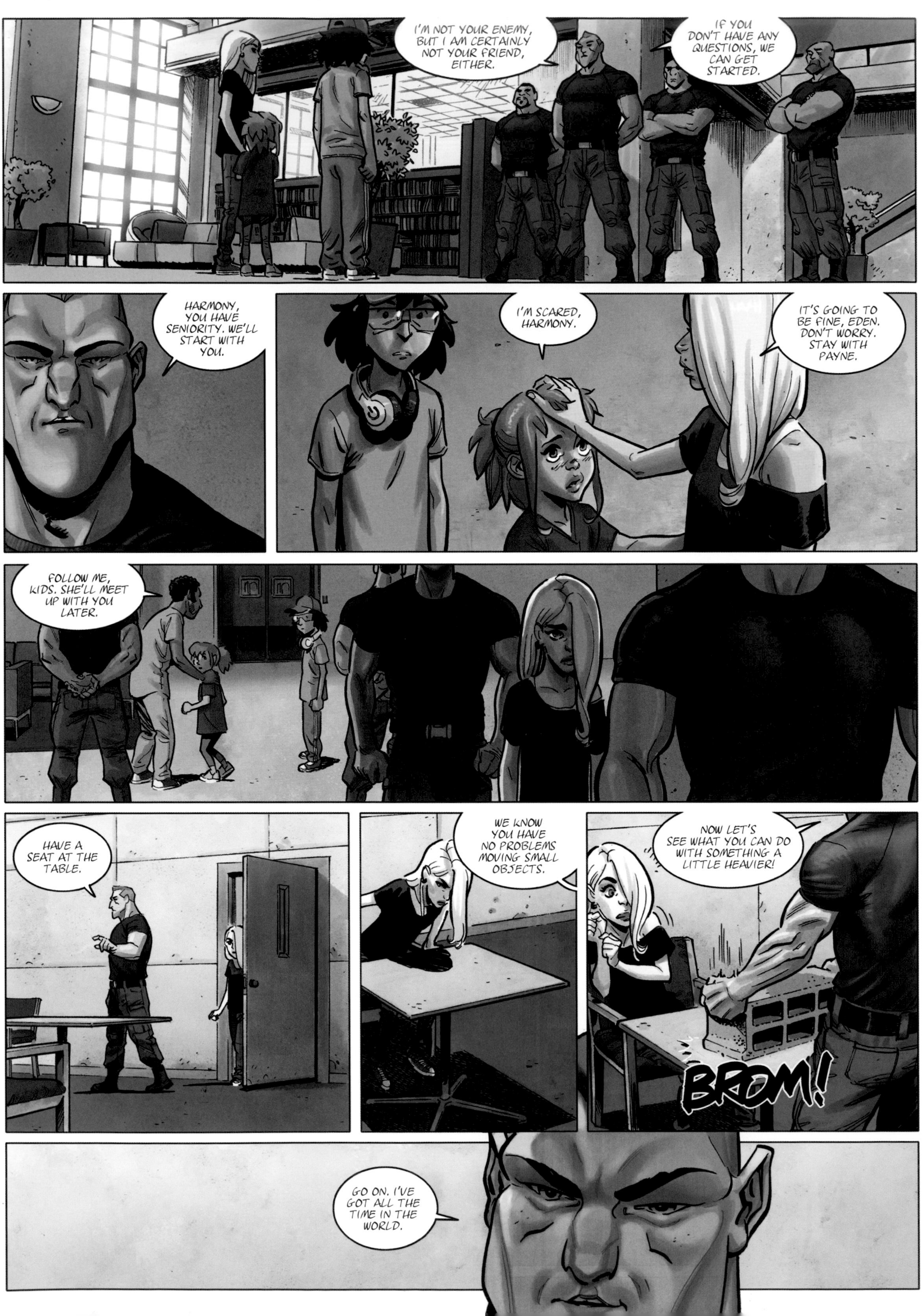
I'M NOT YOUR ENEMY, BUT I AM CERTAINLY NOT YOUR FRIEND, EITHER.
IF YOU DON'T HAVE ANY QUESTIONS, WE CAN GET STARTED.
HARMONY, YOU HAVE SENIORITY. WE'LL START WITH YOU.
I'M SCARED, HARMONY.
IT'S GOING TO BE FINE, EDEN. DON'T WORRY. STAY WITH PAYNE.
FOLLOW ME, KIDS. SHE'LL MEET UP WITH YOU LATER.
HAVE A SEAT AT THE TABLE.
WE KNOW YOU HAVE NO PROBLEMS MOVING SMALL OBJECTS.
NOW LET'S SEE WHAT YOU CAN DO WITH SOMETHING A LITTLE HEAVIER!
BROM!
GO ON. I'VE GOT ALL THE TIME IN THE WORLD.

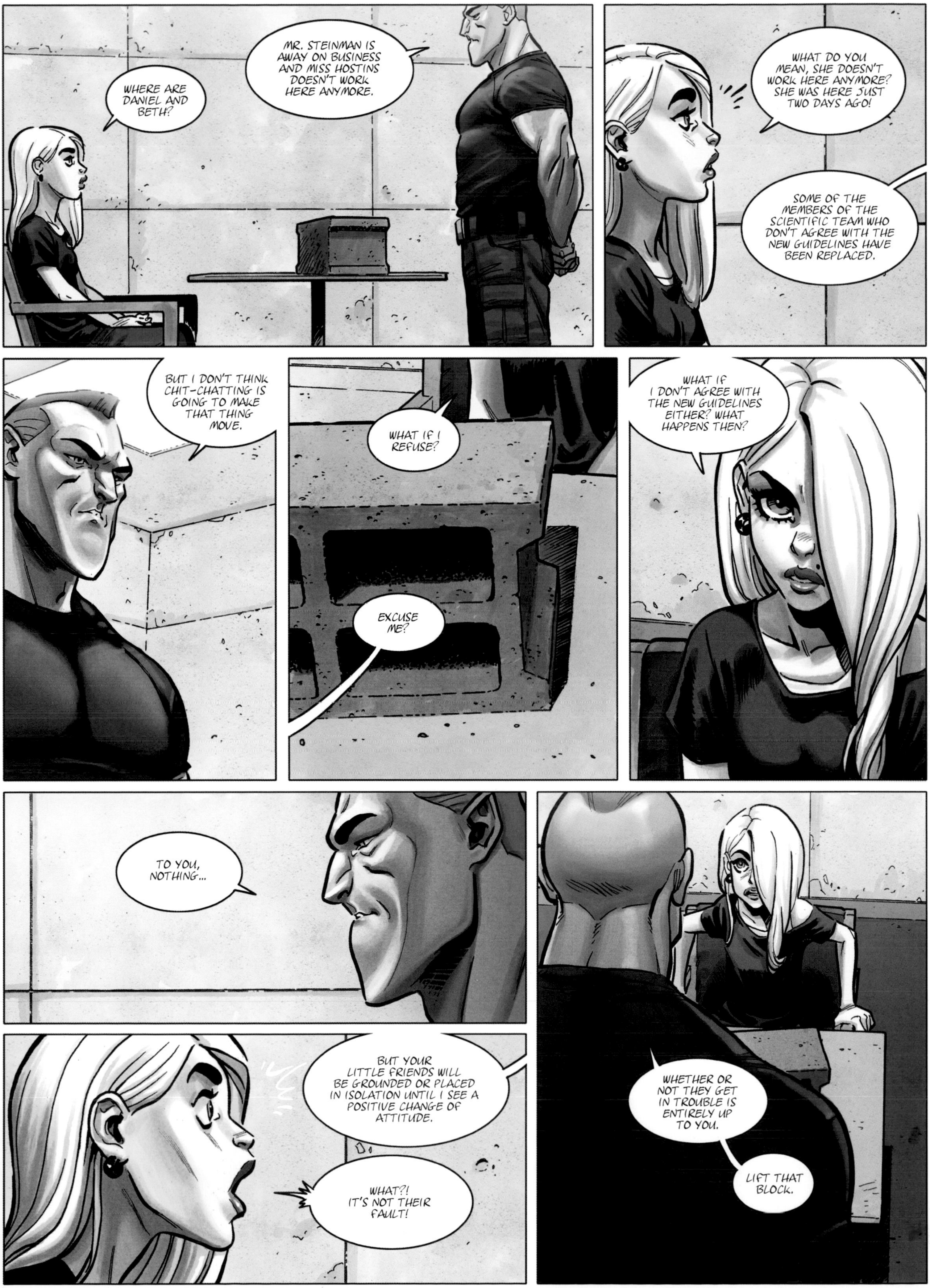
WHERE ARE DANIEL AND BETH?
MR. STEINMAN IS AWAY ON BUSINESS AND MISS HOSTINS DOESN'T WORK HERE ANYMORE.
WHAT DO YOU MEAN, SHE DOESN'T WORK HERE ANYMORE? SHE WAS HERE JUST TWO DAYS AGO!
SOME OF THE MEMBERS OF THE SCIENTIFIC TEAM WHO DON'T AGREE WITH THE NEW GUIDELINES HAVE BEEN REPLACED.
BUT I DON'T THINK CHIT-CHATTING IS GOING TO MAKE THAT THING MOVE.
WHAT IF I REFUSE?
EXCUSE ME?
WHAT IF I DON'T AGREE WITH THE NEW GUIDELINES EITHER? WHAT HAPPENS THEN?
TO YOU, NOTHING...
BUT YOUR LITTLE FRIENDS WILL BE GROUNDED OR PLACED IN ISOLATION UNTIL I SEE A POSITIVE CHANGE OF ATTITUDE.
WHAT?! IT'S NOT THEIR FAULT!
WHETHER OR NOT THEY GET IN TROUBLE IS ENTIRELY UP TO YOU.
LIFT THAT BLOCK.

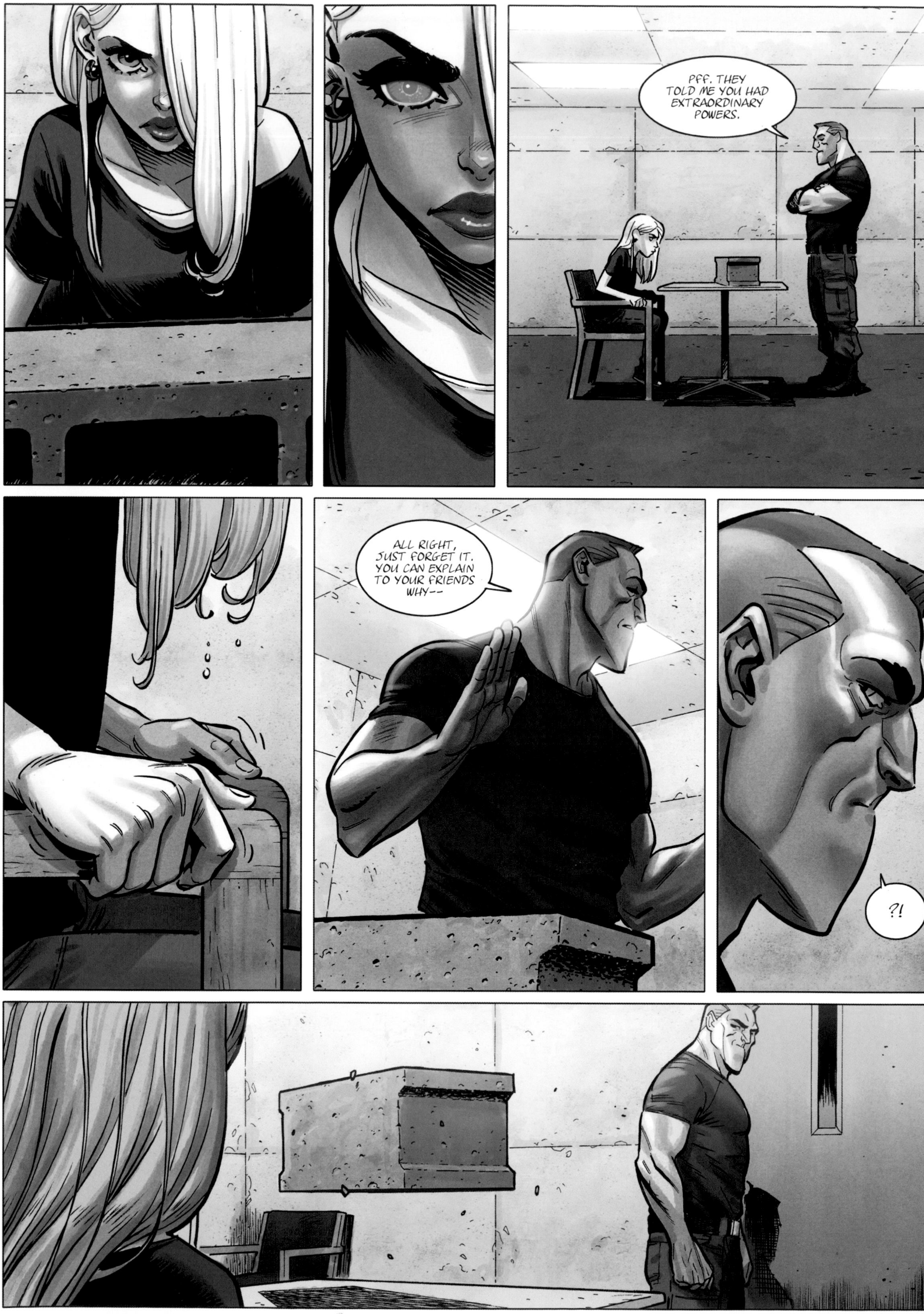
PFF. THEY TOLD ME YOU HAD EXTRAORDINARY POWERS.
ALL RIGHT, JUST FORGET IT. YOU CAN EXPLAIN TO YOUR FRIENDS WHY--
?!

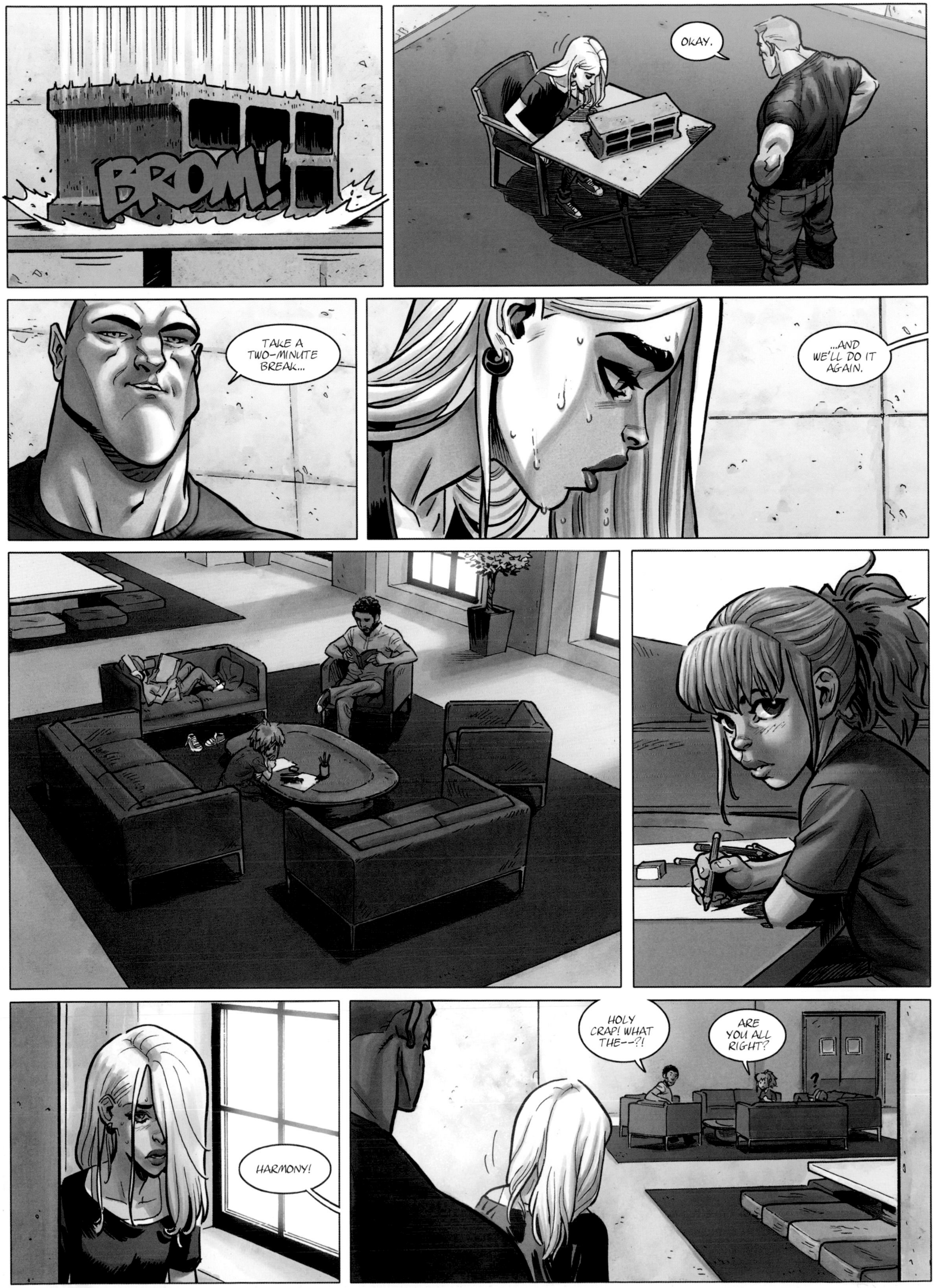
BROM!
OKAY.
TAKE A TWO-MINUTE BREAK...
...AND WE'LL DO IT AGAIN.
HARMONY!
HOLY CRAP! WHAT THE--?!
ARE YOU ALL RIGHT?

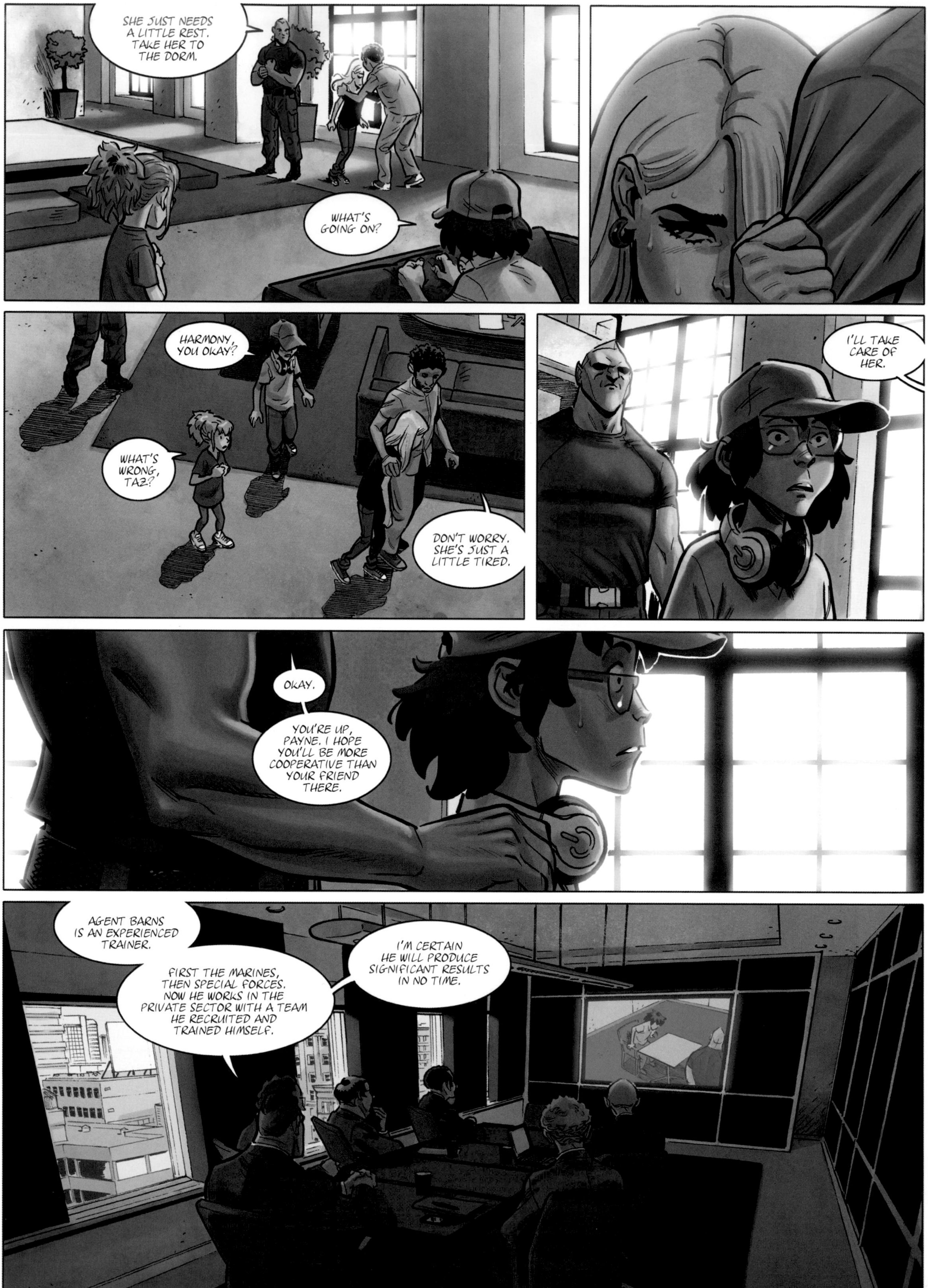
SHE JUST NEEDS A LITTLE REST. TAKE HER TO THE DORM.
WHAT'S GOING ON?
HARMONY, YOU OKAY?
WHAT'S WRONG, TAZ?
DON'T WORRY. SHE'S JUST A LITTLE TIRED.
I'LL TAKE CARE OF HER.
OKAY.
YOU'RE UP, PAYNE. I HOPE YOU'LL BE MORE COOPERATIVE THAN YOUR FRIEND THERE.
AGENT BARNS IS AN EXPERIENCED TRAINER.
FIRST THE MARINES, THEN SPECIAL FORCES. NOW HE WORKS IN THE PRIVATE SECTOR WITH A TEAM HE RECRUITED AND TRAINED HIMSELF.
I'M CERTAIN HE WILL PRODUCE SIGNIFICANT RESULTS IN NO TIME.

DANIEL, YOU WILL CONTINUE OVERSEEING THE CENTER, THE FINANCES, AND THE KIDS' DAILY ROUTINE...

...BUT HE HAS CARTE BLANCHE WHEN IT COMES TO THEIR TRAINING AND CAMPUS SECURITY.

WHETHER YOU AGREE WITH HIS METHODS OR NOT.

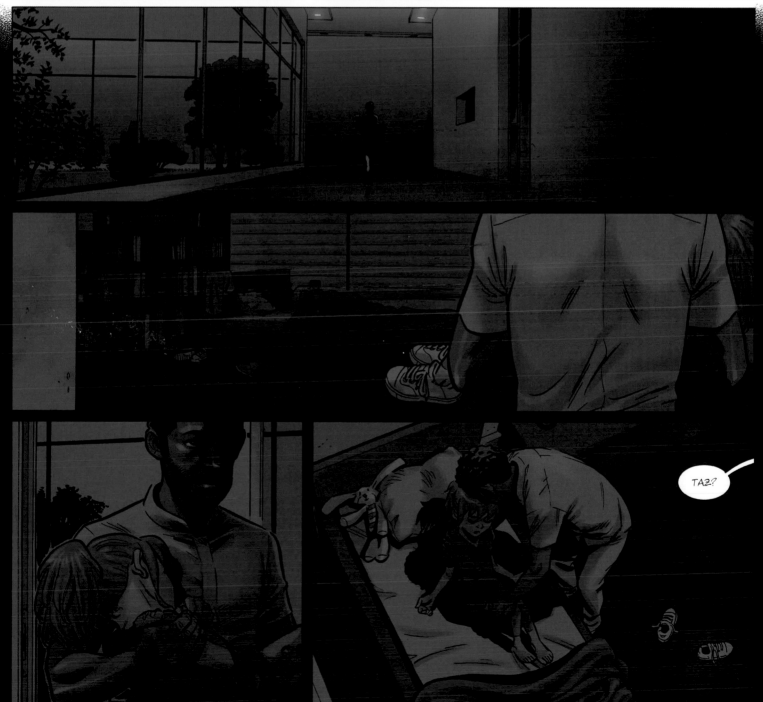

TA?

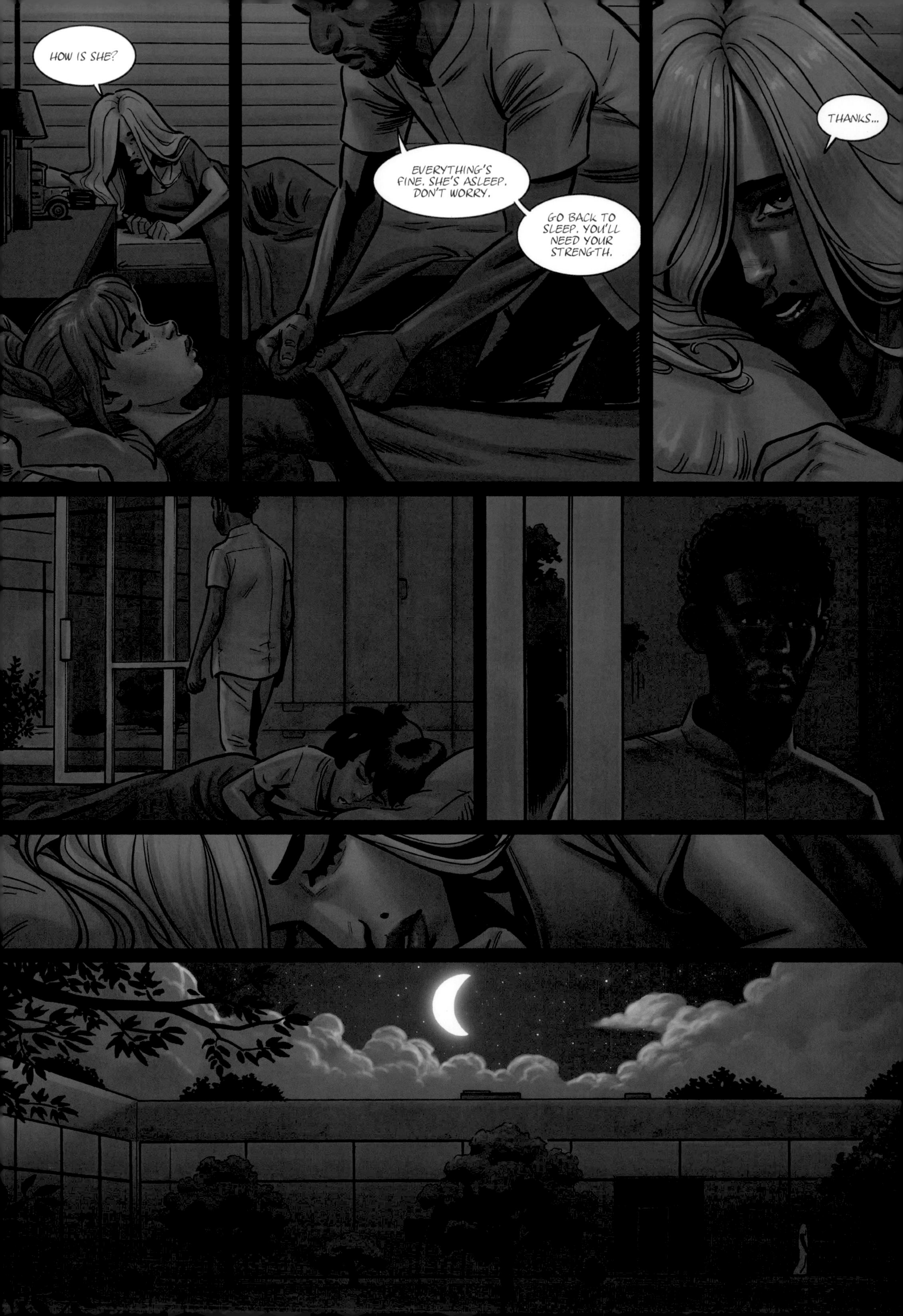
HOW IS SHE?
EVERYTHING'S FINE. SHE'S ASLEEP. DON'T WORRY.
GO BACK TO SLEEP. YOU'LL NEED YOUR STRENGTH.
THANKS...

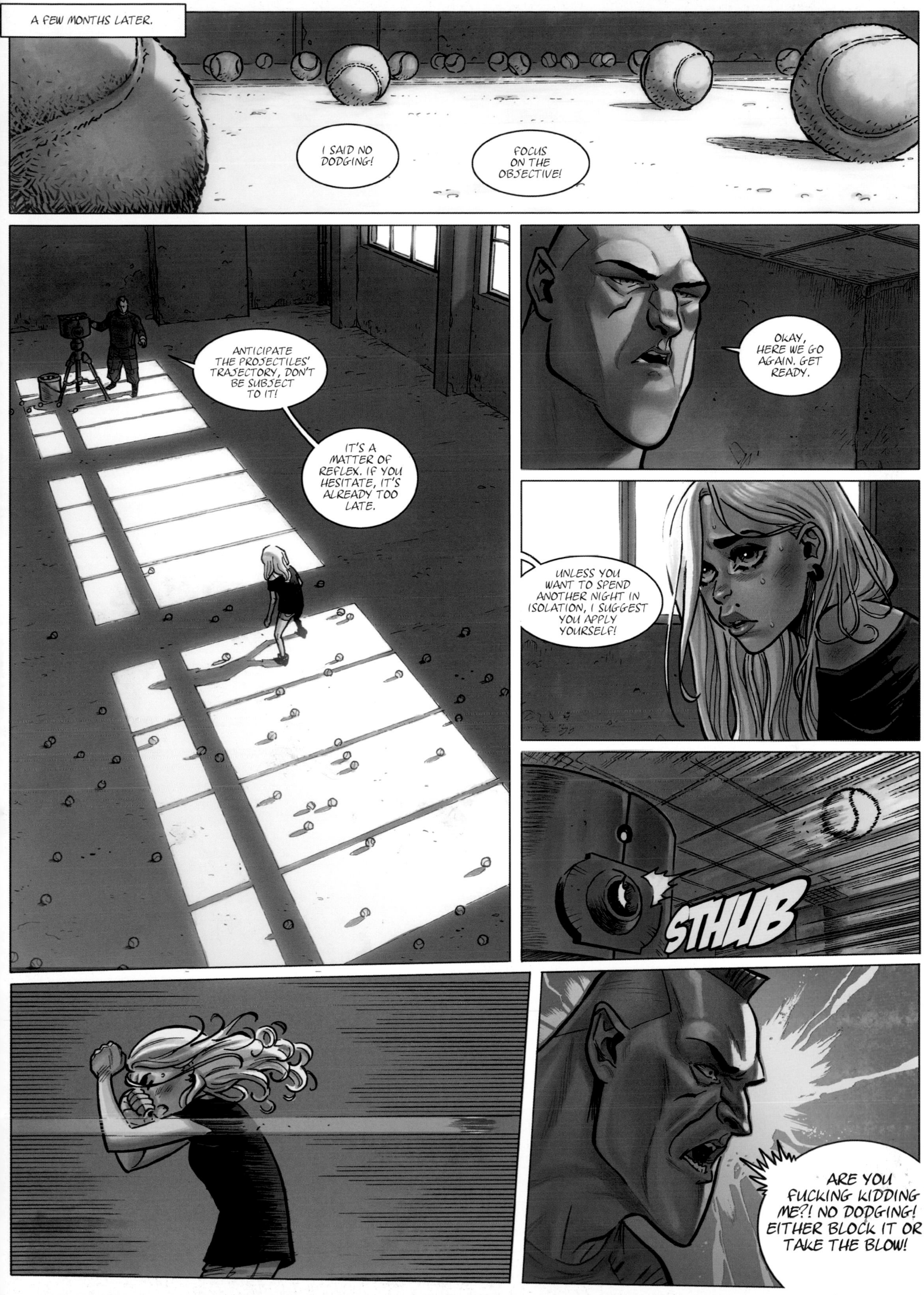
A FEW MONTHS LATER.
I SAID NO DODGING!
FOCUS ON THE OBJECTIVE!
ANTICIPATE THE PROJECTILES' TRAJECTORY, DON'T BE SUBJECT TO IT!
IT'S A MATTER OF REFLEX. IF YOU HESITATE, IT'S ALREADY TOO LATE.
OKAY, HERE WE GO AGAIN. GET READY.
UNLESS YOU WANT TO SPEND ANOTHER NIGHT IN ISOLATION, I SUGGEST YOU APPLY YOURSELF!
STHUB
ARE YOU FUCKING KIDDING ME?! NO DODGING! EITHER BLOCK IT OR TAKE THE BLOW!

IT'S GOING TOO FAST... I CAN'T KEEP UP.

EITHER BLOCK IT OR TAKE IT.

STHUB

KEEP YOUR EYES ON IT!

GOOD. AGAIN!

STHUB   STHUB   STHUB   STHUB

WAIT!

IT'S GOING TOO FAST... I CAN'T KEEP UP.

PAK

OUCH!

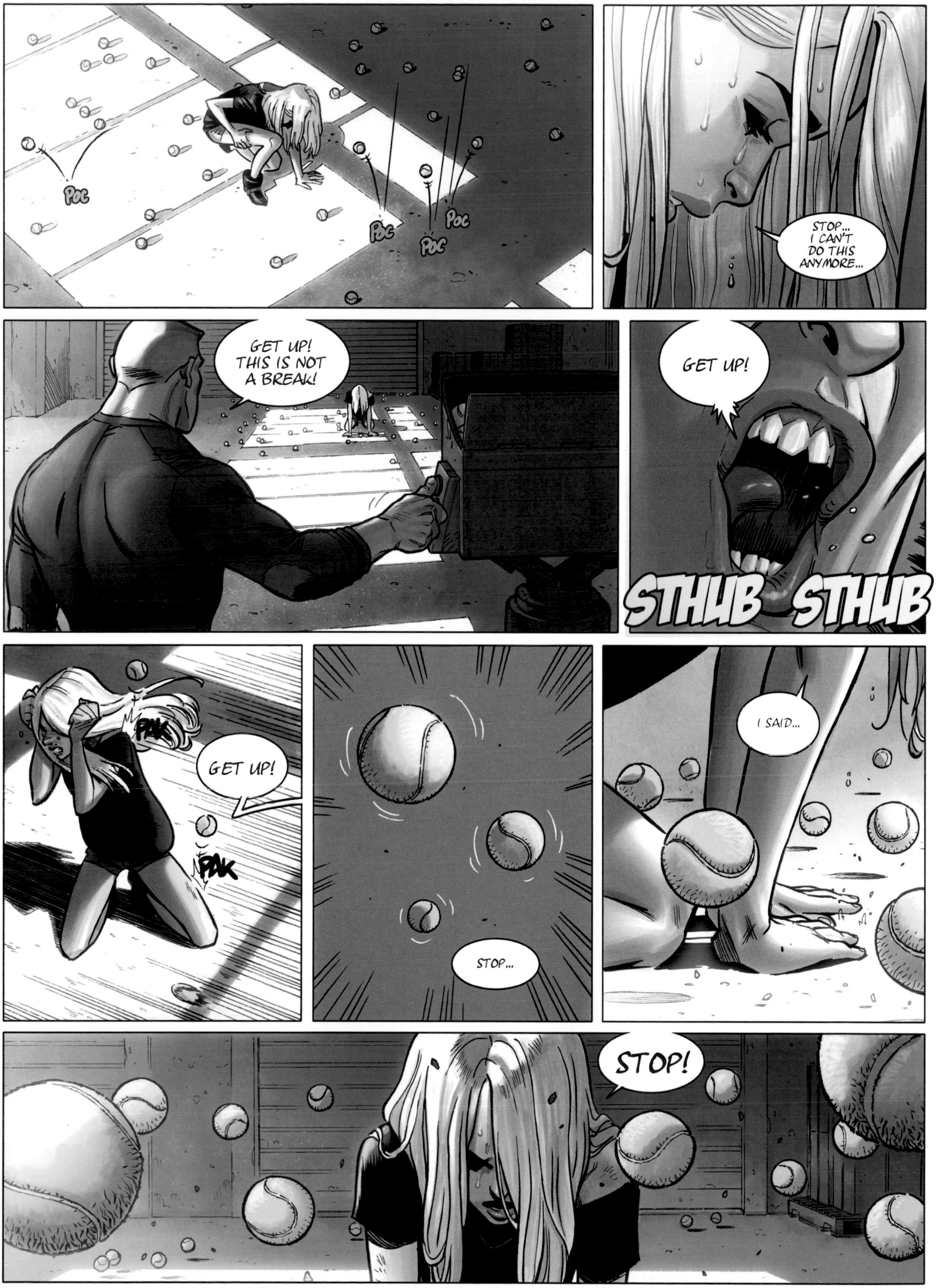
POC
POC
POC
POC
STOP... I CAN'T DO THIS ANYMORE...
GET UP! THIS IS NOT A BREAK!
GET UP!
STHUB STHUB
PAK
GET UP!
PAK
STOP...
I SAID...
STOP!

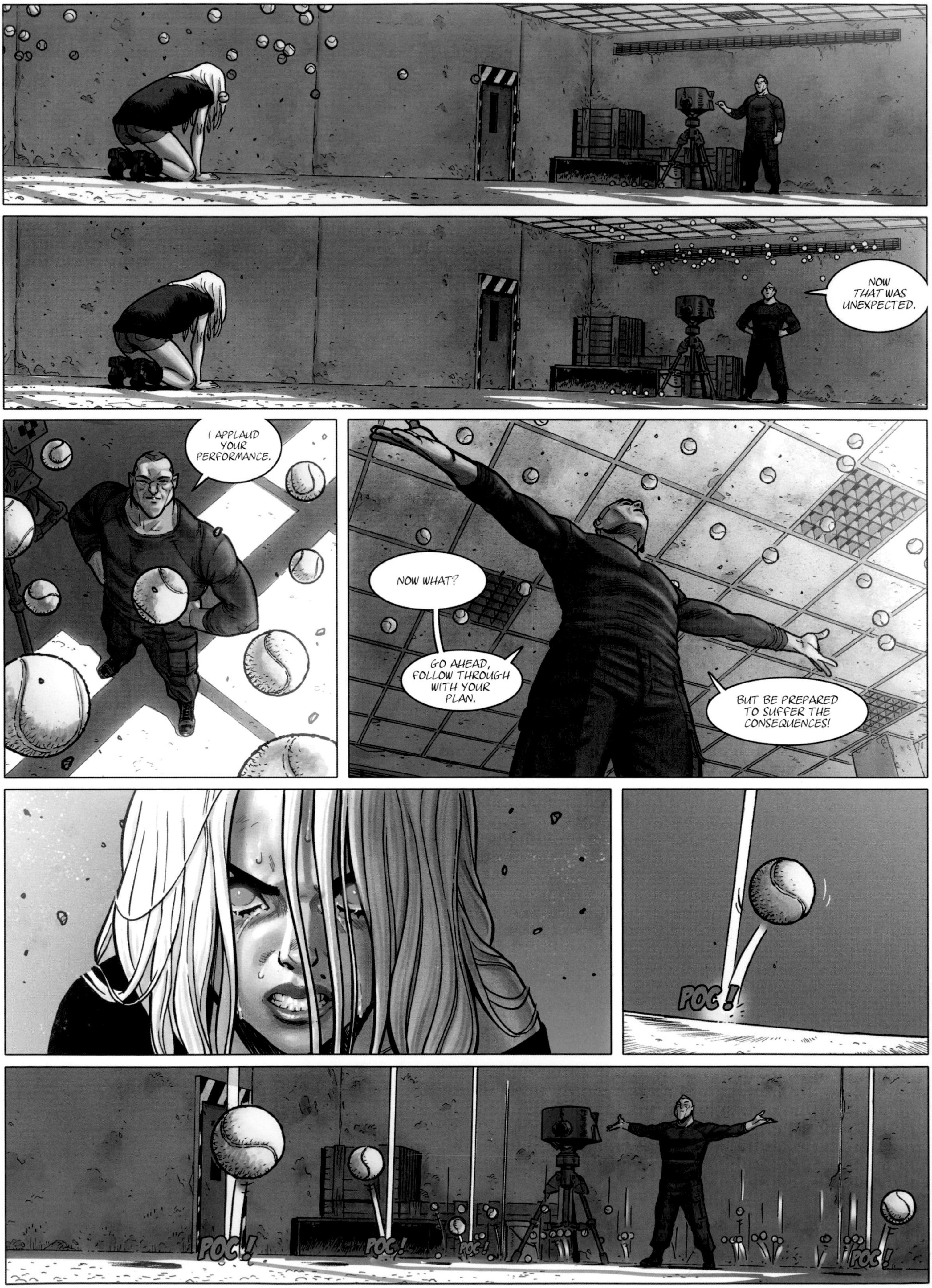
NOW THAT WAS UNEXPECTED.
I APPLAUD YOUR PERFORMANCE.
NOW WHAT?
GO AHEAD, FOLLOW THROUGH WITH YOUR PLAN.
BUT BE PREPARED TO SUFFER THE CONSEQUENCES!
POC!
POC!
POC!
POC!
POC!

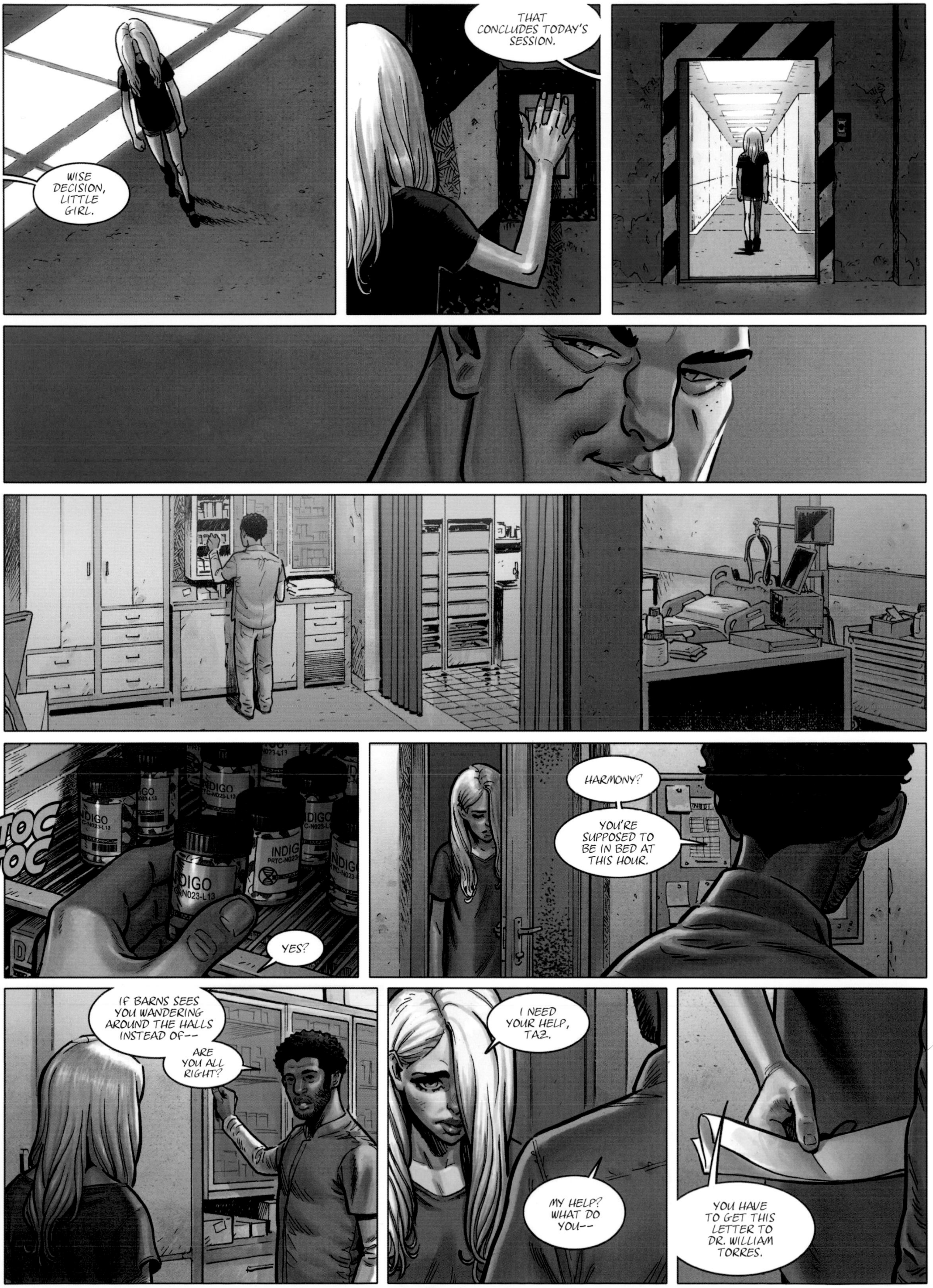
WISE DECISION, LITTLE GIRL.
THAT CONCLUDES TODAY'S SESSION.
TOC
TOC
INDIGO
YES?
HARMONY?
YOU'RE SUPPOSED TO BE IN BED AT THIS HOUR.
IF BARNS SEES YOU WANDERING AROUND THE HALLS INSTEAD OF--
ARE YOU ALL RIGHT?
I NEED YOUR HELP, TAZ.
MY HELP? WHAT DO YOU--
YOU HAVE TO GET THIS LETTER TO DR. WILLIAM TORRES.

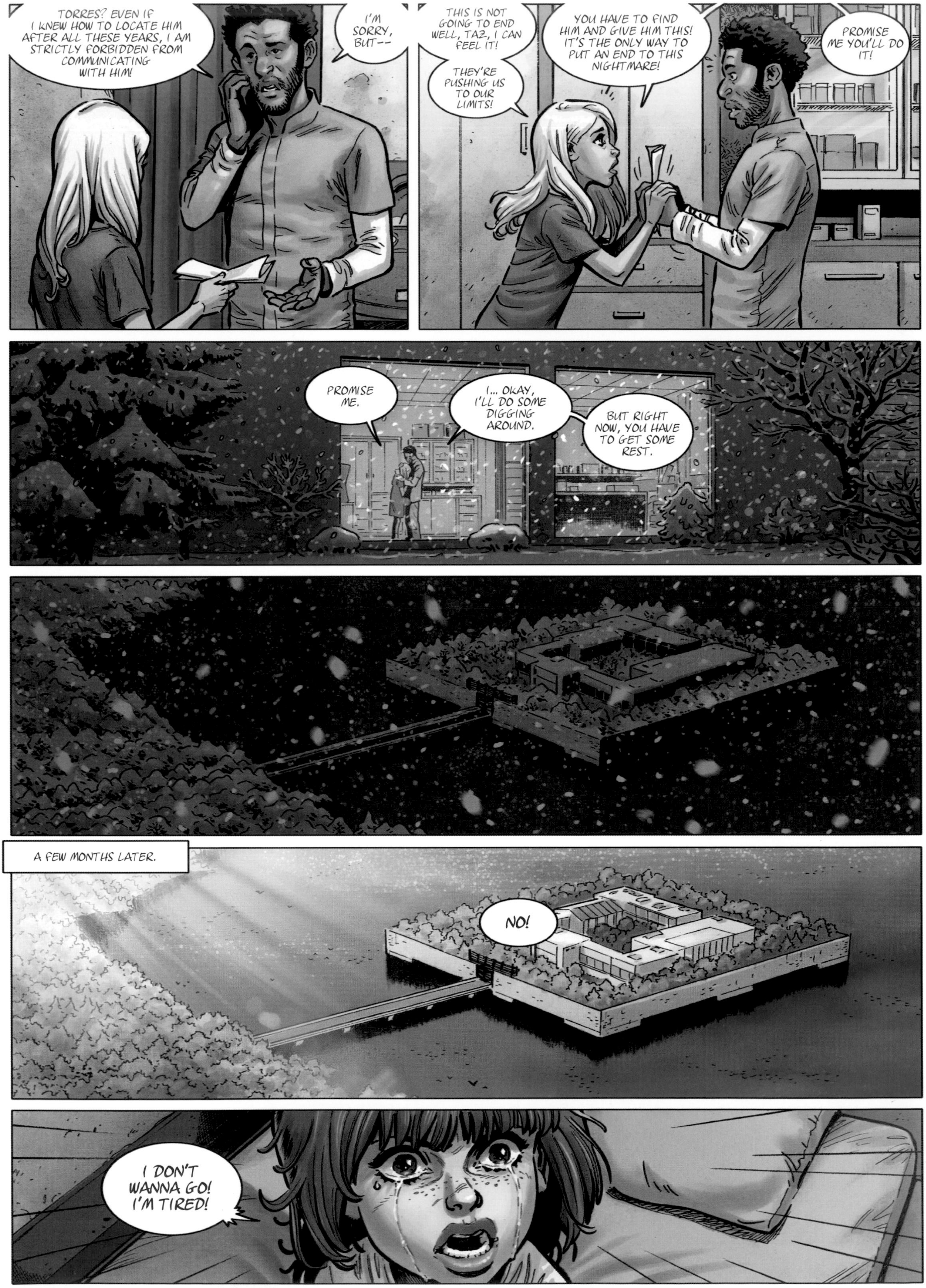
TORRES? EVEN IF I KNEW HOW TO LOCATE HIM AFTER ALL THESE YEARS, I AM STRICTLY FORBIDDEN FROM COMMUNICATING WITH HIM!
I'M SORRY, BUT--
THIS IS NOT GOING TO END WELL, TAZ, I CAN FEEL IT!
THEY'RE PUSHING US TO OUR LIMITS!
YOU HAVE TO FIND HIM AND GIVE HIM THIS! IT'S THE ONLY WAY TO PUT AN END TO THIS NIGHTMARE!
PROMISE ME YOU'LL DO IT!
PROMISE ME.
I... OKAY, I'LL DO SOME DIGGING AROUND.
BUT RIGHT NOW, YOU HAVE TO GET SOME REST.
A FEW MONTHS LATER.
NO!
I DON'T WANNA GO! I'M TIRED!

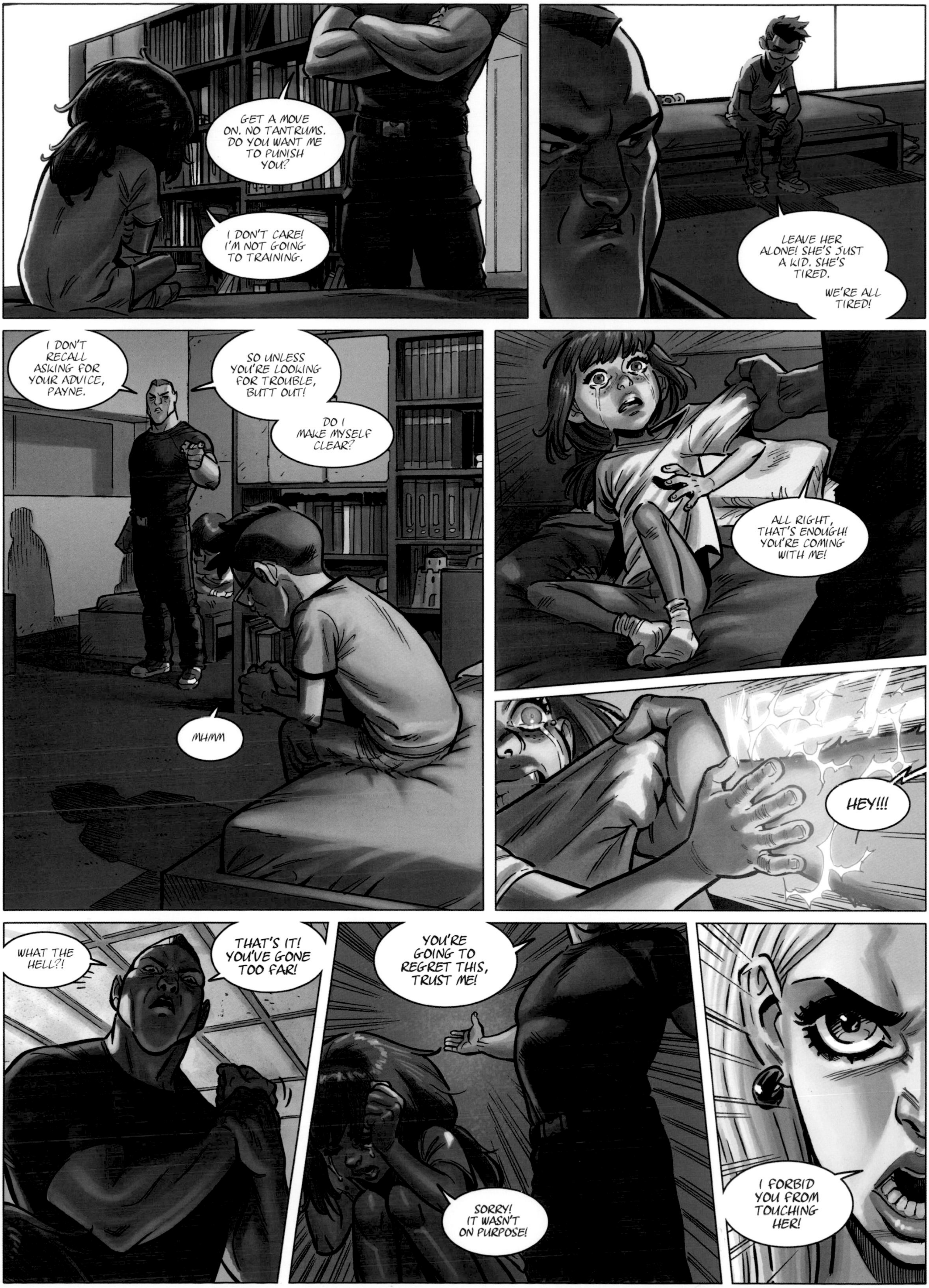
GET A MOVE ON. NO TANTRUMS. DO YOU WANT ME TO PUNISH YOU?
I DON'T CARE! I'M NOT GOING TO TRAINING.
LEAVE HER ALONE! SHE'S JUST A KID. SHE'S TIRED.
WE'RE ALL TIRED!
I DON'T RECALL ASKING FOR YOUR ADVICE, PAYNE.
SO UNLESS YOU'RE LOOKING FOR TROUBLE, BUTT OUT!
DO I MAKE MYSELF CLEAR?
MHMM
ALL RIGHT, THAT'S ENOUGH! YOU'RE COMING WITH ME!
HEY!!!
WHAT THE HELL?!
THAT'S IT! YOU'VE GONE TOO FAR!
YOU'RE GOING TO REGRET THIS, TRUST ME!
SORRY! IT WASN'T ON PURPOSE!
I FORBID YOU FROM TOUCHING HER!

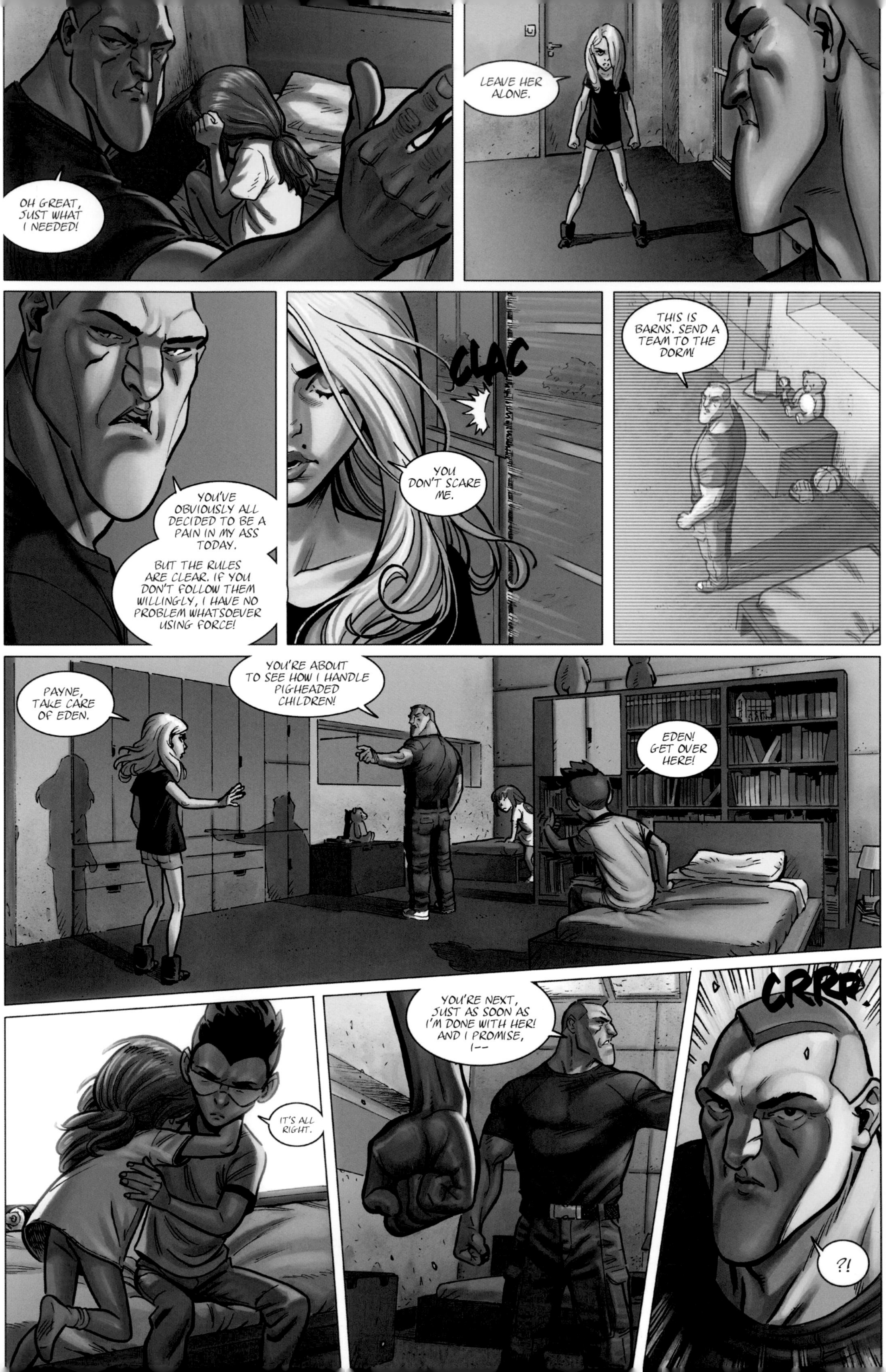
OH GREAT, JUST WHAT I NEEDED!
LEAVE HER ALONE.
YOU'VE OBVIOUSLY ALL DECIDED TO BE A PAIN IN MY ASS TODAY.
BUT THE RULES ARE CLEAR. IF YOU DON'T FOLLOW THEM WILLINGLY, I HAVE NO PROBLEM WHATSOEVER USING FORCE!
CLAC
YOU DON'T SCARE ME.
THIS IS BARNS. SEND A TEAM TO THE DORM!
PAYNE, TAKE CARE OF EDEN.
YOU'RE ABOUT TO SEE HOW I HANDLE PIGHEADED CHILDREN!
EDEN! GET OVER HERE!
IT'S ALL RIGHT.
YOU'RE NEXT, JUST AS SOON AS I'M DONE WITH HER! AND I PROMISE, I--
CRRR
?!

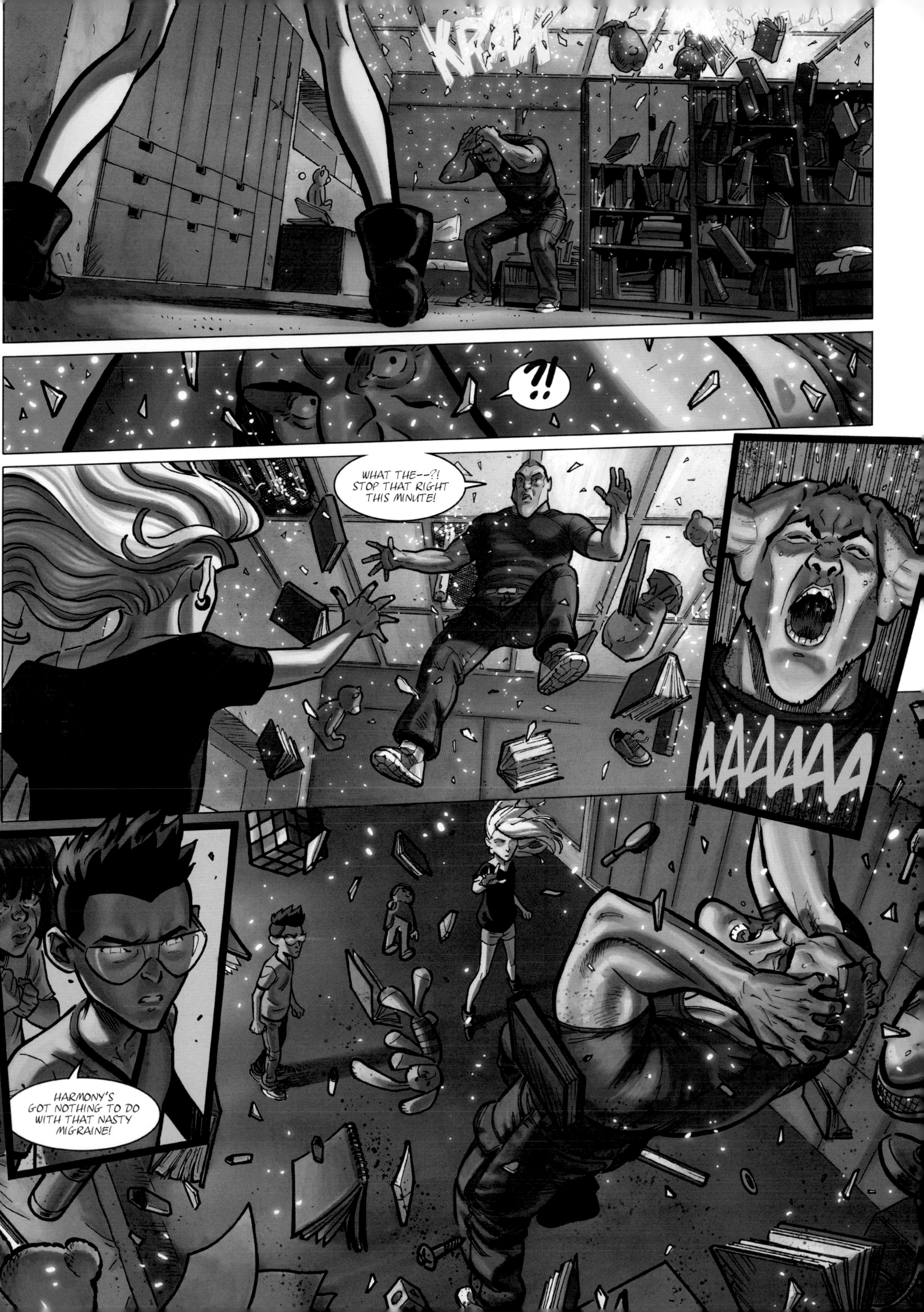
KRAK
?!
WHAT THE--?! STOP THAT RIGHT THIS MINUTE!
AAAAAA
HARMONY'S GOT NOTHING TO DO WITH THAT NASTY MIGRAINE!

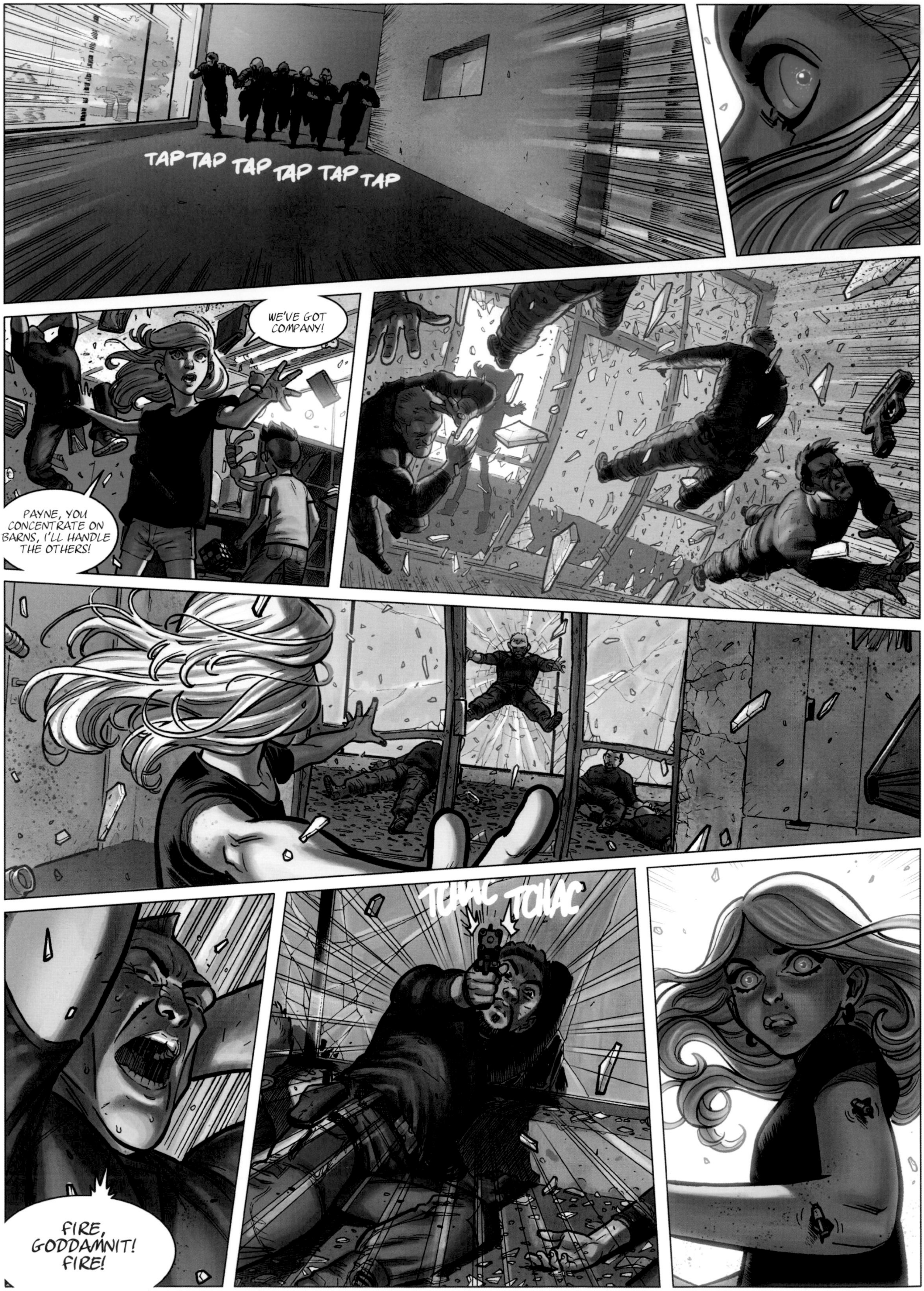
TAP TAP TAP TAP TAP TAP
WE'VE GOT COMPANY!
PAYNE, YOU CONCENTRATE ON BARNS, I'LL HANDLE THE OTHERS!
FIRE, GODDAMNIT! FIRE!
TCHAC TCHAC

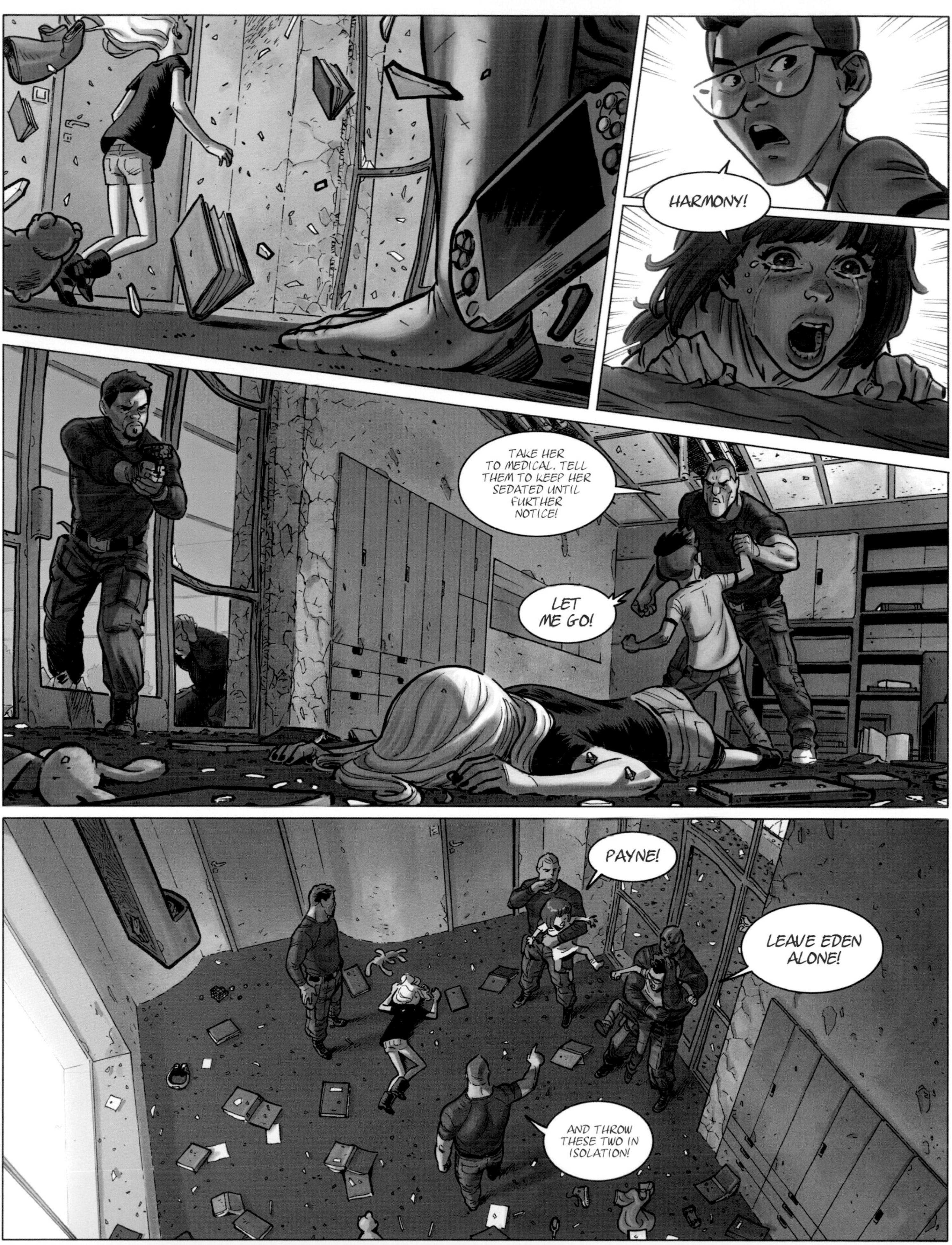
HARMONY!
TAKE HER TO MEDICAL. TELL THEM TO KEEP HER SEDATED UNTIL FURTHER NOTICE!
LET ME GO!
PAYNE!
LEAVE EDEN ALONE!
AND THROW THESE TWO IN ISOLATION!

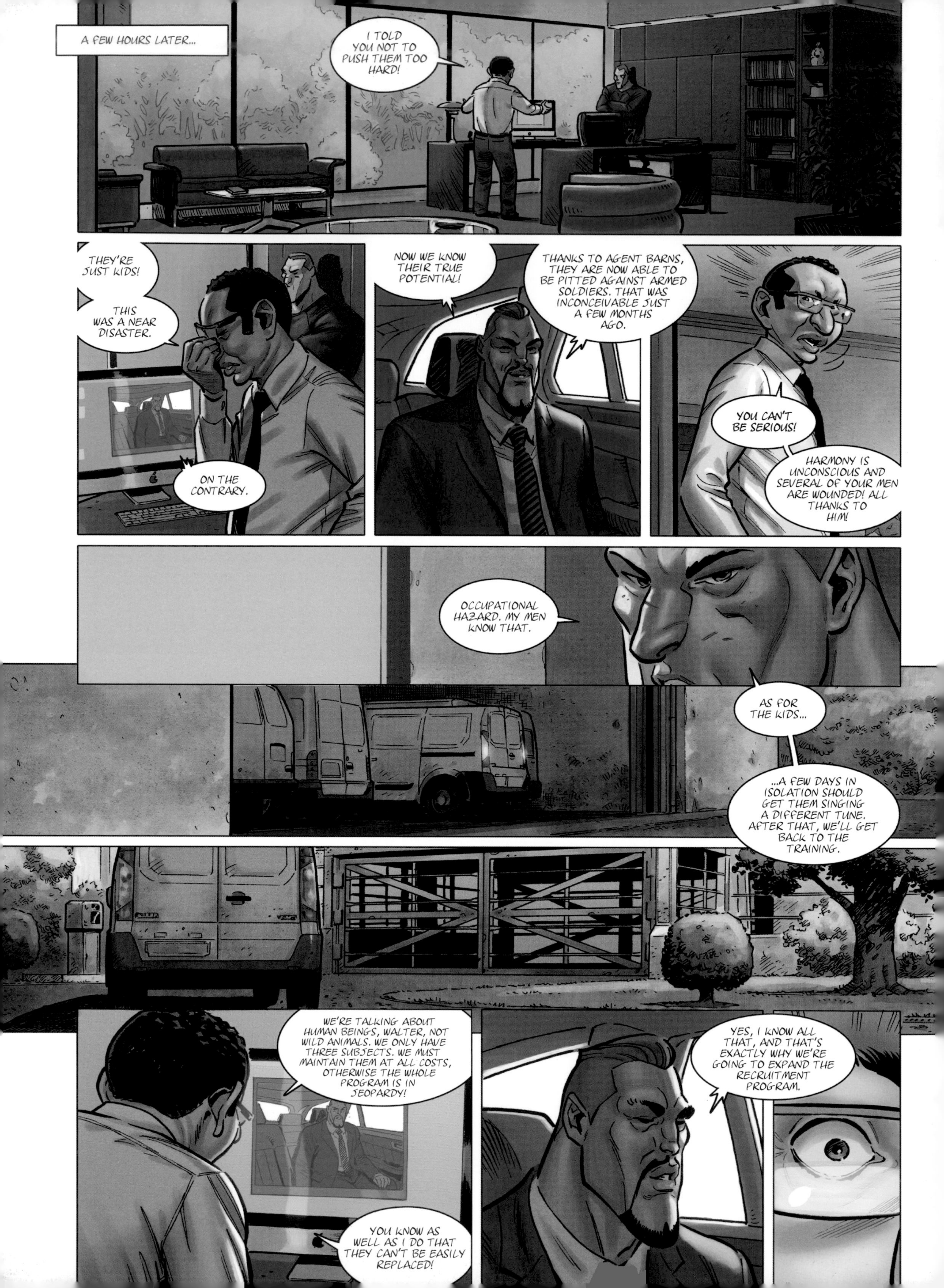
A FEW HOURS LATER...
I TOLD YOU NOT TO PUSH THEM TOO HARD!
THEY'RE JUST KIDS!
THIS WAS A NEAR DISASTER.
ON THE CONTRARY.
NOW WE KNOW THEIR TRUE POTENTIAL!
THANKS TO AGENT BARNS, THEY ARE NOW ABLE TO BE PITTED AGAINST ARMED SOLDIERS. THAT WAS INCONCEIVABLE JUST A FEW MONTHS AGO.
YOU CAN'T BE SERIOUS!
HARMONY IS UNCONSCIOUS AND SEVERAL OF YOUR MEN ARE WOUNDED! ALL THANKS TO HIM!
OCCUPATIONAL HAZARD. MY MEN KNOW THAT.
AS FOR THE KIDS...
...A FEW DAYS IN ISOLATION SHOULD GET THEM SINGING A DIFFERENT TUNE. AFTER THAT, WE'LL GET BACK TO THE TRAINING.
WE'RE TALKING ABOUT HUMAN BEINGS, WALTER, NOT WILD ANIMALS. WE ONLY HAVE THREE SUBJECTS. WE MUST MAINTAIN THEM AT ALL COSTS, OTHERWISE THE WHOLE PROGRAM IS IN JEOPARDY!
YOU KNOW AS WELL AS I DO THAT THEY CAN'T BE EASILY REPLACED!
YES, I KNOW ALL THAT, AND THAT'S EXACTLY WHY WE'RE GOING TO EXPAND THE RECRUITMENT PROGRAM.

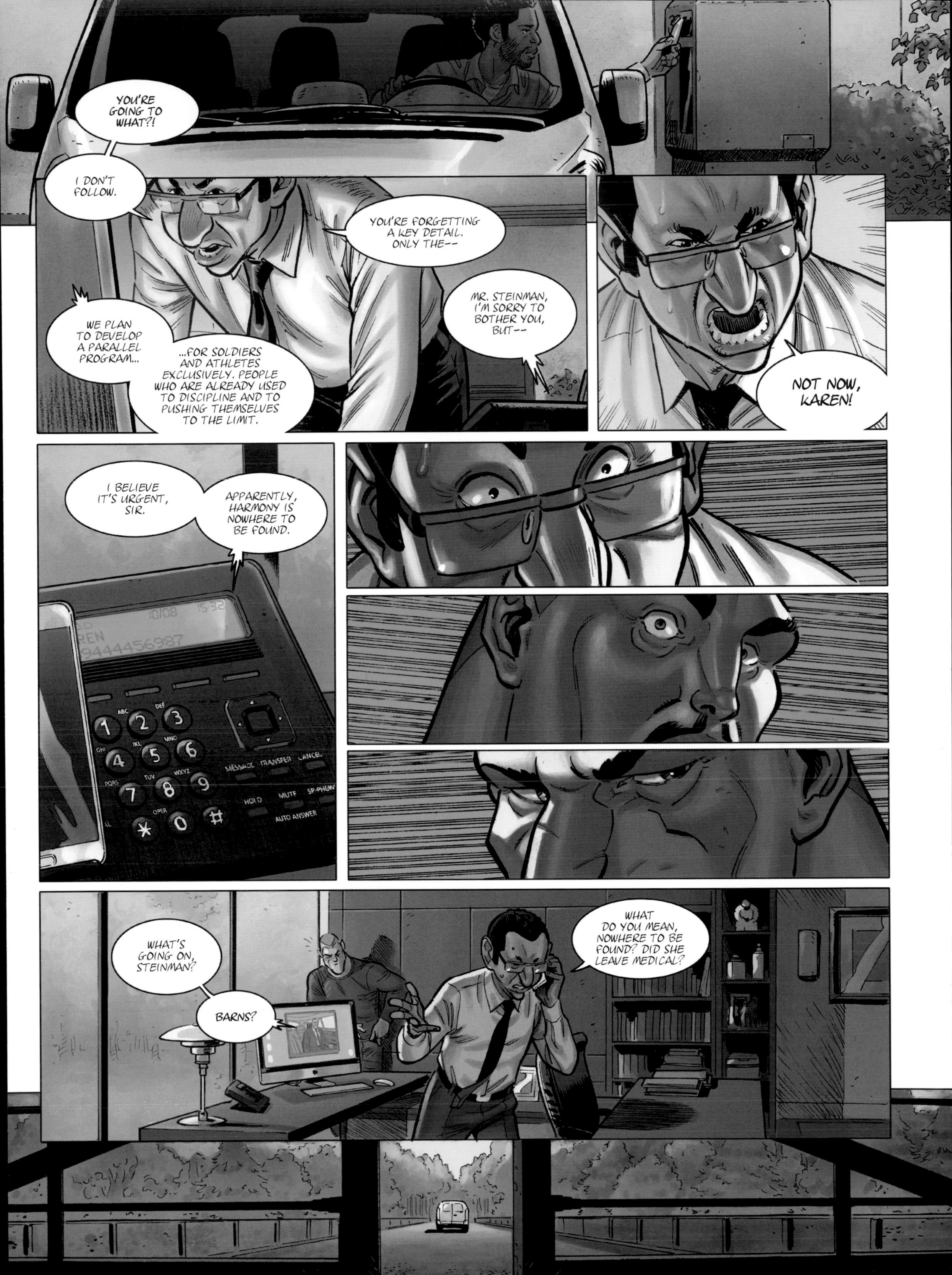
YOU'RE GOING TO WHAT?!
I DON'T FOLLOW.
YOU'RE FORGETTING A KEY DETAIL. ONLY THE--
WE PLAN TO DEVELOP A PARALLEL PROGRAM...
...FOR SOLDIERS AND ATHLETES EXCLUSIVELY. PEOPLE WHO ARE ALREADY USED TO DISCIPLINE AND TO PUSHING THEMSELVES TO THE LIMIT.
MR. STEINMAN, I'M SORRY TO BOTHER YOU, BUT--
NOT NOW, KAREN!
I BELIEVE IT'S URGENT, SIR.
APPARENTLY, HARMONY IS NOWHERE TO BE FOUND.
10/08 15:32
REN
9444456987
MESSAGE TRANSFER CANCEL
HOLD MUTE
AUTO ANSWER
WHAT'S GOING ON, STEINMAN?
BARNS?
WHAT DO YOU MEAN, NOWHERE TO BE FOUND? DID SHE LEAVE MEDICAL?

SHE'S NOT THERE. OR IN THE DORM, OR ANYWHERE ELSE. TOBIAS TAZEKH, ONE OF THE ORDERLIES, HAS ALSO GONE MISSING.

TAZ?

KEEP THE KIDS IN ISOLATION AND CONVENE THE ENTIRE STAFF IN THE HALL!

BARNS?

SEARCH THE ENTIRE BUILDING! REPORT BACK TO ME IN TEN!

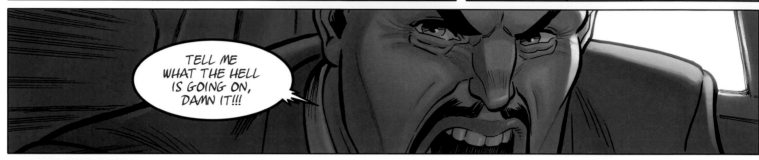

BARNS, HERE! HARMONY AND TAZEKH ARE NOWHERE TO BE FOUND! SECURE THE CAMPUS! BLOCK ALL EXITS!

TELL ME WHAT THE HELL IS GOING ON, DAMN IT!!!

ANYWAY, SO WE MEET FOR A DRINK, TO GET TO KNOW EACH OTHER, RIGHT?

WE HIT IT OFF, SO I SUGGEST GOING FOR A BITE TO EAT SOMEWHERE.

WE GO TO THIS ITALIAN PLACE I LIKE, THEY DO AN AWESOME RISOTTO AND THE PLACE HAS A GREAT VIBE.

ANYWAY, SO WE'RE TALKING, HAVING A GOOD TIME.

SERIOUSLY, IT'S LIKE, A TOTALLY COOL EVENING.

AND THEN ALL OF A SUDDEN, SHE GETS UP, AND SHE'S LIKE: "SORRY, KARL, BUT I'M JUST NOT THAT INTO YOU!"

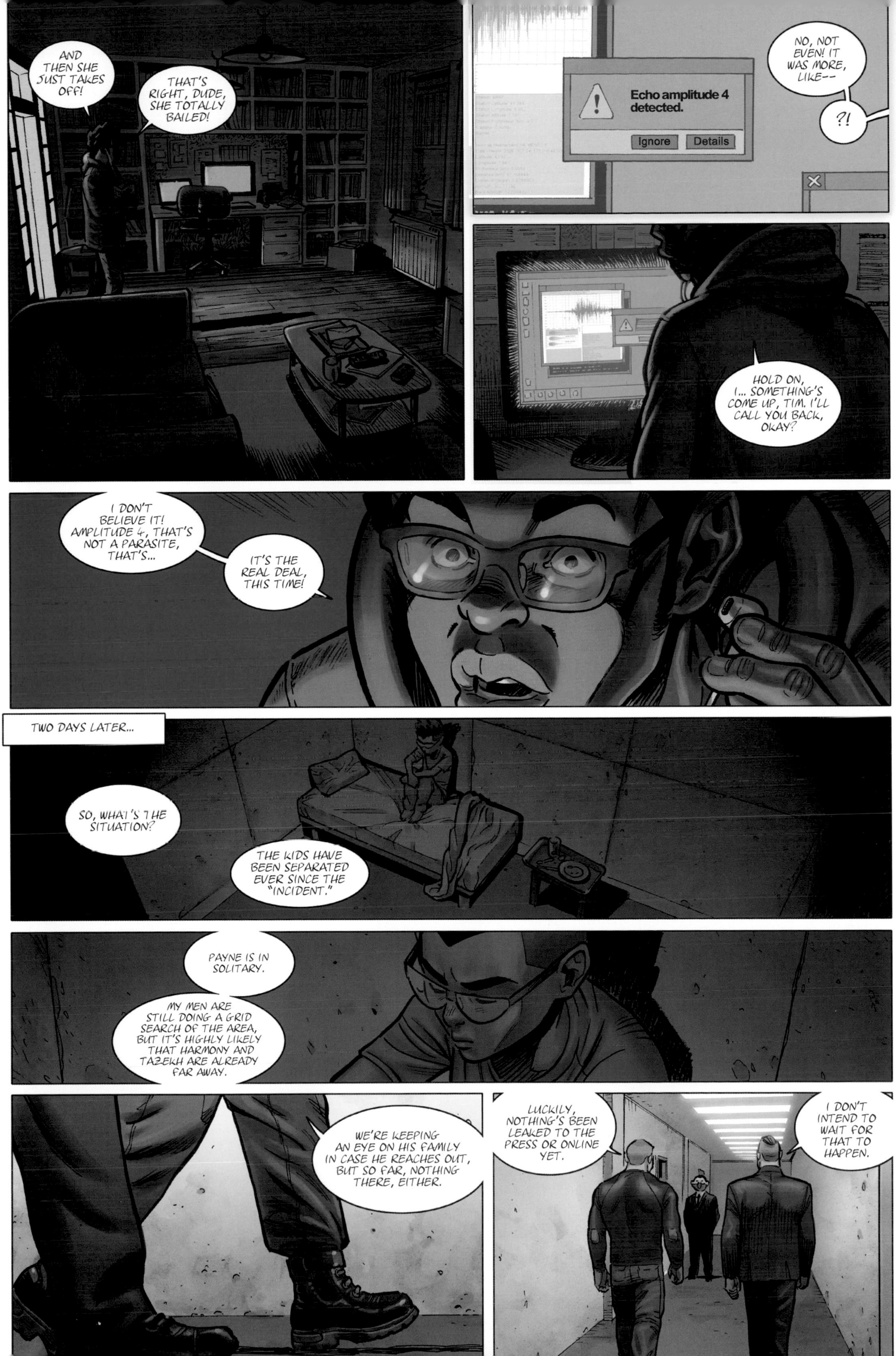
AND THEN SHE JUST TAKES OFF!
THAT'S RIGHT, DUDE, SHE TOTALLY BAILED!
Echo amplitude 4 detected.
Ignore
Details
NO, NOT EVEN! IT WAS MORE, LIKE--
?!
HOLD ON, I... SOMETHING'S COME UP, TIM. I'LL CALL YOU BACK, OKAY?
I DON'T BELIEVE IT! AMPLITUDE 4, THAT'S NOT A PARASITE, THAT'S...
IT'S THE REAL DEAL, THIS TIME!
TWO DAYS LATER...
SO, WHAT'S THE SITUATION?
THE KIDS HAVE BEEN SEPARATED EVER SINCE THE "INCIDENT."
PAYNE IS IN SOLITARY.
MY MEN ARE STILL DOING A GRID SEARCH OF THE AREA, BUT IT'S HIGHLY LIKELY THAT HARMONY AND TAZEKH ARE ALREADY FAR AWAY.
WE'RE KEEPING AN EYE ON HIS FAMILY IN CASE HE REACHES OUT, BUT SO FAR, NOTHING THERE, EITHER.
LUCKILY, NOTHING'S BEEN LEAKED TO THE PRESS OR ONLINE YET.
I DON'T INTEND TO WAIT FOR THAT TO HAPPEN.

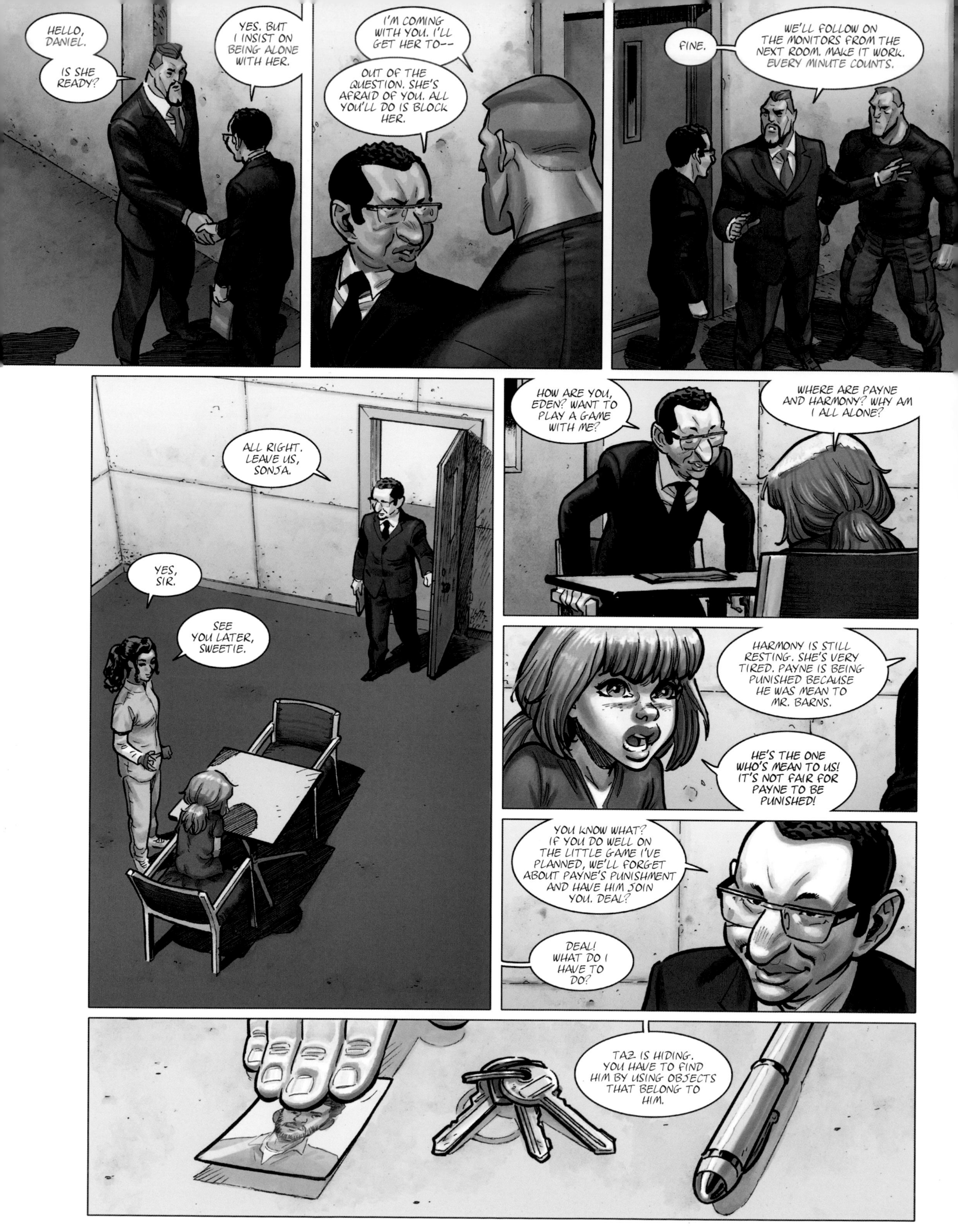

HELLO, DANIEL.
IS SHE READY?
YES. BUT I INSIST ON BEING ALONE WITH HER.
I'M COMING WITH YOU. I'LL GET HER TO--
OUT OF THE QUESTION. SHE'S AFRAID OF YOU. ALL YOU'LL DO IS BLOCK HER.
FINE.
WE'LL FOLLOW ON THE MONITORS FROM THE NEXT ROOM. MAKE IT WORK. EVERY MINUTE COUNTS.
ALL RIGHT. LEAVE US, SONJA.
YES, SIR.
SEE YOU LATER, SWEETIE.
HOW ARE YOU, EDEN? WANT TO PLAY A GAME WITH ME?
WHERE ARE PAYNE AND HARMONY? WHY AM I ALL ALONE?
HARMONY IS STILL RESTING. SHE'S VERY TIRED. PAYNE IS BEING PUNISHED BECAUSE HE WAS MEAN TO MR. BARNS.
HE'S THE ONE WHO'S MEAN TO US! IT'S NOT FAIR FOR PAYNE TO BE PUNISHED!
YOU KNOW WHAT? IF YOU DO WELL ON THE LITTLE GAME I'VE PLANNED, WE'LL FORGET ABOUT PAYNE'S PUNISHMENT AND HAVE HIM JOIN YOU. DEAL?
DEAL! WHAT DO I HAVE TO DO?
TAZ IS HIDING. YOU HAVE TO FIND HIM BY USING OBJECTS THAT BELONG TO HIM.

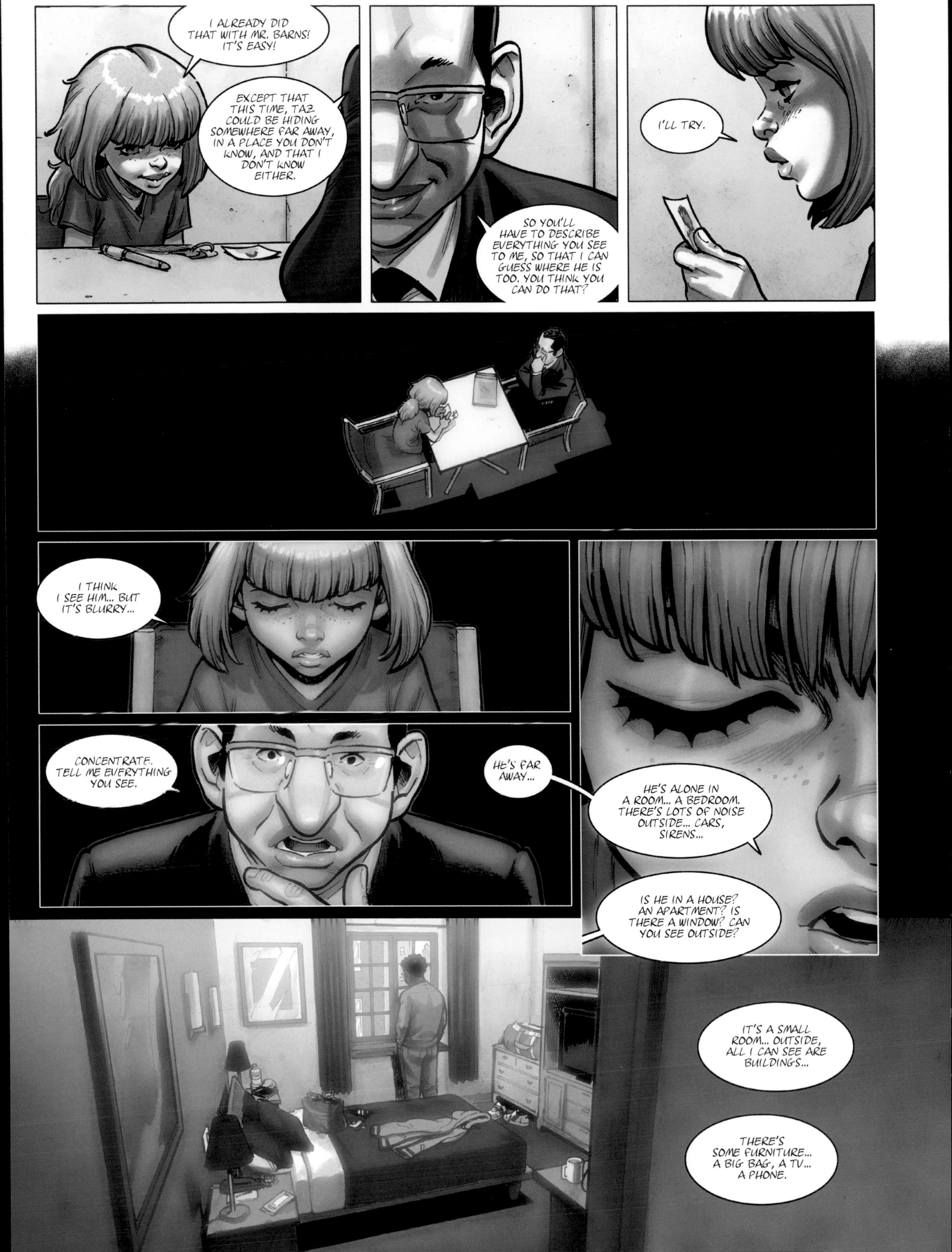
I ALREADY DID THAT WITH MR. BARNS! IT'S EASY!
EXCEPT THAT THIS TIME, TAZ COULD BE HIDING SOMEWHERE FAR AWAY, IN A PLACE YOU DON'T KNOW, AND THAT I DON'T KNOW EITHER.
SO YOU'LL HAVE TO DESCRIBE EVERYTHING YOU SEE TO ME, SO THAT I CAN GUESS WHERE HE IS TOO. YOU THINK YOU CAN DO THAT?
I'LL TRY.
I THINK I SEE HIM... BUT IT'S BLURRY...
CONCENTRATE. TELL ME EVERYTHING YOU SEE.
HE'S FAR AWAY...
HE'S ALONE IN A ROOM... A BEDROOM. THERE'S LOTS OF NOISE OUTSIDE... CARS, SIRENS...
IS HE IN A HOUSE? AN APARTMENT? IS THERE A WINDOW? CAN YOU SEE OUTSIDE?
IT'S A SMALL ROOM... OUTSIDE, ALL I CAN SEE ARE BUILDINGS...
THERE'S SOME FURNITURE... A BIG BAG, A TV... A PHONE.

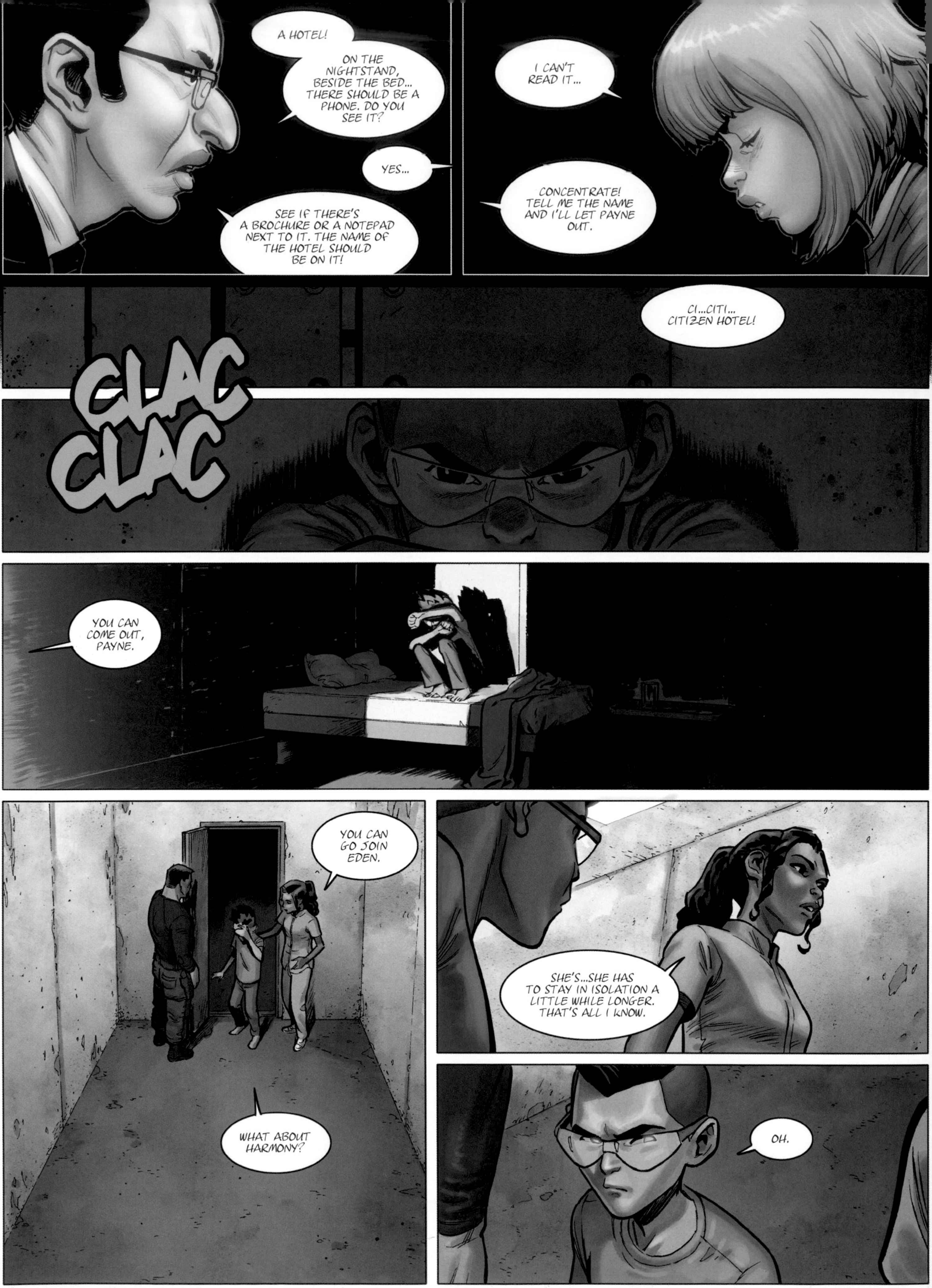
A HOTEL!
ON THE NIGHTSTAND, BESIDE THE BED... THERE SHOULD BE A PHONE. DO YOU SEE IT?
YES...
SEE IF THERE'S A BROCHURE OR A NOTEPAD NEXT TO IT. THE NAME OF THE HOTEL SHOULD BE ON IT!
I CAN'T READ IT...
CONCENTRATE! TELL ME THE NAME AND I'LL LET PAYNE OUT.
CI...CITI... CITIZEN HOTEL!
CLAC CLAC
YOU CAN COME OUT, PAYNE.
YOU CAN GO JOIN EDEN.
WHAT ABOUT HARMONY?
SHE'S...SHE HAS TO STAY IN ISOLATION A LITTLE WHILE LONGER. THAT'S ALL I KNOW.
OH.

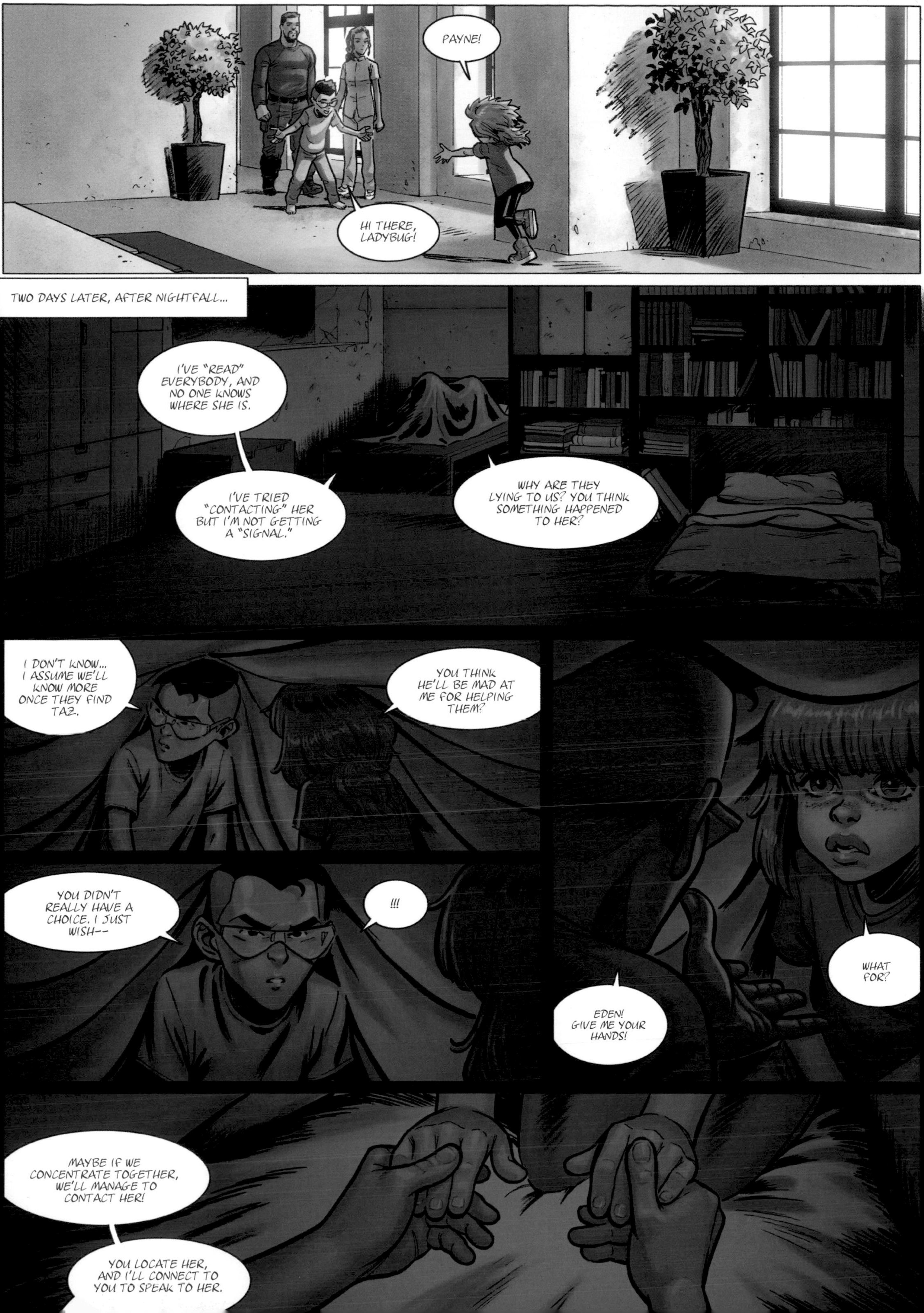
PAYNE!
HI THERE, LADYBUG!
TWO DAYS LATER, AFTER NIGHTFALL...
I'VE "READ" EVERYBODY, AND NO ONE KNOWS WHERE SHE IS.
I'VE TRIED "CONTACTING" HER BUT I'M NOT GETTING A "SIGNAL."
WHY ARE THEY LYING TO US? YOU THINK SOMETHING HAPPENED TO HER?
I DON'T KNOW... I ASSUME WE'LL KNOW MORE ONCE THEY FIND TAZ.
YOU THINK HE'LL BE MAD AT ME FOR HELPING THEM?
YOU DIDN'T REALLY HAVE A CHOICE. I JUST WISH--
!!!
EDEN! GIVE ME YOUR HANDS!
WHAT FOR?
MAYBE IF WE CONCENTRATE TOGETHER, WE'LL MANAGE TO CONTACT HER!
YOU LOCATE HER, AND I'LL CONNECT TO YOU TO SPEAK TO HER.

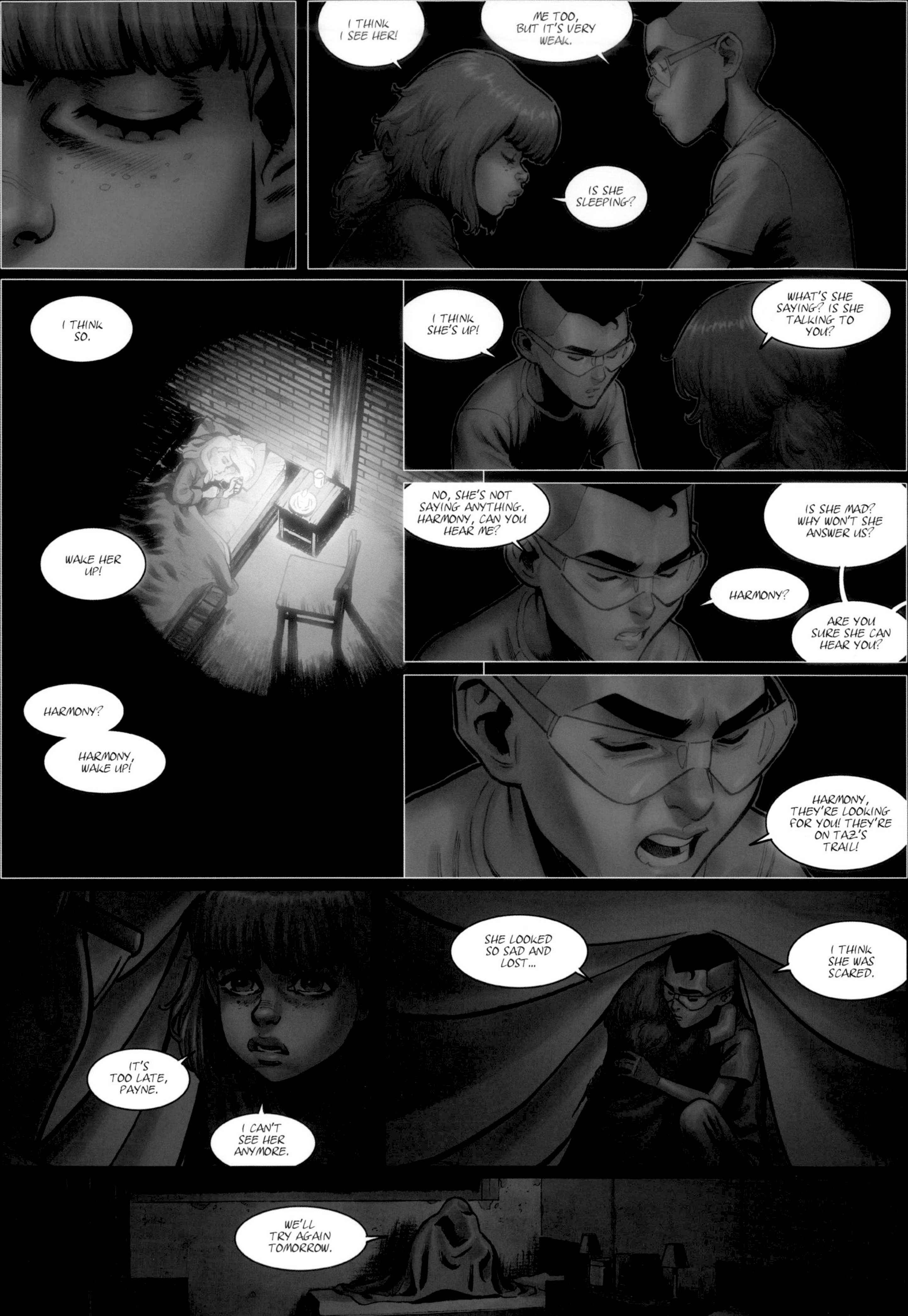
I THINK I SEE HER!
ME TOO, BUT IT'S VERY WEAK.
IS SHE SLEEPING?
I THINK SO.
WAKE HER UP!
HARMONY?
HARMONY, WAKE UP!
I THINK SHE'S UP!
WHAT'S SHE SAYING? IS SHE TALKING TO YOU?
NO, SHE'S NOT SAYING ANYTHING. HARMONY, CAN YOU HEAR ME?
IS SHE MAD? WHY WON'T SHE ANSWER US?
HARMONY?
ARE YOU SURE SHE CAN HEAR YOU?
HARMONY, THEY'RE LOOKING FOR YOU! THEY'RE ON TAZ'S TRAIL!
IT'S TOO LATE, PAYNE.
I CAN'T SEE HER ANYMORE.
SHE LOOKED SO SAD AND LOST...
I THINK SHE WAS SCARED.
WE'LL TRY AGAIN TOMORROW.

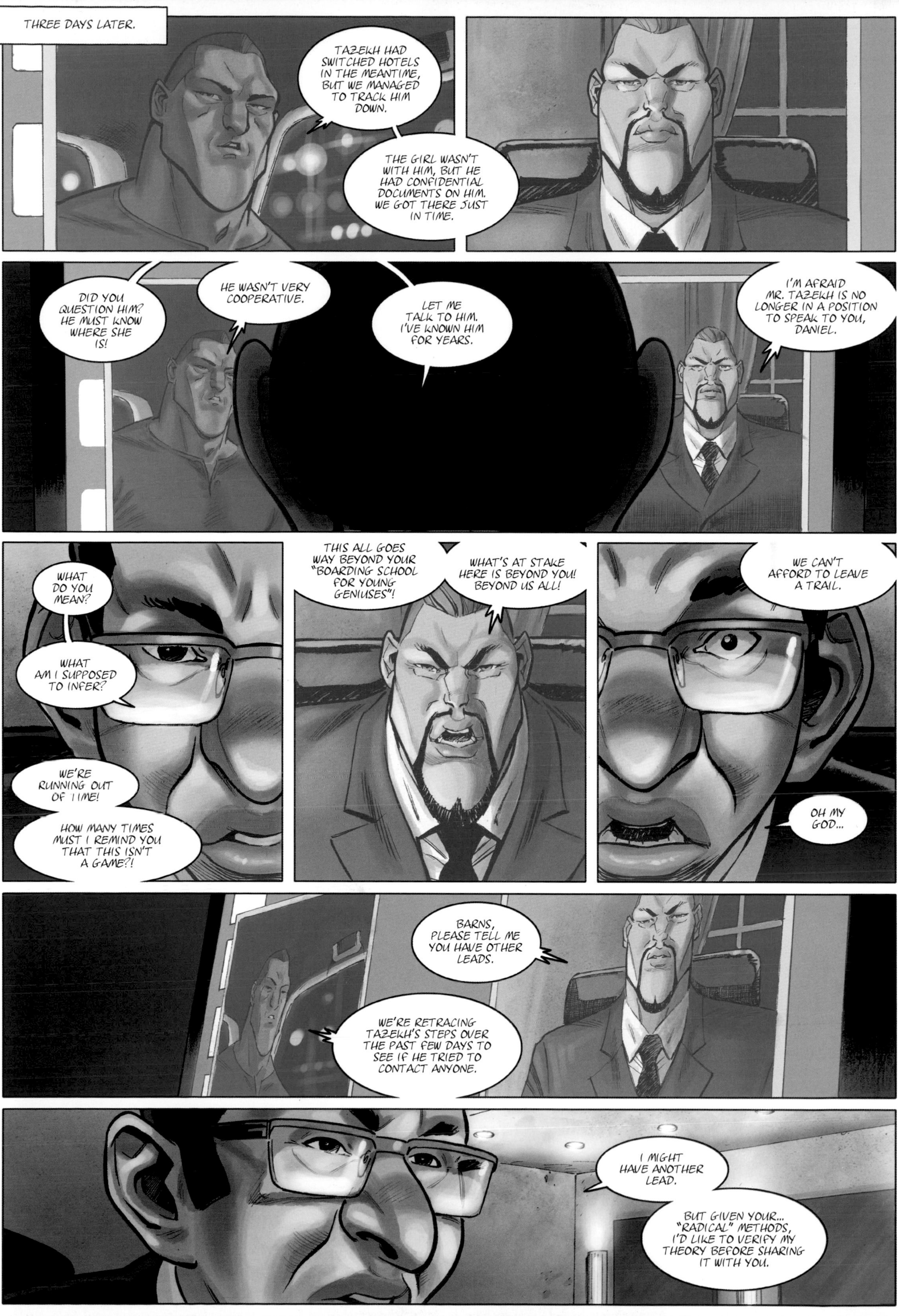
THREE DAYS LATER.
TAZEKH HAD SWITCHED HOTELS IN THE MEANTIME, BUT WE MANAGED TO TRACK HIM DOWN.
THE GIRL WASN'T WITH HIM, BUT HE HAD CONFIDENTIAL DOCUMENTS ON HIM. WE GOT THERE JUST IN TIME.
DID YOU QUESTION HIM? HE MUST KNOW WHERE SHE IS!
HE WASN'T VERY COOPERATIVE.
LET ME TALK TO HIM. I'VE KNOWN HIM FOR YEARS.
I'M AFRAID MR. TAZEKH IS NO LONGER IN A POSITION TO SPEAK TO YOU, DANIEL.
WHAT DO YOU MEAN?
WHAT AM I SUPPOSED TO INFER?
WE'RE RUNNING OUT OF TIME!
HOW MANY TIMES MUST I REMIND YOU THAT THIS ISN'T A GAME?!
THIS ALL GOES WAY BEYOND YOUR "BOARDING SCHOOL FOR YOUNG GENIUSES"!
WHAT'S AT STAKE HERE IS BEYOND YOU! BEYOND US ALL!
WE CAN'T AFFORD TO LEAVE A TRAIL.
OH MY GOD...
BARNS, PLEASE TELL ME YOU HAVE OTHER LEADS.
WE'RE RETRACING TAZEKH'S STEPS OVER THE PAST FEW DAYS TO SEE IF HE TRIED TO CONTACT ANYONE.
I MIGHT HAVE ANOTHER LEAD.
BUT GIVEN YOUR... "RADICAL" METHODS, I'D LIKE TO VERIFY MY THEORY BEFORE SHARING IT WITH YOU.

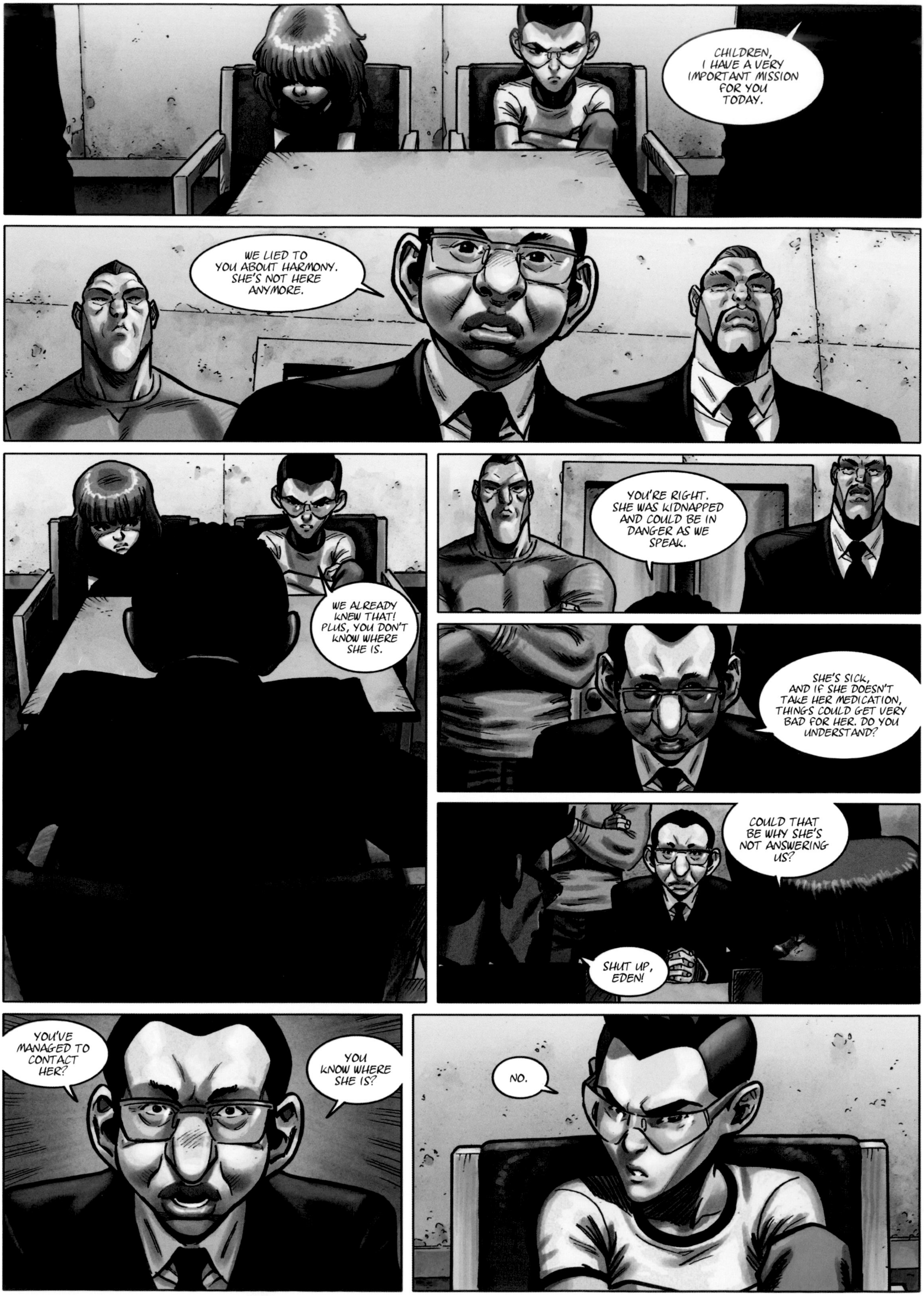
CHILDREN, I HAVE A VERY IMPORTANT MISSION FOR YOU TODAY.
WE LIED TO YOU ABOUT HARMONY. SHE'S NOT HERE ANYMORE.
WE ALREADY KNEW THAT! PLUS, YOU DON'T KNOW WHERE SHE IS.
YOU'RE RIGHT. SHE WAS KIDNAPPED AND COULD BE IN DANGER AS WE SPEAK.
SHE'S SICK, AND IF SHE DOESN'T TAKE HER MEDICATION, THINGS COULD GET VERY BAD FOR HER. DO YOU UNDERSTAND?
COULD THAT BE WHY SHE'S NOT ANSWERING US?
SHUT UP, EDEN!
YOU'VE MANAGED TO CONTACT HER?
YOU KNOW WHERE SHE IS?
NO.

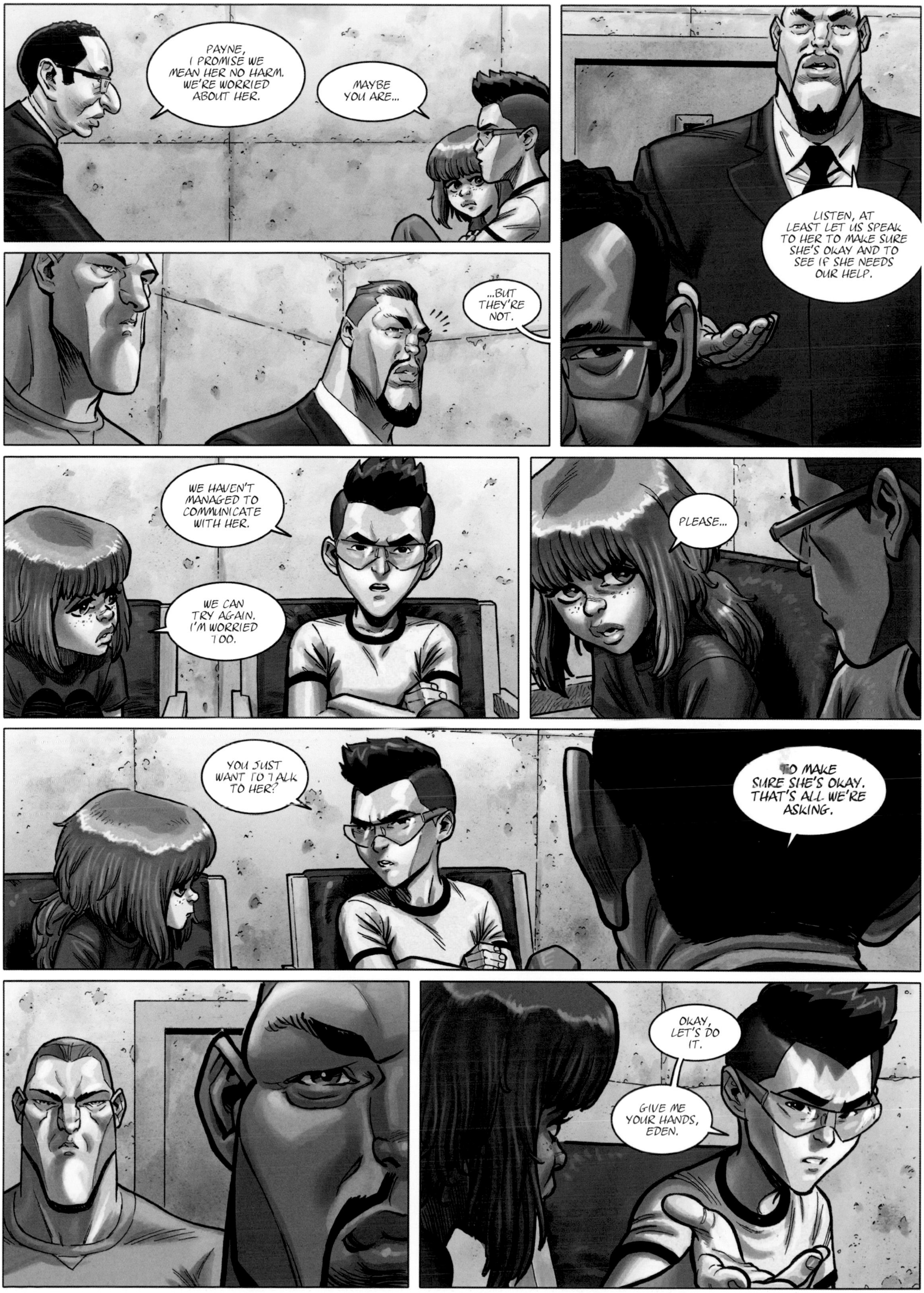
PAYNE, I PROMISE WE MEAN HER NO HARM. WE'RE WORRIED ABOUT HER.
MAYBE YOU ARE...
...BUT THEY'RE NOT.
LISTEN, AT LEAST LET US SPEAK TO HER TO MAKE SURE SHE'S OKAY AND TO SEE IF SHE NEEDS OUR HELP.
WE HAVEN'T MANAGED TO COMMUNICATE WITH HER.
WE CAN TRY AGAIN. I'M WORRIED TOO.
PLEASE...
YOU JUST WANT TO TALK TO HER?
TO MAKE SURE SHE'S OKAY. THAT'S ALL WE'RE ASKING.
OKAY, LET'S DO IT.
GIVE ME YOUR HANDS, EDEN.

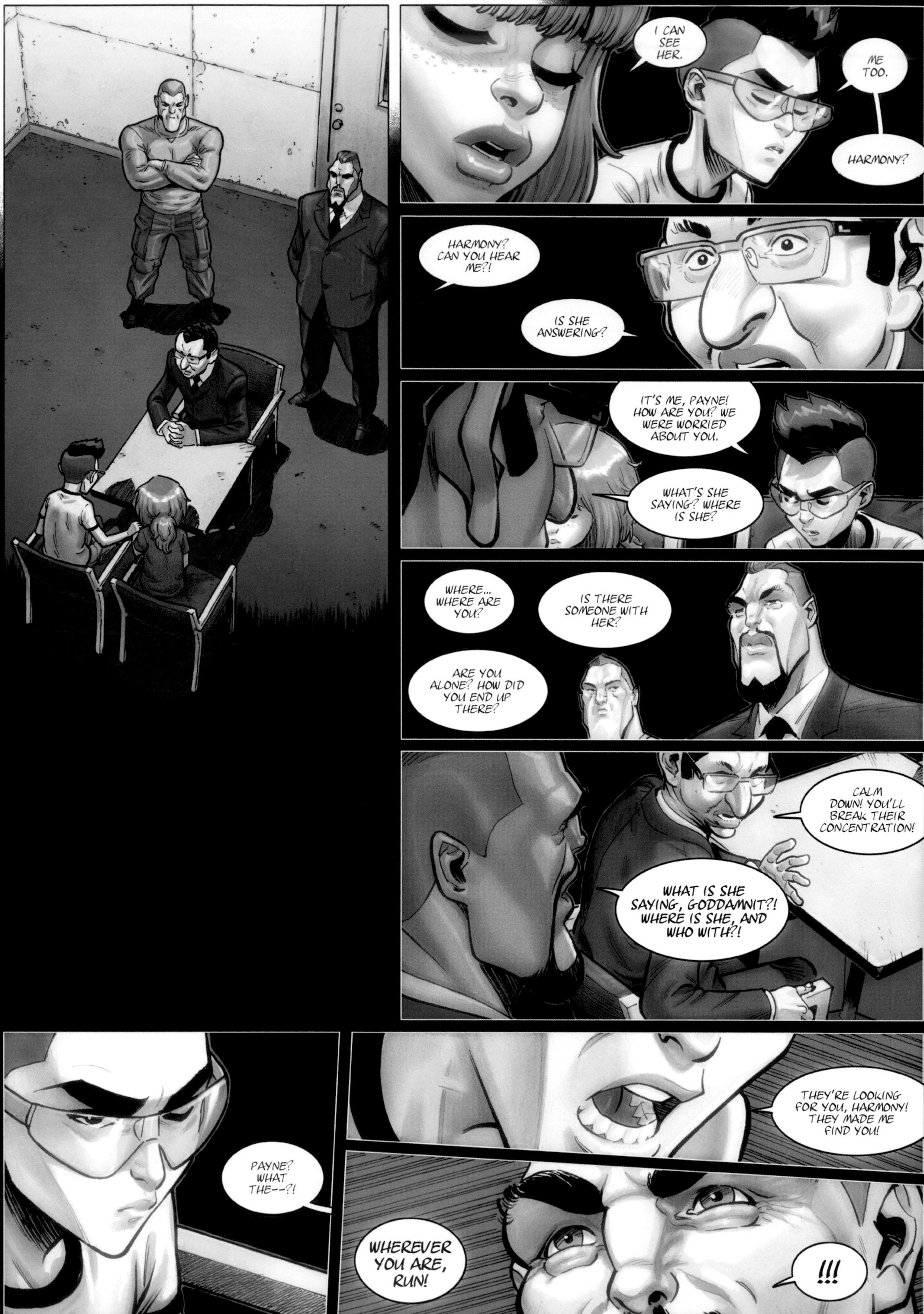
I CAN SEE HER.
ME TOO.
HARMONY?
HARMONY? CAN YOU HEAR ME?!
IS SHE ANSWERING?
IT'S ME, PAYNE! HOW ARE YOU? WE WERE WORRIED ABOUT YOU.
WHAT'S SHE SAYING? WHERE IS SHE?
WHERE... WHERE ARE YOU?
IS THERE SOMEONE WITH HER?
ARE YOU ALONE? HOW DID YOU END UP THERE?
CALM DOWN! YOU'LL BREAK THEIR CONCENTRATION!
WHAT IS SHE SAYING, GODDAMNIT?! WHERE IS SHE, AND WHO WITH?!
PAYNE? WHAT THE--?!
THEY'RE LOOKING FOR YOU, HARMONY! THEY MADE ME FIND YOU!
WHEREVER YOU ARE, RUN!
!!!

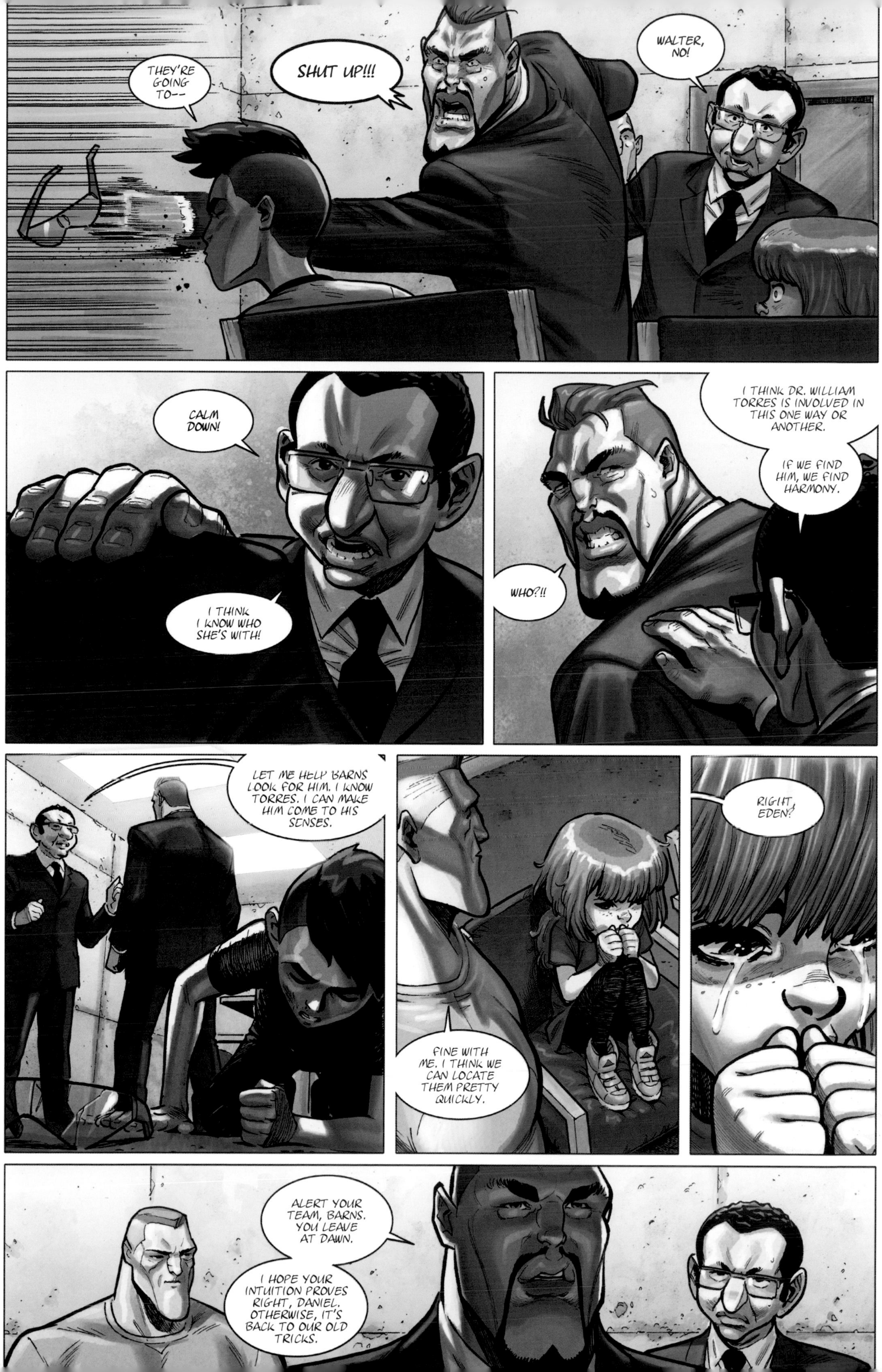
THEY'RE GOING TO--
SHUT UP!!!
WALTER, NO!
CALM DOWN!
I THINK I KNOW WHO SHE'S WITH!
WHO?!!
I THINK DR. WILLIAM TORRES IS INVOLVED IN THIS ONE WAY OR ANOTHER.
IF WE FIND HIM, WE FIND HARMONY.
LET ME HELP BARNS LOOK FOR HIM. I KNOW TORRES. I CAN MAKE HIM COME TO HIS SENSES.
FINE WITH ME. I THINK WE CAN LOCATE THEM PRETTY QUICKLY.
RIGHT, EDEN?
ALERT YOUR TEAM, BARNS. YOU LEAVE AT DAWN.
I HOPE YOUR INTUITION PROVES RIGHT, DANIEL. OTHERWISE, IT'S BACK TO OUR OLD TRICKS.

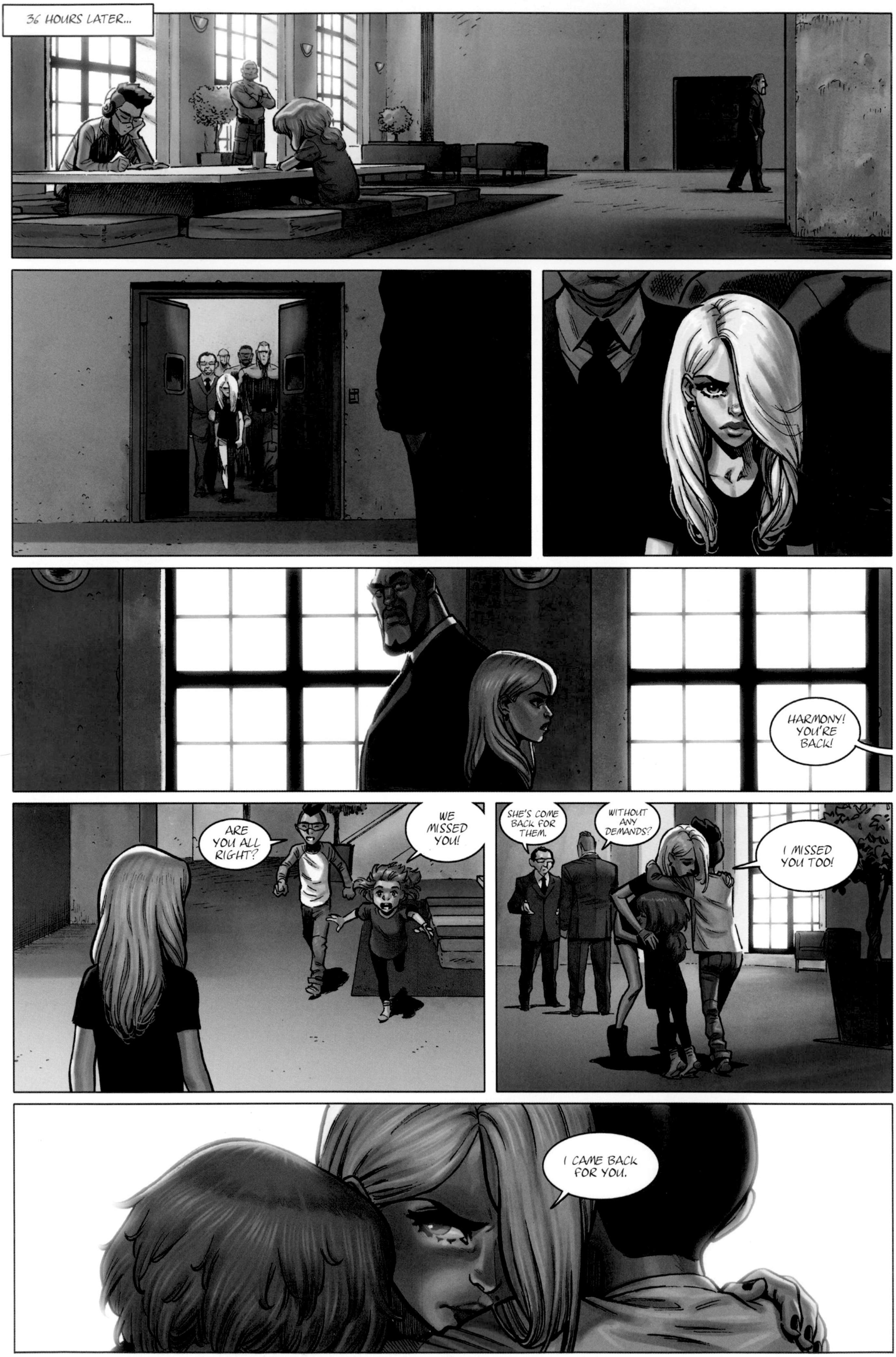
36 HOURS LATER...
HARMONY! YOU'RE BACK!
ARE YOU ALL RIGHT?
WE MISSED YOU!
SHE'S COME BACK FOR THEM.
WITHOUT ANY DEMANDS?
I MISSED YOU TOO!
I CAME BACK FOR YOU.

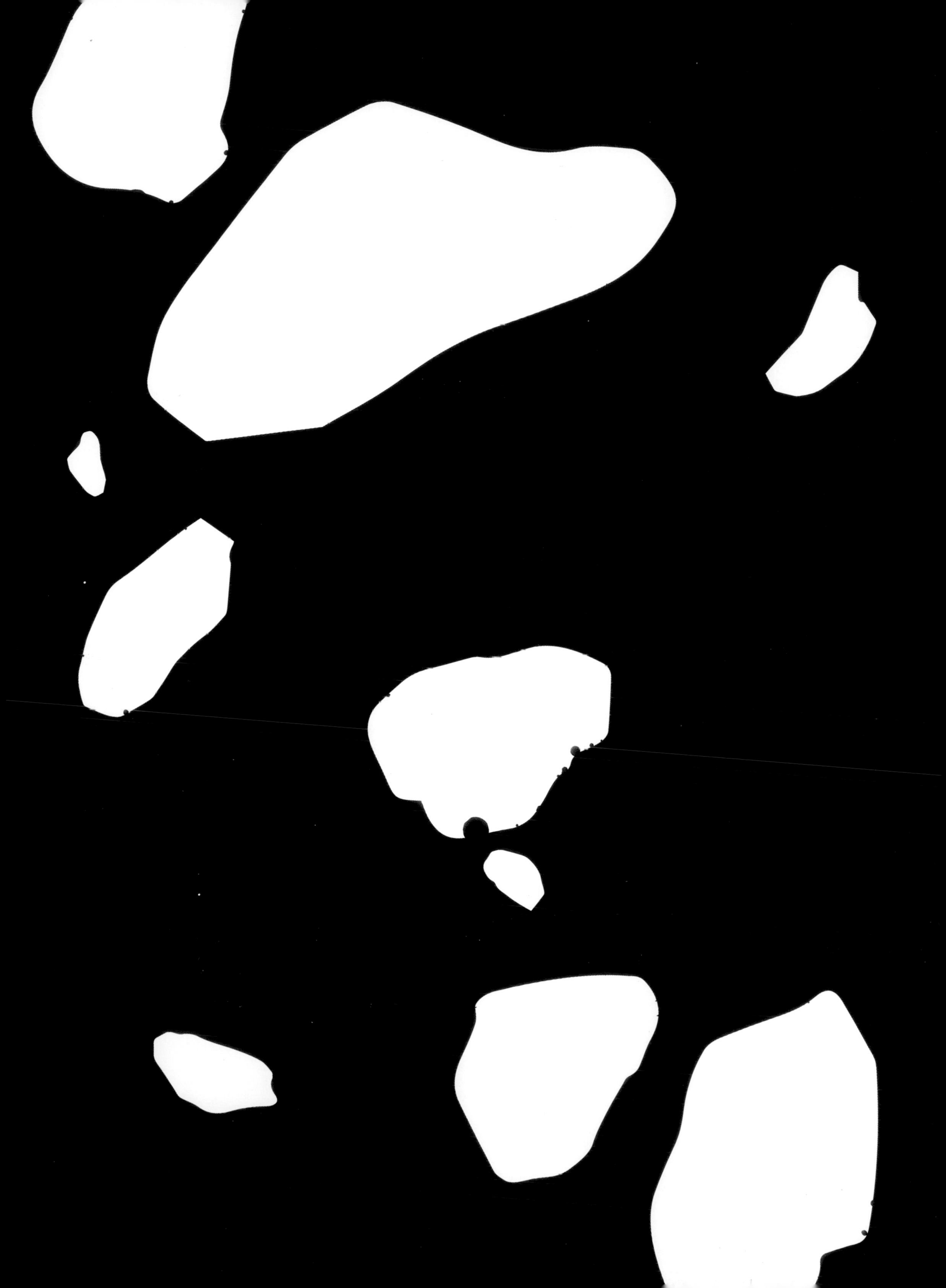

PART THREE

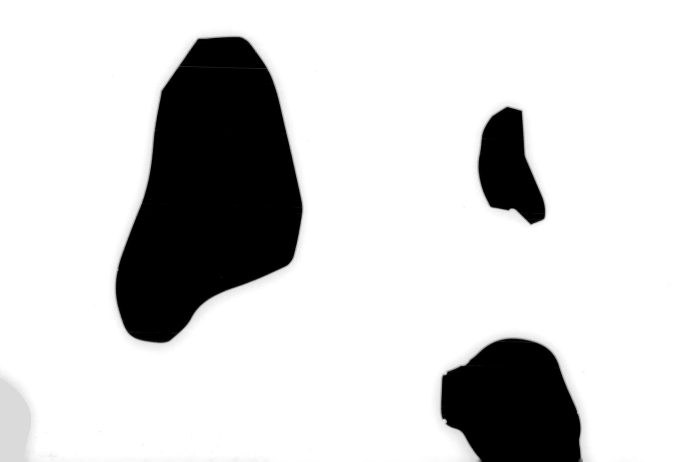

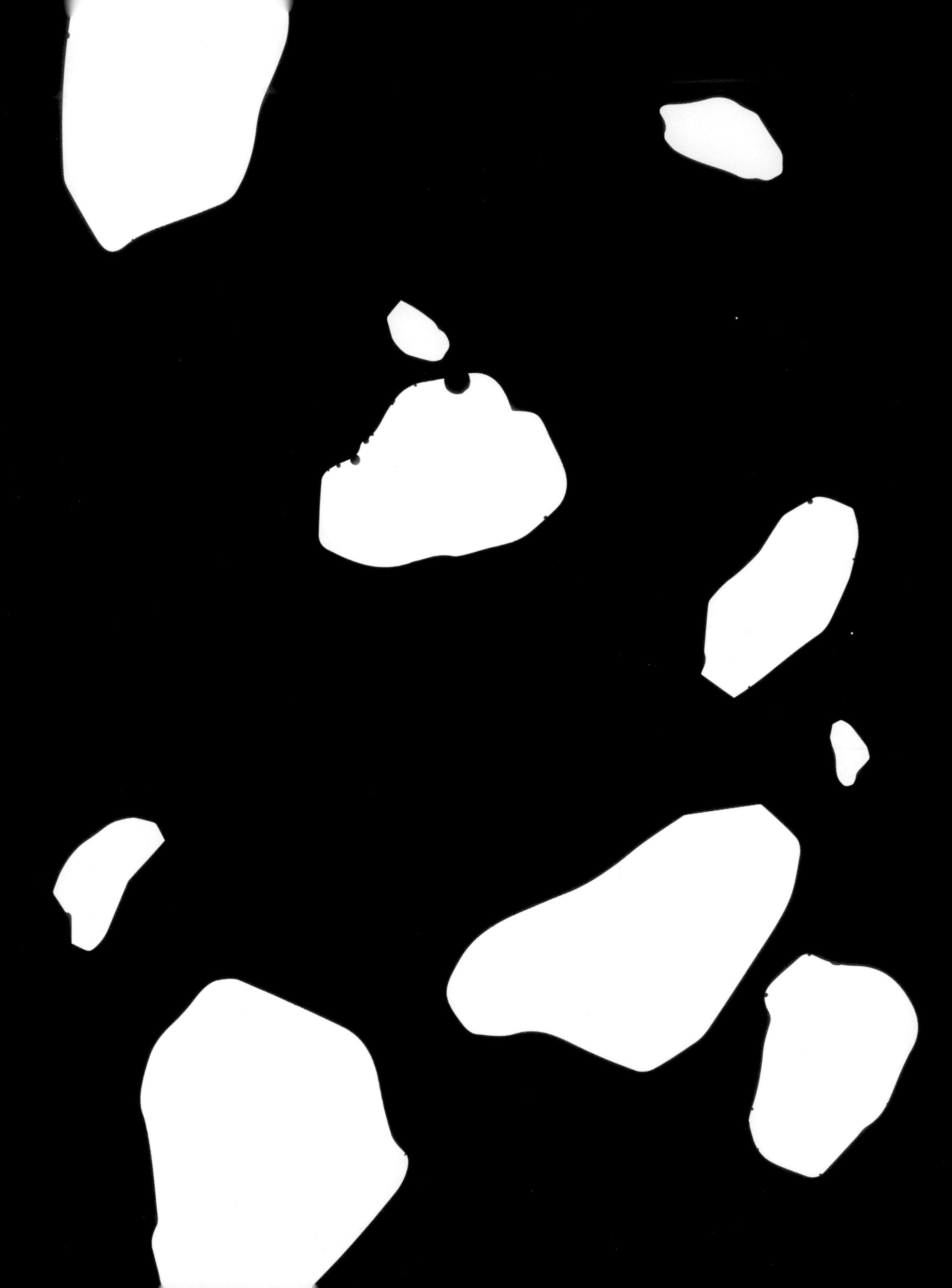

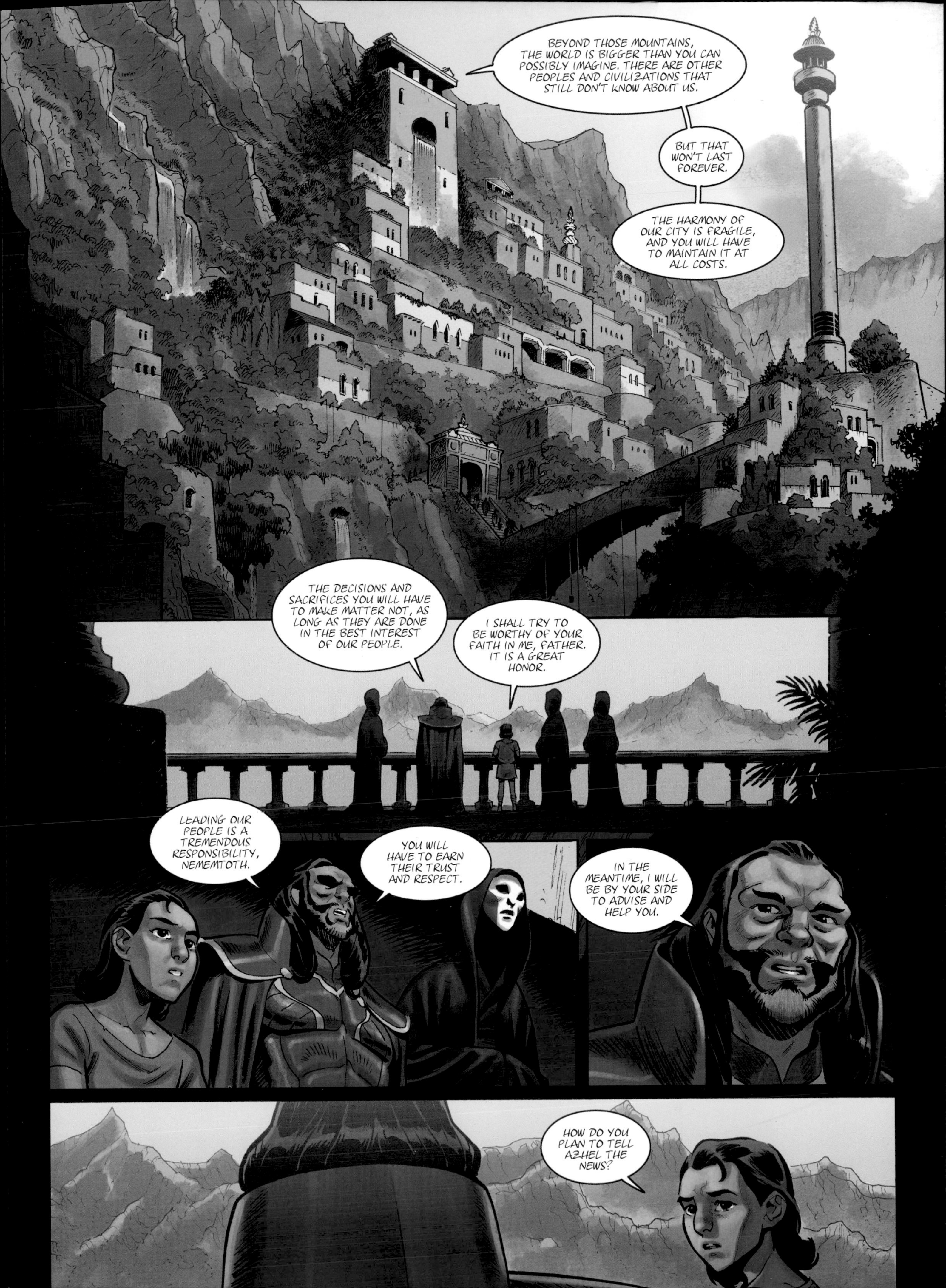
BEYOND THOSE MOUNTAINS, THE WORLD IS BIGGER THAN YOU CAN POSSIBLY IMAGINE. THERE ARE OTHER PEOPLES AND CIVILIZATIONS THAT STILL DON'T KNOW ABOUT US.
BUT THAT WON'T LAST FOREVER.
THE HARMONY OF OUR CITY IS FRAGILE, AND YOU WILL HAVE TO MAINTAIN IT AT ALL COSTS.
THE DECISIONS AND SACRIFICES YOU WILL HAVE TO MAKE MATTER NOT, AS LONG AS THEY ARE DONE IN THE BEST INTEREST OF OUR PEOPLE.
I SHALL TRY TO BE WORTHY OF YOUR FAITH IN ME, FATHER. IT IS A GREAT HONOR.
LEADING OUR PEOPLE IS A TREMENDOUS RESPONSIBILITY, NEMEMTOTH.
YOU WILL HAVE TO EARN THEIR TRUST AND RESPECT.
IN THE MEANTIME, I WILL BE BY YOUR SIDE TO ADVISE AND HELP YOU.
HOW DO YOU PLAN TO TELL AZHEL THE NEWS?

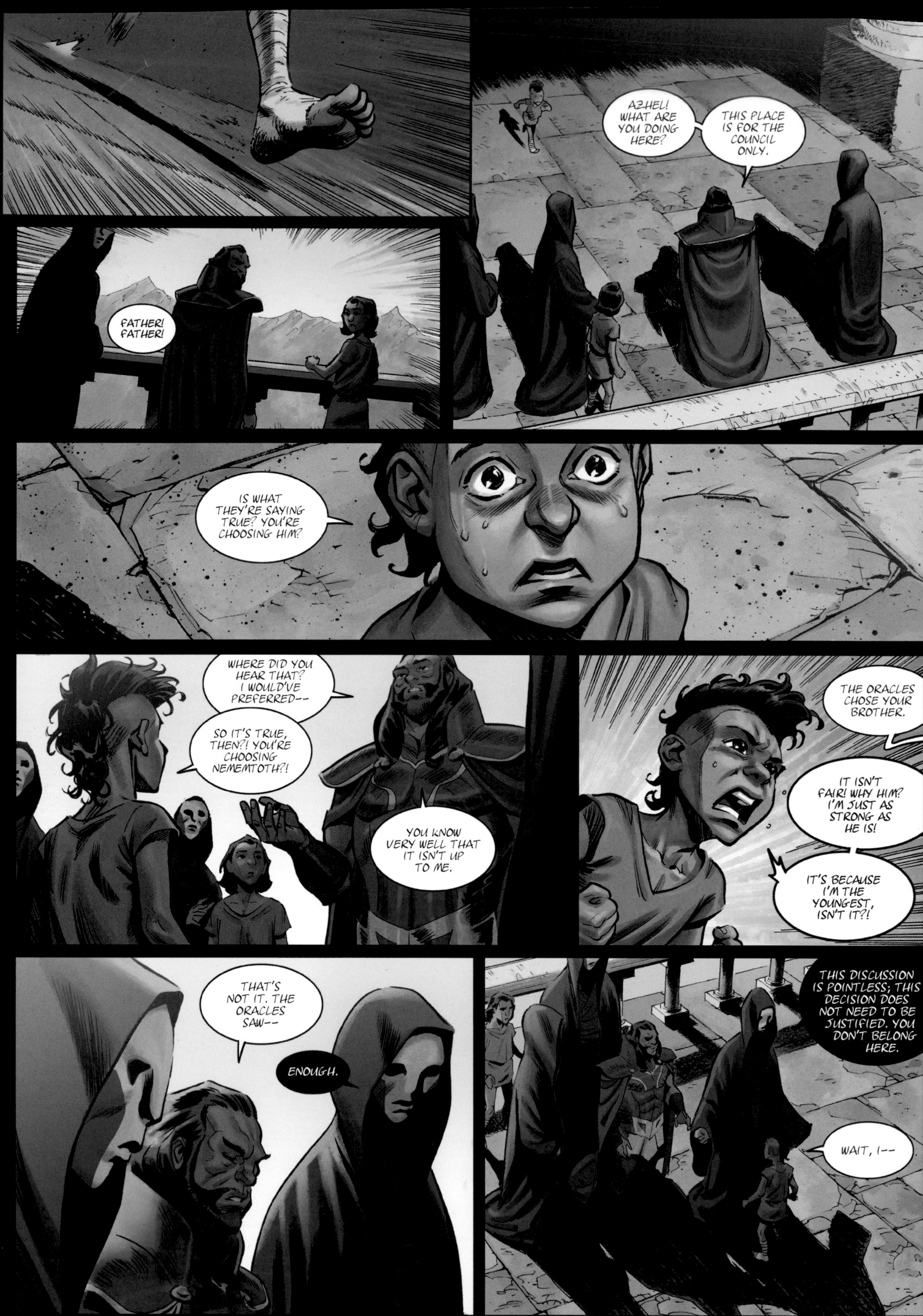
AZHEL! WHAT ARE YOU DOING HERE?
THIS PLACE IS FOR THE COUNCIL ONLY.
FATHER! FATHER!
IS WHAT THEY'RE SAYING TRUE? YOU'RE CHOOSING HIM?
WHERE DID YOU HEAR THAT? I WOULD'VE PREFERRED--
SO IT'S TRUE, THEN?! YOU'RE CHOOSING NEMEMTOTH?!
YOU KNOW VERY WELL THAT IT ISN'T UP TO ME.
THE ORACLES CHOSE YOUR BROTHER.
IT ISN'T FAIR! WHY HIM? I'M JUST AS STRONG AS HE IS!
IT'S BECAUSE I'M THE YOUNGEST, ISN'T IT?!
THAT'S NOT IT. THE ORACLES SAW--
ENOUGH.
THIS DISCUSSION IS POINTLESS; THIS DECISION DOES NOT NEED TO BE JUSTIFIED. YOU DON'T BELONG HERE.
WAIT, I--

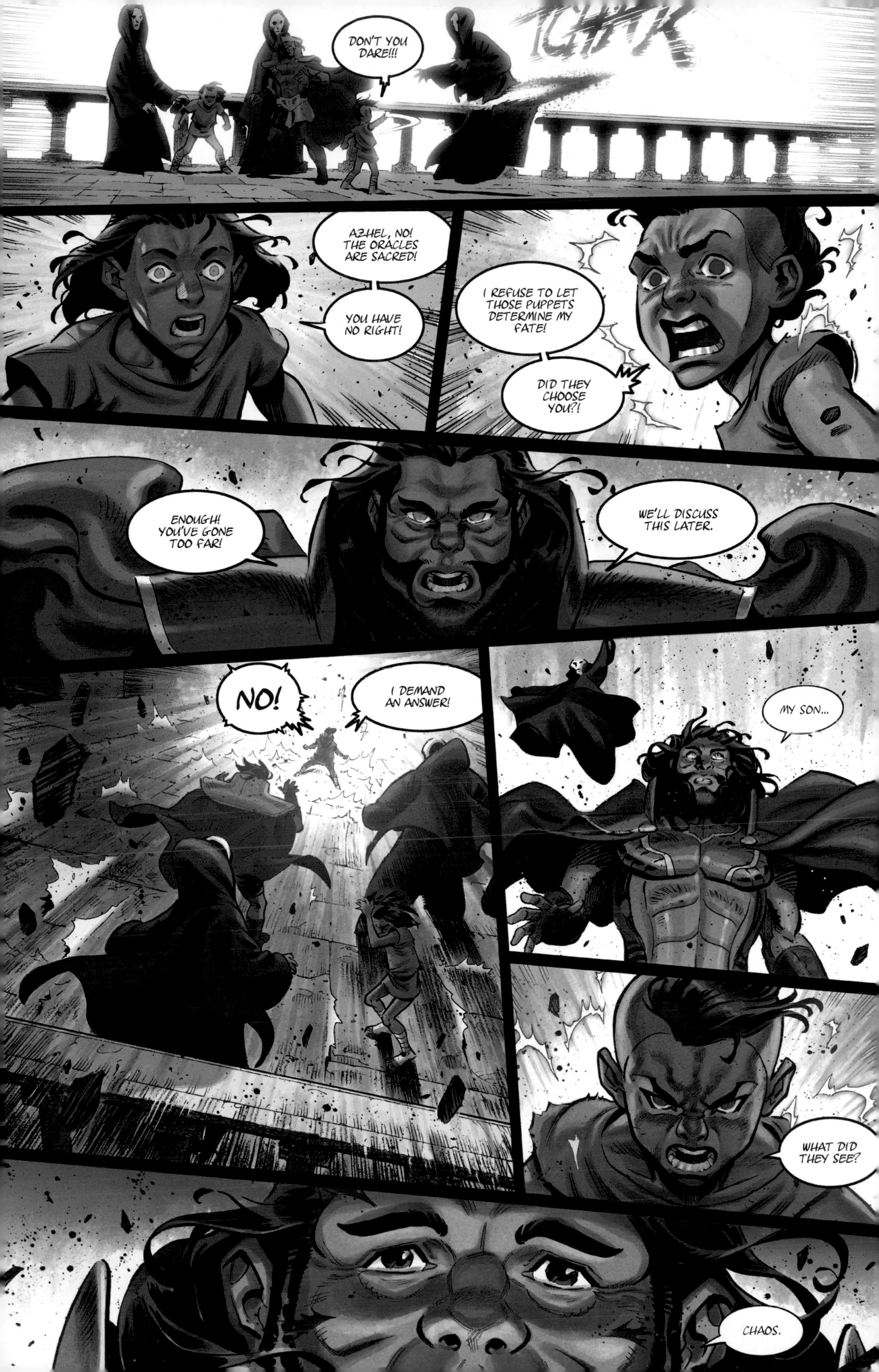
DON'T YOU DARE!!!
TCHAK
AZHEL, NO! THE ORACLES ARE SACRED!
YOU HAVE NO RIGHT!
I REFUSE TO LET THOSE PUPPETS DETERMINE MY FATE!
DID THEY CHOOSE YOU?!
ENOUGH! YOU'VE GONE TOO FAR!
WE'LL DISCUSS THIS LATER.
NO!
I DEMAND AN ANSWER!
MY SON...
WHAT DID THEY SEE?
CHAOS.

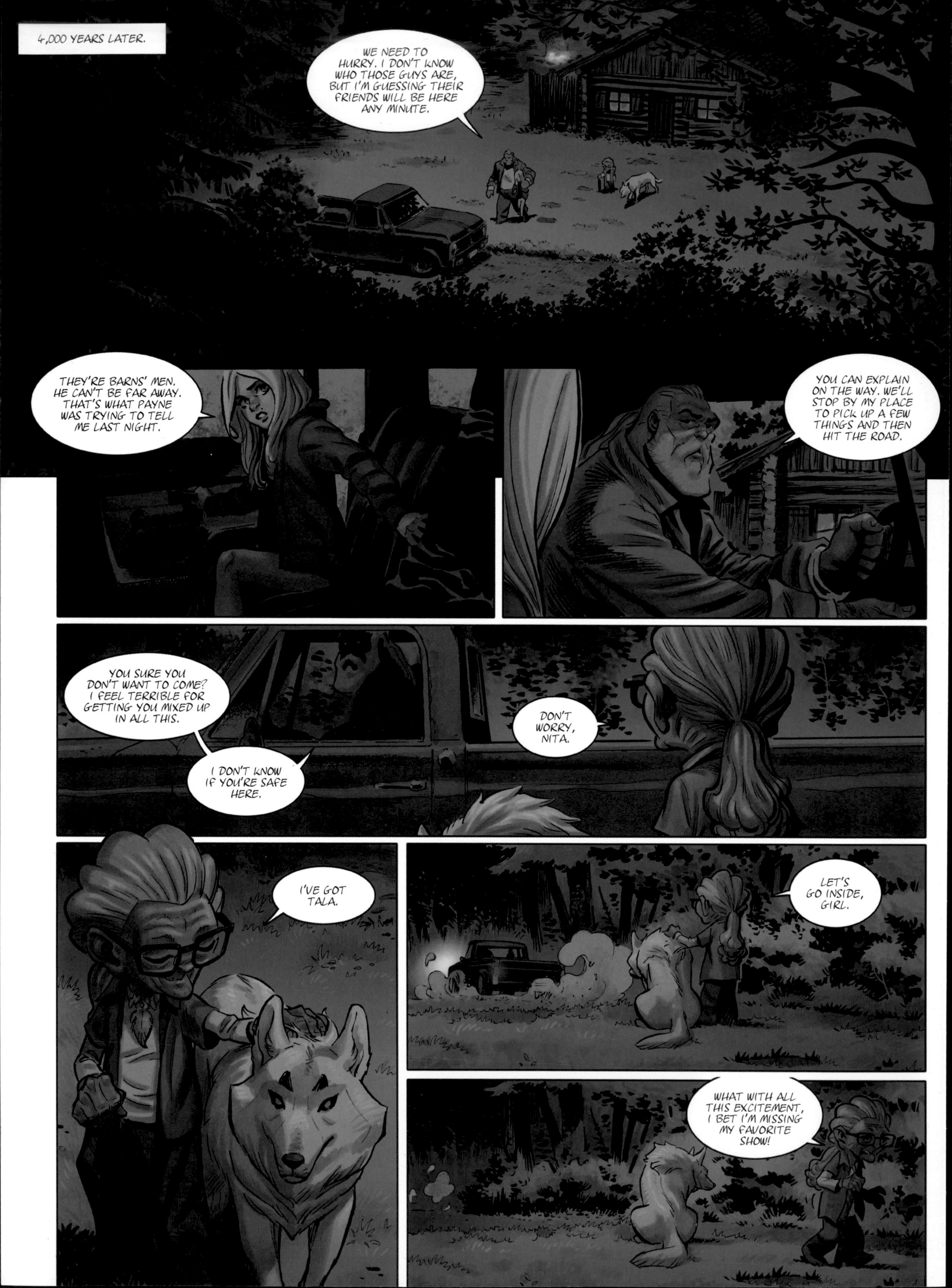
4,000 YEARS LATER.
WE NEED TO HURRY. I DON'T KNOW WHO THOSE GUYS ARE, BUT I'M GUESSING THEIR FRIENDS WILL BE HERE ANY MINUTE.
THEY'RE BARNS' MEN. HE CAN'T BE FAR AWAY. THAT'S WHAT PAYNE WAS TRYING TO TELL ME LAST NIGHT.
YOU CAN EXPLAIN ON THE WAY. WE'LL STOP BY MY PLACE TO PICK UP A FEW THINGS AND THEN HIT THE ROAD.
YOU SURE YOU DON'T WANT TO COME? I FEEL TERRIBLE FOR GETTING YOU MIXED UP IN ALL THIS.
I DON'T KNOW IF YOU'RE SAFE HERE.
DON'T WORRY, NITA.
I'VE GOT TALA.
LET'S GO INSIDE, GIRL.
WHAT WITH ALL THIS EXCITEMENT, I BET I'M MISSING MY FAVORITE SHOW!

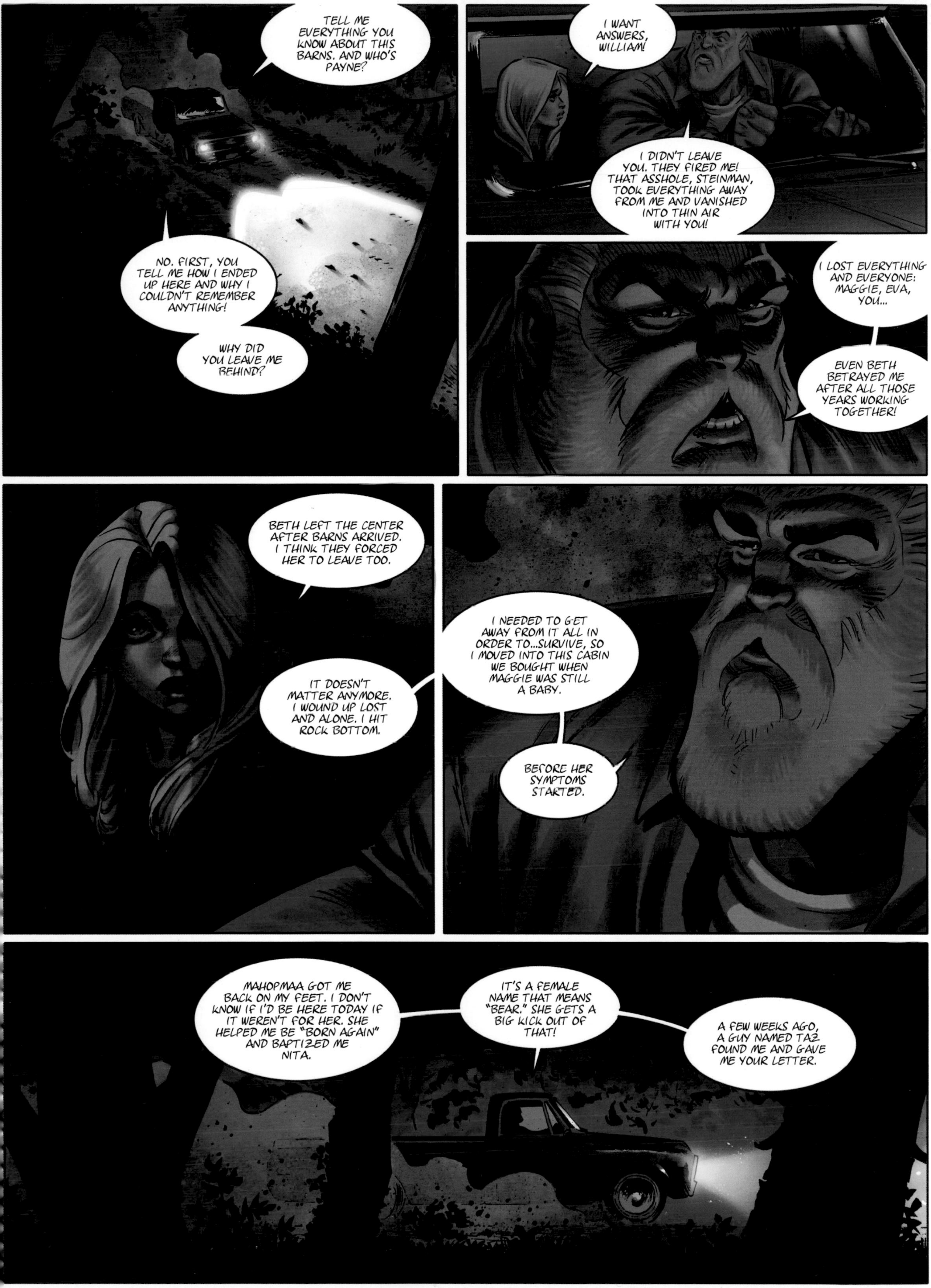
TELL ME EVERYTHING YOU KNOW ABOUT THIS BARNS. AND WHO'S PAYNE?
NO. FIRST, YOU TELL ME HOW I ENDED UP HERE AND WHY I COULDN'T REMEMBER ANYTHING!
WHY DID YOU LEAVE ME BEHIND?
I WANT ANSWERS, WILLIAM!
I DIDN'T LEAVE YOU. THEY FIRED ME! THAT ASSHOLE, STEINMAN, TOOK EVERYTHING AWAY FROM ME AND VANISHED INTO THIN AIR WITH YOU!
I LOST EVERYTHING AND EVERYONE: MAGGIE, EVA, YOU...
EVEN BETH BETRAYED ME AFTER ALL THOSE YEARS WORKING TOGETHER!
BETH LEFT THE CENTER AFTER BARNS ARRIVED. I THINK THEY FORCED HER TO LEAVE TOO.
IT DOESN'T MATTER ANYMORE. I WOUND UP LOST AND ALONE. I HIT ROCK BOTTOM.
I NEEDED TO GET AWAY FROM IT ALL IN ORDER TO...SURVIVE, SO I MOVED INTO THIS CABIN WE BOUGHT WHEN MAGGIE WAS STILL A BABY.
BEFORE HER SYMPTOMS STARTED.
MAHOPMAA GOT ME BACK ON MY FEET. I DON'T KNOW IF I'D BE HERE TODAY IF IT WEREN'T FOR HER. SHE HELPED ME BE "BORN AGAIN" AND BAPTIZED ME NITA.
IT'S A FEMALE NAME THAT MEANS "BEAR." SHE GETS A BIG KICK OUT OF THAT!
A FEW WEEKS AGO, A GUY NAMED TAZ FOUND ME AND GAVE ME YOUR LETTER.

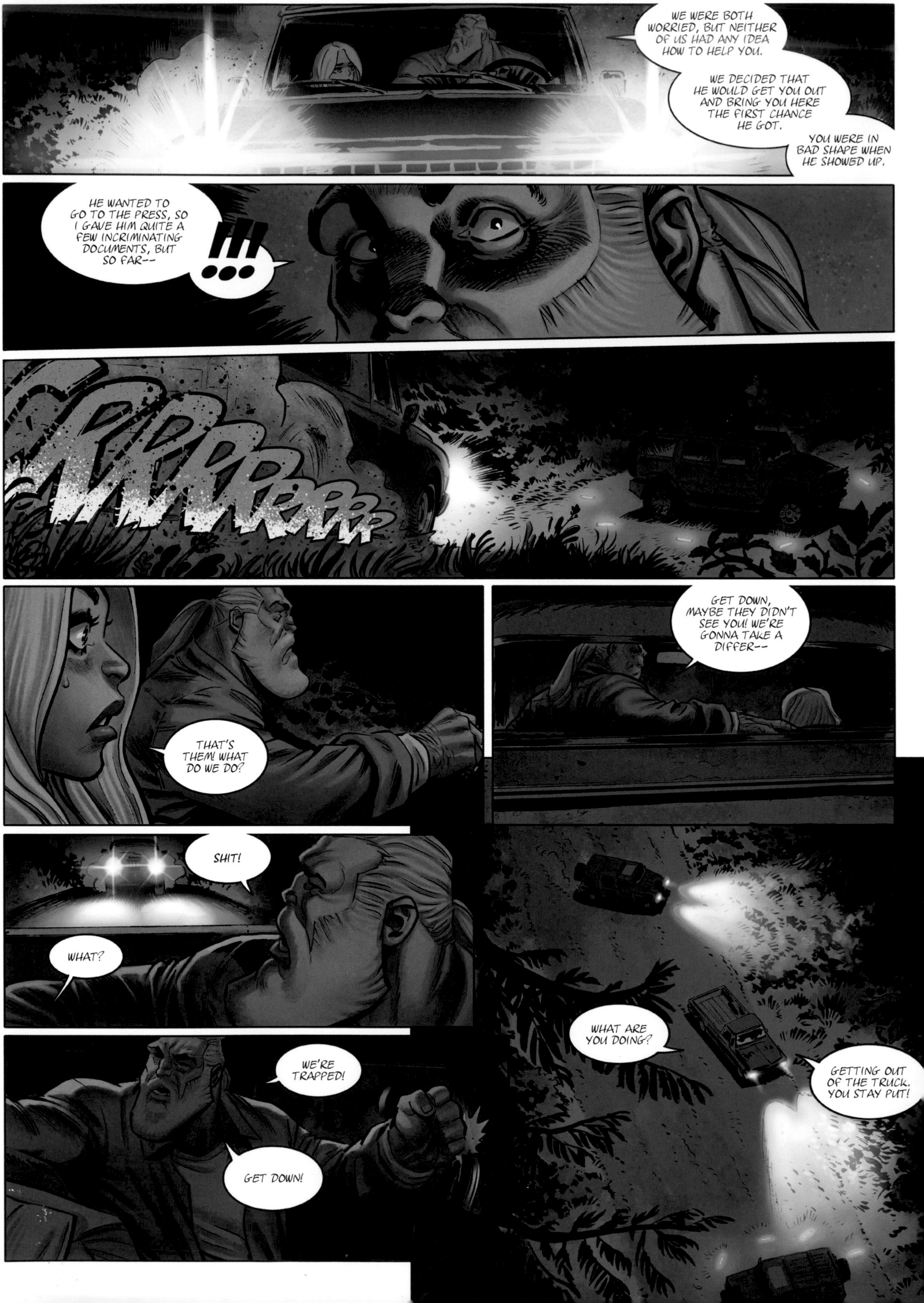
WE WERE BOTH WORRIED, BUT NEITHER OF US HAD ANY IDEA HOW TO HELP YOU.
WE DECIDED THAT HE WOULD GET YOU OUT AND BRING YOU HERE THE FIRST CHANCE HE GOT.
YOU WERE IN BAD SHAPE WHEN HE SHOWED UP.
HE WANTED TO GO TO THE PRESS, SO I GAVE HIM QUITE A FEW INCRIMINATING DOCUMENTS, BUT SO FAR--
!!!
WRRRRRRRRRR
THAT'S THEM! WHAT DO WE DO?
GET DOWN, MAYBE THEY DIDN'T SEE YOU! WE'RE GONNA TAKE A DIFFER--
SHIT!
WHAT?
WE'RE TRAPPED!
GET DOWN!
WHAT ARE YOU DOING?
GETTING OUT OF THE TRUCK. YOU STAY PUT!

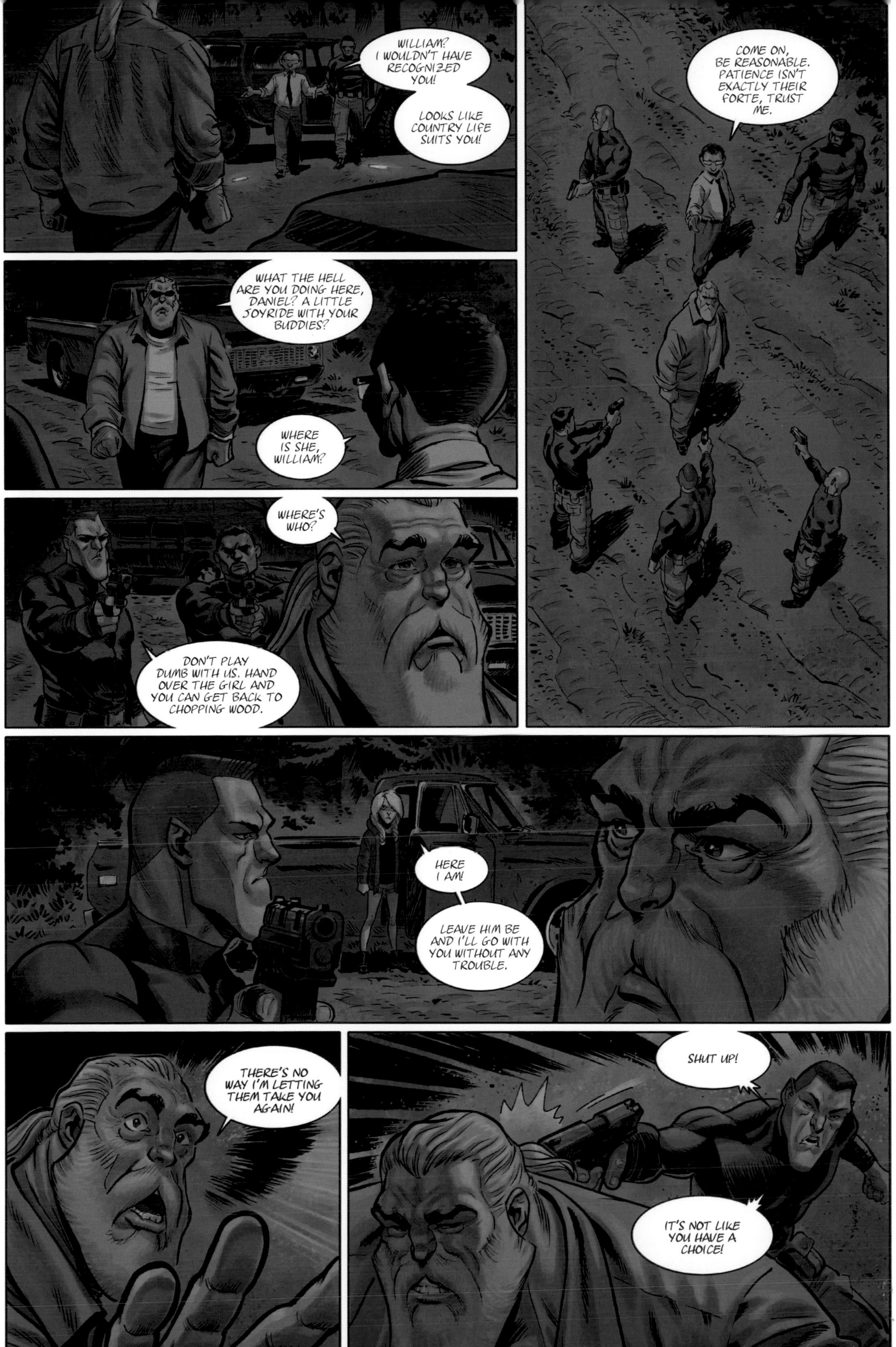
WILLIAM? I WOULDN'T HAVE RECOGNIZED YOU!
LOOKS LIKE COUNTRY LIFE SUITS YOU!
COME ON, BE REASONABLE. PATIENCE ISN'T EXACTLY THEIR FORTE, TRUST ME.
WHAT THE HELL ARE YOU DOING HERE, DANIEL? A LITTLE JOYRIDE WITH YOUR BUDDIES?
WHERE IS SHE, WILLIAM?
WHERE'S WHO?
DON'T PLAY DUMB WITH US. HAND OVER THE GIRL AND YOU CAN GET BACK TO CHOPPING WOOD.
HERE I AM!
LEAVE HIM BE AND I'LL GO WITH YOU WITHOUT ANY TROUBLE.
THERE'S NO WAY I'M LETTING THEM TAKE YOU AGAIN!
SHUT UP!
IT'S NOT LIKE YOU HAVE A CHOICE!

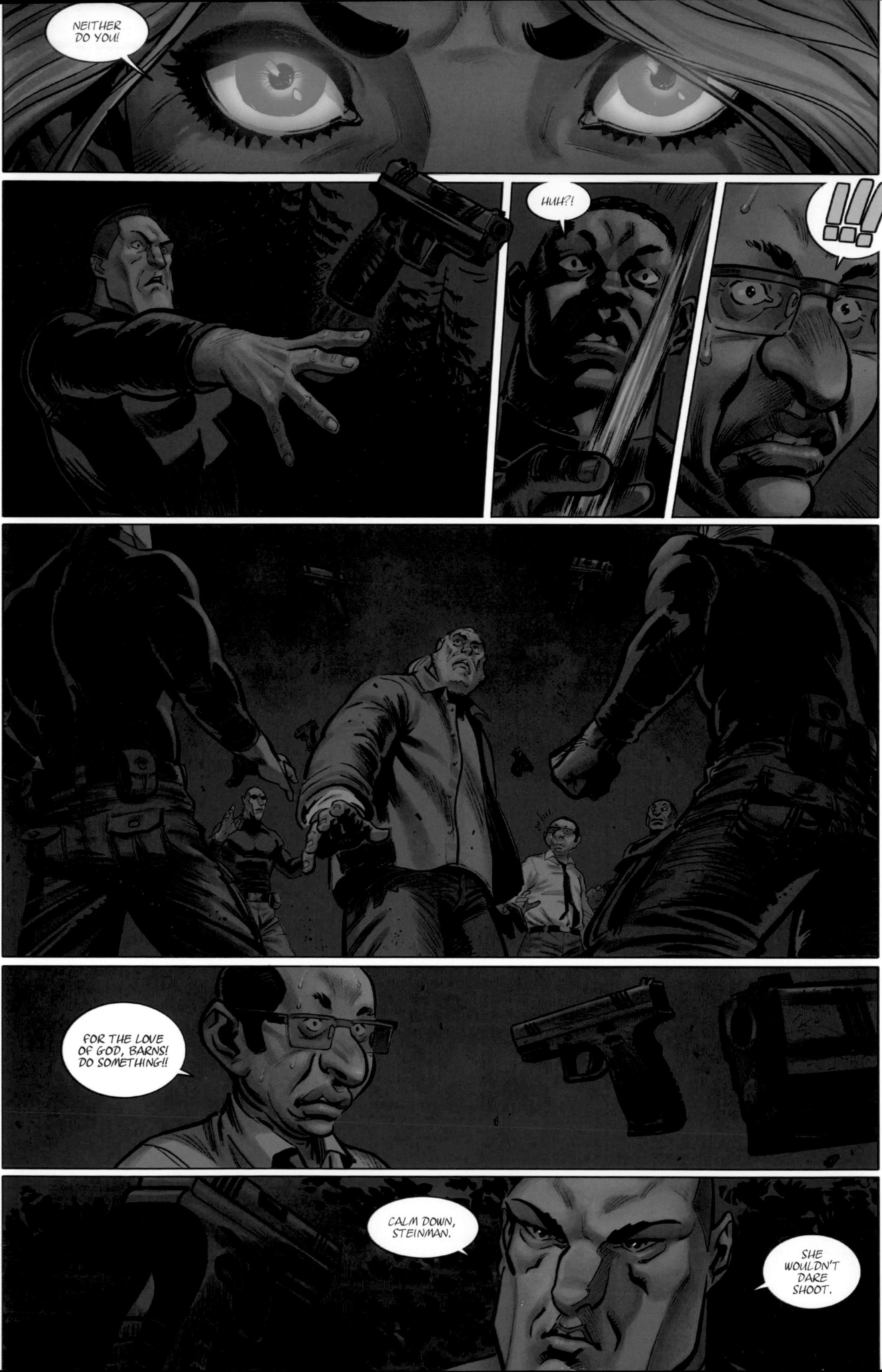

NEITHER DO YOU!
HUH?!
!!!
FOR THE LOVE OF GOD, BARNS! DO SOMETHING!!
CALM DOWN, STEINMAN.
SHE WOULDN'T DARE SHOOT.

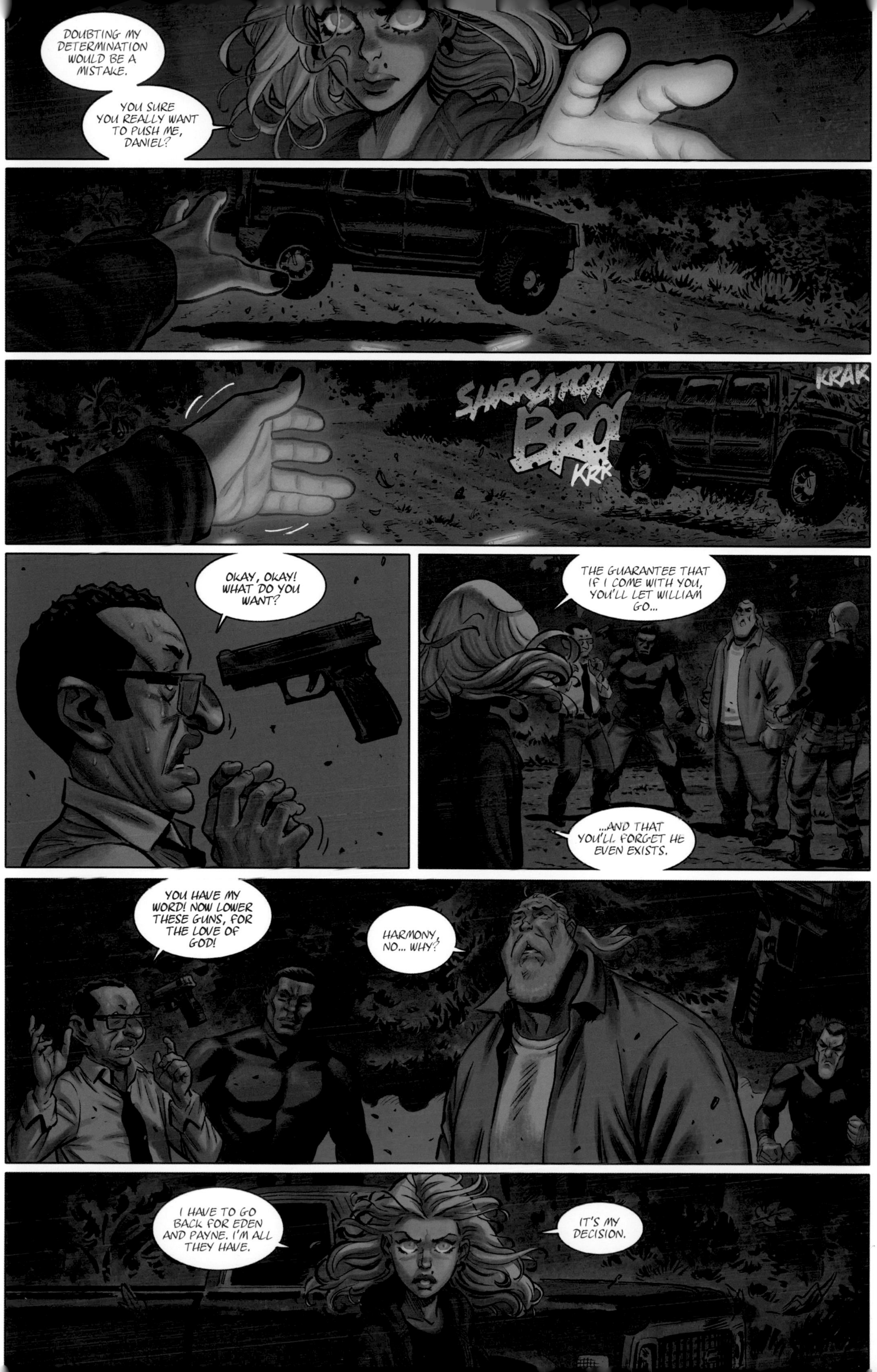
DOUBTING MY DETERMINATION WOULD BE A MISTAKE.
YOU SURE YOU REALLY WANT TO PUSH ME, DANIEL?
SHRRATCH
BRO
KRK
KRAK
OKAY, OKAY! WHAT DO YOU WANT?
THE GUARANTEE THAT IF I COME WITH YOU, YOU'LL LET WILLIAM GO...
...AND THAT YOU'LL FORGET HE EVEN EXISTS.
YOU HAVE MY WORD! NOW LOWER THESE GUNS, FOR THE LOVE OF GOD!
HARMONY, NO... WHY?
I HAVE TO GO BACK FOR EDEN AND PAYNE. I'M ALL THEY HAVE.
IT'S MY DECISION.

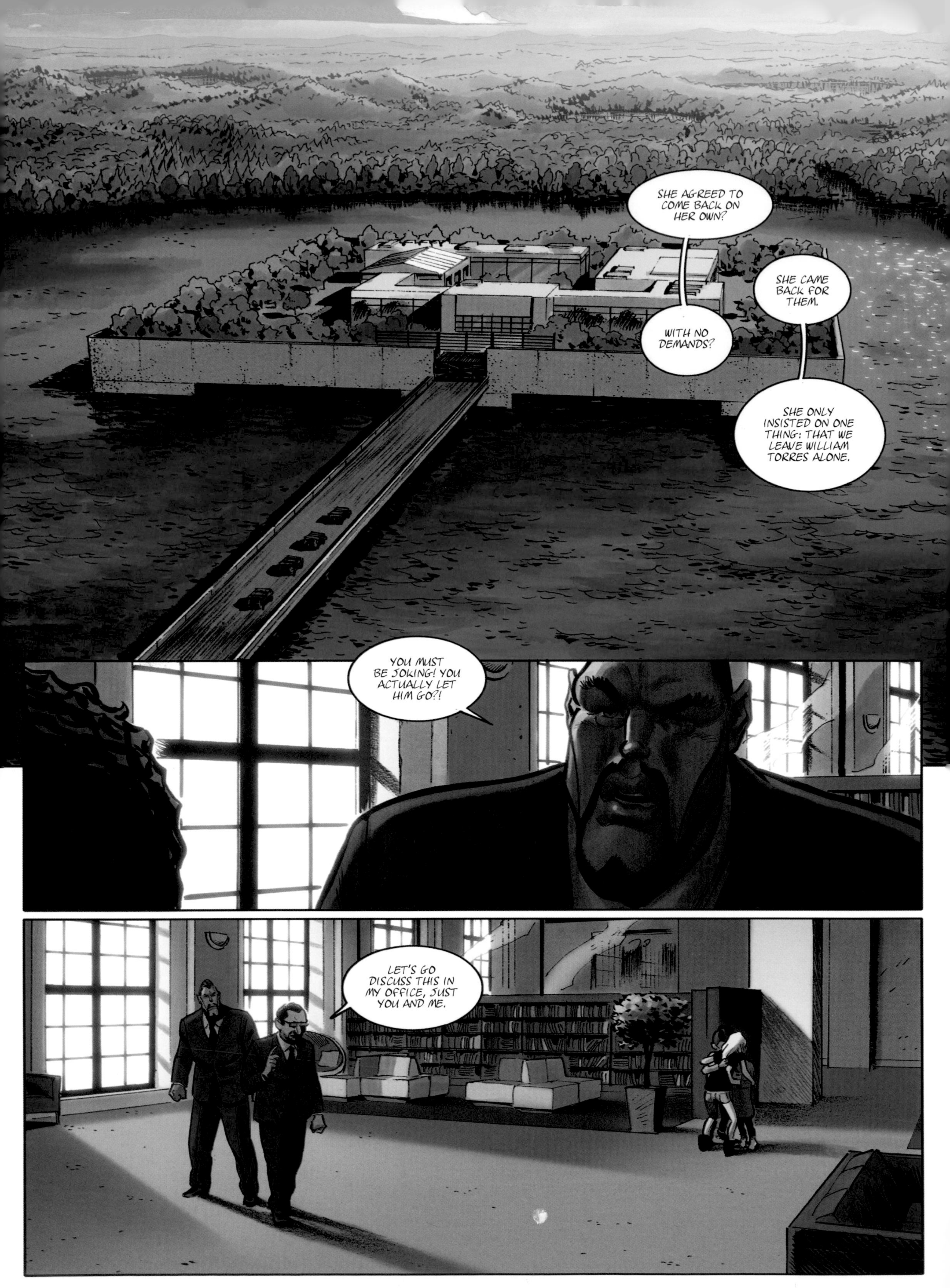
SHE AGREED TO COME BACK ON HER OWN?
WITH NO DEMANDS?
SHE CAME BACK FOR THEM.
SHE ONLY INSISTED ON ONE THING: THAT WE LEAVE WILLIAM TORRES ALONE.
YOU MUST BE JOKING! YOU ACTUALLY LET HIM GO?!
LET'S GO DISCUSS THIS IN MY OFFICE, JUST YOU AND ME.

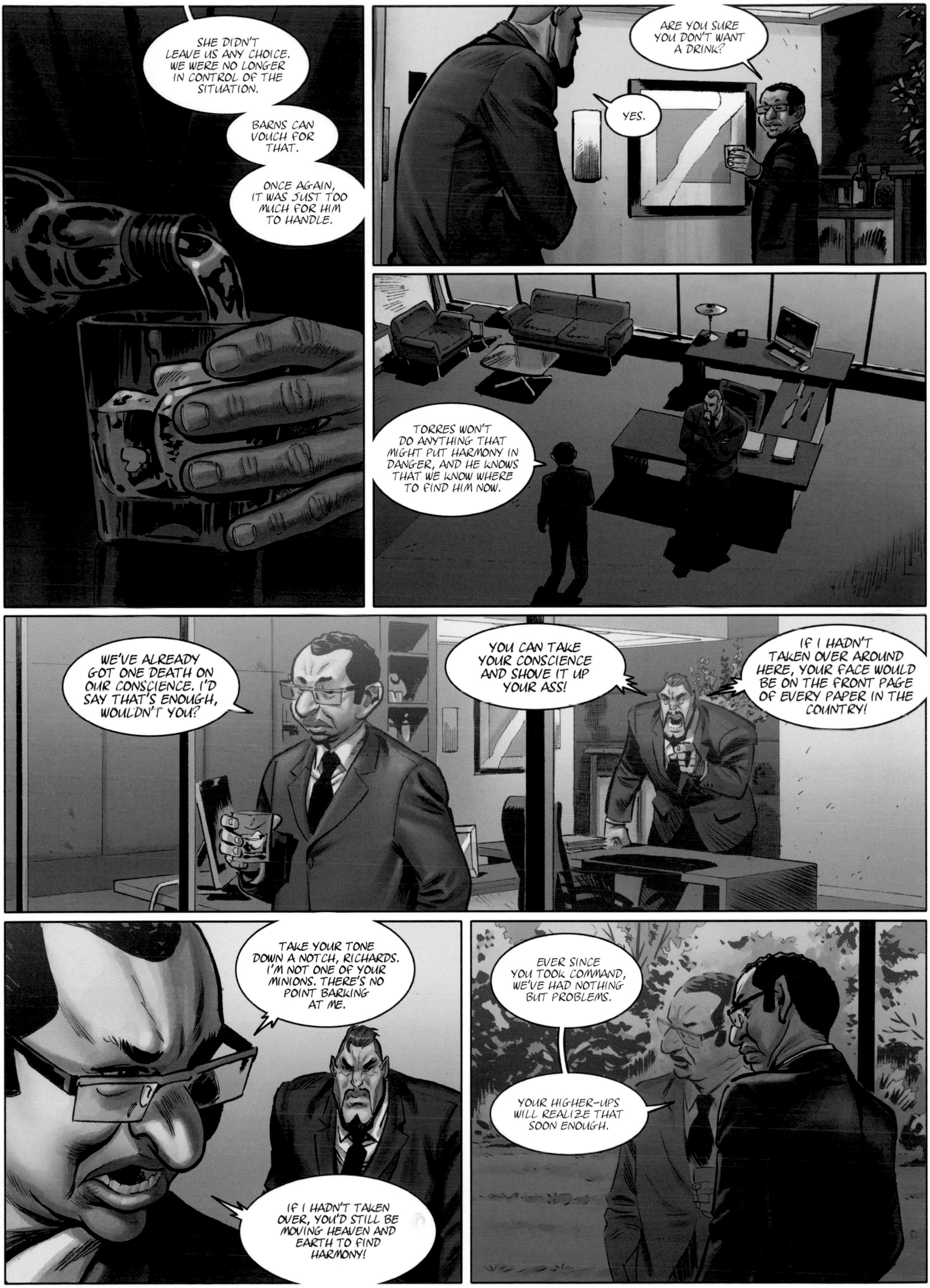
SHE DIDN'T LEAVE US ANY CHOICE. WE WERE NO LONGER IN CONTROL OF THE SITUATION.
BARNS CAN VOUCH FOR THAT.
ONCE AGAIN, IT WAS JUST TOO MUCH FOR HIM TO HANDLE.
ARE YOU SURE YOU DON'T WANT A DRINK?
YES.
TORRES WON'T DO ANYTHING THAT MIGHT PUT HARMONY IN DANGER, AND HE KNOWS THAT WE KNOW WHERE TO FIND HIM NOW.
WE'VE ALREADY GOT ONE DEATH ON OUR CONSCIENCE. I'D SAY THAT'S ENOUGH, WOULDN'T YOU?
YOU CAN TAKE YOUR CONSCIENCE AND SHOVE IT UP YOUR ASS!
IF I HADN'T TAKEN OVER AROUND HERE, YOUR FACE WOULD BE ON THE FRONT PAGE OF EVERY PAPER IN THE COUNTRY!
TAKE YOUR TONE DOWN A NOTCH, RICHARDS. I'M NOT ONE OF YOUR MINIONS. THERE'S NO POINT BARKING AT ME.
IF I HADN'T TAKEN OVER, YOU'D STILL BE MOVING HEAVEN AND EARTH TO FIND HARMONY!
EVER SINCE YOU TOOK COMMAND, WE'VE HAD NOTHING BUT PROBLEMS.
YOUR HIGHER-UPS WILL REALIZE THAT SOON ENOUGH.

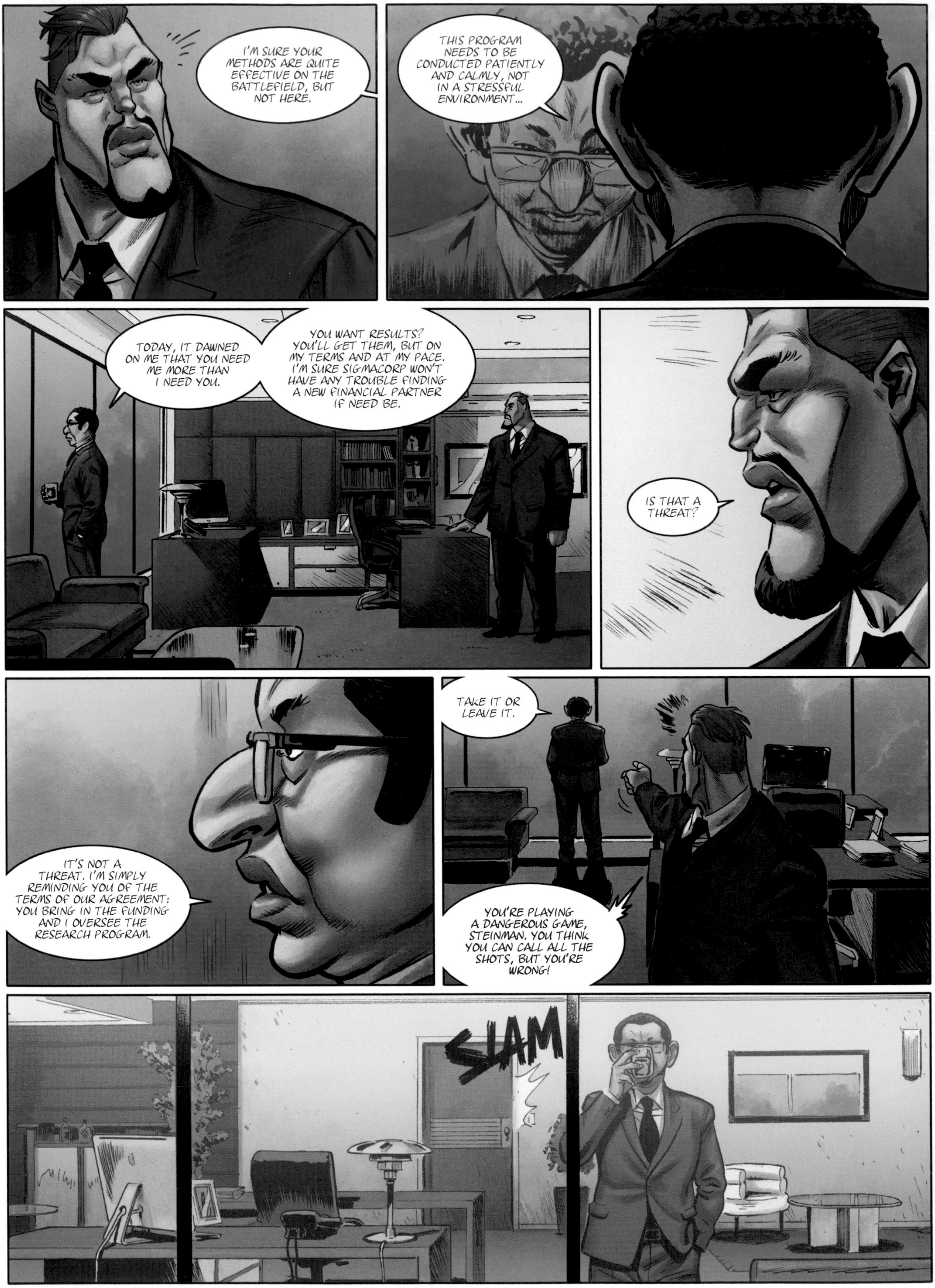
I'M SURE YOUR METHODS ARE QUITE EFFECTIVE ON THE BATTLEFIELD, BUT NOT HERE.
THIS PROGRAM NEEDS TO BE CONDUCTED PATIENTLY AND CALMLY, NOT IN A STRESSFUL ENVIRONMENT...
TODAY, IT DAWNED ON ME THAT YOU NEED ME MORE THAN I NEED YOU.
YOU WANT RESULTS? YOU'LL GET THEM, BUT ON MY TERMS AND AT MY PACE. I'M SURE SIGMACORP WON'T HAVE ANY TROUBLE FINDING A NEW FINANCIAL PARTNER IF NEED BE.
IS THAT A THREAT?
IT'S NOT A THREAT. I'M SIMPLY REMINDING YOU OF THE TERMS OF OUR AGREEMENT: YOU BRING IN THE FUNDING AND I OVERSEE THE RESEARCH PROGRAM.
TAKE IT OR LEAVE IT.
YOU'RE PLAYING A DANGEROUS GAME, STEINMAN. YOU THINK YOU CAN CALL ALL THE SHOTS, BUT YOU'RE WRONG!
SLAM

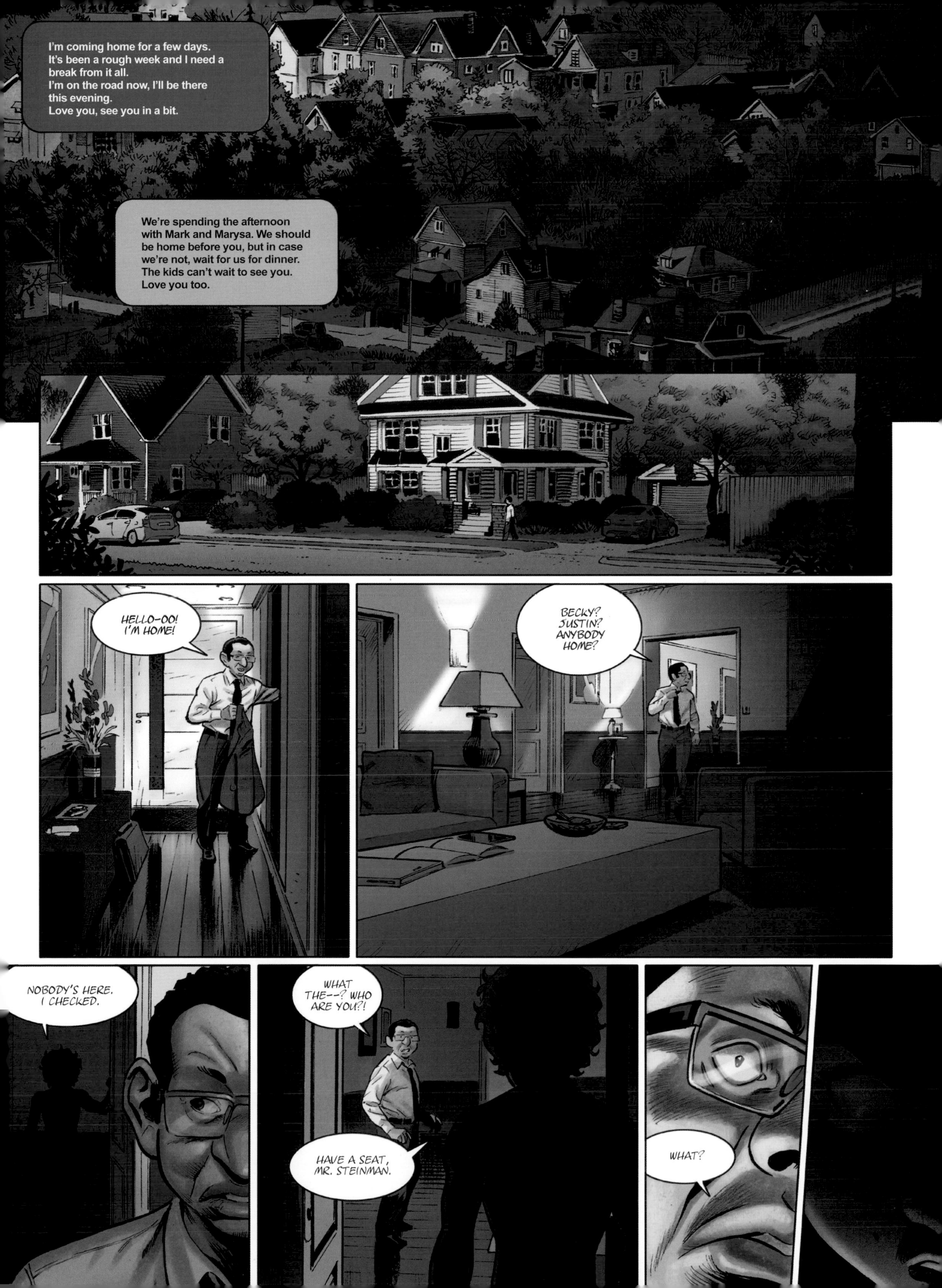
I'm coming home for a few days.
It's been a rough week and I need a break from it all.
I'm on the road now, I'll be there this evening.
Love you, see you in a bit.
We're spending the afternoon with Mark and Marysa. We should be home before you, but in case we're not, wait for us for dinner.
The kids can't wait to see you.
Love you too.
HELLO-OO! I'M HOME!
BECKY? JUSTIN? ANYBODY HOME?
NOBODY'S HERE. I CHECKED.
WHAT THE--? WHO ARE YOU?!
HAVE A SEAT, MR. STEINMAN.
WHAT?

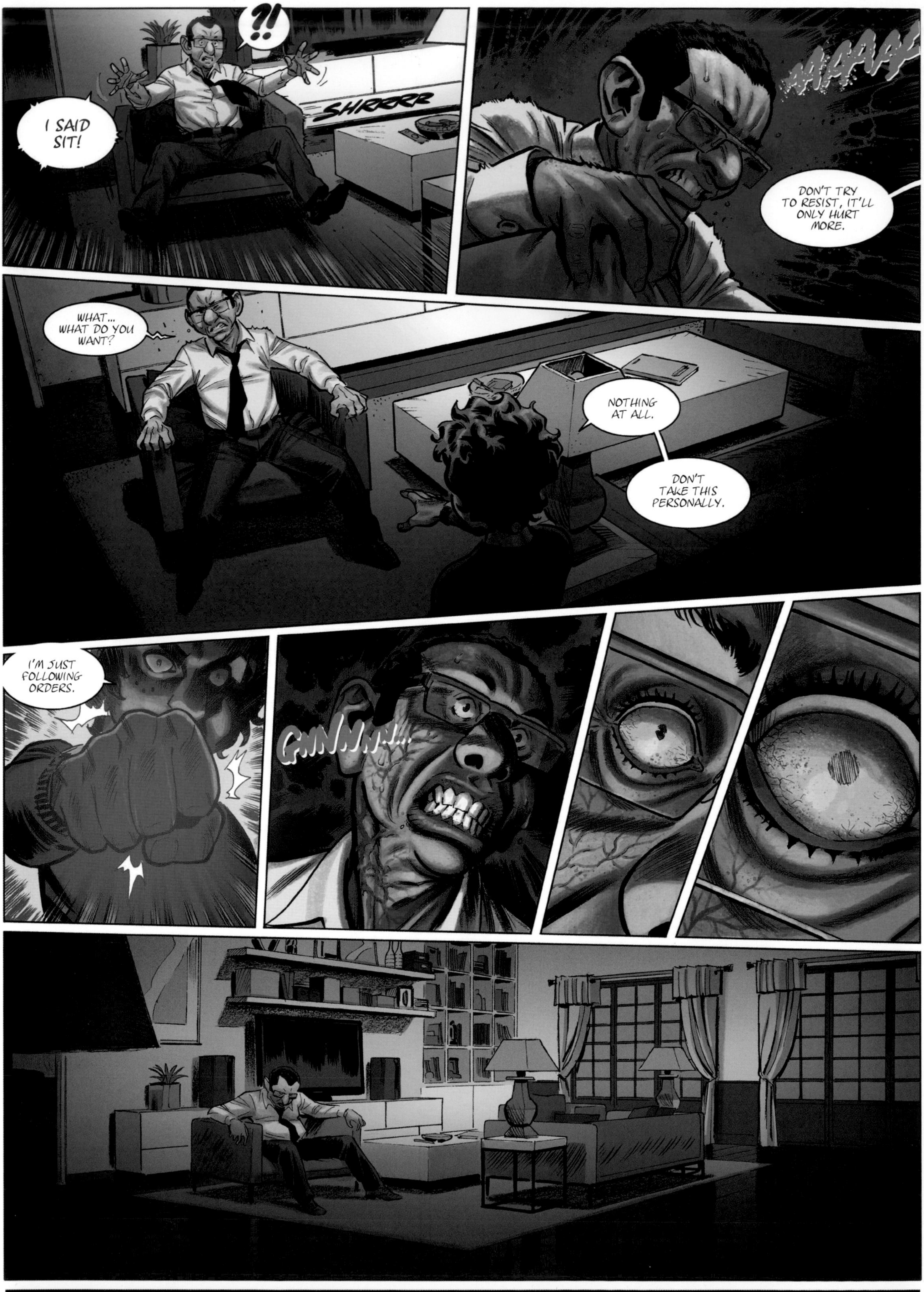
?!
SHRRRR
I SAID SIT!
AAAAA
DON'T TRY TO RESIST, IT'LL ONLY HURT MORE.
WHAT... WHAT DO YOU WANT?
NOTHING AT ALL.
DON'T TAKE THIS PERSONALLY.
I'M JUST FOLLOWING ORDERS.
GNNN...

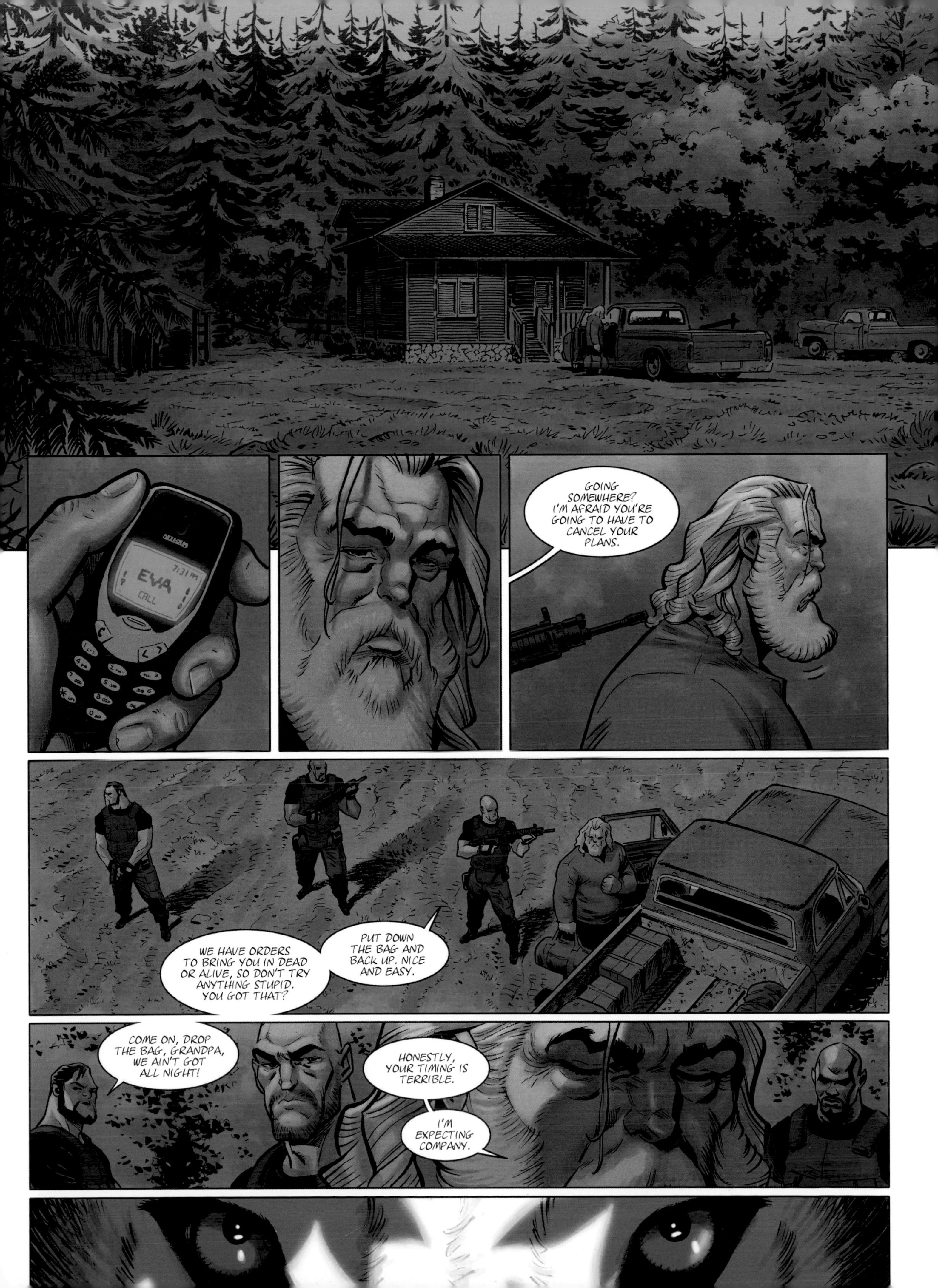
EVA
7:31 PM
CALL
GOING SOMEWHERE? I'M AFRAID YOU'RE GOING TO HAVE TO CANCEL YOUR PLANS.
PUT DOWN THE BAG AND BACK UP. NICE AND EASY.
WE HAVE ORDERS TO BRING YOU IN DEAD OR ALIVE, SO DON'T TRY ANYTHING STUPID. YOU GOT THAT?
COME ON, DROP THE BAG, GRANDPA, WE AIN'T GOT ALL NIGHT!
HONESTLY, YOUR TIMING IS TERRIBLE.
I'M EXPECTING COMPANY.

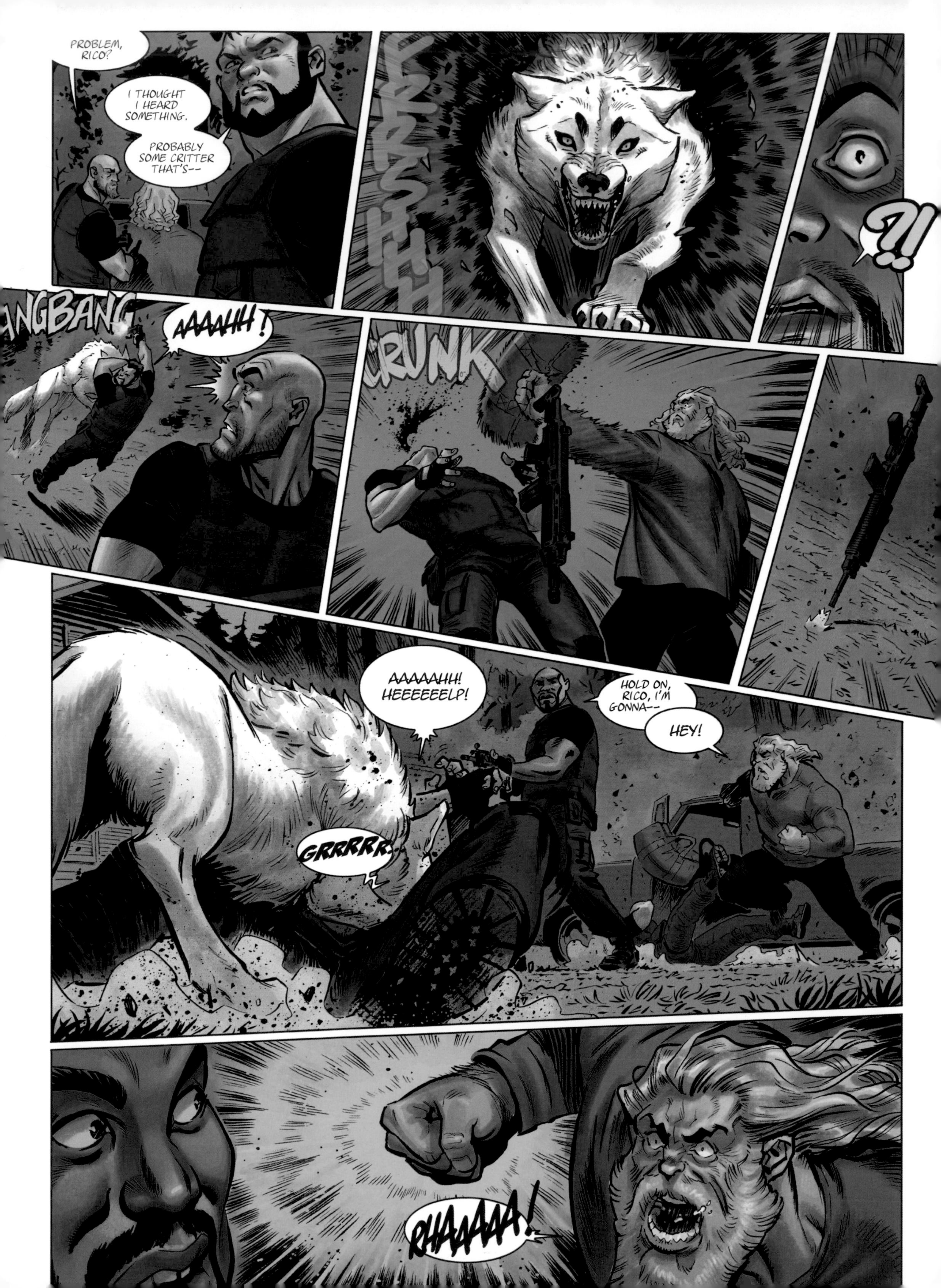

PROBLEM, RICO?
I THOUGHT I HEARD SOMETHING.
PROBABLY SOME CRITTER THAT'S--
?!
ANGBANG
AAAAHH!
CRUNK
AAAAAHH! HEEEEEELP!
HOLD ON, RICO, I'M GONNA--
HEY!
GRRRRR
RHAAAAA!

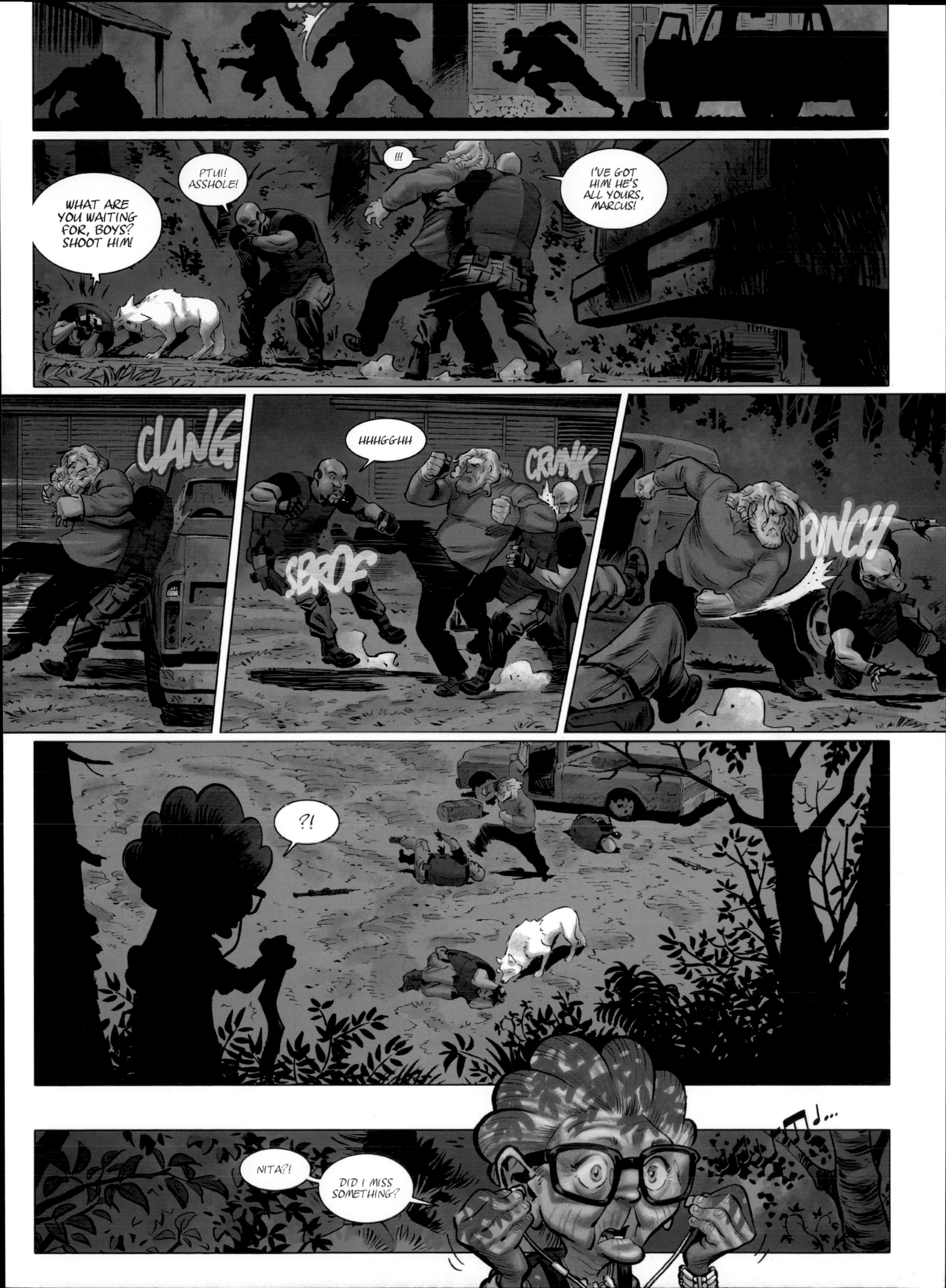

WHAT ARE YOU WAITING FOR, BOYS? SHOOT HIM!
PTUI! ASSHOLE!
!!!
I'VE GOT HIM! HE'S ALL YOURS, MARCUS!
CLANG
HHHGGHH
CRUNK
SBROF
PUNCH
?!
NITA?!
DID I MISS SOMETHING?

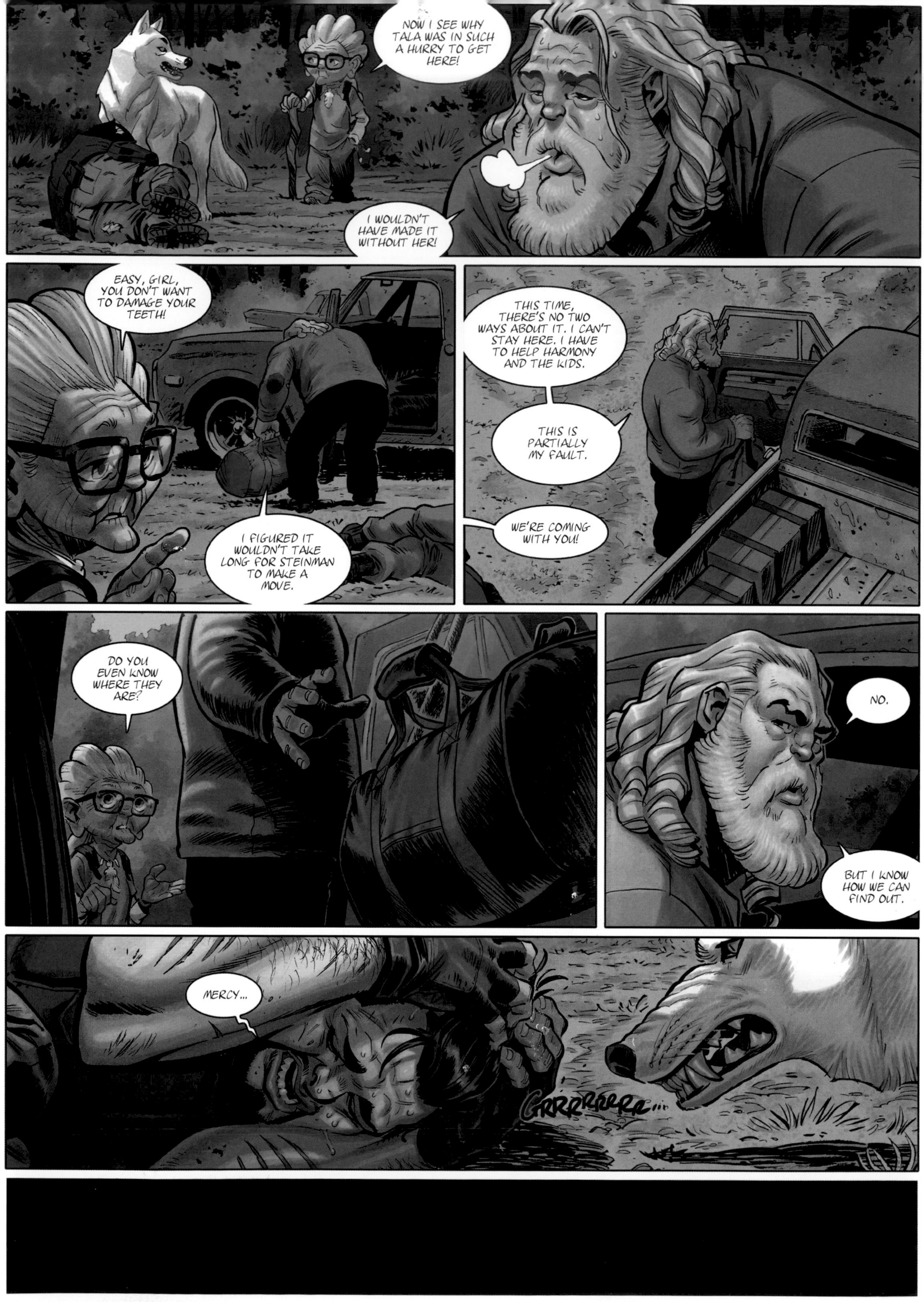
NOW I SEE WHY TALA WAS IN SUCH A HURRY TO GET HERE!
I WOULDN'T HAVE MADE IT WITHOUT HER!
EASY, GIRL, YOU DON'T WANT TO DAMAGE YOUR TEETH!
I FIGURED IT WOULDN'T TAKE LONG FOR STEINMAN TO MAKE A MOVE.
THIS TIME, THERE'S NO TWO WAYS ABOUT IT. I CAN'T STAY HERE. I HAVE TO HELP HARMONY AND THE KIDS.
THIS IS PARTIALLY MY FAULT.
WE'RE COMING WITH YOU!
DO YOU EVEN KNOW WHERE THEY ARE?
NO.
BUT I KNOW HOW WE CAN FIND OUT.
MERCY...
GRRRRRRRR...

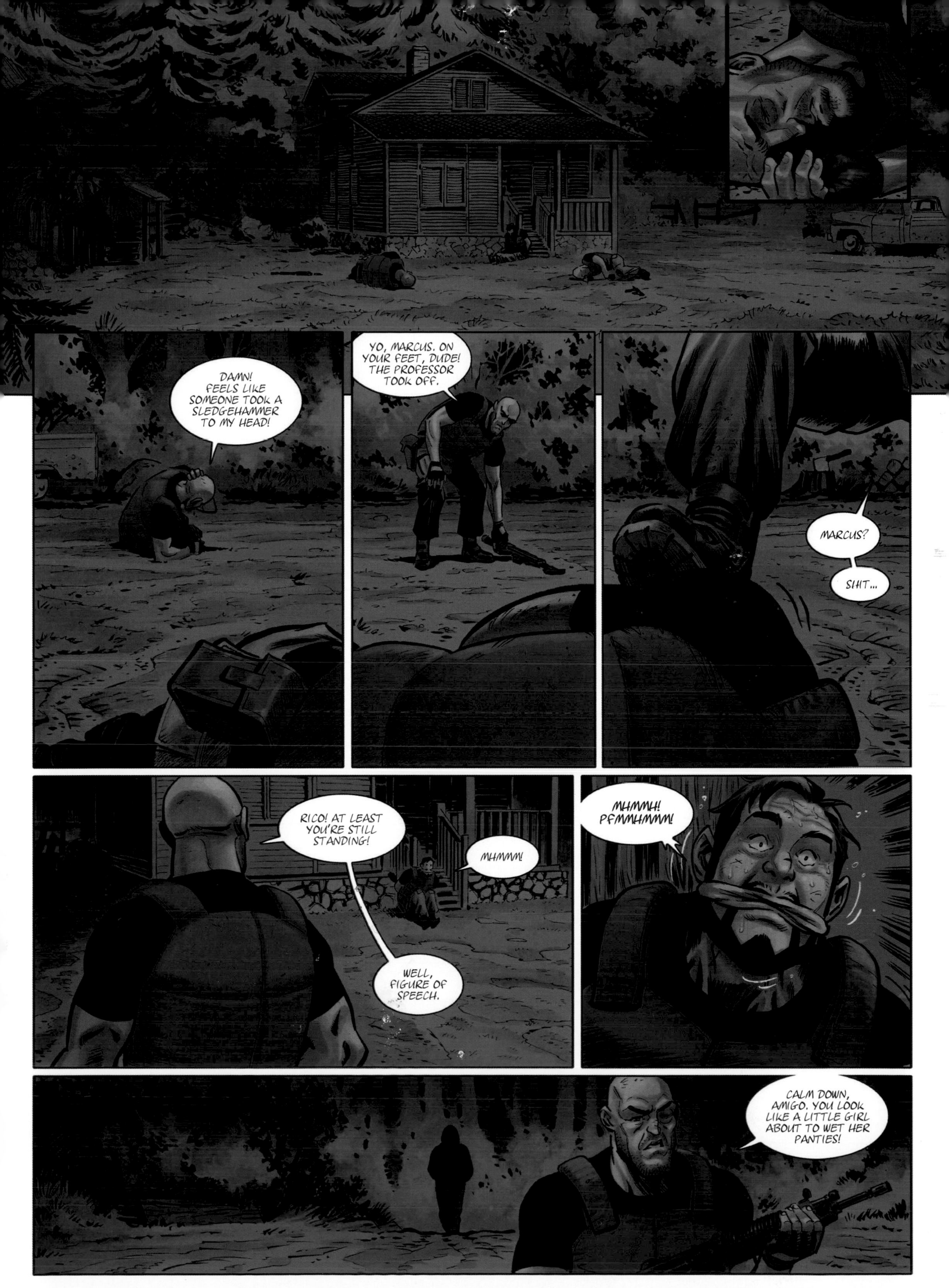
DAMN! FEELS LIKE SOMEONE TOOK A SLEDGEHAMMER TO MY HEAD!
YO, MARCUS. ON YOUR FEET, DUDE! THE PROFESSOR TOOK OFF.
MARCUS?
SHIT...
RICO! AT LEAST YOU'RE STILL STANDING!
MHMMM!
WELL, FIGURE OF SPEECH.
MHMMH! PFMMHMMM!
CALM DOWN, AMIGO. YOU LOOK LIKE A LITTLE GIRL ABOUT TO WET HER PANTIES!

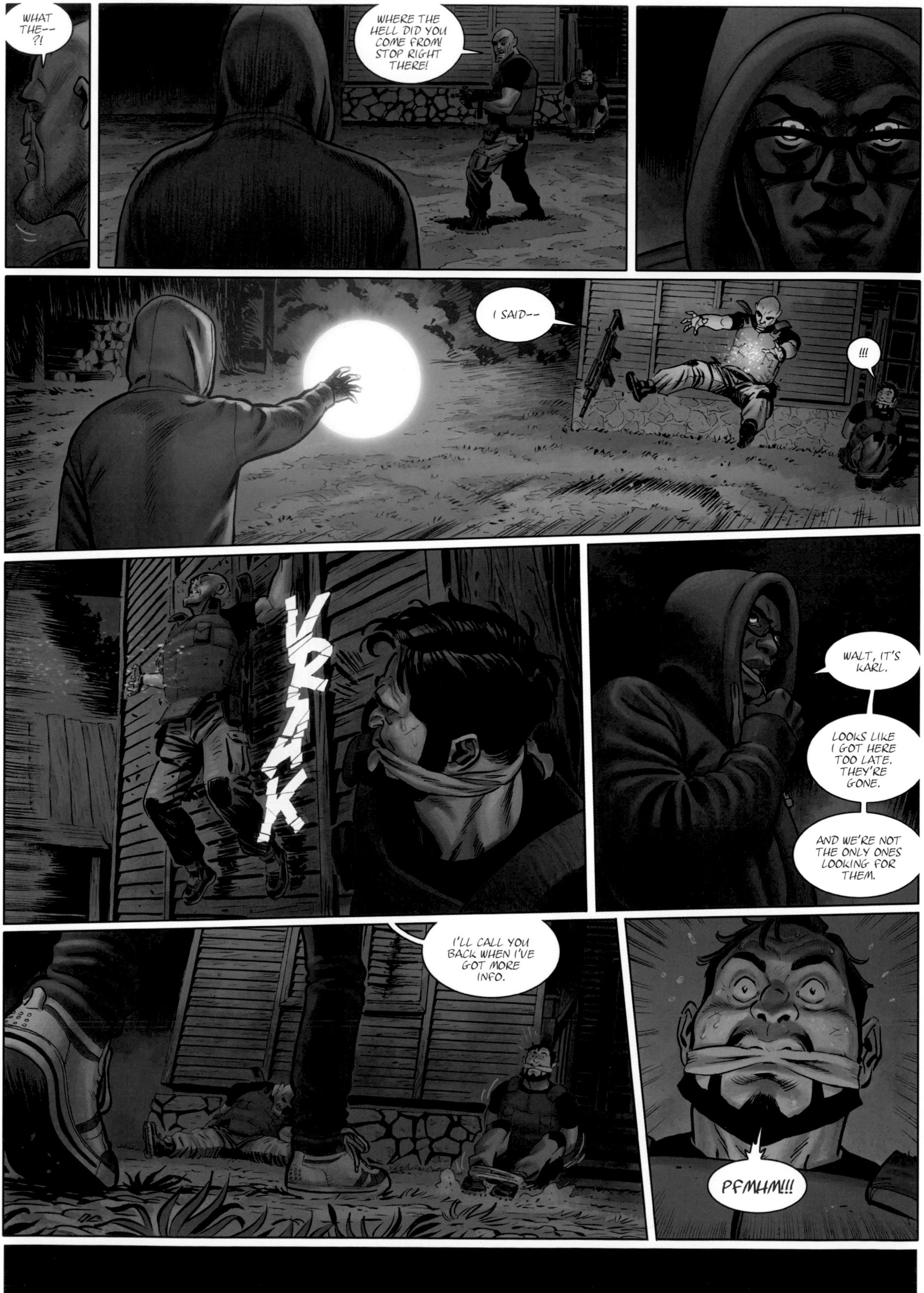
WHAT THE-- ?!
WHERE THE HELL DID YOU COME FROM! STOP RIGHT THERE!
I SAID--
!!!
VRAKK
WALT, IT'S KARL.
LOOKS LIKE I GOT HERE TOO LATE. THEY'RE GONE.
AND WE'RE NOT THE ONLY ONES LOOKING FOR THEM.
I'LL CALL YOU BACK WHEN I'VE GOT MORE INFO.
PFMHM!!!

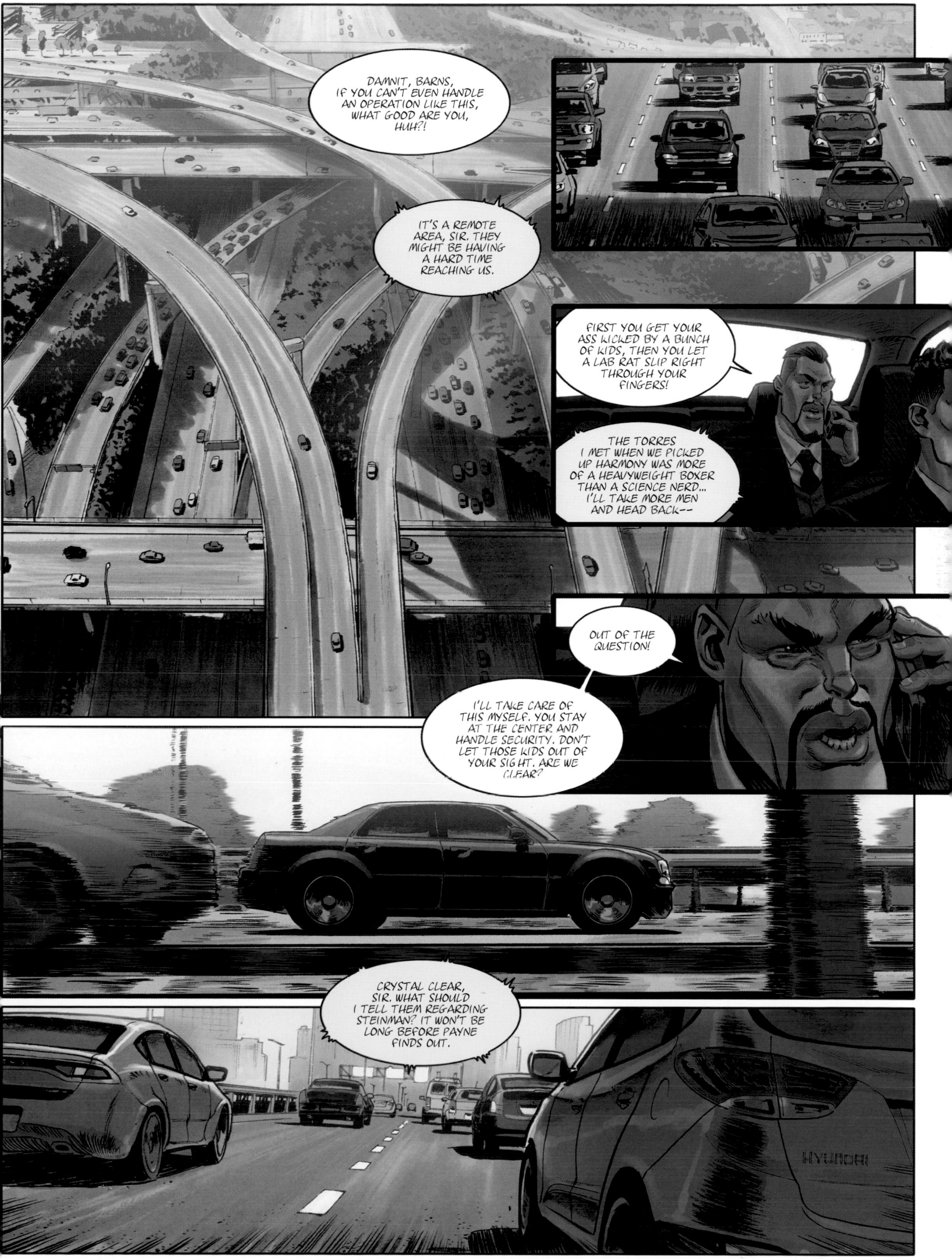
DAMNIT, BARNS, IF YOU CAN'T EVEN HANDLE AN OPERATION LIKE THIS, WHAT GOOD ARE YOU, HUH?!
IT'S A REMOTE AREA, SIR. THEY MIGHT BE HAVING A HARD TIME REACHING US.
FIRST YOU GET YOUR ASS KICKED BY A BUNCH OF KIDS, THEN YOU LET A LAB RAT SLIP RIGHT THROUGH YOUR FINGERS!
THE TORRES I MET WHEN WE PICKED UP HARMONY WAS MORE OF A HEAVYWEIGHT BOXER THAN A SCIENCE NERD... I'LL TAKE MORE MEN AND HEAD BACK--
OUT OF THE QUESTION!
I'LL TAKE CARE OF THIS MYSELF. YOU STAY AT THE CENTER AND HANDLE SECURITY. DON'T LET THOSE KIDS OUT OF YOUR SIGHT. ARE WE CLEAR?
CRYSTAL CLEAR, SIR. WHAT SHOULD I TELL THEM REGARDING STEINMAN? IT WON'T BE LONG BEFORE PAYNE FINDS OUT.
HYUNDAI

IT DOESN'T MATTER. ONCE WE'VE DEALT WITH TORRES, I'LL TELL THEM I'M TAKING OVER THE PROGRAM.

I INTEND TO MOVE INTO THE NEXT PHASE VERY QUICKLY. IT'S IN THEIR INTEREST TO COOPERATE, BELIEVE ME!

WE'RE REACHING A POINT WHERE WE CAN DO WITHOUT THEM IF THEY START ACTING OUT AGAIN.

I'LL ALSO TAKE THE OPPORTUNITY TO REMIND ALL STAFF MEMBERS WHAT'S WHAT BEFORE ANYONE ELSE HAS THE BRIGHT IDEA TO TRY AND BE A HERO.

JUST IN CASE WHAT HAPPENED TO TAZEKH DIDN'T SEND A CLEAR ENOUGH MESSAGE!

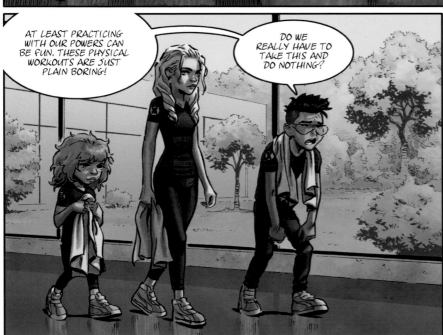

AT LEAST PRACTICING WITH OUR POWERS CAN BE FUN. THESE PHYSICAL WORKOUTS ARE JUST PLAIN BORING!

DO WE REALLY HAVE TO TAKE THIS AND DO NOTHING?

FOR NOW, WE NEED TO GO ALONG WITH THE PROGRAM, BUT AS SOON AS THEY LET THEIR GUARD DOWN--

SHHH! SOMEONE'S COMING!

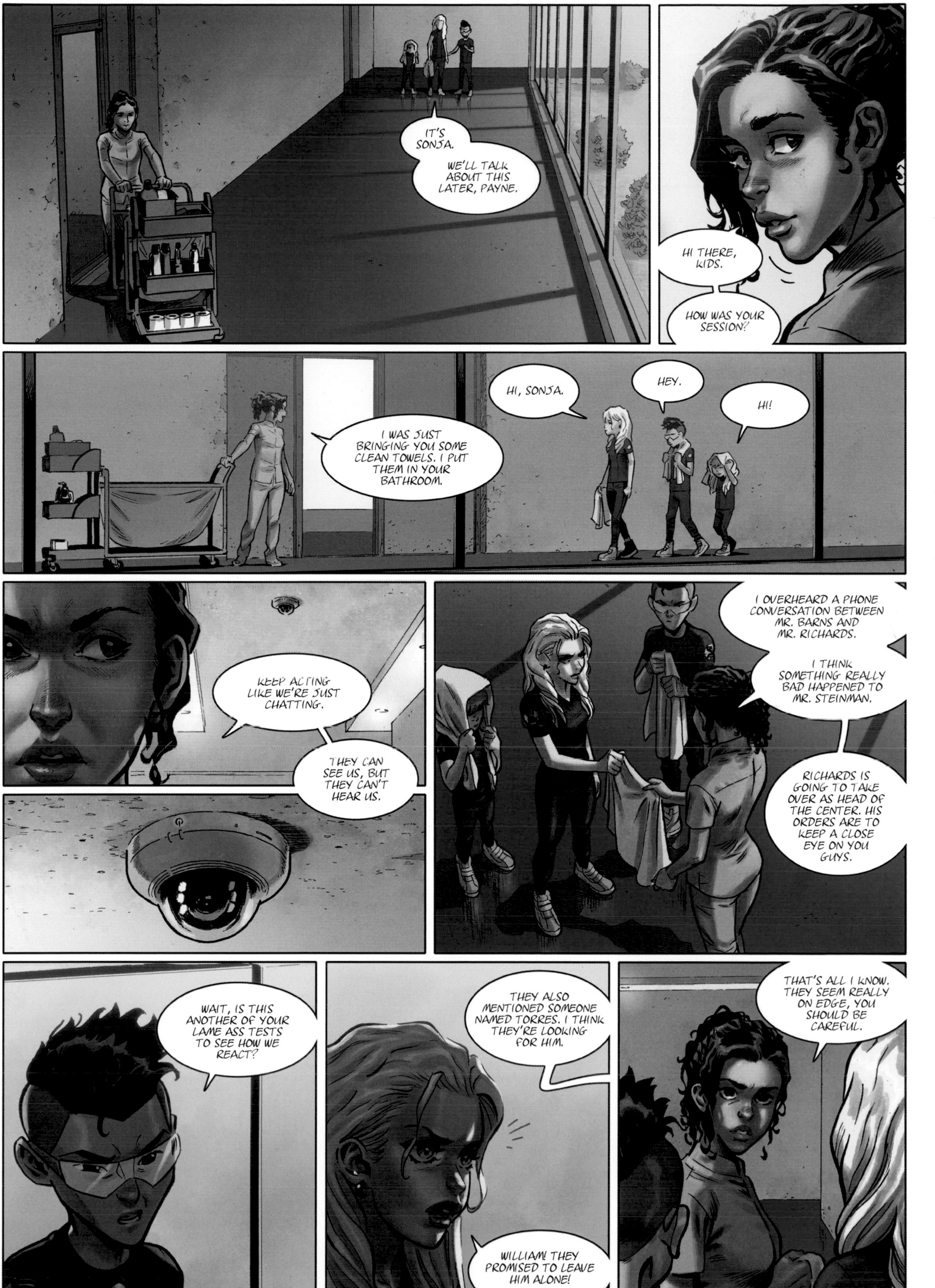
IT'S SONJA.
WE'LL TALK ABOUT THIS LATER, PAYNE.
HI THERE, KIDS.
HOW WAS YOUR SESSION?
I WAS JUST BRINGING YOU SOME CLEAN TOWELS. I PUT THEM IN YOUR BATHROOM.
HI, SONJA.
HEY.
HI!
KEEP ACTING LIKE WE'RE JUST CHATTING.
THEY CAN SEE US, BUT THEY CAN'T HEAR US.
I OVERHEARD A PHONE CONVERSATION BETWEEN MR. BARNS AND MR. RICHARDS.
I THINK SOMETHING REALLY BAD HAPPENED TO MR. STEINMAN.
RICHARDS IS GOING TO TAKE OVER AS HEAD OF THE CENTER. HIS ORDERS ARE TO KEEP A CLOSE EYE ON YOU GUYS.
WAIT, IS THIS ANOTHER OF YOUR LAME ASS TESTS TO SEE HOW WE REACT?
THEY ALSO MENTIONED SOMEONE NAMED TORRES. I THINK THEY'RE LOOKING FOR HIM.
WILLIAM! THEY PROMISED TO LEAVE HIM ALONE!
THAT'S ALL I KNOW. THEY SEEM REALLY ON EDGE, YOU SHOULD BE CAREFUL.

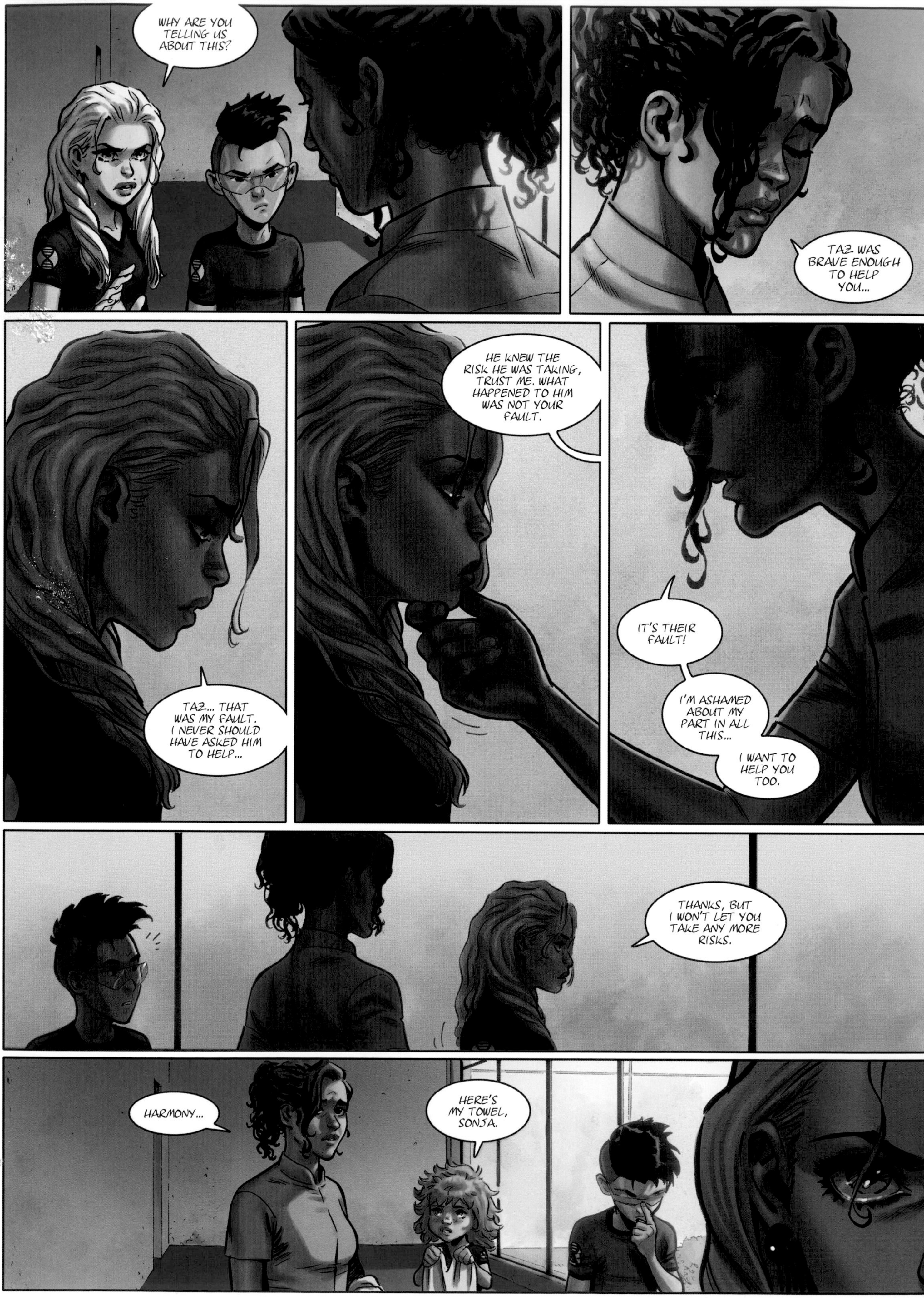

WHY ARE YOU TELLING US ABOUT THIS?
TAZ WAS BRAVE ENOUGH TO HELP YOU...
TAZ... THAT WAS MY FAULT. I NEVER SHOULD HAVE ASKED HIM TO HELP...
HE KNEW THE RISK HE WAS TAKING, TRUST ME. WHAT HAPPENED TO HIM WAS NOT YOUR FAULT.
IT'S THEIR FAULT!
I'M ASHAMED ABOUT MY PART IN ALL THIS...
I WANT TO HELP YOU TOO.
THANKS, BUT I WON'T LET YOU TAKE ANY MORE RISKS.
HARMONY...
HERE'S MY TOWEL, SONJA.

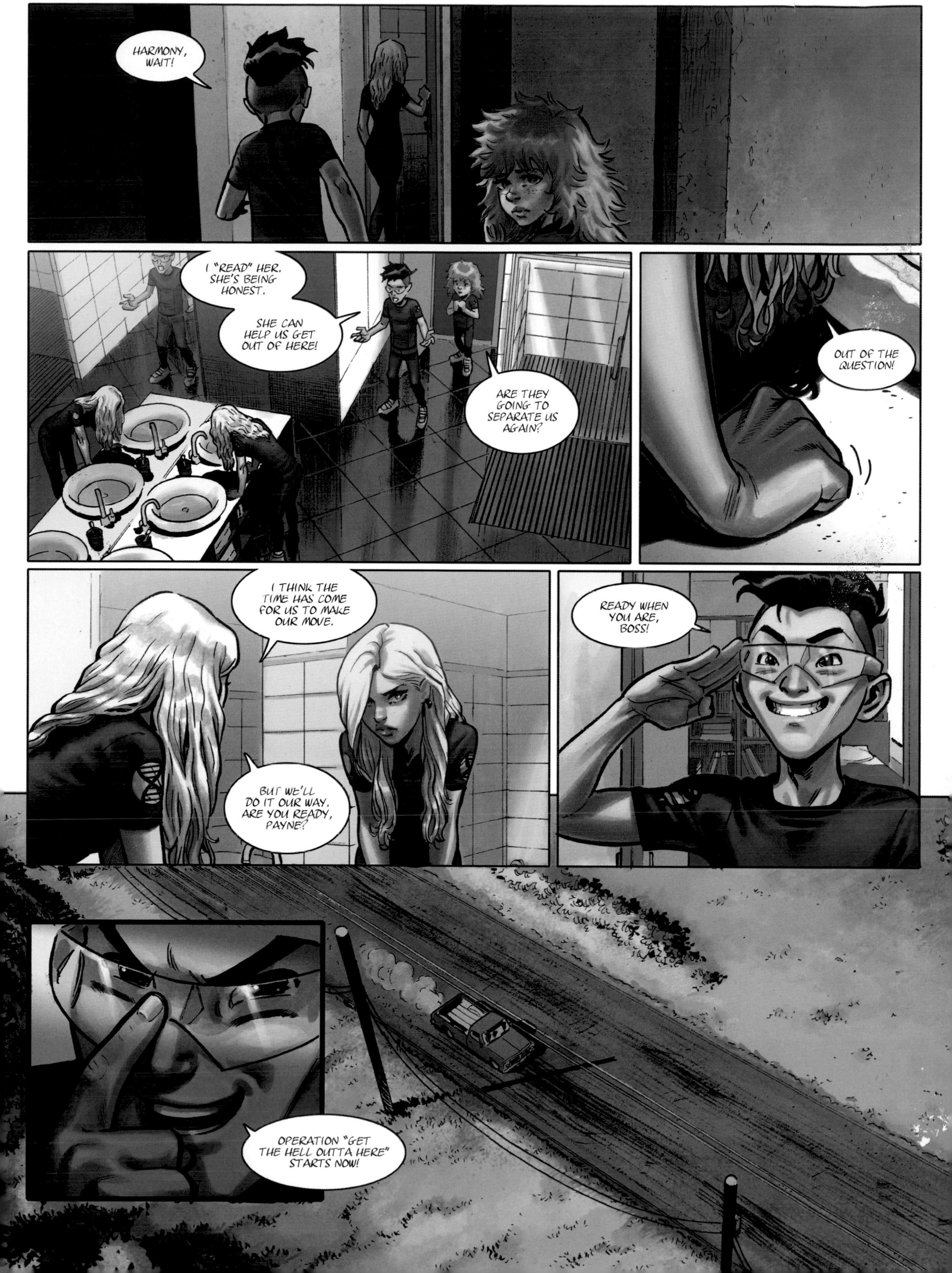
HARMONY, WAIT!
I "READ" HER. SHE'S BEING HONEST.
SHE CAN HELP US GET OUT OF HERE!
ARE THEY GOING TO SEPARATE US AGAIN?
OUT OF THE QUESTION!
I THINK THE TIME HAS COME FOR US TO MAKE OUR MOVE.
BUT WE'LL DO IT OUR WAY. ARE YOU READY, PAYNE?
READY WHEN YOU ARE, BOSS!
OPERATION "GET THE HELL OUTTA HERE" STARTS NOW!

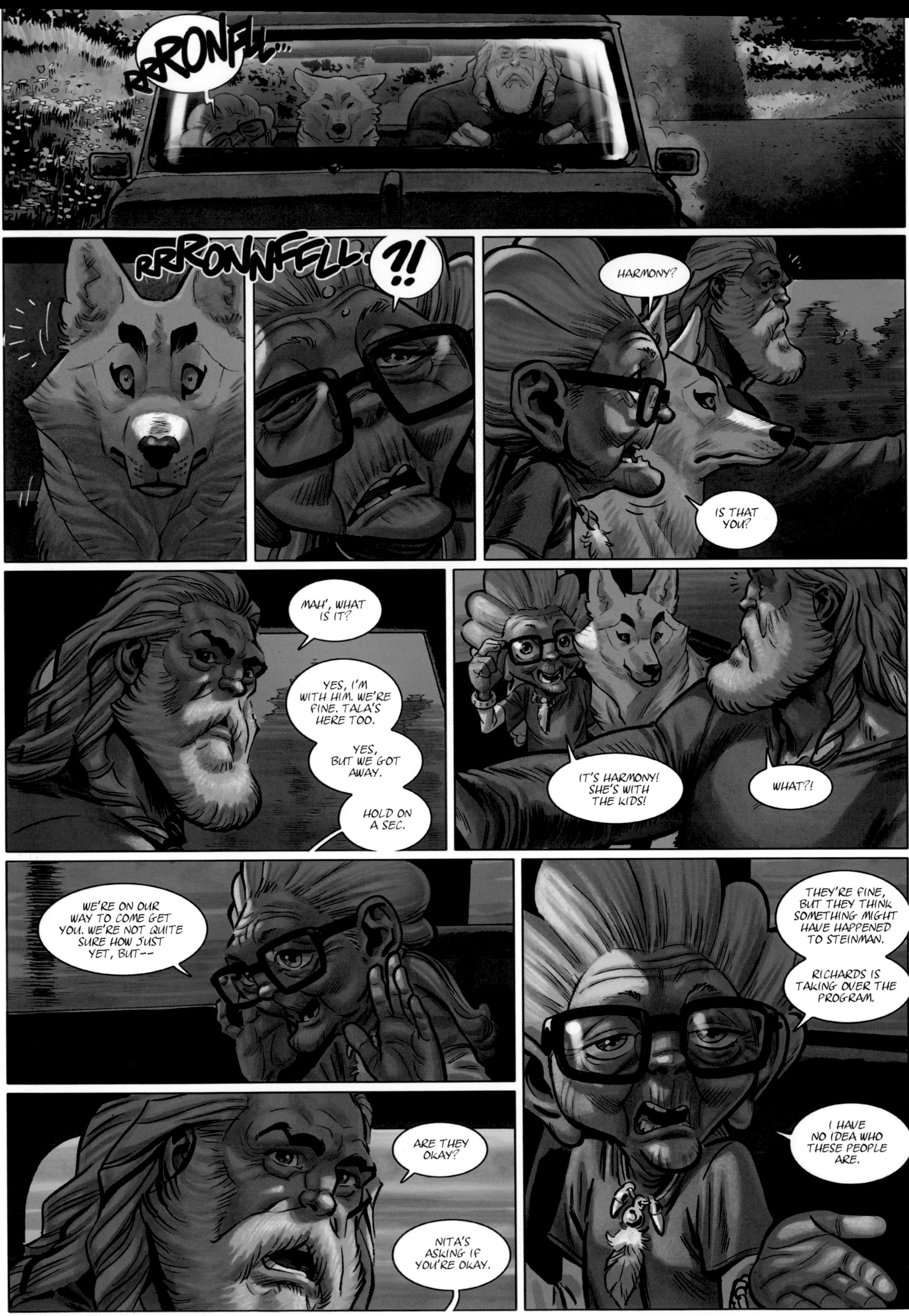
RRRONFLL...
RRRONNFFLL...
?!
HARMONY?
IS THAT YOU?
MAH', WHAT IS IT?
YES, I'M WITH HIM. WE'RE FINE. TALA'S HERE TOO.
YES, BUT WE GOT AWAY.
HOLD ON A SEC.
IT'S HARMONY! SHE'S WITH THE KIDS!
WHAT?!
WE'RE ON OUR WAY TO COME GET YOU. WE'RE NOT QUITE SURE HOW JUST YET, BUT--
ARE THEY OKAY?
NITA'S ASKING IF YOU'RE OKAY.
THEY'RE FINE, BUT THEY THINK SOMETHING MIGHT HAVE HAPPENED TO STEINMAN.
RICHARDS IS TAKING OVER THE PROGRAM.
I HAVE NO IDEA WHO THESE PEOPLE ARE.

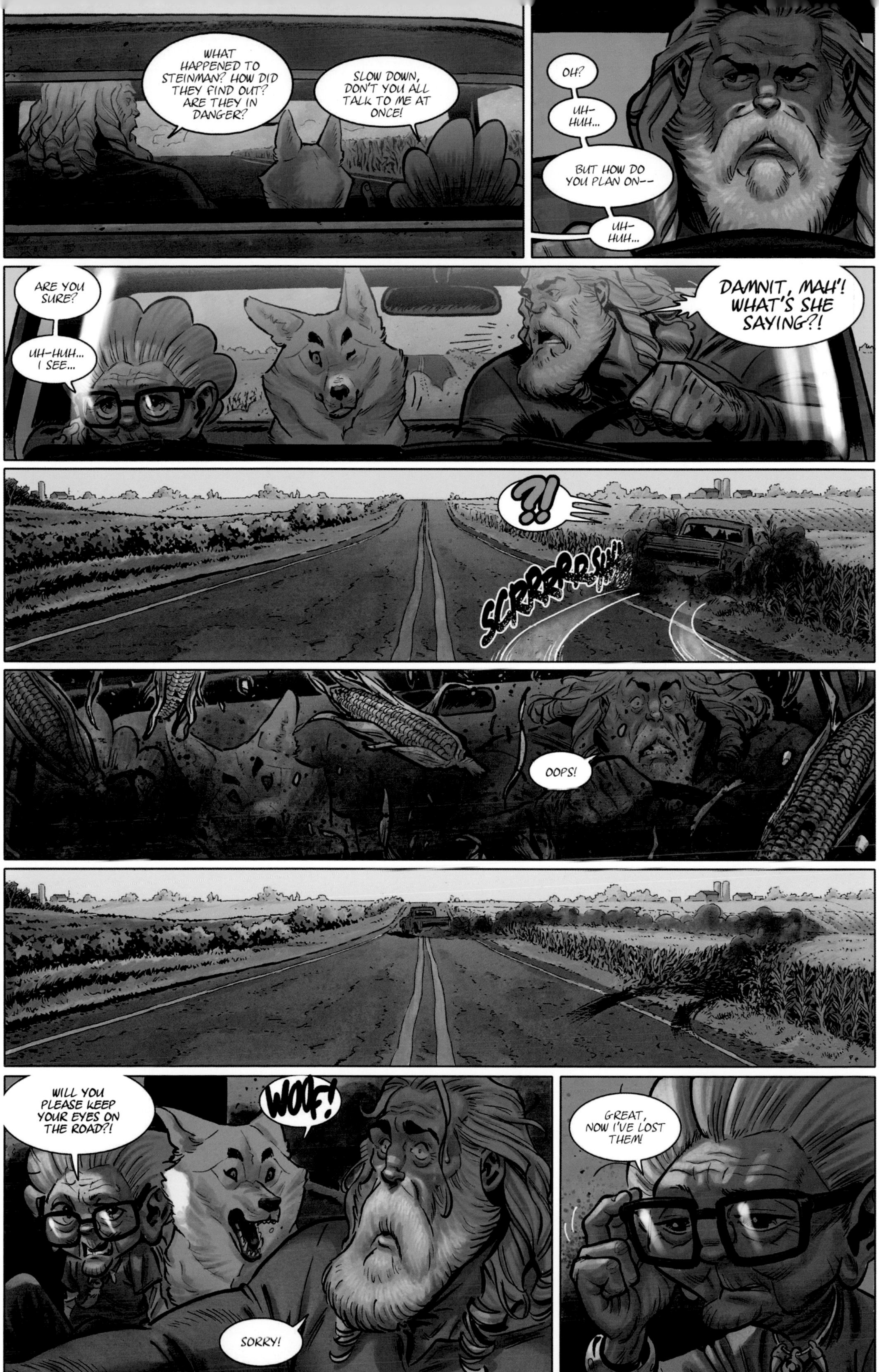
WHAT HAPPENED TO STEINMAN? HOW DID THEY FIND OUT? ARE THEY IN DANGER?
SLOW DOWN, DON'T YOU ALL TALK TO ME AT ONCE!
OH?
UH-HUH...
BUT HOW DO YOU PLAN ON--
UH-HUH...
ARE YOU SURE?
UH-HUH... I SEE...
DAMNIT, MAH'! WHAT'S SHE SAYING?!
?!
SCRRRRSSH!
OOPS!
WILL YOU PLEASE KEEP YOUR EYES ON THE ROAD?!
WOOF!
SORRY!
GREAT, NOW I'VE LOST THEM!

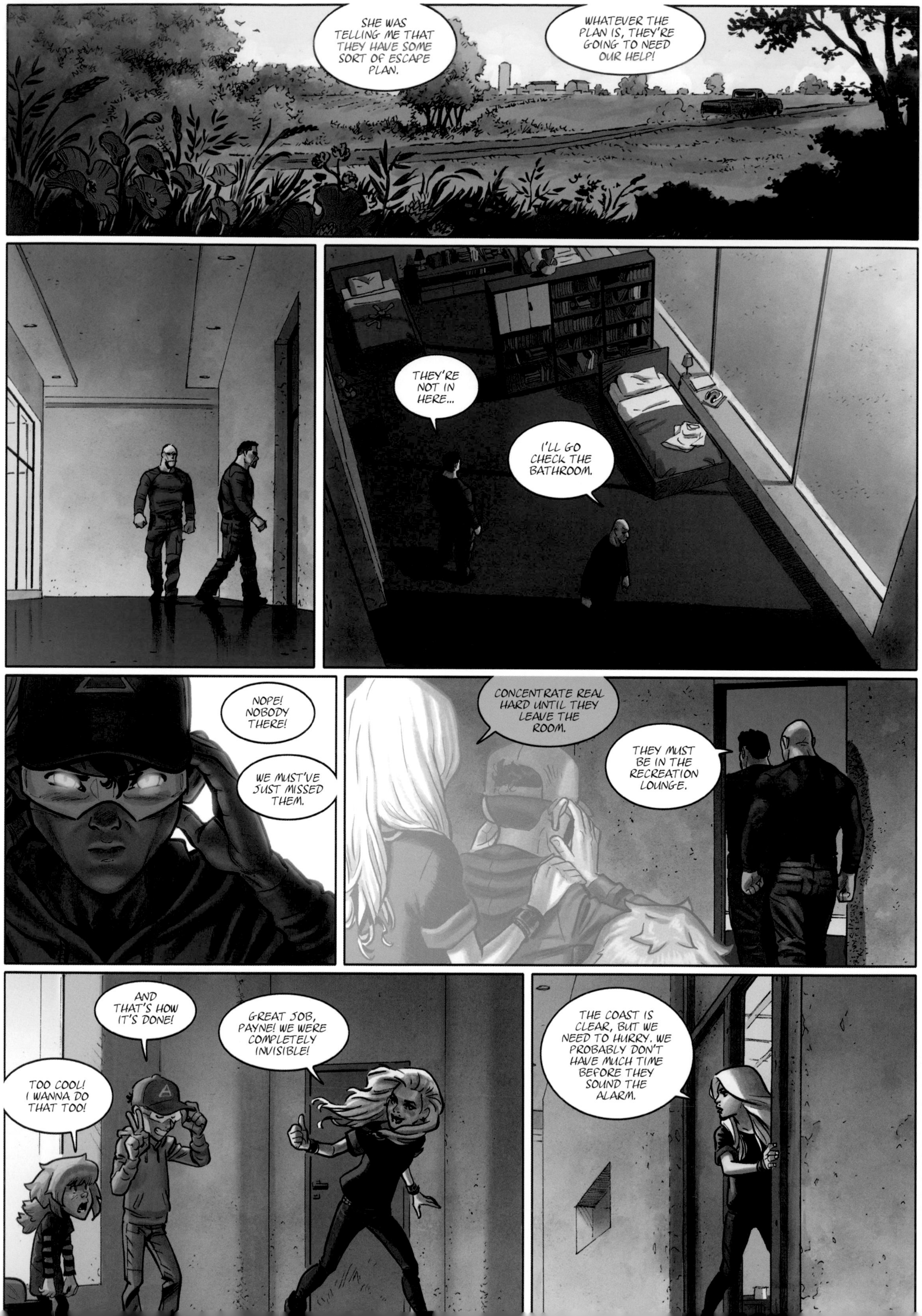

SHE WAS TELLING ME THAT THEY HAVE SOME SORT OF ESCAPE PLAN.
WHATEVER THE PLAN IS, THEY'RE GOING TO NEED OUR HELP!
THEY'RE NOT IN HERE...
I'LL GO CHECK THE BATHROOM.
NOPE! NOBODY THERE!
WE MUST'VE JUST MISSED THEM.
CONCENTRATE REAL HARD UNTIL THEY LEAVE THE ROOM.
THEY MUST BE IN THE RECREATION LOUNGE.
TOO COOL! I WANNA DO THAT TOO!
AND THAT'S HOW IT'S DONE!
GREAT JOB, PAYNE! WE WERE COMPLETELY INVISIBLE!
THE COAST IS CLEAR, BUT WE NEED TO HURRY. WE PROBABLY DON'T HAVE MUCH TIME BEFORE THEY SOUND THE ALARM.

REYNOLDS? IT'S BARNS. PYKE HAS INFORMED ME THAT THE KIDS AREN'T IN THEIR ROOM OR IN THE MAIN LOUNGE.

CAN YOU SEE THEM ON THE MONITOR?

HOLD ON, I'LL PULL UP THE FEED.

YEAH, THEY'RE IN THE SOUTH WING, COMING UP ON BANNISKY.

OKAY, TELL HIM TO INTERCEPT THEM. I'LL SEND PYKE TO PICK THEM UP. I WANT SOMEONE WITH THEM 24/7 FROM NOW ON.

BANNISKY, REYNOLDS HERE. STAY WITH THE KIDS UNTIL PYKE COMES FOR THEM, DO YOU COPY?

I COPY. WHERE ARE THEY?

ARE YOU KIDDING?! THEY'RE RIGHT BEHIND YOU!

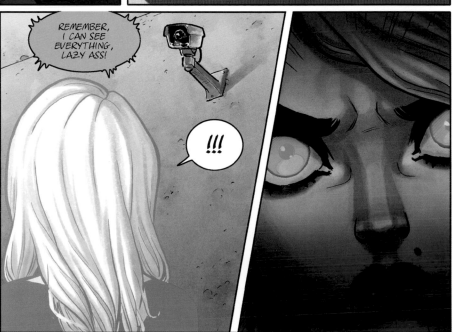

REMEMBER, I CAN SEE EVERYTHING, LAZY ASS!

!!!

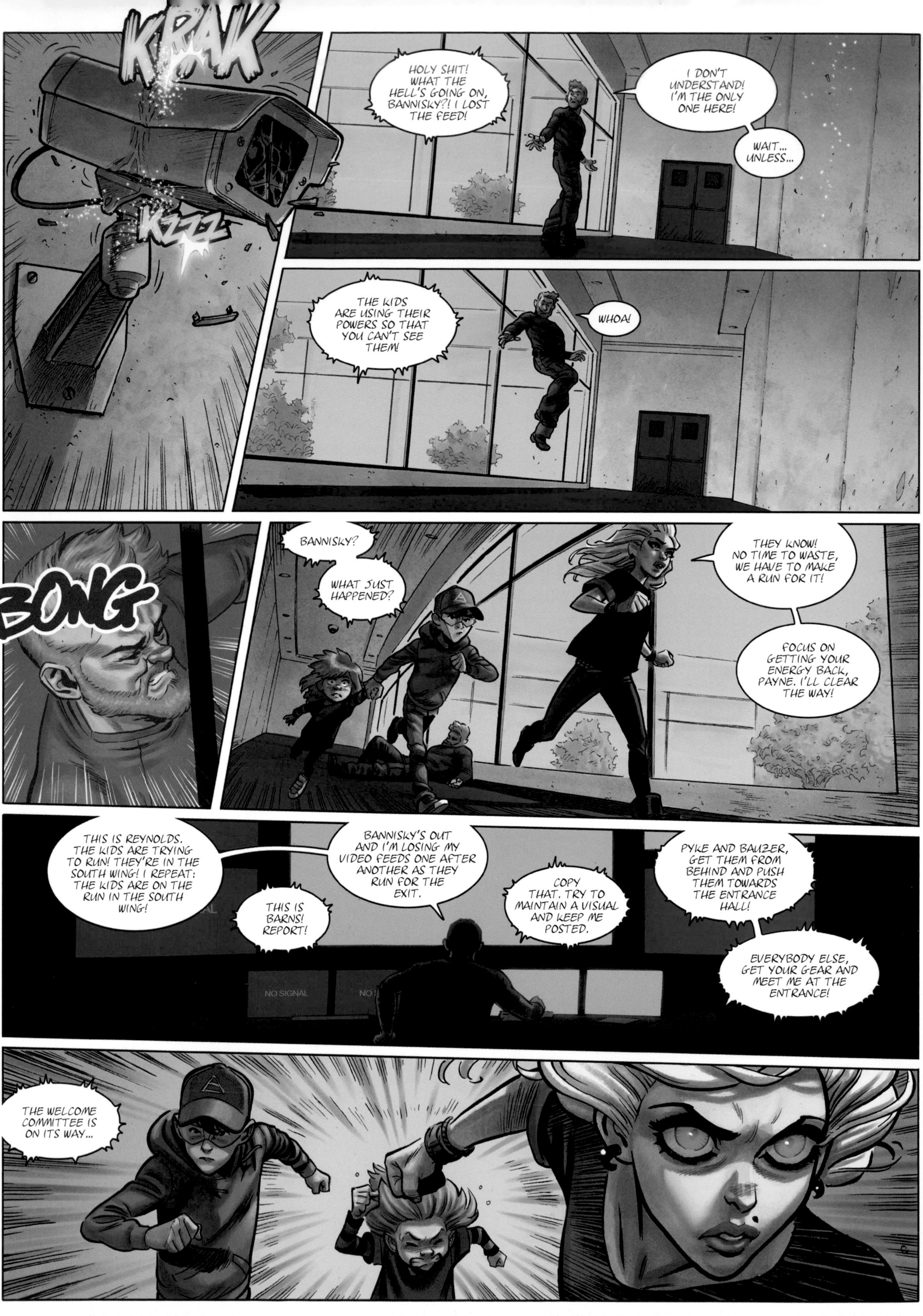
KRAK
KZZZZ
HOLY SHIT! WHAT THE HELL'S GOING ON, BANNISKY?! I LOST THE FEED!
I DON'T UNDERSTAND! I'M THE ONLY ONE HERE!
WAIT... UNLESS...
THE KIDS ARE USING THEIR POWERS SO THAT YOU CAN'T SEE THEM!
WHOA!
BONG
BANNISKY?
WHAT JUST HAPPENED?
THEY KNOW! NO TIME TO WASTE, WE HAVE TO MAKE A RUN FOR IT!
FOCUS ON GETTING YOUR ENERGY BACK, PAYNE. I'LL CLEAR THE WAY!
THIS IS REYNOLDS. THE KIDS ARE TRYING TO RUN! THEY'RE IN THE SOUTH WING! I REPEAT: THE KIDS ARE ON THE RUN IN THE SOUTH WING!
BANNISKY'S OUT AND I'M LOSING MY VIDEO FEEDS ONE AFTER ANOTHER AS THEY RUN FOR THE EXIT.
THIS IS BARNS! REPORT!
COPY THAT. TRY TO MAINTAIN A VISUAL AND KEEP ME POSTED.
PYKE AND BAUZER, GET THEM FROM BEHIND AND PUSH THEM TOWARDS THE ENTRANCE HALL!
EVERYBODY ELSE, GET YOUR GEAR AND MEET ME AT THE ENTRANCE!
NO SIGNAL
THE WELCOME COMMITTEE IS ON ITS WAY...

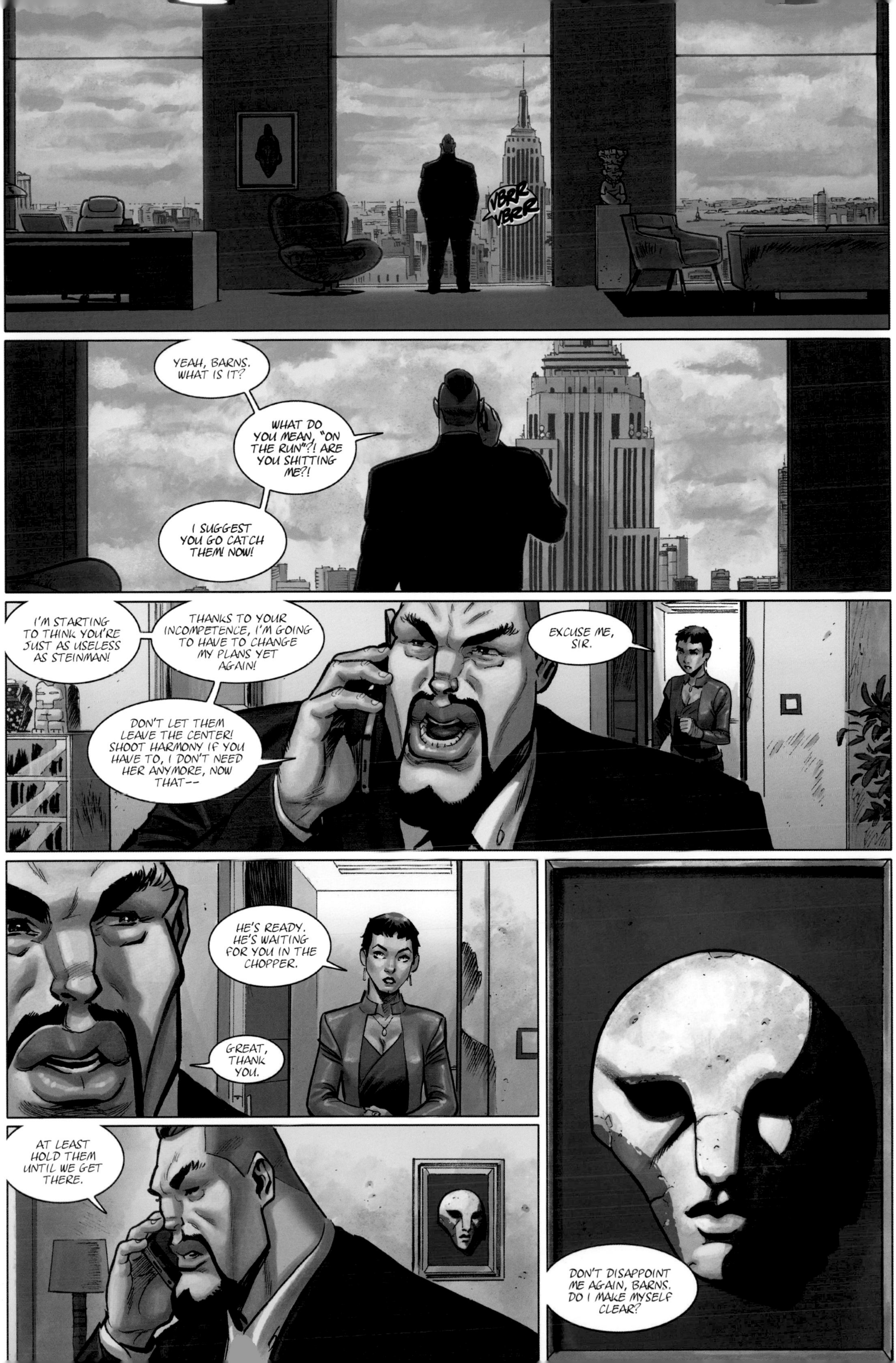
VBRR VBRR
YEAH, BARNS. WHAT IS IT?
WHAT DO YOU MEAN, "ON THE RUN"?! ARE YOU SHITTING ME?!
I SUGGEST YOU GO CATCH THEM! NOW!
I'M STARTING TO THINK YOU'RE JUST AS USELESS AS STEINMAN!
THANKS TO YOUR INCOMPETENCE, I'M GOING TO HAVE TO CHANGE MY PLANS YET AGAIN!
DON'T LET THEM LEAVE THE CENTER! SHOOT HARMONY IF YOU HAVE TO, I DON'T NEED HER ANYMORE, NOW THAT--
EXCUSE ME, SIR.
HE'S READY. HE'S WAITING FOR YOU IN THE CHOPPER.
GREAT, THANK YOU.
AT LEAST HOLD THEM UNTIL WE GET THERE.
DON'T DISAPPOINT ME AGAIN, BARNS. DO I MAKE MYSELF CLEAR?

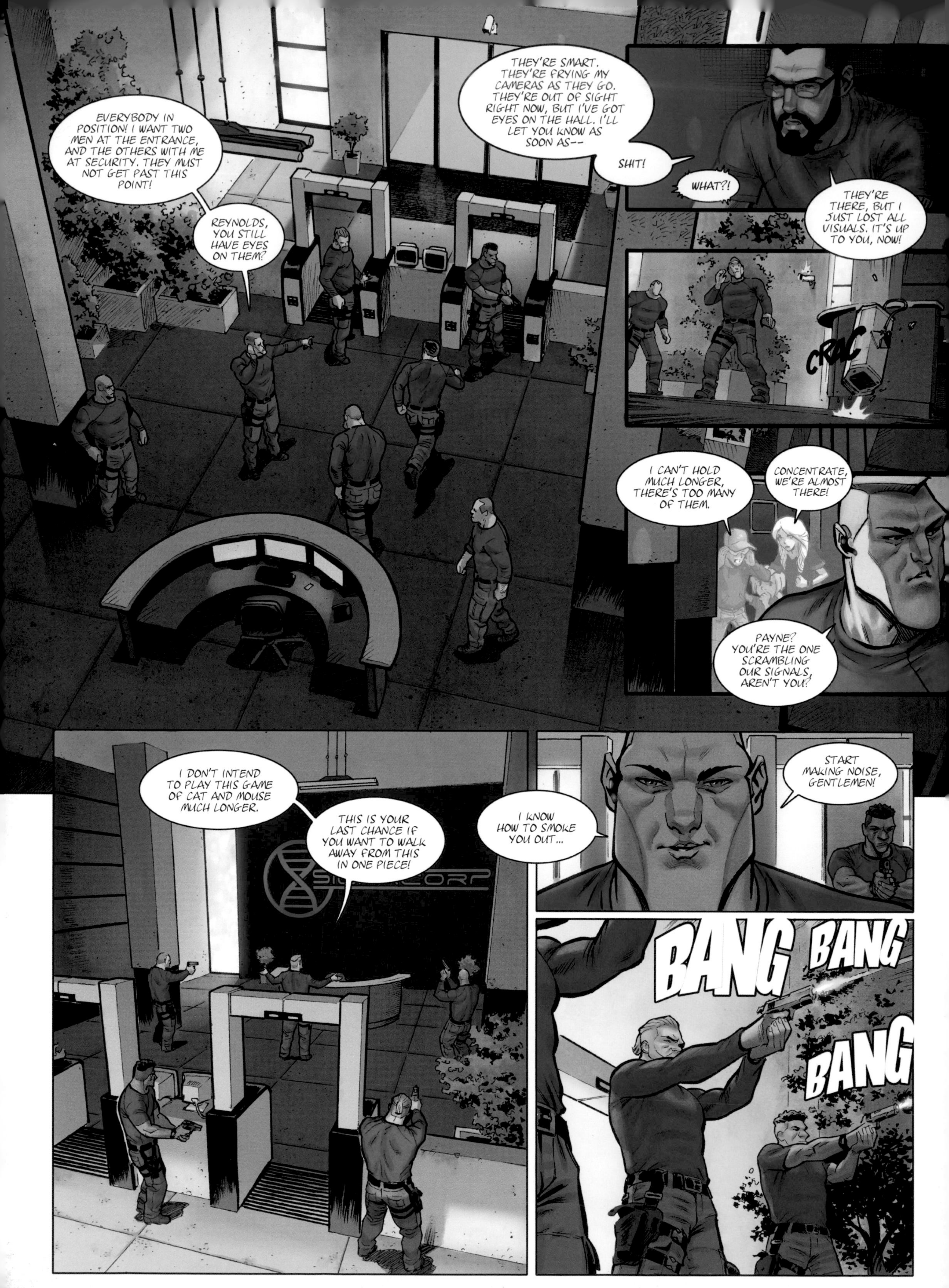
EVERYBODY IN POSITION! I WANT TWO MEN AT THE ENTRANCE, AND THE OTHERS WITH ME AT SECURITY. THEY MUST NOT GET PAST THIS POINT!
REYNOLDS, YOU STILL HAVE EYES ON THEM?
THEY'RE SMART. THEY'RE FRYING MY CAMERAS AS THEY GO. THEY'RE OUT OF SIGHT RIGHT NOW, BUT I'VE GOT EYES ON THE HALL. I'LL LET YOU KNOW AS SOON AS--
SHIT!
WHAT?!
THEY'RE THERE, BUT I JUST LOST ALL VISUALS. IT'S UP TO YOU, NOW!
CRAC
I CAN'T HOLD MUCH LONGER, THERE'S TOO MANY OF THEM.
CONCENTRATE, WE'RE ALMOST THERE!
PAYNE? YOU'RE THE ONE SCRAMBLING OUR SIGNALS, AREN'T YOU?
I DON'T INTEND TO PLAY THIS GAME OF CAT AND MOUSE MUCH LONGER.
THIS IS YOUR LAST CHANCE IF YOU WANT TO WALK AWAY FROM THIS IN ONE PIECE!
I KNOW HOW TO SMOKE YOU OUT...
START MAKING NOISE, GENTLEMEN!
BANG BANG
BANG

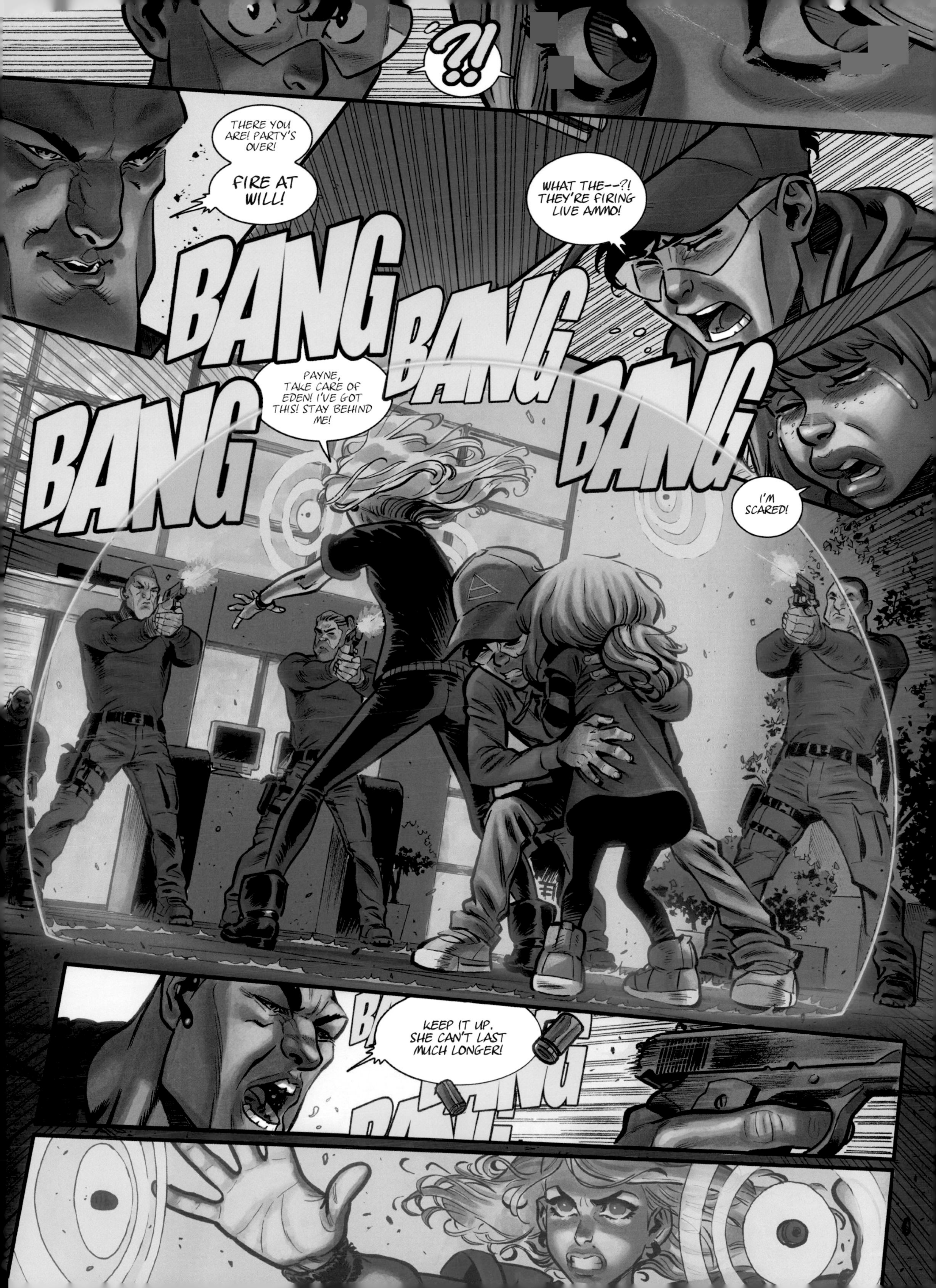
?!
THERE YOU ARE! PARTY'S OVER!
FIRE AT WILL!
WHAT THE--?! THEY'RE FIRING LIVE AMMO!
BANG
BANG
BANG
BANG
PAYNE, TAKE CARE OF EDEN! I'VE GOT THIS! STAY BEHIND ME!
I'M SCARED!
KEEP IT UP. SHE CAN'T LAST MUCH LONGER!

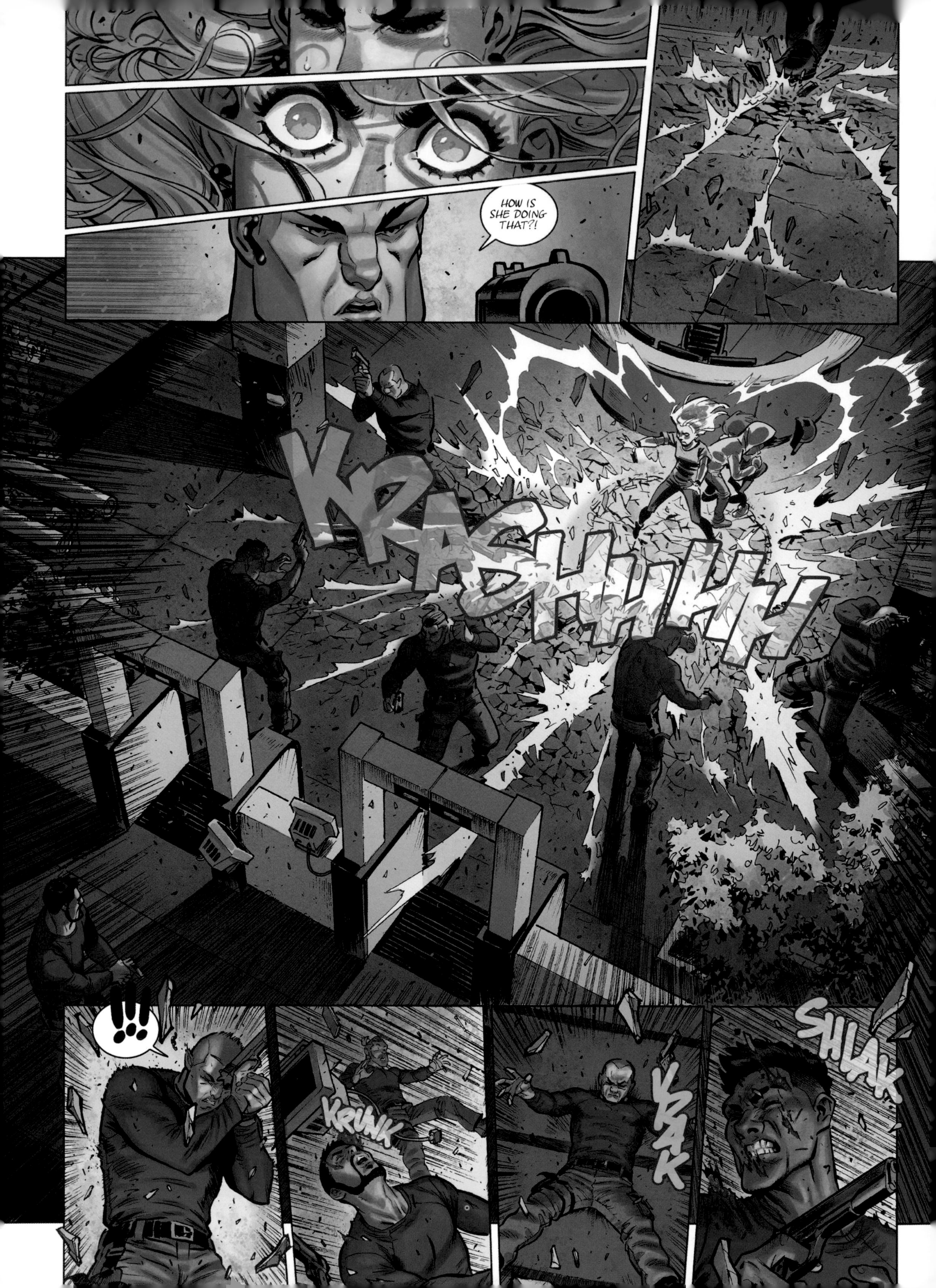
HOW IS SHE DOING THAT?!
KRASHHHHH
!!!
KRUNK
VRAK
SHLAK

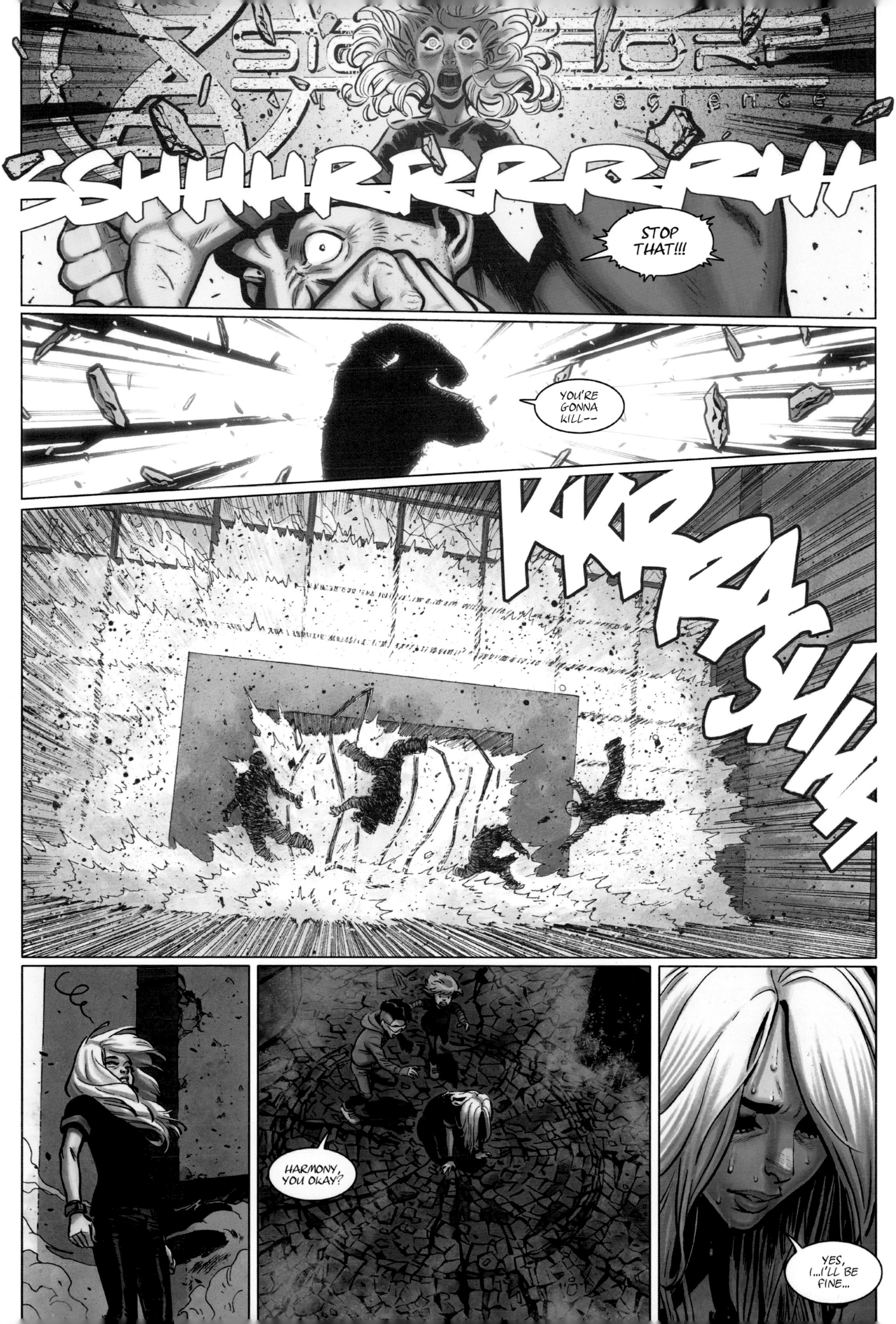

science
SHHHRRRRRH
STOP THAT!!!
YOU'RE GONNA KILL--
KKRRASHH
HARMONY, YOU OKAY?
YES, I...I'LL BE FINE...

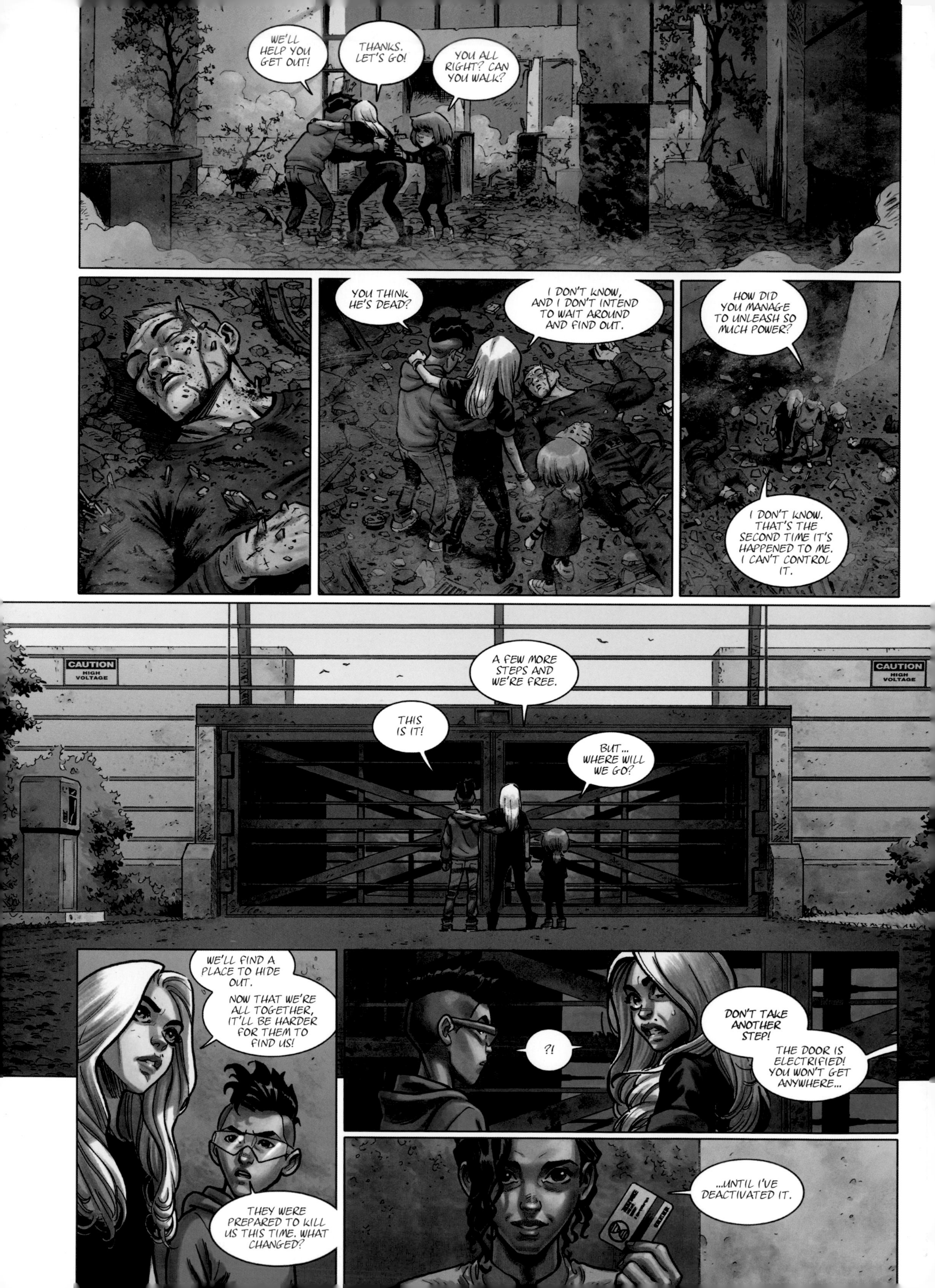
WE'LL HELP YOU GET OUT!
THANKS. LET'S GO!
YOU ALL RIGHT? CAN YOU WALK?
YOU THINK HE'S DEAD?
I DON'T KNOW, AND I DON'T INTEND TO WAIT AROUND AND FIND OUT.
HOW DID YOU MANAGE TO UNLEASH SO MUCH POWER?
I DON'T KNOW. THAT'S THE SECOND TIME IT'S HAPPENED TO ME. I CAN'T CONTROL IT.
CAUTION HIGH VOLTAGE
CAUTION HIGH VOLTAGE
A FEW MORE STEPS AND WE'RE FREE.
THIS IS IT!
BUT... WHERE WILL WE GO?
WE'LL FIND A PLACE TO HIDE OUT.
NOW THAT WE'RE ALL TOGETHER, IT'LL BE HARDER FOR THEM TO FIND US!
THEY WERE PREPARED TO KILL US THIS TIME. WHAT CHANGED?
?!
DON'T TAKE ANOTHER STEP!
THE DOOR IS ELECTRIFIED! YOU WON'T GET ANYWHERE...
...UNTIL I'VE DEACTIVATED IT.

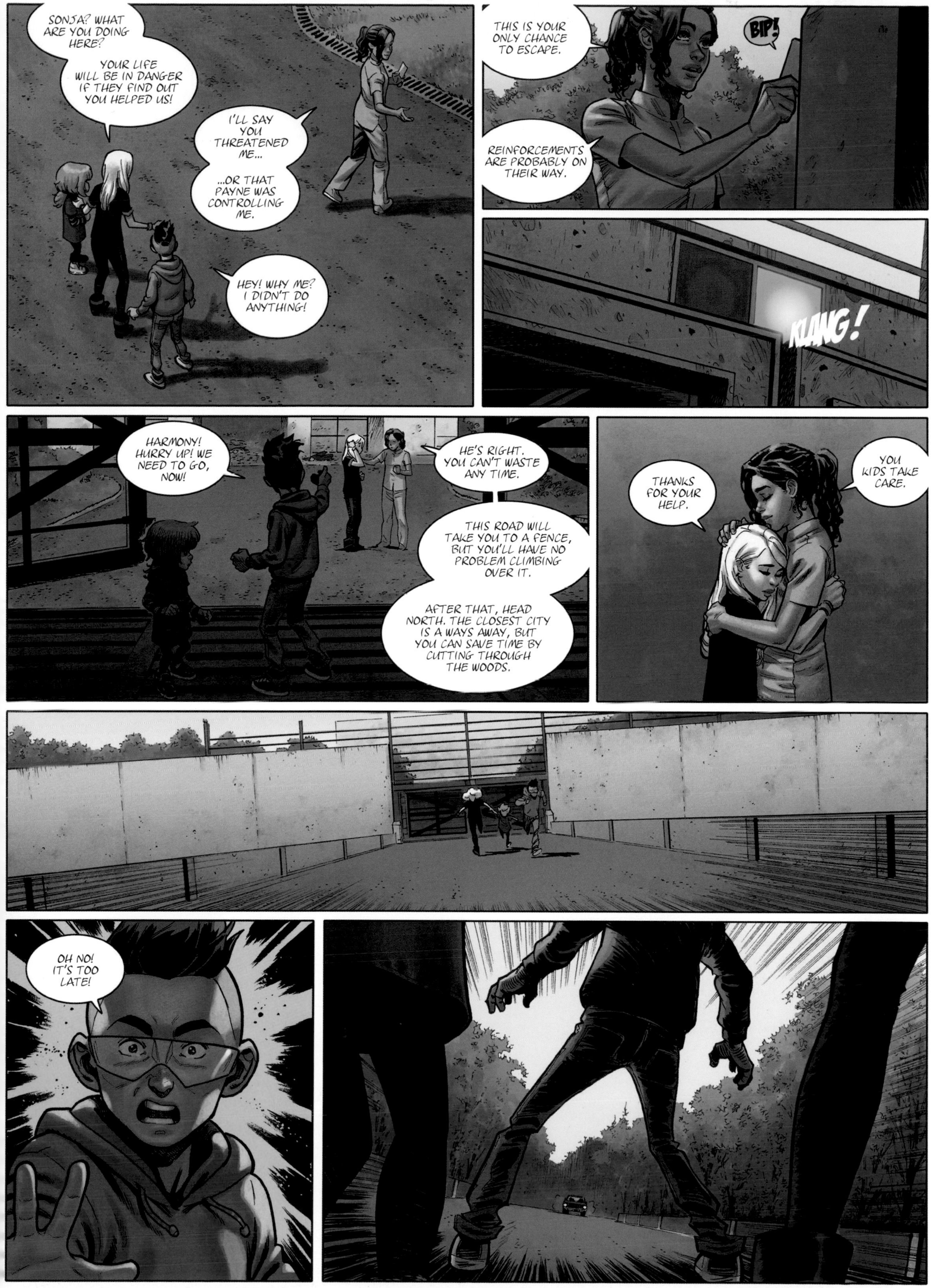
SONJA? WHAT ARE YOU DOING HERE?
YOUR LIFE WILL BE IN DANGER IF THEY FIND OUT YOU HELPED US!
I'LL SAY YOU THREATENED ME...
...OR THAT PAYNE WAS CONTROLLING ME.
HEY! WHY ME? I DIDN'T DO ANYTHING!
THIS IS YOUR ONLY CHANCE TO ESCAPE.
BIP!
REINFORCEMENTS ARE PROBABLY ON THEIR WAY.
KLANG!
HARMONY! HURRY UP! WE NEED TO GO, NOW!
HE'S RIGHT. YOU CAN'T WASTE ANY TIME.
THIS ROAD WILL TAKE YOU TO A FENCE, BUT YOU'LL HAVE NO PROBLEM CLIMBING OVER IT.
AFTER THAT, HEAD NORTH. THE CLOSEST CITY IS A WAYS AWAY, BUT YOU CAN SAVE TIME BY CUTTING THROUGH THE WOODS.
THANKS FOR YOUR HELP.
YOU KIDS TAKE CARE.
OH NO! IT'S TOO LATE!

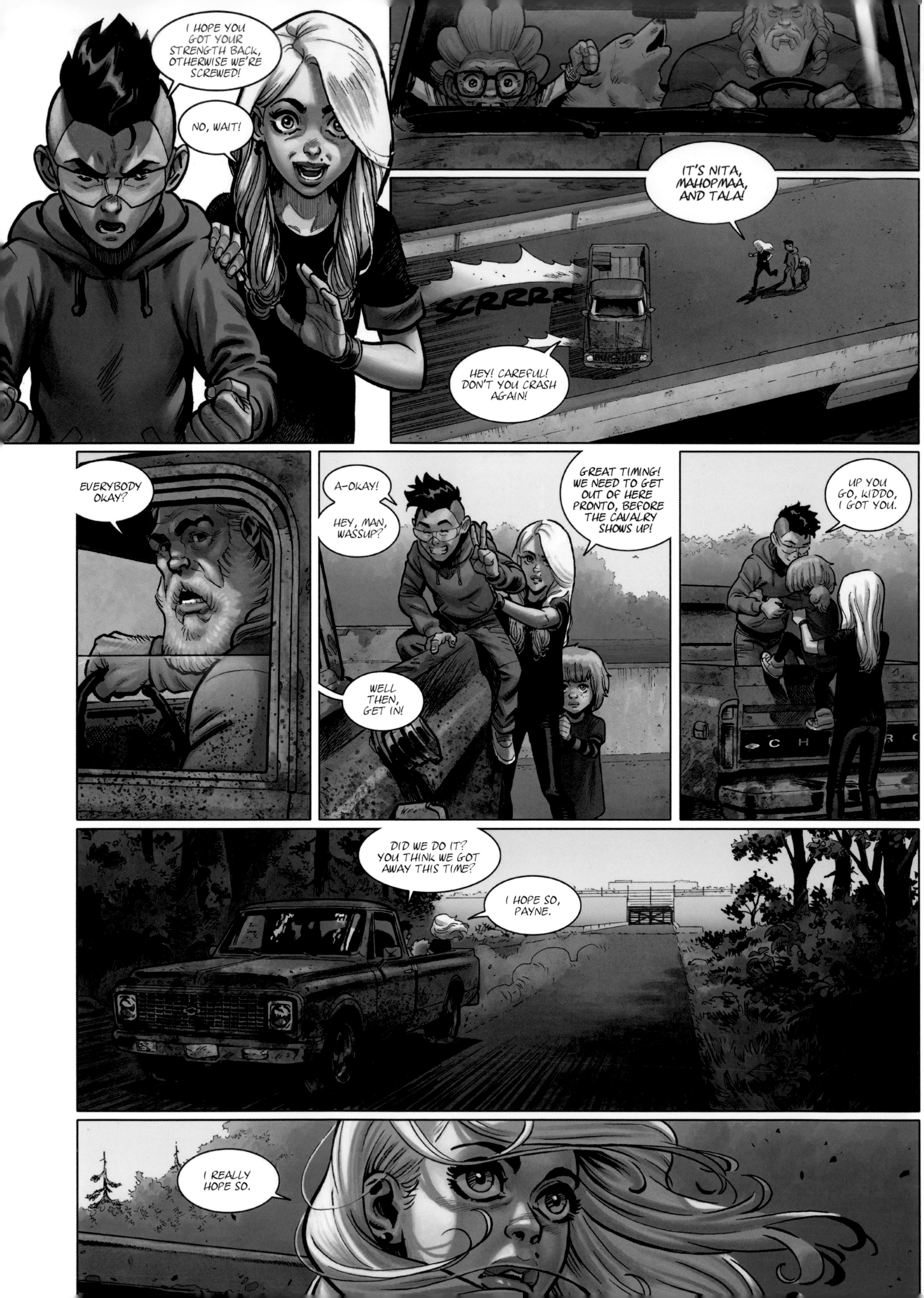
I HOPE YOU GOT YOUR STRENGTH BACK, OTHERWISE WE'RE SCREWED!
NO, WAIT!
IT'S NITA, MAHOPMAA, AND TALA!
SCRRRR
HEY! CAREFUL! DON'T YOU CRASH AGAIN!
EVERYBODY OKAY?
A-OKAY!
HEY, MAN, WASSUP?
GREAT TIMING! WE NEED TO GET OUT OF HERE PRONTO, BEFORE THE CAVALRY SHOWS UP!
WELL THEN, GET IN!
UP YOU GO, KIDDO, I GOT YOU.
DID WE DO IT? YOU THINK WE GOT AWAY THIS TIME?
I HOPE SO, PAYNE.
I REALLY HOPE SO.

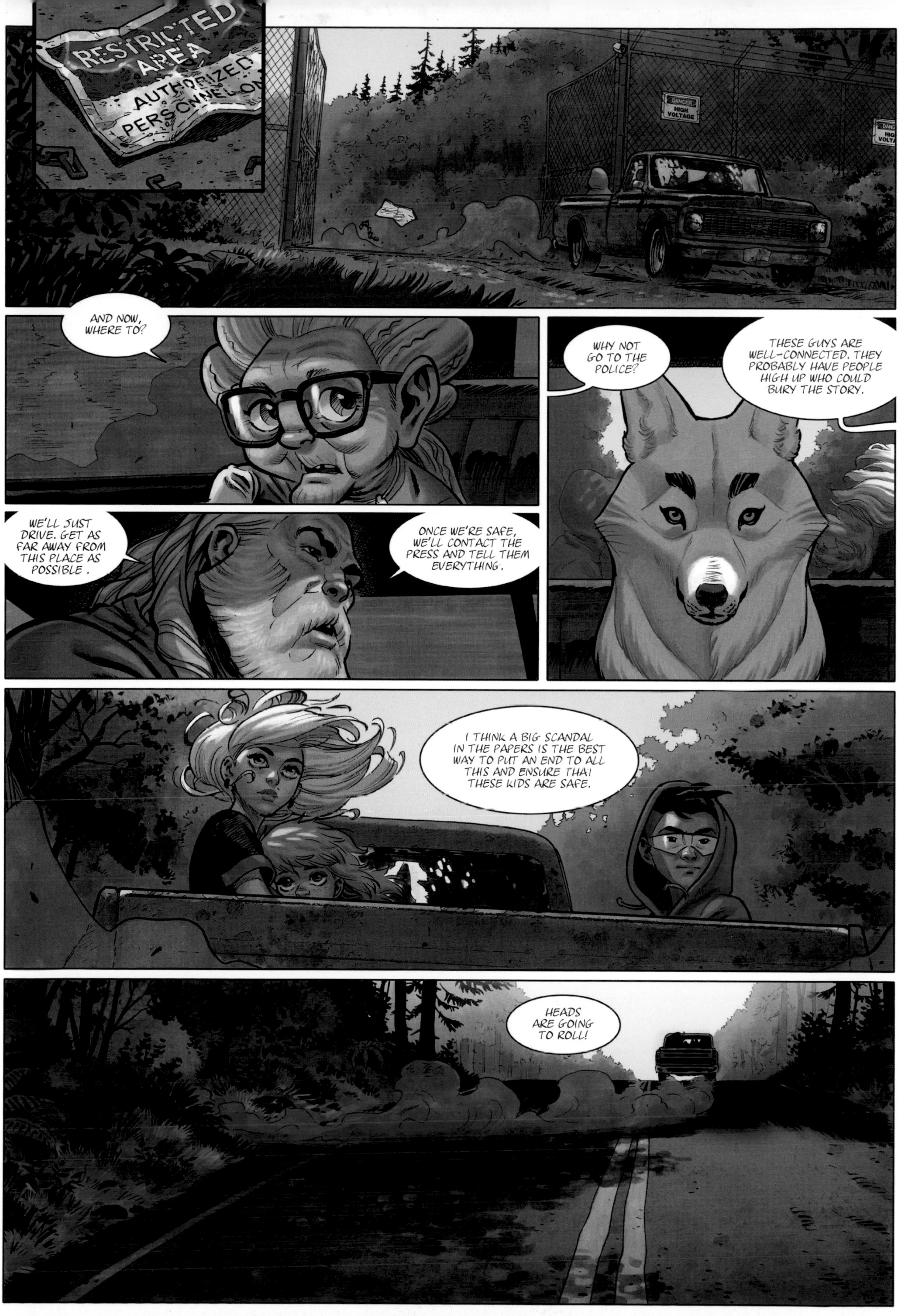
RESTRICTED AREA
AUTHORIZED PERSONNEL ON
DANGER HIGH VOLTAGE
AND NOW, WHERE TO?
WHY NOT GO TO THE POLICE?
THESE GUYS ARE WELL-CONNECTED. THEY PROBABLY HAVE PEOPLE HIGH UP WHO COULD BURY THE STORY.
WE'LL JUST DRIVE. GET AS FAR AWAY FROM THIS PLACE AS POSSIBLE .
ONCE WE'RE SAFE, WE'LL CONTACT THE PRESS AND TELL THEM EVERYTHING.
I THINK A BIG SCANDAL IN THE PAPERS IS THE BEST WAY TO PUT AN END TO ALL THIS AND ENSURE THAT THESE KIDS ARE SAFE.
HEADS ARE GOING TO ROLL!

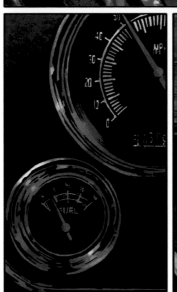

RRRr...

I NEED TO FILL UP THE TANK BEFORE WE HAVE OURSELVES A LITTLE SITUATION.

GRRRR...

DON'T WORRY, GIRL. WE STILL HAVE PLENTY OF GAS FOR NOW.

WHAT'S GOING ON?!

IT FEELS LIKE...

HARMONY? IS THAT YOU?!

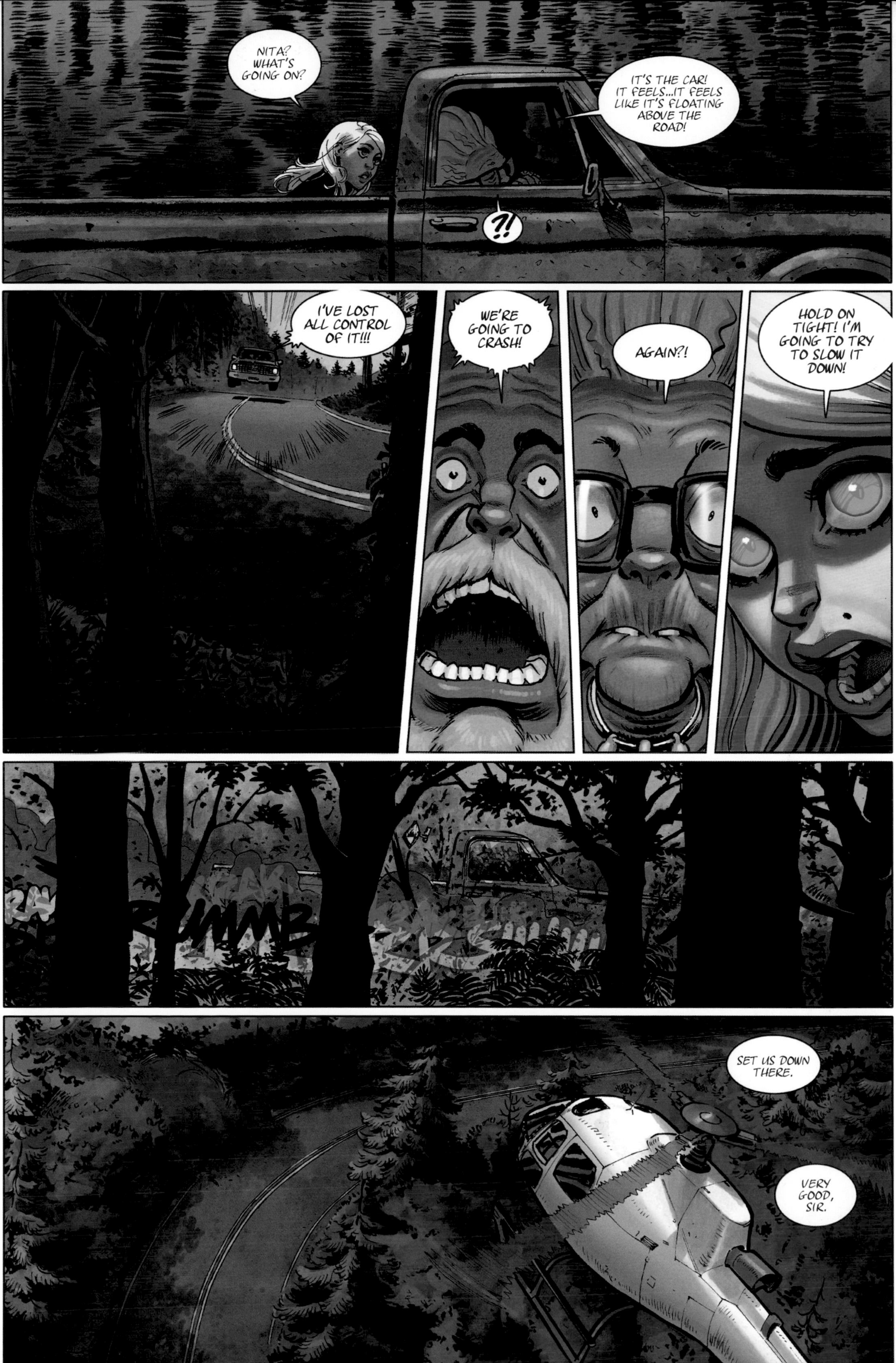
NITA? WHAT'S GOING ON?
IT'S THE CAR! IT FEELS...IT FEELS LIKE IT'S FLOATING ABOVE THE ROAD!
?!
I'VE LOST ALL CONTROL OF IT!!!
WE'RE GOING TO CRASH!
AGAIN?!
HOLD ON TIGHT! I'M GOING TO TRY TO SLOW IT DOWN!
SET US DOWN THERE.
VERY GOOD, SIR.

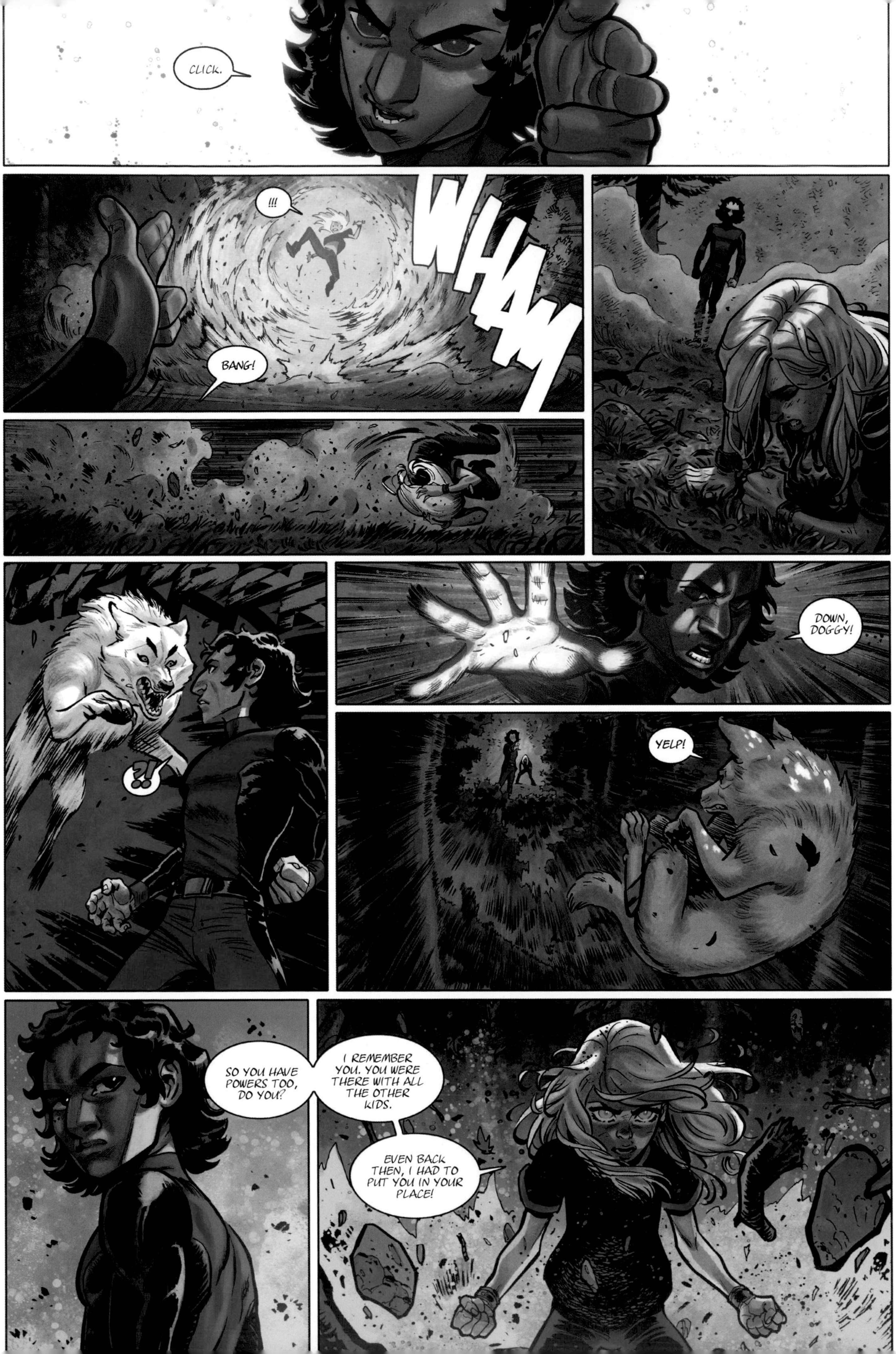
CLICK.
!!!
BANG!
WHAM
DOWN, DOGGY!
YELP!
SO YOU HAVE POWERS TOO, DO YOU?
I REMEMBER YOU. YOU WERE THERE WITH ALL THE OTHER KIDS.
EVEN BACK THEN, I HAD TO PUT YOU IN YOUR PLACE!

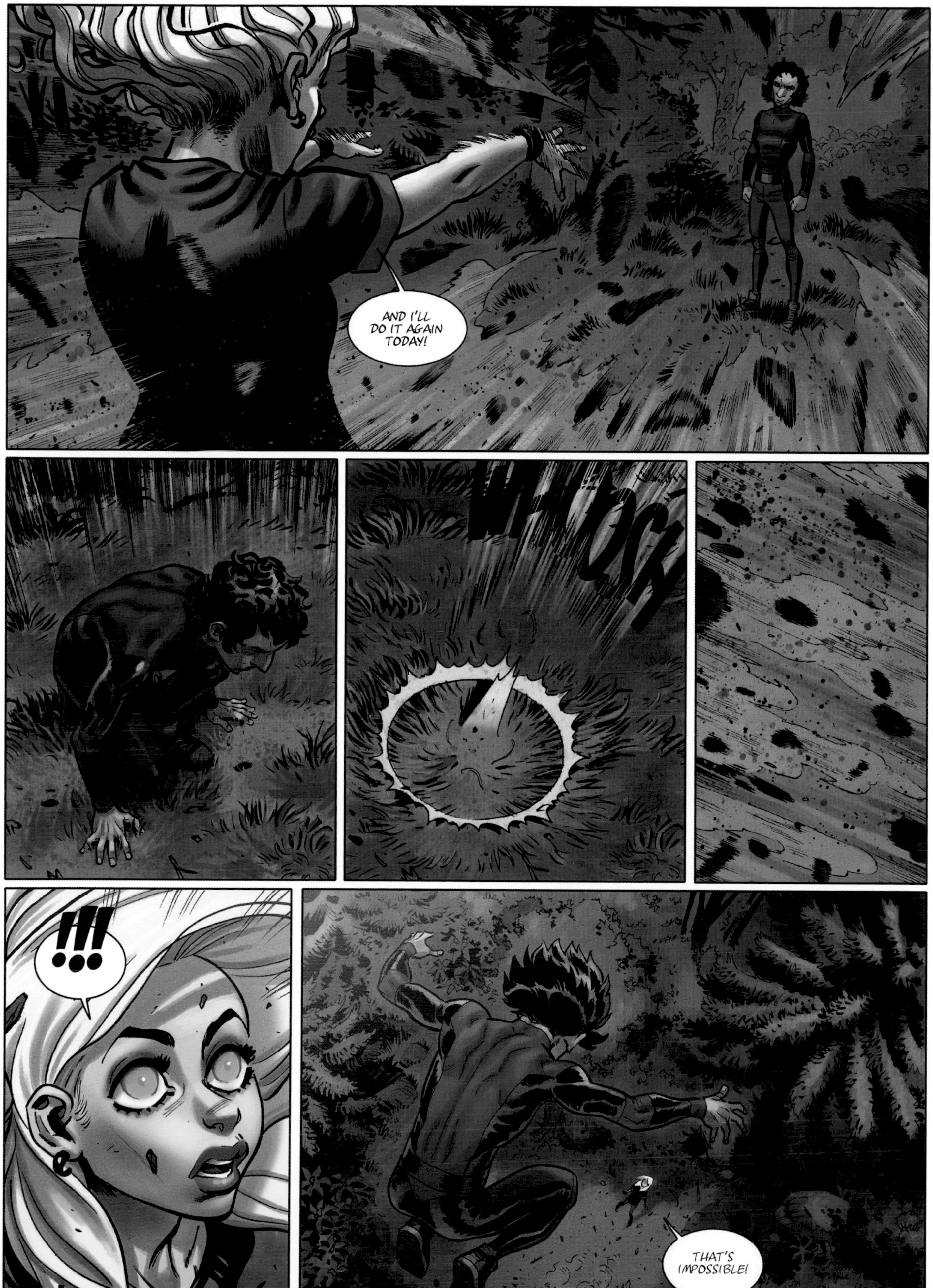
AND I'LL DO IT AGAIN TODAY!
!!!
THAT'S IMPOSSIBLE!

HA HA! LOOKS LIKE I'M THE ONE WITH THE ELEMENT OF SURPRISE THIS TIME!

WHY...WHY ARE YOU DOING THIS?

I GET A KICK OUT OF IT.

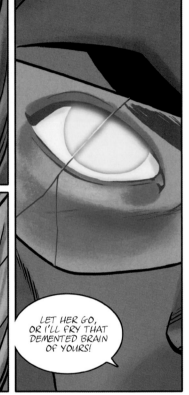

ARGHH!

LET HER GO, OR I'LL FRY THAT DEMENTED BRAIN OF YOURS!

THANKS, PAYNE!

WATCH OUT FOR HIM!

DON'T WORRY, I'M NOT LETTING HIM GO!

WHO IS THIS GUY?

GNNN!

COUGH! HE'S GOT POWERS, LIKE US. COUGH!

HE'S... COUGH! WITH RICHARDS.

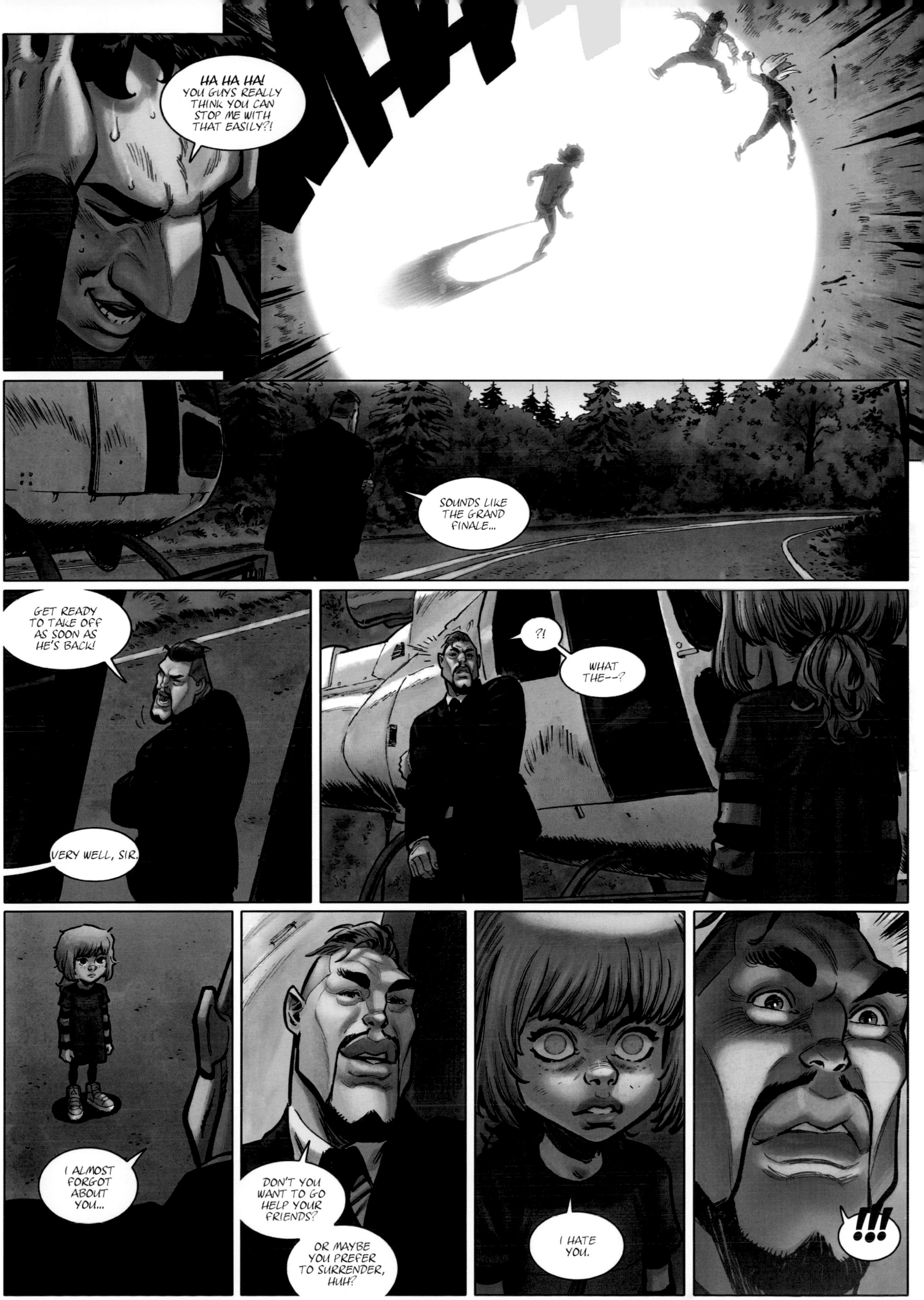
HA HA HA! YOU GUYS REALLY THINK YOU CAN STOP ME WITH THAT EASILY?!
SOUNDS LIKE THE GRAND FINALE...
GET READY TO TAKE OFF AS SOON AS HE'S BACK!
VERY WELL, SIR.
?!
WHAT THE--?
I ALMOST FORGOT ABOUT YOU...
DON'T YOU WANT TO GO HELP YOUR FRIENDS?
OR MAYBE YOU PREFER TO SURRENDER, HUH?
I HATE YOU.
!!!

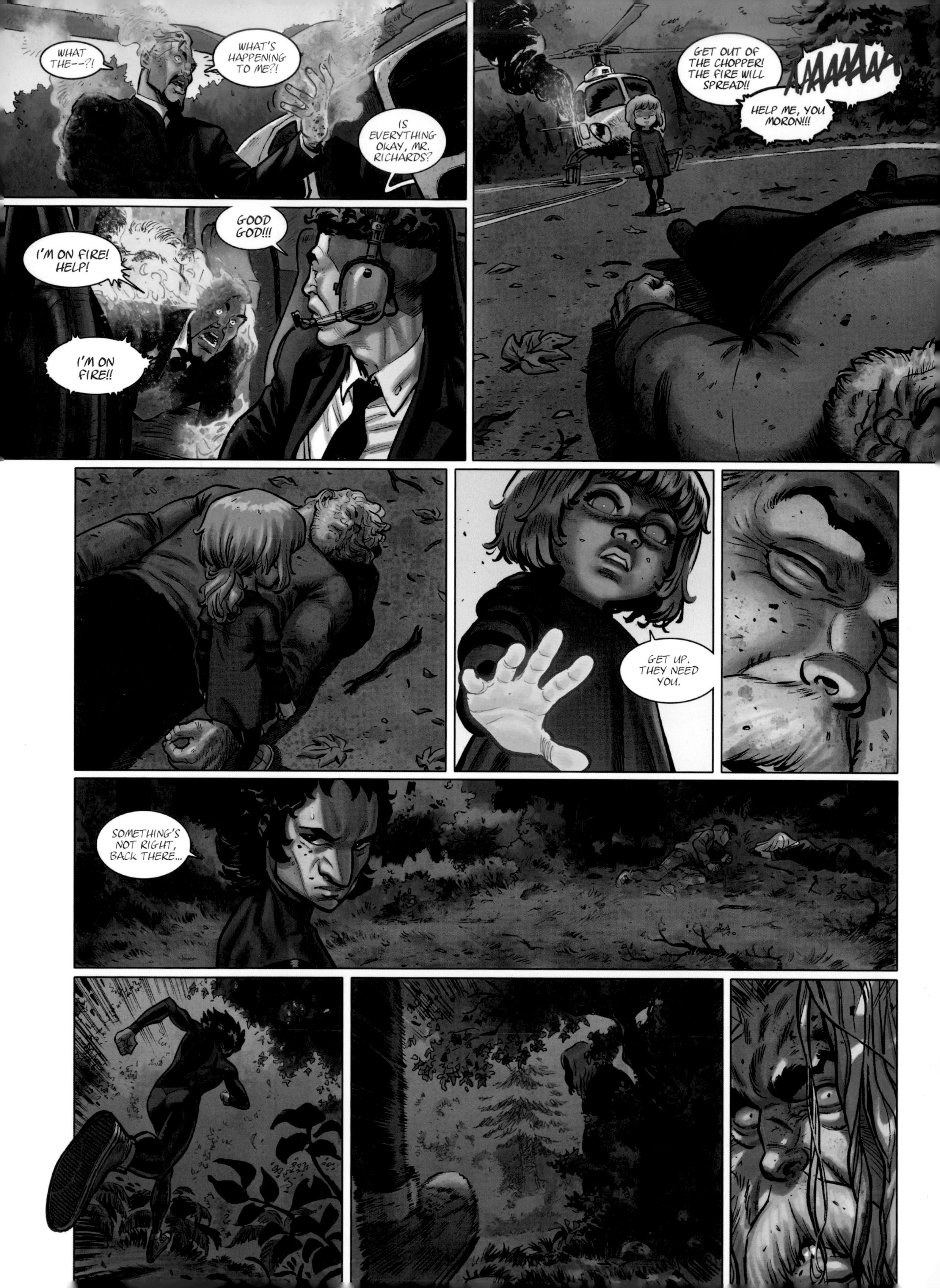
WHAT THE--?!
WHAT'S HAPPENING TO ME?!
IS EVERYTHING OKAY, MR. RICHARDS?
GOOD GOD!!!
I'M ON FIRE! HELP!
I'M ON FIRE!!
GET OUT OF THE CHOPPER! THE FIRE WILL SPREAD!!
AAAAAAAA
HELP ME, YOU MORON!!!
GET UP. THEY NEED YOU.
SOMETHING'S NOT RIGHT, BACK THERE...

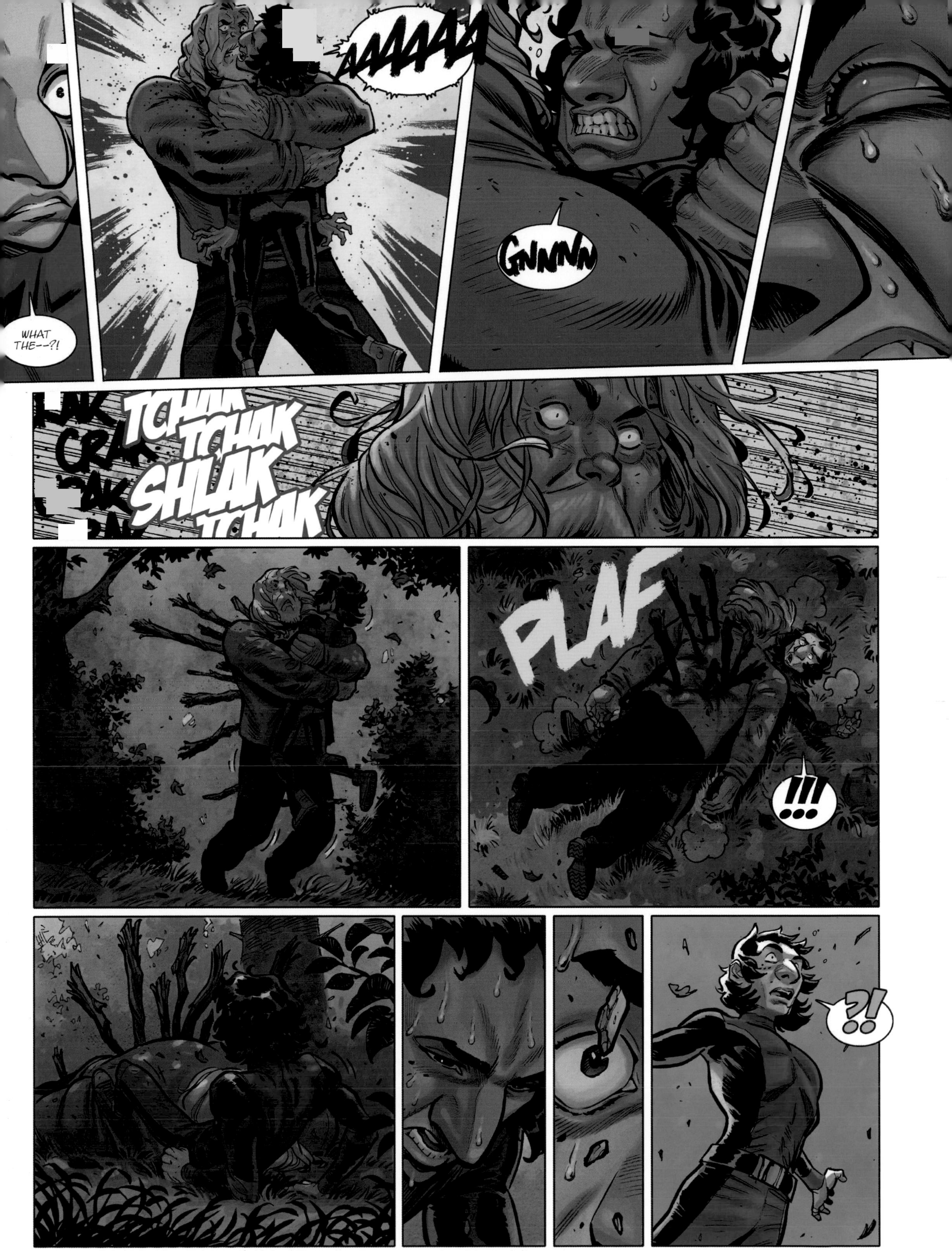
WHAT THE--?!
GNNNN
TCHAK
TCHAK
SHLAK
PLAF
!!!
?!

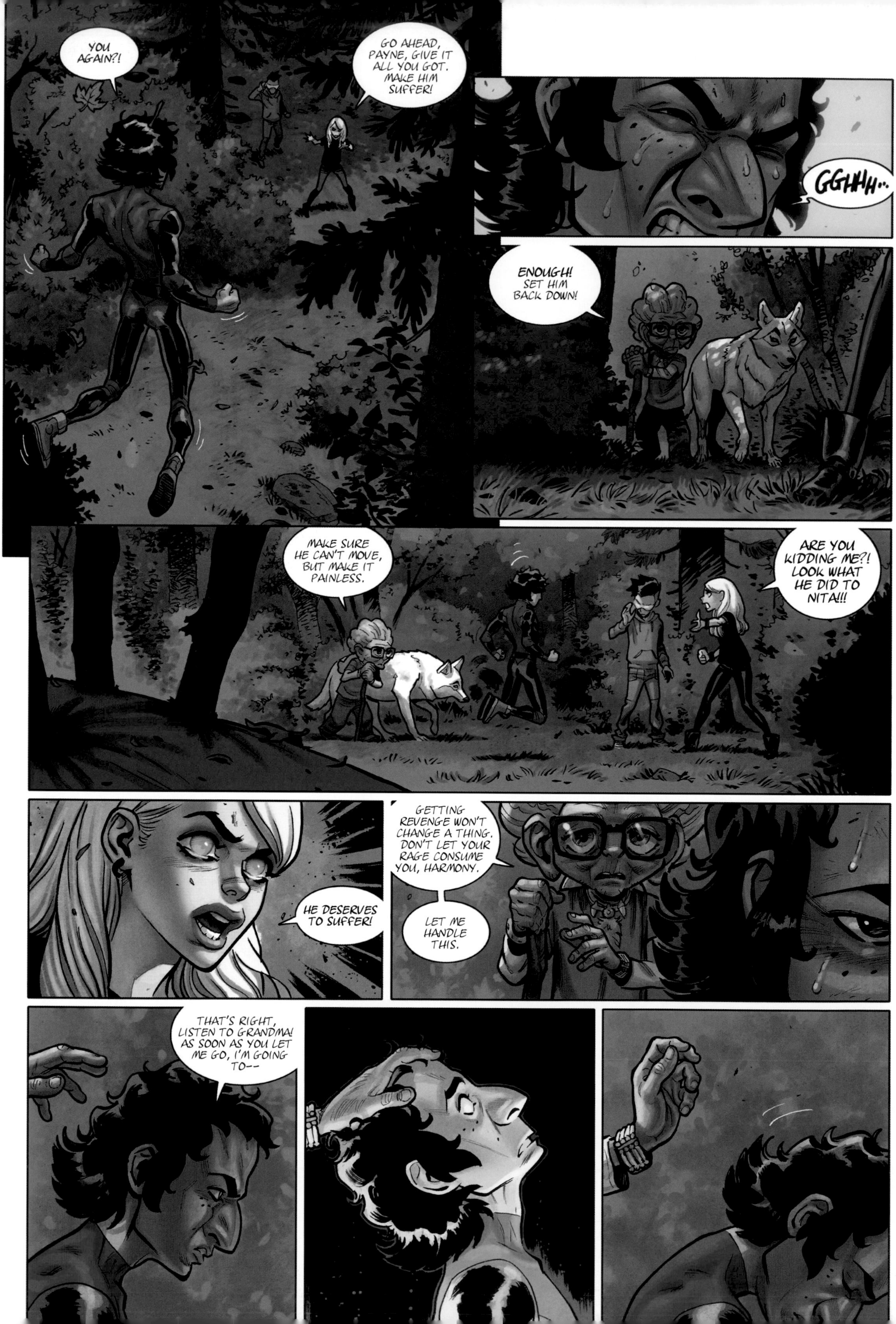

YOU AGAIN?!
GO AHEAD, PAYNE, GIVE IT ALL YOU GOT. MAKE HIM SUFFER!
GGHHH...
ENOUGH! SET HIM BACK DOWN!
MAKE SURE HE CAN'T MOVE, BUT MAKE IT PAINLESS.
ARE YOU KIDDING ME?! LOOK WHAT HE DID TO NITA!!!
HE DESERVES TO SUFFER!
GETTING REVENGE WON'T CHANGE A THING. DON'T LET YOUR RAGE CONSUME YOU, HARMONY.
LET ME HANDLE THIS.
THAT'S RIGHT, LISTEN TO GRANDMA! AS SOON AS YOU LET ME GO, I'M GOING TO--

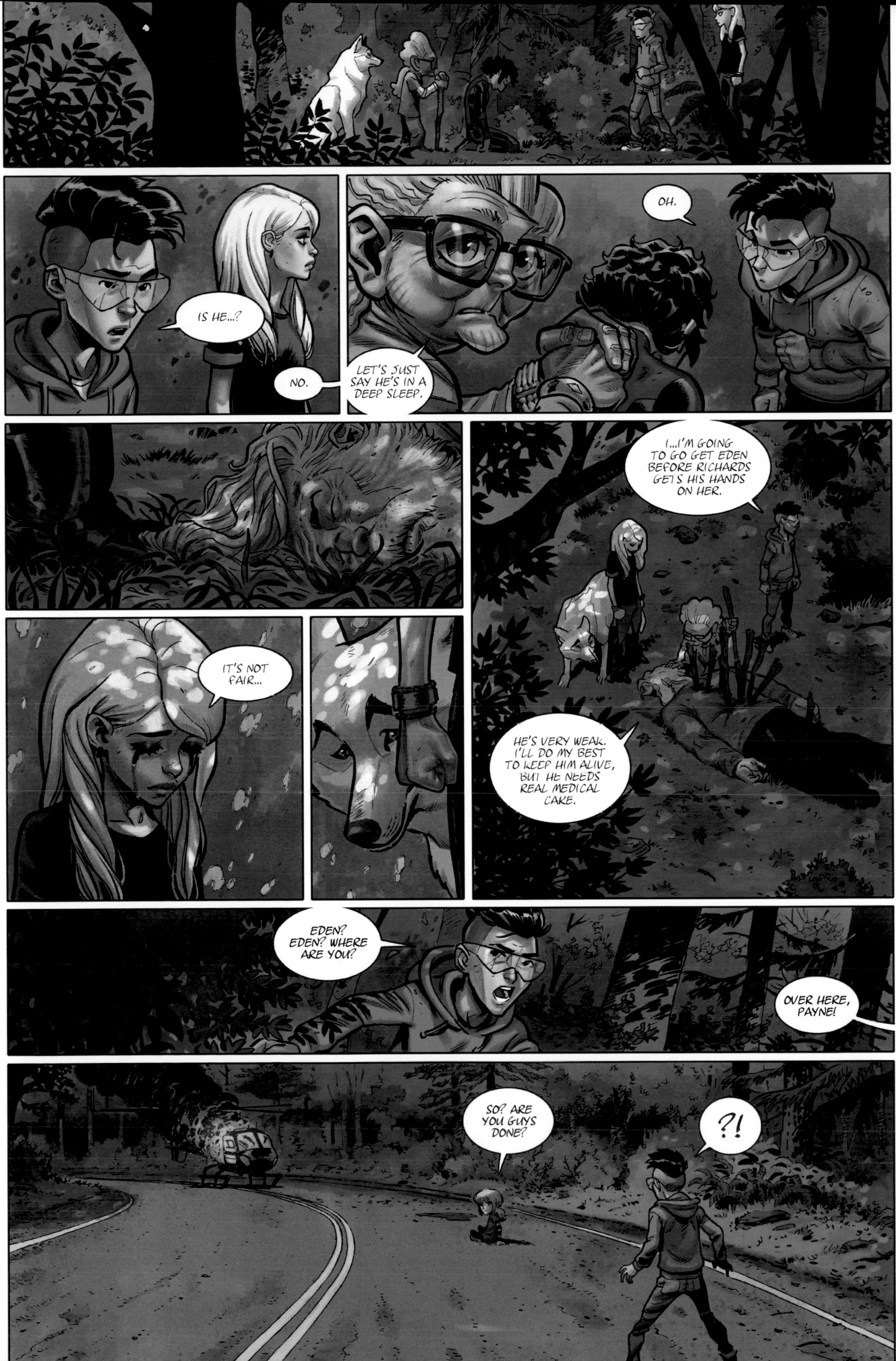
IS HE...?
NO.
LET'S JUST SAY HE'S IN A DEEP SLEEP.
OH.
IT'S NOT FAIR...
I...I'M GOING TO GO GET EDEN BEFORE RICHARDS GETS HIS HANDS ON HER.
HE'S VERY WEAK. I'LL DO MY BEST TO KEEP HIM ALIVE, BUT HE NEEDS REAL MEDICAL CARE.
EDEN? EDEN? WHERE ARE YOU?
OVER HERE, PAYNE!
SO? ARE YOU GUYS DONE?
?!

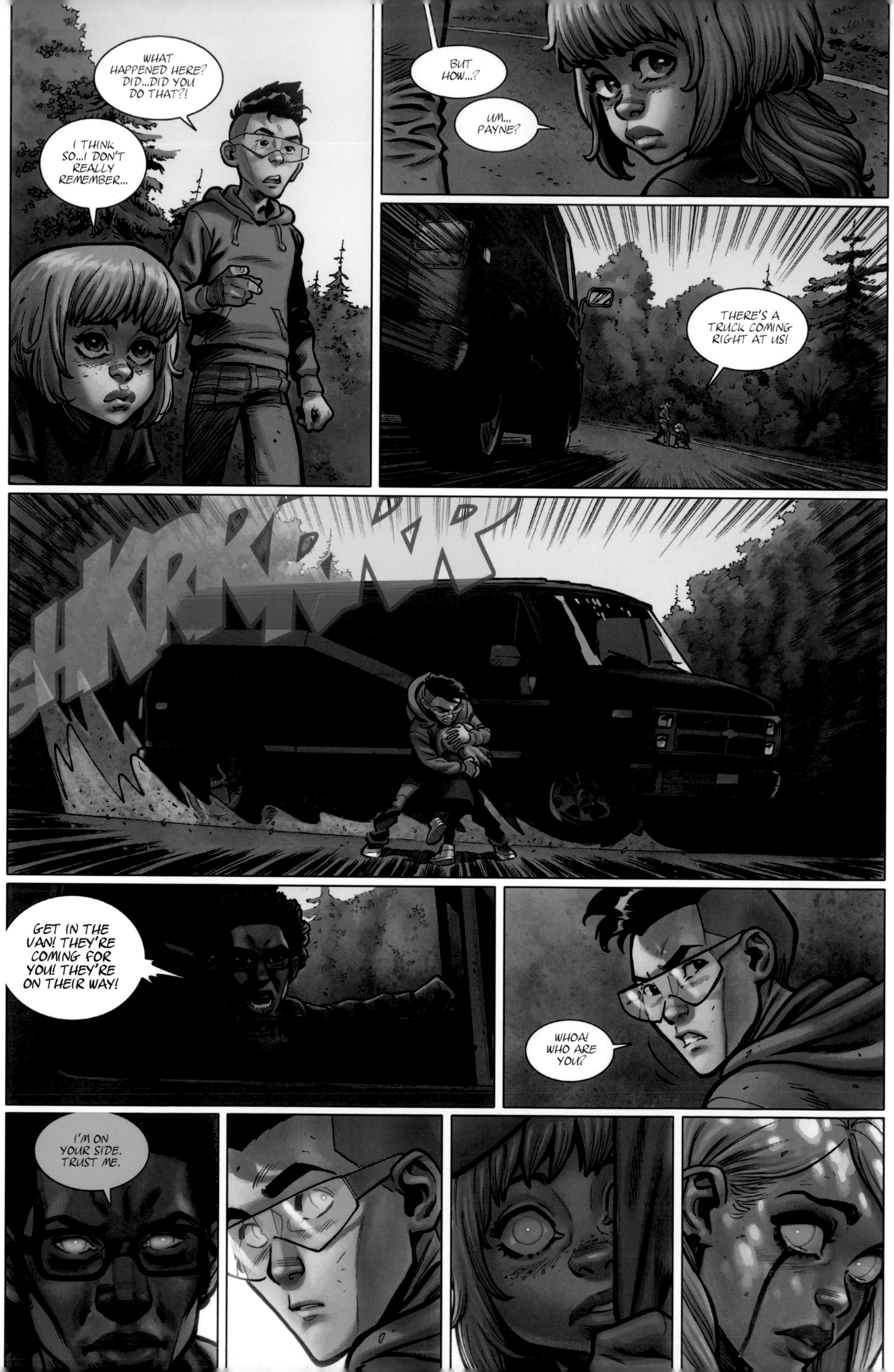
WHAT HAPPENED HERE? DID...DID YOU DO THAT?!
I THINK SO...I DON'T REALLY REMEMBER...
BUT HOW...?
UM... PAYNE?
THERE'S A TRUCK COMING RIGHT AT US!
SHKRRR
GET IN THE VAN! THEY'RE COMING FOR YOU! THEY'RE ON THEIR WAY!
WHOA! WHO ARE YOU?
I'M ON YOUR SIDE. TRUST ME.

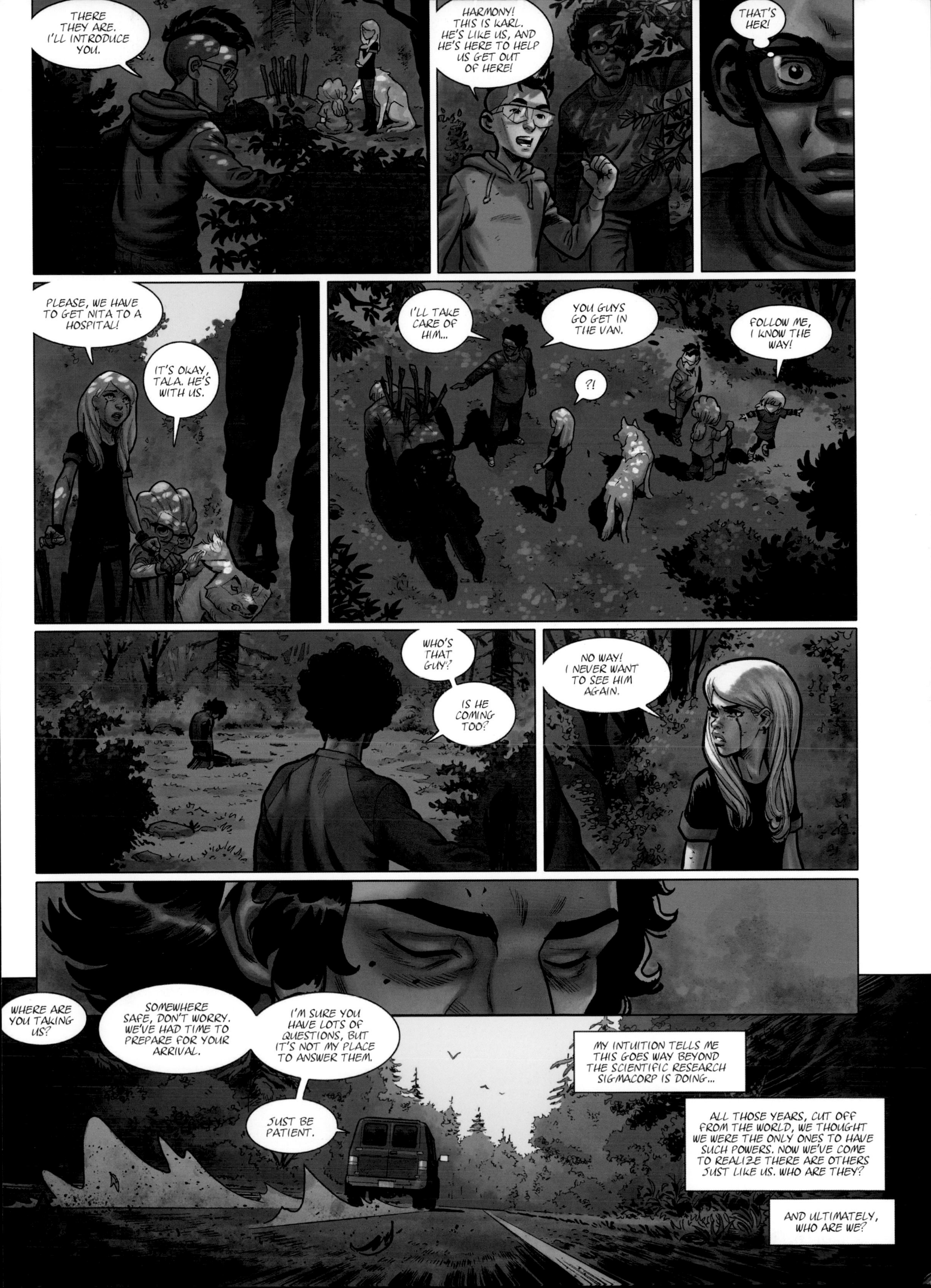
THERE THEY ARE. I'LL INTRODUCE YOU.
HARMONY! THIS IS KARL. HE'S LIKE US, AND HE'S HERE TO HELP US GET OUT OF HERE!
THAT'S HER!
PLEASE, WE HAVE TO GET NITA TO A HOSPITAL!
IT'S OKAY, TALA. HE'S WITH US.
I'LL TAKE CARE OF HIM...
YOU GUYS GO GET IN THE VAN.
?!
FOLLOW ME, I KNOW THE WAY!
WHO'S THAT GUY?
IS HE COMING TOO?
NO WAY! I NEVER WANT TO SEE HIM AGAIN.
WHERE ARE YOU TAKING US?
SOMEWHERE SAFE, DON'T WORRY. WE'VE HAD TIME TO PREPARE FOR YOUR ARRIVAL.
I'M SURE YOU HAVE LOTS OF QUESTIONS, BUT IT'S NOT MY PLACE TO ANSWER THEM.
JUST BE PATIENT.
MY INTUITION TELLS ME THIS GOES WAY BEYOND THE SCIENTIFIC RESEARCH SIGMACORP IS DOING...
ALL THOSE YEARS, CUT OFF FROM THE WORLD, WE THOUGHT WE WERE THE ONLY ONES TO HAVE SUCH POWERS. NOW WE'VE COME TO REALIZE THERE ARE OTHERS JUST LIKE US. WHO ARE THEY?
AND ULTIMATELY, WHO ARE WE?

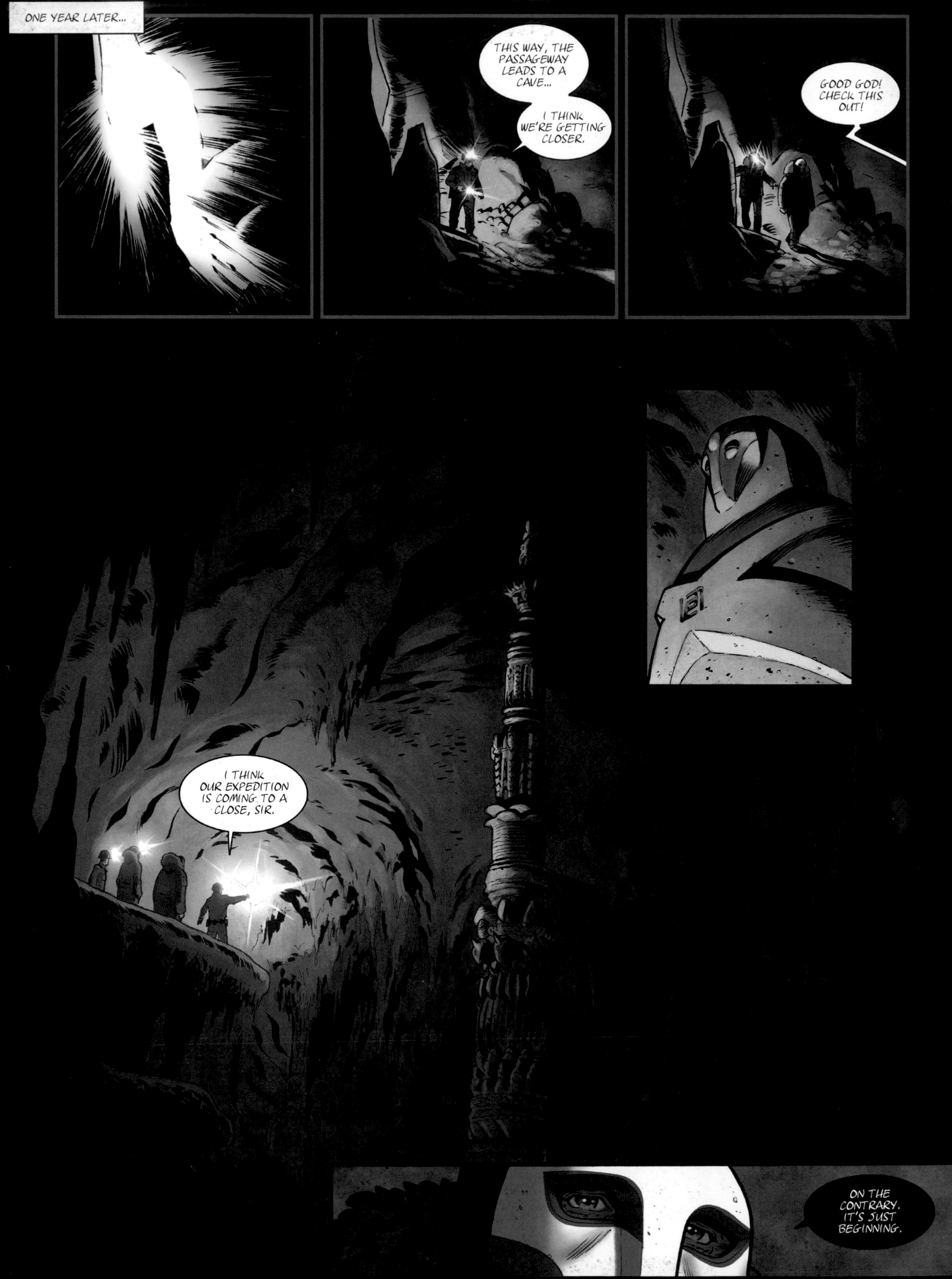
ONE YEAR LATER...
THIS WAY, THE PASSAGEWAY LEADS TO A CAVE...
I THINK WE'RE GETTING CLOSER.
GOOD GOD! CHECK THIS OUT!
I THINK OUR EXPEDITION IS COMING TO A CLOSE, SIR.
ON THE CONTRARY. IT'S JUST BEGINNING.

END OF THE FIRST CYCLE

An Imprint of Insight Editions
PO Box 3088
San Rafael, CA 94912
www.insightcomics.com

Find us on Facebook:
www.facebook.com/InsightEditionsComics

Follow us on Twitter:
@InsightComics

Follow us on Instagram:
Insight_Comics

HARMONY-COMPILATION 1

Harmony 1 - Memento
© DUPUIS 2016, by Reynès,

Harmony 2 - Indigo
© DUPUIS 2016, by Reynès,

Harmony 3 - Ago
© DUPUIS 2017, by Reynès,

www.dupuis.com

Published in the United States in 2020 by Insight Editions.
Originally published in French by Dupuis, Belgium, in 2016.

Library of Congress Cataloging-in-Publication Data available.

ISBN: 978-1-68383-785-5

Publisher: Raoul Goff
President: Kate Jerome
Associate Publisher: Vanessa Lopez
Creative Director: Chrissy Kwasnik
VP of Manufacturing: Alix Nicholaeff
Designer: Brooke McCullum
Executive Editor: Mark Irwin
Associate Editor: Holly Fisher
Senior Production Editor: Elaine Ou
Production Associate: Eden Orlesky

Insight Editions, in association with Roots of Peace, will plant two trees for each tree used in the manufacturing of this book. Roots of Peace is an internationally renowned humanitarian organization dedicated to eradicating land mines worldwide and converting war-torn lands into productive farms and wildlife habitats. Roots of Peace will plant two million fruit and nut trees in Afghanistan and provide farmers there with the skills and support necessary for sustainable land use.

Manufactured in China by Insight Editions

10 9 8 7 6 5 4 3 2 1